# Elspeth, The Living Dead Girl

by

## Stuart R. West

**Elspeth, The Living Dead Girl**

Cover Art by *Lea Schizas*

The Wild Rose Press, Inc.
PO Box 708
Adams Basin, NY 14410-0708
Visit us at www.thewildrosepress.com

Publishing History
First Edition, 2023
Trade Paperback ISBN 978-1-5092-5012-7
Digital ISBN 978-1-5092-5013-4

Previously Published 6/2014 MuseItUp Publishing
Published in the United States of America

## Dedication

I'd like to dedicate this book to my wife and daughter, my support team. And trust me, these two women could teach Elspeth a thing or two.

Chapter One

*Elspeth*

"So, Susan, have you ever made out with a girl?"

"What? No! Ewww."

I knew she never had. Truth be told, I hadn't either. But I enjoyed busting my roommate's chops. Her expressions were always well worth it. I took my kicks where I could find them.

"Relax. I'm kiddin'!"

Susan stood by the door, her fingertips pressed against her lips in horrific contemplation. I rolled over on my bed, my leather jacket creaking like a tree limb in the wind. "It's not like it was an *offer* or anything."

"Elspeth, honestly!" She practically vanished when she sat on her bed. Only Susan would color coordinate her sweater with the ugly aqua-colored bedspread. "Have *you,* um, ever kissed a girl?"

Guess I had unleashed her inner beast.

"No." I kicked my feet into the air. "I'm bored. Bored, bored, *bored!*" Everything about my living arrangement was boring. Our small bedroom was a simple dorm room, decorated in bland pastel colors—a sixties nightmare. The walls were constructed of cold, harsh cinder blocks at odds with the decor. A few paintings of doe-eyed children hung on the walls, attempting to spruce the joint up. Delivered the opposite effect.

Ho-hum. As I said, boring.

Thirty years ago, when I first woke up, I honestly thought I'd gone to hell. I encountered Ms. Pillows first. The name fit her to a T. Tightly packaged into her purple dress, her lumps bulged everywhere. And I remember thinking, *the devil's an overweight, blue-haired woman wearing cat-eyed glasses.*

\*\*\*\*

"Am I dead?" I had asked.

"Well, child, that's a hard distinction to make here."

"Okay."

"I'm Ms. Pillows. I suppose you can say I'm the welcoming committee."

I sat up and studied the room. "So, hell is pastel colored?" Whether it was hell or not, it may as well have been. I absolutely despised light colors, preferring everything dark.

"Oh! Oh, my!"

I had shocked the devil, probably not an easy thing to do.

"No, Elspeth, not at all! You're in a very special place now."

"Heaven?"

"Let's just say it's somewhat of a way station." She beamed at me in a grandmotherly fashion, waiting for her nonsensical words to affect me. "Tell me, Elspeth, what's the last thing you remember?"

I closed my eyes, attempting to erase dark memories. But they came flooding back with a vengeance. "I was at a nightclub in New York. I glommed onto some guys. They took me out into the alley. They beat me, robbed me, and…" My voice grew ragged. I fought back tears. I didn't want to appear weak. Since there was no way I could finish my tale without breaking down, I just shook my head and embraced silence.

"It's okay now, Elspeth," she said, patting my hand. "Those days are behind you." She smiled sadly, knowingly, her eyes crinkling at the corners. "Everything's fine now."

I sacked up and pulled my act together. Couldn't keep me down for long. "Okay. So, what is the deal, anyway?"

"Elspeth, you've been given another chance. Your life was forfeited before your natural time. It happens sometimes." She shook her head apologetically, as if bureaucratic incompetence were to blame for my death.

"So, what does that mean, exactly? Am I alive? Did the doctors save me? Or what?" I rose from the small bed and grabbed my jacket from the back of a chair. Feeling woozy, I immediately crashed back onto the mattress.

"Now, now. It's going to take you a little while to become acclimatized to your new existence." She placed her hand on my forehead. "Just relax. You're not going anywhere for a while."

"Ms. Pillows! Would you please tell me what the hell is going on?"

Ms. Pillows blinked her eyes at my blasphemy. But I felt the fate of my soul was kinda, you know, important.

"Oh, my! Language please, Elspeth." Her lips turned white, and all but vanished into a tight grimace. "As I said, you've been given a second chance. I'm afraid you have left the mortal world as you know it."

"All right."

"However, there are certain individuals we encounter from time to time whom we feel are worthy of a second chance. Sometimes, it's because a mistake was made and as a consequence, they're taken before their previously scheduled time. Other times, we feel a person has special qualities—talents—that can be used to make the mortal world a better place."

"Which kind am I?"

"A little bit of both."

"Well, let's get going, then!" I swung my boots over the side of the bed. "How's this work?"

"Patience, Elspeth, patience." She grabbed my feet, attempting to hoist them back into bed. After huffing and panting, she gave up, leaning back in her chair. "Youth today. No patience." She clucked disapprovingly. "I'm afraid it's not as simple as going back to the mortal world and picking up where you left off. You'll be assigned a host body."

"A 'host body'?"

"That's correct, Elspeth!"

*Where's my damn gold star?*

"Your host will be someone your age, sharing similar physical qualities. It will be up to you to make her understand what's happening. We can't have an unwilling host body, after all." She giggled toward the ceiling as if sharing a private joke with God.

"Yeah. We can't have that."

"Anyhoo. You'll have to share the host's body. And, mind you, it's just a temporary thing. We can't be expected to inhabit your host full time!"

"Of course we can't."

"Yes, well…"

"So. What's the catch?"

"Excuse me?" She pushed her glasses up along her nose.

"I know damn well…"

Ms. Pillows gasped.

"There's gotta be a catch. You guys aren't doing this just because you're nice! *Whoever* you are!"

"So cynical. Yet, in this case, you're correct. You will be asked to do certain things. Sometimes, they might even prove to be dangerous."

"Kick ass!" Primed for action, I pumped my fist into the air.

"Oh, my." Ms. Pillows fanned herself with her hand, quite in danger of passing out. "Yes, well…oh, my. Anyhoo, the jobs you will be assigned typically have something to do with crimes of various natures. Do you believe you're up to the challenge, Elspeth?"

Didn't really sound like I had a choice. "Does a bear crap in the woods?"

She gasped again. I knew right there and then that I was going to have fun with her. "Well! Disregarding the rather vulgar nature of your rhetorical question, yes, I suppose a bear does…" She leaned in to whisper the next word. "Defecate in the woods. I suppose this means you're on-board?"

"Who are you guys? You never answered my question! Before I sign anything or whatever, I want to know whom I'm dealing with. I don't want to sign a contract with the devil!" Obviously, I had pulled Ms. Pillows' trigger again. Sometimes I just couldn't help myself.

Her face turned pale underneath her rosy-cheeked

makeup. "We are certainly not in alignment with the devil, young lady!"

"So, you're admitting the devil exists?"

"I'm not saying anything of the sort!"

"So, then, you're denying it."

"I'm not denying it either!"

"What can you tell me, Ms. Pillows?"

She released a huge, cleansing sigh. "I'm afraid it's not up to us to know everything about what goes on here. I can safely tell you this is neither heaven nor hell." She glanced skyward as if waiting for enlightenment. Or a lightning bolt. "As I said, it's a waiting station before the next part of your journey."

"So…" I cracked my knuckles. "We're in limbo."

Ms. Pillows sighed. "If we must put labels on things, Elspeth, then, fine. Call it what you will." She stood, her dress bunched with wrinkles. "Now get some rest, you're going to need it. Tomorrow we will begin your education."

"Wait…*what?*"

"You will not go on assignments without the proper education, young lady."

"I don't do so well with organized education. I'm sorta…self-educated." Organized groups weren't my thing. They drained individuality and were one step away from group mentality mobs.

"Well," she puffed. "You're just going to have to get over that, Elspeth!" She wagged her finger in my face. "Perhaps if you paid more attention in school back on Earth, you wouldn't be here." Her voice drifted away as she realized what she'd said.

I jumped to my feet, crossed my arms, and shot her a glare.

"I'm truly sorry I said that, Elspeth. It wasn't proper." Once again, her gaze climbed toward the ceiling. I guess she lived in a constant state of divine fear. She extended her arms and patted my shoulders from a safe distance. I stood my ground, arms still folded. "I *am* sorry for what became of you, Elspeth. It's not fair."

"Yeah, fine."

She finally broke her awkward half-of-a-hug. "Splendid! Now, in addition to education, you'll have an introductory session, a tour, training courses—"

"Training? What kind of training?"

"Why, self-defense, of course."

"Kick ass!" I kickboxed the air and spun around.

"Yes, well. Perhaps some proper etiquette training, as well." She stumbled toward the door, right hand placed flat upon her chest in dismay.

\*\*\*\*

Most people probably don't accept their fate as easily as I did. But it was just the way I rolled. Early on, I learned to accept the unexpected, and to go with the punches fate delivered, but that didn't make me a punching bag.

I grew up with two loving parents in a middle-class home in New York. But even as a kid, I knew I was different. A rebel with a mind of my own, I rallied against any perceived intolerance and ignorance. My parents didn't escape the backlash. The more people pushed me to do something dumb, the harder I fought back. Honestly, I had no personal causes to fight. Simply put, I was in love with the idea of rebellion. Thought it romantic, I supposed, in a weird way.

Being a New York City teen in the '80s supplied

me with the perfect venue for my one-girl war against stupidity. I experimented with drugs and booze, skipped school, stayed out all night, snuck into bars, saw cool bands. I perfected getting into trouble as an art form.

In retrospect, my wild lifestyle didn't work out so well for me. Duh.

My biggest regret was the pain I caused my parents. If I could go back, and tell them my death wasn't their fault, that I was okay, I would. They didn't deserve their grief. I asked Ms. Pillows once if I could see my parents. She said absolutely not. Against the rules. Stupid, pointless rules, arbitrarily drawn up. Yet, what I'd have given to hug my mother one last time, blanket her with some sense of comfort, of closure. Even if it was a huge-ass rule breaker. Whatever.

My first week of education in limbo was a crashing bore. The same basics of reading, writing, and arithmetic once again pummeled into my head. Heavy emphasis placed on religion with an obvious slant toward Christianity. My constant questions about faith, belief, and just why other religions were considered wrong made me a pariah. The teachers grew to dislike me, branding me as a troublemaker. My fellow students—sort of a bland, young Christian rally— shunned me, choosing to run in their own packs. Just like high school. No matter. I'd always been somewhat of a loner and intended to remain one. I knew I could count on myself.

I shined in the self-defense classes. The Asian teacher—who never gave his name, but I swear he was Bruce Lee—took a shining to me, particularly when I landed a round-about kick to his chest, knocking him to the mat on our first session. When I helped him off the floor, his eyes filled with shock, maybe even a little admiration. Soon, the gym beckoned me. I improved my skills, transforming myself into one badass piece of work. The teacher approved of me. He even gave me a spare key to the gym. However, the one-on-one spars stopped after I felled him several more times.

Upon meeting my roommate Susan Patterson, I wanted to run the other way. Blond, pretty in a dull mid-western manner, and dumb as a box of rocks. Fuzzy sweaters were her blouse of choice. Calf-length skirts in checkered patterns, high heels, hair braids, and a constant toothy smile were her adornments. On Earth, she'd died from pneumonia in the early sixties. She had even *died* boring. I had to give it up to her, though. She tried to be friendly to me, unlike the rest of the "God Squad." Still, I made her squirm as much as possible. Sure, it was mean, but as I said, I had to get my kicks any way I could.

'Cause it was dead boring in limbo.

****

I groaned, staring up at the popcorn-spattered ceiling. The boring popcorn-spattered ceiling. "I'm bored!"

"Elspeth, you've already said that." Susan sat on the bed, posture perfect, hands folded demurely in her lap. "Why don't you go work out?"

"Already did that. I'm getting itchy. It's been practically a year since I went on a mission." I had to wonder what type of missions they sent Susan on. She was pretty tight-lipped about them, but it was hard to imagine her coping with anything dangerous. Like my last couple of missions. Maybe she dealt with church crises where the wine offerings have soured or something.

"I haven't been out in a while, either." She twirled her blond hair around a finger, deep in thought. Or as deep as she could muster. "But I really like it here. So many nice people!" Her face scrunched up into a ball of sunshine. I fought the impulse to kick that ball out of the stadium.

"Yeah. *So* many nice people." Deadly dull people more like. Even though they hadn't really befriended me, everyone here was superficially sugary sweet, smiley. So mind-numbing. If I ever heard "have a nice day!" again—by anyone, living or dead—I'd gouge my eyes out.

"Elspeth, you should really try to join some of the other groups. They're not so bad, you know." The pink eyesore rotary telephone rang. Apparently, in limbo, technology hadn't caught up yet. "I'll get it!" screamed Susan, lunging for the receiver. "Hello?" Based on her obvious disappointment, it wasn't Biff or whoever was asking her out for ice cream. "I'll tell her." She hung up the phone. "Elspeth, Ms. Pillows would like to see you."

"Awesome!" I cartwheeled off the bed. Saved by the bell from "Little Susan Sunshine"!

Halfway out the door, Susan called after me. "Elspeth?"

"Yeah?"

"If you're going on a mission, be careful, okay? I know they send you on dangerous ones sometimes." The corners of her mouth drooped down, ever the worrywart.

"Thanks, Susan. Don't worry, I'll be careful."

As I ran out into the hallway, a thought crossed my

mind. *Is it possible for me to die again?*

\*\*\*\*

In the narrow hallway, I sat on a wooden bench next to an old, bald Indian man in a *khurta*. I think his name was Goulash or something like that; he was supposed to be a big deal. He nodded a greeting, his eyes magnified through his wire-rim glasses.

"Got any gum?" I asked.

He looked at me as if I'd spoken gibberish. "Young lady, I do not indulge in items of unnecessary, instant, and frivolous self-gratification, particularly those of a sugar-based nature—"

"So, you don't have any?"

He sighed loudly and leaned back, his bony shoulders pressed up against the cold, cement wall. "No, young lady, I do not." He closed his eyes, shutting me out.

More people sat on the benches, exchanging nervous glances. I knew a lot of them dreaded their missions. Not me. I lived for them.

On the wall opposite me, a red light was caged behind a wire enclosure. A nice prison-like effect. I'd never seen the light flash on before, prompting the question, *just what does constitute a limbo emergency?* A painting by limbo's favorite accursed artist hung above me; the subject was another child with hugely abnormal eyes. Less than inspirational, and not at all attractive. Hell, must've had a starving artist sale and limbo cleaned up.

The fluorescent bulbs set into the ceiling cast a sickly suffusion over the tiled floor. The refraction rippled like a wave all the way to Ms. Pillows' oak door at the end of the hallway. It felt like old times, waiting to see the school principal.

The door squeaked open. My fellow bench-sitters straightened, waiting for their date with destiny. A thin man in a light blue suit stood in the doorway. He consulted the small booklet in his hand. "Ms. Chambers?"

I turned to Goulash and whispered, "They make sugarless gum now, you know?"

His small eyes widened, his mouth flapping open and shut.

"Just sayin'."

I moved down the hallway. The blue-suited man stepped aside to usher me into Ms. Pillows' office. She perched behind her desk, stylishly frumpy in her flower-patterned dress. Straining to see over the top of her cat-eye glasses, she gestured toward the chair across from her. Her assistant closed the door, hovering by it like a guard.

The office seemed at once familiar and alien. It looked like any other chamber of horrors from the principals of my past. Except that where most principals proudly displayed photos of their wives and children, Ms. Pillows decked her desktop with plant photography. Whereas degrees and awards usually decorated walls, more paintings of demonic, unnaturally huge-eyed devil spawn ogled me. "Hellish Moments" could be the name of the painting series.

"And how are we today, Elspeth?" she asked, stacking a ream of paper onto her desktop.

"Oh, I guess 'we're' doing just fine." I kicked my boots up on top of her desk and leaned back, fingers entwined behind my neck. She pointed at my feet and sniffed. I swept them to the floor with a double clump.

"It's time for you to go back into the field, Elspeth."

"All right!"

"Yes, well. Ahem. Your methods of doing things have been rather, how do I put this? Unorthodox, to say the least." She glared at me, awaiting my response. I had none. "But you do tend to provide results."

"I aim to please, Ms. Pillows."

She narrowed her eyes, scrutinizing me, uncertain whether I was messing with her. "Now, your host..." She shuffled her papers. "Elizabeth Blackmer. How is your relationship with her?"

"I wouldn't exactly say we have a relationship, Ms. Pillows." I shrugged. "She's a rich spoiled brat. But I guess you could say we tolerate one another."

"Tolerate?"

"You know. We don't want to kill one another." Ms. Pillows choked and looked at her assistant for help. He stifled a laugh and averted his gaze out the window. "We wouldn't ever play tea party together or anything. But she understands the deal. As long as she gets into an Ivy League college and I don't harm her body or her wardrobe, she seems to be okay with it. I guess."

"Yes, well. We certainly don't want to have an inhospitable host, now do we?"

"No, 'we' certainly don't." My fake politeness never fooled anyone. But genuine politeness just didn't come naturally to me.

"Now, we have another problem at Clearwell High School in Kansas. I know you're familiar with the school."

I nodded while buffing out a scratch on my boot.

"We have a situation. One involving drugs." Her eyelashes fluttered like butterfly wings.

13

"Okay." My voice dropped to a near whisper. Pillows had caught me off guard. Drugs made me extremely uncomfortable these days.

"I know your past with drugs. I'm hoping this won't be a problem for you." While she smiled sympathetically, her eyebrows arched.

I picked the snow globe off her desk, turning it over and over. The fake flakes spun about in a white whirlpool. Weird for Ms. Pillows to have a snow globe. It never snowed in limbo. "Yeah, I used drugs in my past life. But if you're asking me if I'll be tempted," I shook my head. "Ain't gonna happen. I learned my lesson. I won't be going down that dark alley again."

"Terrific." With some effort, she reached across her desk, grabbed the globe from my hands, and returned it to its roost. "We do feel you're best suited for this particular operation. You have certain skills—and knowledge—that could prove quite beneficial."

"Okay. I know we're dealing with drugs here, but what else can you tell me?"

"Several days ago, there was a drug-related death involving one of Clearwell's seniors. It appears there's been a sudden influx of drugs made available to the student body. Before there are any other deaths, we need you to seek out the source of the drugs."

"You want me to find the dealer? Sounds easy enough."

"Well, things are never as easy as they appear, Elspeth. You should know this by now." She stood, staring out her window at the flat fields of green grass that seemed to go on forever. I thought they might, too. Grass was the only thing I ever saw when I went outside.

"I've word from on high this could be a dangerous case."

"What did your higher-up say exactly?"

She dropped back into her chair, wagging her head. "Elspeth, you know I can't divulge that information to you. We've been through this already."

"Yeah, yeah, I get it. Keep me in the dark even though I do the dirty work." I tossed out some finger quotes. "'The higher-ups move in strange and mysterious ways and it's not for us to ask why'." From behind me, Ms. Pillows' assistant snorted. She shot him an icy, disapproving stare.

"Yes, well. As I was saying, things could prove to be dangerous. People may not turn out to be who you— or Elizabeth—take them to be. It is vitally important you be careful whom you trust. There's a darkness falling upon Clearwell."

"Again."

Ms. Pillows' sour expression spoke volumes. "Anyhoo, the drugs are tearing the school apart. The damage is increasing. We fear it will grow considerably worse unless we put a stop to it. We mustn't allow any more untimely deaths. It upsets the natural order of things."

This time, I lifted my eyebrows. "What exactly *is* the natural order of things, Ms. Pillows?"

"Elspeth…" She dragged my name out with several additional syllables.

"Okay, fine, whatever. What *can* you tell me? I mean, I don't even know what time of year it is in Clearwell." No one has watches or calendars in limbo. To me, every day is Monday.

"It's nearing the end of the school year. Your

host," she said, consulting her papers once again, "Elizabeth is readying for graduation. She's also running for prom queen."

I rolled my eyes. Of course Elizabeth would. "I'm not going to wear a stupid crown." Once again, Ms. Pillows' assistant chuckled before she shot him down with her evil glare.

"Well, Elspeth, let's hope it doesn't come to that," she said. "Anything else you would like to know?" She slapped her papers onto her desk, signifying the end of our "exit interview".

I stood up. "Yeah, actually there's tons of stuff I'd like to know. But, as always, I'm sure you won't give me the answers."

"You will be given important information on a need-to-know basis, Elspeth."

I fought the urge to salute her. "Any other parting words?"

"Just one." I was way overdue to rattle Ms. Pillows with a new expletive. *"Bitchin'!"* When Ms. Pillows turned several shades of puce, I stored the magical moment away in my brain. Then I high-fived the assistant on my way out the door.

Time to prepare for my trip to Clearwell. And whatever was waiting for me there.

Chapter Two

*Elizabeth*

"Oh, my God!" shouted Addison, pitched between excitement and shock. "Did you guys hear about Charles Durbin?" Addie stood straight, shoulders back, the way I taught her. "Did you hear, Elizabeth?"

First of all, I hadn't heard. Second, I had no idea who Charles Durbin was. "No. What's going on, Addie?" I stood several feet in front of my locker in the packed hallway. If anyone needed to get around me, they could take the long path. I was not a locker-hugger.

"He *died* last night!"

High drama was never a good thing. "Inside voice, Addie, inside voice." I waved my hand, slowly and firmly, as if stroking my pony. "Deep cleansing breath." Addie followed my directive and breathed in deeply. "Calm now?" Addie nodded. "Tell me what happened. And who is…was…Charles Durbin?"

"Charles Durbin was in our class, Elizabeth! He was an okay guy. Kinda quiet, stayed to himself. But he had some friends." She fanned herself, fingers splayed. Very unbecoming. "I wouldn't ever consider him popular, but he was well-liked."

My first thought was, if he was so well-liked, why didn't I know him? But maybe that was a little too insensitive. "How did he die?"

Addie threw her hands up, slapping them down loudly onto her khaki shorts. Her Tiffany charm bracelet jangled, punctuating her excitement. "It's really, really weird. He was driving his car late last night. They say he was up to one hundred miles per hour. And he crashed it into a house. He died in an ambulance a little bit later!"

"That's awful, Addie." I tapped my lips in a refined fashion. "Was it suicide? Or drugs?"

"Don't know. But I never thought Charles was a druggie."

"Huh." Down the hall two girls—underclassmen, I believed—were crying and hugging in front of their open lockers. Word spread quickly. "That's a real shame." I was not heartless. I just couldn't get worked up over the—tragic as it was—demise of a student I didn't know. And even though this was an extremely crucial year for me, I had way too much pride—too much good taste—to try to make this tragedy my own. On the other hand, it might garner me some sympathy votes for prom queen. Something I was sure Charlotte Drayton was no doubt working on. She probably already had a grievance committee marching their way through the hallways. And I was positive she didn't know who Charles Durbin was either.

With a shudder, Addison's eyes brimmed with tears. I leaned in and gave her a short, tasteful hug. One of the few things I'd learned from boys. They knew how to provide quick, subtle hugs that didn't outlast their welcome.

"Thank you, Elizabeth," said Addie between sniffles. "I knew I could count on you."

Addison Harcourt was probably my "Best Friend Forever," maybe the best BFF I'd ever had. Hard to believe we'd remained close for so long. I had met her four years earlier and it seemed like a lifetime ago.

**** 

During the Clearwell freshman orientation session, I had sat in the cafeteria waiting for the festivities to begin. Though it was a brand new school for me, I felt confident in myself, having put all of my childhood friends behind me. They'd served their purpose in my formative years. But it became apparent they were holding me back from the social status I deserved. One couldn't continue going through life fantasizing about popular boy bands and which boy in school has the nicest smile. I had bigger fish to fry, and larger aspirations to hook, in my pursuit of stature and wealth.

Addison immediately captured my attention when she walked into the cafeteria. Her fear and lack of confidence were obvious, the proverbial rabbit caught in the headlights. Yet her wardrobe spoke of good style and money: a nice pink oxford and flats. I thought her checkered skirt looked like a designer knock-off, but if it was, it was a forger's dream. With subtly applied mascara, the rest of her makeup looked subdued and naturally sunny. Her blond hair was a bit of a mess, asymmetrical waves streaming down both sides of her face. No matter, though. I could work with it.

I called out to her, "Hi. Why don't you sit with me?"

"Thank you." She seemed greatly relieved she wouldn't be destined for outcast status before school even started.

"I love your oxford. It totally works for you."

She studied my clothing. I wore a cardigan over a yellow button-down shirt, a matching skirt tailored just above my knees (nothing too short!) and Topsiders. "I like your clothes, too." *Well, of course she does.* She squinted at my pearls. "That's daring of you to wear pearls."

"Are you kidding me? They are the new fashion accessory. Even though they're old as the hills!" I jangled the pearls around my neck. "Just raid your mother's jewelry box. They may be old, but they cost—"

"Oh, I don't live with my mother." She traced a line on the Formica tabletop before catching herself, and then folded her hands in front of her. Good upbringing.

"I'm sorry. I didn't mean to bring up something uncomfortable for you." I leaned forward, expressing my best sympathy. "Has she passed away?"

"I wish! No, another divorce casualty."

"Ah." Actually, divorce was much more trending these days than having a deceased parent. "I'm Elizabeth, by the way." I held my hand out and she accepted it. I shook it firmly, twice, and dropped it the way Daddy taught me.

"I'm Addison."

"So, Addie…may I call you Addie?"

Her smile grew. "Yes, I'd like that very much. Can I call you Liz?"

"No."

"Oh. I'm sorry."

"Don't worry about it. It's just…Liz is so gauche, don't you think?"

"I suppose it is," she said quietly.

"Anyway, do you live with your father?"

She nodded.

"What does he do?"

"He's a real estate developer. He builds condos. He's been pretty successful at it."

"Addie, I think we're going to hit it off just fine." We both giggled at the prospect of having found someone so mutually compatible on our first day of school. Luck of the Irish, Daddy would say.

And hit it off we did. Like crazy. During our first month of friendship, I decided to help her in any way I could. Her crippling lack of confidence had to be dealt with. I started slow, with trips to the hair salon, pedicures, manicures, the works. Once a girl starts feeling good about her outward appearance, the rest flows naturally. I taught her the importance of good posture; it's not just for boys. Walk proudly, shoulders back, chin out, straight strides that announced you were going places. The results were amazing. Sure, some of the more idiotic boys started calling us "twins," but I didn't see it that way. Of course, we wore similar clothing—there weren't that many great stores to choose from—and we both had long, straight blond hair. But we couldn't be any more different.

Addie's lack of experience in dealing with boys was another issue, one that surprised me. For a pretty girl such as her to have next to no knowledge about handling boys seemed deplorable, to say the least. She had an absolutely appalling taste in boys. Her only criterion was that they be "cute." She had no parameters, no bars to set high. When she'd point out a boy she liked, nine times out of ten, she was *way* out of their league. I soon taught her there was more to boys than their "cuteness" factor. Why settle for the cream when you can slaughter the cow?

Next up in my tutorial came the fine art of flirting, a true talent bestowed upon very few girls. Not only was it fun, but if done properly, it was an amazing way to get boys to do things for you.

"Okay, Addie, how would you approach a boy?" I asked her at our initial training session.

She swayed back and forth uncertainly in her flats. "I don't know. I guess I'd go up to him and ask him if he's going to the spring formal—"

*"Wrong!"* I turned the full-length mirror toward her. "Addie, pretend your image is the boy you desire." I quickly put a stop to her eye rolling with a glare. "First, you never act desperate! Desperation is a tool reserved for those lacking in self-confidence. You may as well wear a sign, saying, 'I'm desperate! Someone— *anyone*—date me!'"

"Elizabeth, I don't know—"

"I know, Addie. That's why you have me." I flashed my perfect teeth at her. "Okay, now sashay!"

"Um, what?"

*"Sashay!* Sashay in front of the boy, taking extra care to not look him in the eyes."

"Okay." Addison moved her hips back and forth like she'd lost her point of gravity. She turned to me, giggling. "Elizabeth, I feel silly."

"You do look silly. Who taught you how to sashay, anyway? Madame Olga of the house of ill-repute?"

Addison snorted, attempting to cover the uncouth sound with her hand.

"Okay, we do not sashay like common hos. Watch." I walked toward the mirror, chin jutting out, shoulders balanced and back, legs close together, eyes locked firmly in front of me. I paused in front of the mirror, and flung my hair back before continuing. "Did you see what I did there?"

"Wow…yeah." I had totally earned the admiration in her voice.

"Now you try." It took Addison longer than two hours before she mastered the subtle, yet classy, sashay. And this was only the first lesson in how to deal with boys. A slow student, but I felt she'd be worth the effort.

"Where did you learn how to do that, Elizabeth?"

"I suppose I learned a lot of it from my mother. She's a bona fide trophy wife. We could both learn a lot from her. Okay, once you get the boy's attention, what do you do next?"

Addison stared into the mirror, a goofy smile plastered across her face. "Hi! I'm Addison. Are you going to the dance?"

*"Wrong!"* I clapped my hands together loudly, startling her. "Addie, Addie, Addie, what are we going to do with you?" Although the question was rhetorical, I stared at her expectantly, letting her realize the severity of her situation. "Here's what you do next…*nothing.*"

"Nothing?"

"Absolutely nothing*.*"

"Huh."

"Once you master the first steps, and it will take practice and determination, you might try a backward glance, followed by a brief smile—mouth closed, no teeth showing. But since you're a beginner, just skip that part for now."

"But what if it puts him off?"

I hung my head, shaking it like a bobblehead. "Addie, do you trust me?" She nodded emphatically, her eyes wide with adulation. "Fine. You obviously don't know boys. It's bred into their nature to enjoy a challenge. They have to think they're the ones in charge, the ones who make the conquest. So, we let them think that. What they don't know is we're the ones who pull the strings on these silly little would-be macho marionettes."

Addison laughed.

"Just trust me, Addie. You repeat this first step several times—just like treating your hair, wash, rinse, repeat—and soon, they'll be chasing you around, doting on your every word and command."

"Awesome!"

"But—and this is very important—never say or do anything unladylike. We may be flirts, but we're not hos."

"Got it."

Addison proved to be a better student than I had initially thought. Her enthusiasm was boundless. Before too long she caught on, nearly my equal—amazed at her own transformation, and with a mind-boggling number of boys calling on her. Of course, I had to steer her away from a few of her choices—she still didn't quite get the importance of choosing good stock and how it reflected upon her—but that came with time as well. Over the next few years, she cut a swath through several boyfriends, none of them lasting too long. That was okay, though. She developed an uncanny knack for picking boys then dropping them with the ebb and flow of school public opinion. She filled me with pride. She was a great best friend, and I couldn't have asked for a better "number two".

****

As I walked Addison to her class, my arm lightly draped around her shoulder for support (but not in a gaudy fashion, mind you), I noticed the student body's collective emotions had taken a decided change. April, with graduation just around the corner and the prom coming up. Soon. Until today, giddiness abounded in the hallways, expectations soaring about the bright future some of us had to look forward to. And I couldn't help but suspect my fellow students were just as excited about the crowning of the prom queen and king.

But today, things seemed different, quieter. Students wandered the halls aimlessly, lost in thought. Smaller groups adjourned, sharing hugs. Some of the tears and outbursts sounded gut-tugging. Maybe people were sad they hadn't grasped the opportunity to know Charles Durbin. I must admit I felt a twinge of guilt. Had I missed out on a friend worth knowing? Charles Durbin apparently affected a lot of people. How could this be possible when I didn't even know who he was?

I air-kissed Addie's cheeks and headed off to my environmental science class. Walking down the middle of the hallway—my chosen path, as I didn't let the dictates of traffic force me to walk on the right side of the hallway—I kept my gaze locked ahead, acknowledging others only when they spoke to me first.

My eyes wandered to one of my prom queen posters hanging above a row of lockers. Tastefully done, the focal point was a photograph of me wearing a white cardigan sweater and sitting in my father's study in front of the fireplace. My knees were locked together tightly, my cat Sparkles on my lap. I had one hand forcefully pointing outward with the slogan emblazoned across the bottom, "Elizabeth Blackmer...I Want to Be YOUR Prom Queen."

At least the poster *used* to be tasteful. Someone had defaced it. Juvenile devil's horns were scribbled on top of my hair, ludicrous fangs scrawled into my mouth. "Prom Queen" had been replaced with the word "Bitch."

I knew my mature, refined manner might have been misconstrued by others as "bitchiness," but that wasn't the case here. Not at all. I had donated some of Daddy's money to charities from time to time and even helped out a few causes I believed in. If anything, I was misunderstood. But this was personal. *Hugely* personal. And I had a good idea who was behind it, too.

****

I huffed into class ten minutes early and took my seat at the back of the room. It wasn't where I generally chose to sit, but it was where Mr. Dawson placed me. I had the distinct feeling Mr. Dawson didn't care for me, a feeling I was totally unaccustomed to. Whatever. It didn't matter, really. Environmental science was a stupid class anyway, something I picked for an easy A.

The new skinny kid sauntered in and sat down in front of me. A stale cigarette stench wafted off him, filling my nostrils with the stink. Ewww. He wore tripp pants, ridiculous chains jangling whenever he moved, and a metal band T-shirt Today's outlaw. The only thing I knew about him other than his poor choice in wardrobe? His name, Tim Matthews. And he'd been expelled from some other school for unknown reasons. He sank into his chair, turned, and stared at me. When he smiled, the overhead lights glinted off his braces. Not the good kind of braces designed for perfection either, but the barely functional kind, fitted to correct heinous genes.

"Can I *help* you?"

He quickly turned around without saying a word. The rest of the class was abuzz about the demise of Charles Durbin. I caught pieces of information here and there. Half of the class thought it was a suicide while others swore drugs were involved.

I slammed my books onto the table—backpacks were *much* too common—and placed my designer purse by my feet. I just wanted to be left alone. No sense in my totally sucky day getting even worse.

Lance bounced in, happy as usual. "Morning, Elizabeth." He sidled in next to me. Noticing my dour demeanor, he said, "What's the matter, girl? Did somebody get up on the wrong side of her pretty, pretty pony this morning?" He laughed loudly, *way* too loudly.

Lance Nguyen was my environmental science lab partner, chosen at random by Mr. Dawson. Actually, I didn't mind him so much. Lance was Asian, eternally optimistic, and came from money. In fact, Daddy had had some dealings with his father in the past. Lance had impeccable taste in clothing, although for the life of me, I'd never understood his fascination with ankle-pants. They looked like what less privileged kids might wear when they couldn't afford new clothing to accommodate their growth spurts.

Lance was also proudly, openly gay. Although I was defiantly Republican, I'd managed to make homosexuality work in my worldview. Times were a-changing and maybe it was time for a new breed of Republican. The stodgy old school should move over and make way for those better suited to adapt to the ever-evolving world. And I was fully prepared to lead the way.

But Lance wasn't someone I'd welcome into my close circle. By his own choice, he surrounded himself with those of a lower standing, obviously not heeding the saying that people judge you by who you hang out with. Still, while not a friend exactly, Lance was an acquaintance whom I tolerated and sometimes even liked. When he wasn't getting on my nerves.

"Oh, shut up, Lance."

He stopped laughing when he noticed the grave atmosphere permeating the room. "Hey, what's going on?"

"You haven't heard?"

He shook his head, his eyes expressing dread.

"Charles Durbin died last night."

"Oh…oh…" He leaned forward, resting his head on the table.

"Did you know him?"

He sat up, averting his eyes. "I didn't know him well, but he was always nice to me. How did it happen?"

Tim Matthews turned to look at me again. Without saying a word, I spun my finger around. He obeyed, like a well-trained puppy. "I'm not sure. He crashed his car into a house and died in an ambulance on the way to the hospital."

"That's…that's not like him." Lance's voice cracked. "I don't understand this."

"I know, Lance. I know." Tempted to give him a

hug, I thought better of it, not wanting to cause a scene.

Mr. Dawson's entrance saved me from an emotional dilemma. He dropped into a chair behind his desk. His bushy mass of black, curly hair puffed out from his head, while his huge, outdated rope of a mustache drooped down. Leaning back, he studied the ceiling. I was used to these long periods of Mr. Dawson's contemplation; he lapsed into them often enough. I suspected if he wasn't a current recreational drug user, he was definitely weaned on them in the '70s. Yeah, that old. Obviously, a tree-hugger, he loved sharing his liberal agenda while presenting his lessons. Might've been why he didn't like me.

Finally, Mr. Dawson broke the interminable silence. "Class, I'm sure by now you've heard of the unfortunate passing of Charles Durbin." A few random sobs acknowledged we had. "I didn't have the fortune to know him well, but from what I understand, Charles was a good student, a good kid. Cool kid, cool kid. Now I wanna break it down to your level. Mr. Dawson is in the hizzy-ouse."

*Oh, good God.* Whenever Mr. Dawson "broke it down" for us, I wanted to scream. But I imagined it would've been inappropriate given the circumstances. Still, if he ever started freestyle rapping, even I wouldn't be able to maintain my dignity.

"From what I hear, drugs might have been involved. This is just what I hear, mind you, nothing has been confirmed as of yet, so stay cool." He strolled in front of his desk, sat, and hitched one leg over the side. His "easy-going, just one of the kids" pose. "Now, I think this might be a good opportunity to address the drugs issue."

One kid groaned. A few snickered. Tim Matthews hunkered farther down into his chair, clearly a topic hitting too close to home for him.

"Lately, there appears to be a sudden flood of drug usage and sales going on around campus—"

A hand shot up, followed by an earnest voice. "How do you know this, Mr. Dawson?" A few more chuckles arose. Mr. Dawson didn't fool anyone about *his* after-hours recreational hobbies.

"Well, Bobby, it's what I've been told," he said, looking him squarely in the eyes. "Now, I know some of you, on occasion, might be curious about experimenting with a little marijuana, a little pot." He held two fingers to his mouth and inhaled the air. "That's to be expected. What's not to be expected are the types of drugs that're being peddled around here!" *Splat!* He whacked his fist into his palm. "We're talking prescription drugs, cocaine, even heroin! And then there's talk about home-made synthetic drugs. I hear it all, guys. All of it. It needs to stop! It's a bad scene, dudes. Bad!" Placing his arms akimbo, he swiveled his head across the classroom. "If any of you, *any* of you, know anything about who's dealing this poison to your fellow students, then please let us know. I implore you, just let us know." He flailed his hands about his mountain of hair, definitely on a roll. "Furthermore, what's the stupidest thing you could possibly do? Anyone?"

"Take drugs!" yelled out some lame-o.

Mr. Dawson sighed. "Well, yes, but don't any of you ever get behind the wheel of a car if you're impaired. Smoke your weed behind closed doors and keep it inside. It's not cool. Just un-cool." A very melodramatic usage of finger quotes. "Such a tragedy. It's tragic what happened to Charles Durbin. Just don't let it happen to you or your friends." Mr. Dawson walked back behind the comfort of his desk. "Don't do it, people. Okay, let's begin."

I had to admit Mr. Dawson's words were stirring. Except for his slang slaughter. But I had a difficult time seeing the relevance of the situation as it pertained to me. I wanted to help, but I didn't know anyone who used or sold drugs.

How wrong I would prove to be.

\*\*\*\*

My trustworthy steed waited for me outside the doorway, as he always did.

"Hi, Elizabeth." He leaned in to kiss me.

"Donovan." I swiftly turned my head so his lips fell upon my cheek. No need for tacky PDAs.

\*\*\*\*

Donovan Goode had been my boyfriend for the past two years and had damn well better be the prom king to my queen-in-waiting. I met him at the beginning of my junior year at a "Young American Christians" meeting (the less said about that group, the better!). When he strolled into the room, his confidence overpowered everyone else's. He owned the crowd. I watched as he made his way through the gathering, personally greeting as many Young American Christians as possible. What some may have called grandstanding, I saw as genuine. I *felt* it. Totally electrifying. At that moment, I knew I'd found my special other.

I played coy, as I instructed Addie to do, and like a moth drawn to the flame, he eventually flew to my table.

"Hello." He offered his hand. I accepted his, presenting an award-winning reticent performance. He enclosed his other hand on top of our clasped hands like a stamped seal to a Royal message. "I'm Donovan Goode."

"Elizabeth Blackmer." I snatched my hand back, but not too quickly. A girl should never linger too long lest the wrong message be implied.

"I know who you are. I've seen you around school." I'd actually seen him as well, but he didn't need to know that. "May I sit with you?"

"Be my guest."

"You haven't been to a meeting before."

"It's my first one." I'd never been what you might call a "religious person." Yes, my parents made me attend church every Sunday (Protestant, natch), but I sorta attended because of the societal acceptance and possible networking connections that may have arisen from it. And after my dealings with Elspeth, I knew there was at least some form of life after death. When in doubt, best to hedge one's bets. Something Daddy taught me early on.

"I certainly hope it's not your last meeting, Elizabeth." He sparkled dazzlingly white teeth at me. Extremely well groomed and not a hair out of place in his coiffed, wavy hair. His eyes, warmly brown, twinkled, filling me with—I was hesitant to say lust (vulgar!)—passion. I'd have to be careful around this boy. Otherwise, my inner desires would get the better of me and I could easily have ended up as one of those girls who "travels" for nine months.

"We'll just have to see how it goes." I studied his

wardrobe as I did with everyone I met. Respectable, but quite possibly from a cheap retail outlet. But I could work on that. "Are you religious?"

"I consider myself a Christian, yes. I think we should all strive to expand our minds and hearts." Wow. Spoken like a true politician. Safe, yet sincere.

"So, what is it you want to do with your life, Donovan?" Forward, sure, maybe, but life is short.

His eyes bore into mine, dancing with sincerity. "I'm interested in politics. As you may know, I was just elected head of the student council."

"Hmmm. Maybe I do recall that." Of course I did. But if I let on, it'd immediately go to his head. Everyone knew the dynamics of all relationships were defined early. Best to lay down the ground rules up-front, so there weren't any surprises later. "I'm interested in politics as well." Which was true. Behind every great politician, a great woman pulls the strings. "If not that, a career in finance or law is a viable option."

"Wow, just, wow."

I had him. He was probably used to the dumb, obedient cheerleader type.

"That's quite impressive, Elizabeth."

"I know it is."

At the end of the meeting, he asked me out. I told him I'd think about it, but left him with an alluring smile that purposefully gave him conflicting messages. Besides, if he didn't keep trying, he was not quite the man I thought him to be. He made several more attempts, and I finally consented. Although, secretly, I'd given in to him the minute I spotted him at the YAC meeting.

33

I pre-warned Daddy that he wasn't from a wealthy family. Not poor, just tiresomely middle-class; his father a salesman, his mother a housewife. But there was something special about Donovan; his determination and ambition would easily propel him to the top.

Daddy wasn't happy about it at first. But, then again, he never liked *any* boy—regardless of financial stature—who dated me. Okay, so I was "Daddy's Little Girl". It'd worked out so far.

On our first date, I couldn't help but be disappointed when I spied Donovan pulling up in a Celica. Sigh. Okay, he was merely *next* to perfection. Once the doorbell rang, I assumed my customary hiding spot on the upstairs landing and listened in on the proceedings.

"Yes?" Daddy growled, even though he knew full well who to expect.

"Hello, Mr. Blackmer, my name is Donovan. Donovan Goode." Donovan greeted him with his stellar handshake. "I'm here to escort your daughter—with your permission, of course—to a movie."

I melted a little bit. Old-fashioned gentlemen were a rare commodity at Clearwell High.

"Please don't worry, sir," continued Donovan. "It's a PG-rated film, and I intend on having her home by ten o'clock. I respect Elizabeth's curfew and that it's a school night."

"Come in, come in," said Daddy, his voice lightening in tenor a couple of notches. Daddy's gruff billy-goat demeanor vanished, yet he still sounded guarded. None of my suitors ever made it that far. "Can I get you something to drink, Donovan?" Daddy laid his trap. One I knew Donovan would have no trouble avoiding.

"No, thank you, sir. I never touch alcohol, and I would *never* get behind the wheel of a car if I partook in any. The offer is appreciated, however."

"Fine," said Daddy. "Why don't you join me in the study while I have one?" Okay, time to let Donovan off the hook, especially since they were going into Daddy's private chambers. No one was ever allowed in there, not really.

I flew down the stairs, keeping my skirt pressed down at my sides. My heart leapt to my throat as I saw the large, mahogany doors close, a warning against trespassers. With a great amount of trepidation, I knocked.

"Enter!" I opened the doors and the two men in my life were facing one another in Daddy's oversized fireplace chairs. Daddy dangled a drink in his hand while Donovan's hands were clasped reverentially in his lap. "Elizabeth." Daddy afforded me a rare, wry smile. "Donovan was just getting ready to tell me about his father's work."

Uh-oh. I had arrived at just the right moment. "That's great, Daddy." I walked behind him and draped my arms around his neck, a proven method to soften his bluster. "But our movie starts in thirty minutes. We should really get going."

Daddy half-rose from his chair, ready to interject like a crabby lawyer.

Donovan said, "That's okay, Elizabeth. We have time. I'm more than happy to tell your father what mine does."

*Great.* My first big high school romance was about

to be torpedoed before it had a chance to get ocean bound. I stood between their two chairs, ready to play arbiter if necessary.

"Mr. Blackmer, my father is a hard-working salesman, has been all his life. He makes a good honest living and provides for my mother and me. He worked his way up from the bottom, was the first member of his lineage to go to college, and has a dream to retire early."

Daddy swirled his drink, staring at the clinking ice cube. "What does he sell?" He lifted a gray eyebrow, as if the answer would determine my future romantic happiness.

"Computer software programs. He works one-on-one with the designers so he has an idea of the product he's putting out there. Then he puts together presentations, taking them to large corporations across the—"

"What are some of the corporations, son?" I couldn't tell if he meant "son" as a term of endearment, derision, or intimidation. Knowing Daddy, probably a mixture of the three.

"Um…" Donovan stuttered, the first time I'd ever seen his calm composure dry up. But he rebounded and listed a number of corporations much too boring for me to recall.

Daddy raised his hand authoritatively. "And do you wish to pursue this line of work, Donovan?"

"No, sir. I'm interested in politics." The ticking of the grandfather clock in the corner tapped away the seconds it took for Daddy to process this information. I felt like a criminal on trial awaiting a jury's verdict.

"I see. Which party, if I may be so bold to ask?"

"Republican, sir." Donovan's wide smile returned. He knew he had answered correctly.

Daddy grinned back. "Is that right? Well, tell me more, son, tell me more." He leaned forward, displaying a light, breezy air I hadn't seen in years. Donovan regaled him with his student council triumphs.

After five minutes of their mutual admiration society, I'd had enough. "Okay, Daddy, Donovan and I must be going! *Ta.*" I leaned over and kissed Daddy's forehead. Donovan stood, straightening the pleats in his slacks.

"Okay, you kids have a good time." Obviously remembering his role as watchdog, Daddy added, "And don't be late."

"We won't, sir. I promise."

Donovan and I fairly raced for the door, both of us holding our breaths. Once into the safe confines of the front yard, we burst out laughing.

"Wow—that was just—*wow,*" said Donovan.

"I know, right?"

We headed for the car, still giggling over our victory. To my surprise, our hands had interlocked. Didn't know when it happened, but it felt natural.

Our date, as expected, went great. A true gentleman, Donovan opened doors, and insisted on paying for everything. At the end of the night, he walked me to my doorstep, never once being too forward. Instead, he bowed to me gracefully and shook my hand. He asked if he could call me again. I told him yes. When I went to bed that night, I couldn't help but wish he had kissed me. The heck with the third date rule!

That date led to many, many more, which inevitably

led to exclusivity. I'd have it no other way. Our first month together was primarily spent getting to know one another, sharing our ambitions and dreams, and most importantly, improving Donovan's wardrobe. He grumbled a bit but was receptive. He soon learned cheap retail clothing was strictly forbidden. Knock-offs? Don't even *think* about it.

"But, Elizabeth," he whined in his adorable way, "I don't have an unlimited expense account like you do. These clothes are expensive." He eyeballed the price tags of the shorts and belt without even admiring the quality of the clothing.

"Donovan, do you want a career in politics?" He nodded sheepishly. "Well, then let's get the clothes. Daddy always says 'clothes make the man'. You wanna play the part, you gotta look the part."

"But I'm telling you, I don't have the money. I don't make much at my job." His part-time job as a waiter was a little embarrassing, but cute. I tolerated it. Just a temporary fix until he was ready for his real life to begin.

"I'm going to help you with your first wardrobe as a real politician." I didn't mind. It was my future at stake as well, after all.

"I'm not going to let you do that, Elizabeth! I can't take your money."

Seeing how adamant he was, I tossed him a bone. "I'm not giving you the money, silly. It's a loan until you can pay me back."

He held the shorts up, turning them around as if inspecting for flaws. Like he'd find any. "And you really think these shorts will help me attain my goals?" He sounded doubtful, but definitely wavering.

"Trust me, Donovan." I graced him with my most flirtatious smile. "You're going to look great."

"I suppose a loan might be all right," he muttered. "But I'm paying it back with interest."

"Deal."

"And could you not tell anyone? Please?" The one trait Donovan shared with every other boy in school was his arrogant, misplaced, machismo pride. But it's how boys are built.

"Okay, fine."

"But I'm not so sure about the pink polo shirt. Don't you think pink's a little…" —he lowered his voice— "gay?"

I slapped his shoulder. "Donovan Goode! First of all, really? Secondly, didn't I ask for your trust?"

Even though it was a struggle to get Donovan into pink and other brightly colored polo shirts, our mutual trust had been forged. Whole-heartedly. Respect the name of the game, including when it came to sexual boundaries. Our relationship, other than some heavy petting, remained chaste. We both wanted it that way, neither of us desiring to jeopardize our futures with one clumsy mistake brought on by pesky, raging hormones. Sure, temptation was always there—maybe a little bit of frustration, too—but we held true to our convictions, our beliefs, our driving desires to take the world by storm.

Besides, I knew I'd one day marry Donovan Goode, becoming his First Lady in more ways than one. Maybe as soon as when we graduated from college. My heart always kicked up a notch when I thought about it.

\*\*\*\*

"What's the matter, Elizabeth?" asked Donovan

outside my classroom. "Are you upset about Charles Durbin?" He placed his strong hands on my shoulders and peered into my eyes.

"No…I don't know. Maybe. I guess." Durbin's death bothered me more than I expected it to. Was I jealous, missing out on an obviously emotional experience? Maybe the defaced prom queen poster was right. Was I a bitch?

"I'm sorry. Come here." Donovan embraced me. Usually this was a no-no for me in public. But I needed it. "I wasn't even aware you knew Charles."

I pushed away. "I didn't! That's the problem. Everyone's torn up about this and I feel like I should be, but…" It was only then I noticed Donovan's red eyes. "Oh. Oh, Donovan, I'm so *way* sorry. Here I've been going on about my silly problems. Did you know Charles?"

When he shook his head, his hair remained an immaculate helmet, a perfect reflection of his steely resolve. "No. It's just sad, Elizabeth. Everyone said Charles was a nice guy."

"That's what I understand." It sounded weak, but I really needed to find a way not to make this about me. "They say it might have been drugs."

Donovan's eyes closed. One teardrop crawled along his eyelashes before finally splashing down onto his cheek. "It's terrible. Just terrible. Why did it have to be drugs? I had no idea."

"I don't think anyone did, Donovan." This time, I thrust my arms around him. Lady-like or not, let the haters talk.

Donovan had already pulled back his tears, ready to take on his next challenge. "I'm just surprised he was into that stuff. I mean, it's a shock and everything…I'm just…"

"I know." The general consensus. Even though practically everyone—except me—had known Charles, no one *truly* knew him.

I wondered who Charles Durbin really was. And what he was into that caused his death.

****

That night, I slept miserably. When I could sleep, I had nightmares of cars crashing into houses, drug usage amongst my friends, Charlotte Drayton being crowned prom queen…endless torture. And this kind of restless sleep, punctuated by fever dreams, usually signified something I was all too familiar with.

A troublesome visitor coming my way.

Sometimes I hated always being right.

"I'm here, my dear. *Get used to it!*" Elspeth lay next to me in her full leather regalia. "Do you like my slogan? It took me a while to come up with it."

Chapter Three

*Elizabeth*

"Cute," I said. *"Elspeth."*

"Thanks for calling me cute. How's it goin', Elizabeth?" She leaned up on one elbow, grinning at me like we were at a slumber party. "Miss me?"

She wasn't really in my bedroom. Well, sort of.

****

Elspeth Chambers and I had a complicated relationship. At least that was how I described it on my fave social networks. It all started years ago when I was in the ninth grade. Some mornings I'd wake up to find my items—makeup, clothing, important stuff—misplaced. At first, I blamed it on sleepwalking and thought nothing of it.

Then things escalated. Some of my skirts were cut to inappropriate lengths, nothing more than raggedy miniskirts. Gag. Like I'd do that even in my sleep. And the pack of cigarettes I found on my dresser! I knew then I wasn't sleepwalking. No one would sell cigarettes to a minor, let alone a sleepwalking one. I began having small blackouts, nothing too big, but glaring enough to leave tiny lapses in my memory. I'd wake up tired every morning. It left me terrified, questioning my sanity. No Ivy League college would ever accept an insane student.

Even though I dreaded it, I had no other choice but to tell my parents. At first, Daddy totally negated the idea. He thought I was just seeking attention, something I'd grow out of. Mother, on the other hand, went to the opposite extreme. She decided I should be seen by as many of the best child psychiatrists money could buy.

Reluctantly, I went. Mentally probed, questioned, studied, written about, consulted over, tested, and run through the psychoanalytical ringer. When the head psychiatrist asked me if I had an imaginary playmate, I studied the way she posed the question. Her eyes narrowed, her lips pursed, her pen poised to write me off as delusional. I developed an acute sense of how to read people, how to respond to get the desired effect I wanted. My game plan quickly changed. I admitted to making it all up to win my parents' attention. I knew my parents would be angry, but they always forgave my very few trespasses against them. As I suspected, Daddy felt validated in his beliefs, brandishing a triumphant smile. Mother remained quiet, but kept a keen eye on my every move. I played the part well.

Soon, the notes started showing up. Each morning I found a poorly written note penned with my eyeliner. The first note instructed me to keep lying to my psychiatrist, tell her I made it up. She added she could help me and signed it "Elspeth." I took solace in this. I knew I wasn't going psycho.

One night, I wrote a note back, asking "Elspeth" who she was and what she wanted. The written reply stated she was a channeled spirit and we'd be sharing a body for a while. She further explained she could help me because she knew things, things no one else could possibly be privy to. The kicker? She said she could help me get into the college of my choice. *Dealmaker.*

But I wanted proof. The next morning she told me Sally's boyfriend was cheating on her. I didn't believe it for a minute. I mean, who'd cheat on Sally? But something compelled me to approach Sally's boyfriend and flat out accuse him of cheating. He admitted to it. Elspeth appeared to be on the level.

But before I allowed this to go any further, I made sure Elspeth understood we were traveling a two-way street. My body, my rules. She needed to leave my clothes alone. She would never put my body into a potentially damaging situation, either physically, morally, or one that would compromise my reputation. Absolutely no smoking, drugs, alcohol, or sex. Finally, she would never interfere with my life-plan and had to agree to aid me in my goals.

Elspeth agreed, although she had an initial problem with the clothing rule. Unbelievably, she didn't like my wardrobe. I met her halfway and bought her some clothes to her liking, mostly retro punk stuff (it worried me someone would spot me at a thrift store. I traveled a good hour out of town to do the icky shopping). When I found a box of jet-black hair dye on my dresser, I quickly revised our written agreement. I bought her a couple of black wigs. I mean, *no one* touches the hair!

Even though we agreed she wouldn't appear at school, I finally consented to keep a set of her clothes in my locker. "Just for emergencies, just in case," she wrote. Apparently, there had been quite a few "emergencies" over the past two years as she had surfaced at Clearwell several times. Actually, she—we—had been instrumental in capturing a couple of killers. Too bad I couldn't put that on my resume.

I never knew too much about Elspeth or her past. I had no idea where she went when she wasn't me. Not my problem. Just as long as she upheld her promise about helping me achieve my future goals.

The last time Elspeth appeared—late last school year—our bond grew stronger. We no longer had to communicate via written notes. On occasion, I could hear her in my head, barking out a demand or warning about impending danger. The first time she appeared to me in my sleep, I totally freaked out. There she was in my bedroom, talking to me like she was an actual living entity. She found it hilarious when I attempted to pinch myself awake.

"Just where are we, Elspeth?" I asked. "Am I in hell?"

In a stone-cold serious tone, she replied, "No, but they're looking for you." After she saw my horrified expression, she added, "Just kidding."

"Not funny. So, what's the deal here? Where are we?"

"Well, as you can see…" She waggled her black-painted fingernails about the room. "It's your bedroom." She rudely smirked at my primarily pink décor. "Well, okay, it's not really your bedroom, but I thought it best to meet in a place you're comfortable with."

"Is this limbo?" Not a concept I believed in, but she'd already disqualified hell, and I knew heaven wouldn't hire Elspeth as my greeter.

"Hardly," she roared. "Let's just call it Dream Space. You know, sorta like your beloved computer hangouts…only not."

"Huh. So this is in my head?"

"Kind of. You are asleep, but this is most definitely real. It's just sorta a different take on reality, I guess. They don't really tell me everything either, you know." Didn't I know it. Every time I had asked her a pertinent question in the past—like, say, I don't know, am I in danger of *losing my life?*—she brushed me off and pleaded ignorance.

****

So, I woke up, finding myself back in Dream Space. Seriously unsettling here. Like a waking dream, everything felt and looked real. Yet there was a certain sluggishness to my thought process, like a warm comfort wrapped in helplessness.

"Did I miss you?" I asked. Elspeth nodded, mischief dancing in her eyes. And what gorgeous eyes she had. They were the same as mine, after all. "Would you believe me if I said, maybe a little bit?" I held my thumb and forefinger slightly apart. I couldn't believe I admitted it, the most dumbfounding thing being it was true. I didn't like relinquishing my body, but I'd missed our Dream Space chats. I could slouch, sit any way I desired, not wear makeup, and say things to her I wouldn't dare say to anyone else. The sister I never had.

When I saw her on the verge of bursting out laughing at my proclamation, I quickly recanted. "But not really."

The corners of her mouth curled up. "It's okay, Elizabeth. I think I might've missed you a little bit, too." She imitated my thumb and finger demonstration.

"So, what is it this time, Elspeth?"

She bounced off the bed and strolled across the room, staring at my wall hangings. "You're not still

46

into boy bands, are you?" I was, but I wasn't going to tell her that. Maybe I didn't miss her so much, after all. "How's Tex and Olivia?"

"I don't know. They're your friends, not mine."

"Oh, come on, Elizabeth. I know you sorta like Tex and can even tolerate Olivia. You don't have to put on a show for me."

Elspeth was right. Over the past two years, I'd become involved with Tex and Olivia, helping them in their quest to seek out murderers, of which there seemed to be no short supply at Clearwell High. Tex had grown on me, and while not an out-and-out friend, I didn't hate him. The jury was still out on Olivia, though—definitely not my cup of tea. "Oh, whatever! I guess Tex is at K.U. and Olivia is at junior college. I think they're still together. It's not like I chat with them every day or anything."

"How sweet."

"Cut to the chase, Elspeth."

"You kids today." She smacked her lips, adopting a mock-parental frown. "Always in such a hurry."

"Whatever. I know you're the same age as me. Well, basically!" I really had no idea when Elspeth had died. "Why are you back this time?"

"What do you know about the drug problem at Clearwell High?" She turned toward me, hands behind her back, not unlike Mr. Dawson's grandstanding earlier today.

I shrugged. "I guess it's bad. I don't know, really. I mean, it's not like I hang out with druggies or anything like that."

"Huh. Well, you know about Charles Durbin, right?"

47

"Yeah. I didn't know him. But it's sad, anyway." I momentarily ditched my mask of righteous indignation, allowing a few seconds of grief. "So, did Charles die because he was stoned?"

Elspeth closed her eyes as if dredging up a half-forgotten memory. "I'm not sure. I know Durbin's the key to this whole drug thing, but it's not clear how far his involvement goes. All I was told was that there's more to his death than meets the eye."

"Cryptic much?"

"I know, right? I don't know much more than you do, Elizabeth. My 'keepers' are a bunch of close-mouthed, tight-asses."

Extremely vulgar, but I laughed anyway. "Who— or what—are your 'keepers'?"

"No clue." Obviously, she noted my frustration. "No, really. You know what I know."

"Okay, so big deal. We know next to nothing. You say Charles Durbin's death is not what it looks like. Because your oh-so-mysterious keepers say so. So what? I mean, it's sad and everything, but what does it have to do with me? Or with us?"

"We're supposed to bring the drug dealer down." Elspeth tightened her mouth into a tiny black-ringed circle.

"Really?"

"'Fraid so."

"And how am I supposed to do that?"

"How are *we* supposed to do that?" she corrected me.

"Okay, fine. We! It's not like I can just go up to a drug dealer and say, 'Hey, can I buy some acid or bad-ass dope?'"

Elspeth snickered. "Elizabeth, you'd make the worst undercover agent in the world. No, that's an advantage I have. No one knows me. And I look the part and can be pretty damn convincing. But I can't exactly skulk around the school either. Your buddy, Hastings, would be all over me." She sneered at the mention of our vice principal, Arville Hastings. "But you're gonna have to do some ground work. Point me in the right direction. Do some research, sniff 'em out—"

"But I don't know any dopers!"

"Well, start with Charles Durbin. Talk to his friends."

"But as far as I can tell, he didn't have any friends. Not close ones."

Elspeth sprang across the room and hopped onto the bed. She sat against the bed board, pulling her leather-clad knees underneath her chin. "Oh, wake up, Elizabeth. You're so caught up in your insular world, you think just because you're not aware of something, it doesn't exist."

"That's not true." Although, maybe it was.

"Whatever." Elspeth waved her hand as if erasing the lie off the chalkboard of my soul. "Everyone has at least one friend. And you know one of his best friends."

"I hardly think I—"

"Tina Bottoms."

The name tore threw me like a double-barreled shotgun blast from the past. "What?"

"Tina Bottoms."

"I cannot just waltz up to Tina Bottoms and ask her about Charles Durbin, Elspeth! It's impossible." I grabbed my stuffed pink pony, cradling it for support.

"Why not?" Elspeth hefted an eyebrow. "Because of what you did to her in ninth grade?"

"I didn't do anything to Tina Bottoms!"

"Yes, you did. And it sucked."

I glowered at Elspeth, squeezing my anger out on my plush pony. "You do not get to judge me. You haven't walked in my shoes."

"Actually, yes, I have."

"You know what I mean!"

Elspeth snatched my comfort pony away from me. She held it in front of my face, shaking it. Imitating an annoying little girl's voice, she said, "Awww, what's the matter, snookums? Mr. Pinky thinks you're having a rotten day. Is your past coming back to haunt you?" Her lips puffed out in a pout. She tossed my pony back to me and mercifully resumed her normal voice. "Ponies aren't pink."

"Her name is Snowcone!"

Elspeth chortled. I wrung my fists and roared toward the ceiling. "Don't you mock me."

"I'm not mocking you." She did the finger and thumb bit again. "Well, maybe a little."

"And stop doing that…that thing with your hand!" I took several deep breaths, finding my center as I'd learned to do in yoga class.

"Better?"

Couldn't believe I thought I missed Elspeth earlier. "I can't do this. Ask me anything else, but not—"

"Oh, suck it, Elizabeth. Just talk to her. It's the only lead we have right now. Don't put your vanity ahead of this. You're stronger than you think."

"I know I'm strong. I know my strengths."

"What about weaknesses?" Elspeth rolled over on

her stomach, her legs kicking behind her. She frowned. A rare and troublesome look for her. "Elizabeth, this might be a bad one. I have a feeling we both might be tested."

"What do you mean?"

She shrugged, her leather jacket cracking slightly. "Don't know, really. Just a feeling."

I fell back into bed, tossing my hands over my eyes. "Oh my God, Elspeth. Fine! I'll try to talk to Tina, but don't blame me if she won't talk to me!"

"All you can do is try."

"Gah! Your timing sucks, Elspeth. This is a majorly important time for me. I can't get distracted by—"

"What's so majorly important? Your graduation? Or…" She smirked. "Being a prom queen?"

"They're both important, thank you very much! Being prom queen is major."

Elspeth shook her head, her black faux-hawk wagging. "Honestly, Elizabeth, is it really all that to you?" I nodded determinedly. "Really? You know it's only important to those running in this pointless competition. No one else at the school cares. They're worried about their future, not some stupid, worthless popularity contest. It won't matter to anyone once you get out of school. Or do you plan on wearing your tiara to college?"

I wouldn't let Elspeth know her words stung like a thousand bees. "It's important to me." When my voice cracked, I clamped one hand over my mouth, the other over my eyes to hide the welling tears.

A long moment of silence ensued before Elspeth swatted my shoulder. "Elizabeth, I'm sorry about what I said. It was harsh. Saying whatever's on my mind has always gotten me in trouble."

Once I knew I was back in control, I said, "Elspeth, why are we doing this?"

"To save lives."

"Okay." The first thing I had heard that made any sense.

Elspeth clapped her hands twice as if summoning a genie. "Now, it's off to bed with you, Elizabeth."

"Wait! I have more questions!"

"I'll be in touch. Right now, I'm going to take us out for a spin."

"Wait a minute! Where are you—" Before I could finish my objections, Elspeth clapped once more, sending me into a deep, restful sleep. Bitch.

**\*\*\*\***

*Elspeth*

I probably shouldn't have done that to Elizabeth, but I'd been chilling my heels in limbo for nearly a year, itching to get out. One can only take so many endless fields of grass and cinder block walls. Girl's gotta live. Well, such as it was.

The night air felt warm. A light breeze kissed my face. Tree limbs greeted me, waving their limbs. Leaves whispered, almost as if wondering where I'd been. It felt great to be out again.

Several hollow thumps echoed throughout the empty street. A tall boy, dressed in a T-shirt and jeans, bounced a basketball in the driveway next to Elizabeth's house. An outdoor bulb, posted above the garage, spotlighted him in a yellow oval. He tossed the ball, missing the hoop by a long shot. The ball clanged off the backboard and rolled into the street. I stopped it with my foot.

"Hey," I said.

Startled, the boy brushed back his long sandy hair and replied, "Hey."

"You're not very good." I kicked the ball up into my hands.

He smiled, exposing pearly white teeth. "You think you can do any better?"

"I know I can." I dribbled the ball to the end of the driveway. "Wanna make a bet I can sink it from here?"

He looked at the distance between the goal and myself and grinned. "Sure, why not?"

I bounced the ball twice, aimed, and tossed. The ball soared through the air, perfectly sinking into the net. *Swoosh.*

Slack-jawed, the boy retrieved the ball. "How'd you do that?"

I strutted toward him victoriously. "Just one of my many talents. I'm Elspeth."

"Kevin. Kevin Bartholomew." He swiped his hair out of his eyes and held out his hand. I shook it firmly. "Kind of late for you to be out, isn't it? I mean, for a school night and everything."

"What about you? It's after midnight. Kinda late to be playing with your balls."

He chuckled. "I couldn't sleep. Basketball helps relax me."

"How can something you totally suck at be relaxing? You really need to step your game up." I held my hands out for him to toss the ball. Catching it in one hand, I continued the momentum, swooping my arm over my head. The ball swished into the basket. If you can show off, why not? "I can probably teach you a thing or two."

Running after the ball, he called out, "Yeah, I think maybe you could." With two hands, he paddled the ball back up the driveway. "You live around here, Elspeth?"

I shook my head. "No. Just out for a walk."

"Huh. So late?"

"What can I say? I like the night."

"Where do you go to school?"

"I don't." I folded my arms and flashed him a smile. "What's your story?"

"I'm home from college. If you don't go to school, what *do* you do?" He leapt into the air, slamming the ball off the backboard. Another complete miss.

"What am I gonna do with you, Kevin? It's all about the follow-through. Use your hand to guide the ball and roll it off your fingers. Control the ball." I grabbed the ball and demonstrated my perfect aim. "Anyway, I do whatever I want to do. Let's just say I'm sorta a free agent."

"Really? Huh. How old are you?"

"Old enough." Damn if I wasn't flirting. But it felt good. "Now try it like I showed you."

When he threw the ball, it fell short of the hoop. He tossed his hands into the air. "Okay, so I suck."

"Putting it mildly." I snatched the rebounding ball and dribbled it in a circle around him. He impotently waved his hands in the air, trying to block me. Squatting, I jumped into the air, throwing the ball into the hoop. Again. Sucked being awesome.

"Maybe you should play basketball, Elspeth." Apparently tired of being upstaged by a girl, he tucked the ball under his arm for safekeeping.

"Nah. Sports aren't my thing." They were

Elizabeth's thing, however. She spent two years on the girls' basketball team before taking up golf and more feminine pursuits. "So, you never said what I'd win."

"What?"

"For the bet. I bet you I could make the basket from the end of your driveway. Now I want my winnings." I slowly sauntered toward him.

"Okay, what do you want?"

I threw my hands around his neck, stretched up on my tiptoes, and kissed him. He stumbled back. Always best to keep people off guard. The ball slid from underneath his arm and rolled into the yard. I broke off the kiss and nudged him away. His eyes widened with exhilaration and shock. "That's what I wanted."

Trotting down the driveway, I couldn't resist a look back. He stood speechless, as if the air had been knocked out of him. Pretty much had, too. "Gotta say, I thought it'd be better than that," I called out.

"Wow," he sputtered. "Wait!"

I stopped, tapping my boot onto the street until he caught up to me.

"Could we…maybe…go out for a coffee or something? Sometime?" His easygoing poise had vanished. He stuttered, trying desperately to form a coherent sentence.

I played my hand along his jawline. "We'll see, Kevin." I turned, giddily leaping away for a hasty retreat.

"What? Wait! How can I get hold of you?"

"I'll be around." I ran for tree coverage, plentiful in Elizabeth's neighborhood. From my hiding place, I saw Kevin sitting at the end of the driveway on his basketball, shaking his head. Thunderstruck by

Hurricane Elspeth.

I thought I might enjoy my stay this time.

\*\*\*\*

*Elizabeth*

Pounding noises dragged me back into consciousness. Elspeth's clothes lay sloppily discarded by my dresser. Ugh. Raised in a barn. By wild wolves, no doubt.

I quickly took a personal inventory, ensuring my body remained damage free. I didn't know what Elspeth got up to half the time and it scared me to death. But I damn sure was going to have words with her later. I couldn't believe she put me to sleep and then took my body out. Didn't seem like an emergency, either.

The cracking noises continued. I had first thought the sounds were part of a dream. The kind of horrible, unexplained sounds that sometimes plague one's nightmares. But, no, the hollow explosions were definitely of the waking realm. My kitty clock displayed 1:15 a.m. I was never going to get my required eight hours of sleep tonight.

I pulled the blinds up and looked outside my window. Some idiot was playing basketball next door. Growling, I pulled on my pink robe and slippers, ready to raise some hell. But not before stealing a quick glimpse into my vanity. At least Elspeth had taken off her gaudy makeup this time. In years past, several times I'd wakened looking like a trollop.

I stormed out the door, heading straight for the new neighbor's house. The Bartholomews had arrived less than a month ago. I had only seen a middle-aged man and woman puttering about in their yard, never a sign of any children. Other than an occasional wave, I didn't really know them. Obviously, the onus was on them to get to know me. I had lived here long before they moved in.

With his back turned and his head down he dribbled the ball incessantly. The resounding bangs bounced back into my head, each thump a nail in my sleep-deprived brain.

"Hey!"

He whipped around, the ball slipping from his grasp. I startled him. Good. The ball rolled toward me at the end of the driveway. Cinching my robe with one hand, I scooped the ball up with the other. "What do you think you're doing? It's after one-thirty in the morning! Some of us need our sleep, you know!"

The boy squinted, staring at me with a quizzical look. "Wait…what?"

"No habla inglés?" I said. "I'm trying to sleep!"

He approached me warily. "Elspeth?" he asked uncertainly.

Uh-oh. She was back for one night and already making my life a living hell. "No! I'm Elizabeth! I don't know any Elspeth!"

He cocked his head and grinned. "Come on. Is this some sort of joke or something?" He took another few steps toward me. When I held the ball up as if to throw it at him, he stopped.

"Look, I have no idea what you're talking about. I'm just trying to get some sleep. And you're out here tossing around your stupid ball!"

His idiotic grin slipped away like a forgotten dream. "But you were just here about an hour ago. Although you were dressed a lot differently and had different hair and—"

"Still have no idea what you're talking about."

"You kissed me."

Crap. Strike three, Elspeth. Throwing down now! "I don't know what sort of gross fantasy you think you had, but I did not kiss you!" I snorted. "As if! I would never kiss you. I've never even met you."

"Huh. Well, you don't have a twin or anything, do you? I mean, you have very distinctive eyes and—"

"I do not have a twin. Hello! They broke the mold when they made me." I almost felt sorry for him. He questioned his hold on reality. Been there, done that. But *almost* didn't cut it. "Are you crazy or something? You're playing basketball at one-thirty in the morning! And you're obviously deluded or whatever!"

"Okay, my bad," he stammered. "Huh. Weird. Anyway, I'm Kevin." He offered his hand.

I glared at him, ignoring his introductory gesture. "And I already told you I'm Elizabeth."

"Okay. Hi, Elizabeth. It's um, nice to meet you. I'm home from college and—"

"What part of one-thirty in the morning do you not understand? This isn't exactly the time for social hour."

"Oh, right. Sorry, I—"

"Now are you done playing basketball?" He nodded like a properly chastened child. "Good!" With all my might, I heaved the basketball into the tall hedges surrounding his house.

"Oh, man." With an annoying sigh, he chased after the ball.

Stomping back to my house, I called to him, "Don't make me come out here again."

I couldn't believe Elspeth kissed the neighbor.

With my body! And now Kevin Bartholomew seemed to suspect we were one and the same. She had put our damn secret at risk. So help me, I was going to make sure Elspeth stayed away from him.

As I pulled up my bedspread, I smiled at a sudden revelation. The neighbor was kinda cute. For an idiot.

Chapter Four

*Elizabeth*

"Good morning, Daddy!" I dropped my arms around his neck and kissed his cheek. He lowered the *Wall Street Journal* and grunted at me. Our usual morning routine.

"Good morning." He vanished behind his newspaper again, occasionally reaching for his coffee mug.

"A beautiful day." Mother dropped an egg-white omelet in front of me. She knew the importance of staying fit. "And how did you sleep?"

*Terrible.* "Just fine." No sense in worrying them again. "Except for the stupid neighbor kid. Did you hear him playing basketball in the middle of the night?"

Daddy tossed the paper onto the table and grimaced. He did that a lot these days. In his early sixties, Daddy was quite a bit older than Mother. Over the past year, his hair had transformed from distinguished salt-and-pepper into elderly snow white. The tiny wrinkles that used to hint at character had grown, crisscrossing his face like a weathered road map. He relied ever more on his glasses, having only used them before when he read. I would never call Daddy "animated". A stern demeanor defined his disposition. Yet he was never this withdrawn or sullen before. Having a conversation with him was like talking to his ever-present newspaper. Mother said work stressed him out, something she pooh-poohed away as nothing but a temporary nuisance.

Mother sat next to me. "No, I didn't hear anything. And don't call him stupid, dear. It's uncouth." She smiled, her teeth radiant in a beauty pageant style. In her early forties, Mother didn't look a day over thirty-something—blessed with gorgeous brunette hair, hazel eyes, and a figure I envied.

When she was fresh out of college, she had met Daddy through mutual friends at a big to-do party. Six months later, they married. She never worked a day in her life, her busy schedule filled with socializing, manicures, pedicures, workouts, massages, and country club living. I learned a lot from her. "That must be Kevin, the Bartholomews's son. Kathryn told me he was coming back from K.U. for a visit. Did you meet him, dear?"

I rolled my eyes. "Yeah, if that's what you want to call it. I had to go out there last night and tell him to stop the noise."

"Hmmm," said Daddy, rattling the newspaper.

"Well, I certainly hope you weren't too harsh on him, dear." She patted my hand and hummed her way back into the kitchen.

"I understand a boy died in your class, Elizabeth." Daddy looked like I wasn't the only sleep-deprived Blackmer in the house. "Did you know him?"

I shook my head once. "No, I didn't."

"How did he die?"

"There's talk about drugs, maybe."

He frowned, the gravity of his newly developed

jowls dragging his face down. "Drugs are terrible. Just terrible."

"I know, Daddy." The longest conversation I'd had with Daddy in some time. His version of an anti-drug speech, I supposed. And he seemed very uncomfortable tackling it. "And you know I'd never touch drugs, right?"

When he smiled, he nearly looked like the Daddy from my youth, the one who used to bounce me on his knee. He coughed once and resumed his paper reading.

The doorbell rang. Mother answered it, loudly making over our visitor in her usual fashion, even though we all expected Donovan every school morning. He appeared in the dining room doorway looking much more robust than the last time I saw him.

"Good morning!" From his delivery, it sounded like he found the morning not only good but great. I dashed my napkin discretely at my lips, folded it properly, and ran to Donovan. I threw my hands around his neck like I did with Daddy, but that's where the similarities stopped. Never kiss in front of your parents. I rested my head on his chest.

"And how are you this morning, Elizabeth?"

"Fine. And you?"

"Great. Just great." Not only a morning person, Donovan thrived on being a "twenty-four-hour person." Always on. I didn't realize until now how unsettling it was to see him so distraught yesterday. Having my Donovan back thrilled me.

He strolled up next to Daddy. "And how are you, sir?" His hand jutted out.

"Just fine, Donovan." Donovan had the ability to rouse Daddy from his stupor more than anyone did these days. Daddy stood and accepted Donovan's double-handed shake.

It hadn't taken long for Donovan to weave his magic on Daddy. After their first several meetings, it became commonplace for them to retreat to Daddy's study for some quality male bonding to which I was never invited. Jealousy struck me, yet to have my two favorite men share mutual admiration more than made up for it. Soon, Daddy even asked Donovan to come work for him as an intern of sorts. The job was nothing more than a glorified "go-for" where he ran errands and performed paperwork tasks, but it paved the way for Donovan to quit his menial, low-paying job. And Donovan went on at great lengths about how much he had learned regarding business and finance from Daddy.

"Are you coming by the office after school?" asked Daddy.

"Just try and keep me away, sir."

After they finished slobbering all over each other, we walked out to Donovan's car. I still held out hope he'd trade up soon, purchasing an automobile more befitting of his stature. *Give it time,* I reminded myself. *Give it time.*

"I hope this won't be an imposition, Elizabeth, but I told Kip I'd give him a ride." From his reluctance to meet my gaze, I knew he dreaded dropping this bombshell on me.

I wrinkled my nose and sighed. "Why?"

"Kip's Beemer's in the shop. He was in a pinch. Sorry."

Kip Aldrich was absolutely gorgeous, charming, well-groomed, wealthy, and the captain of the lacrosse team. And a total tool. Addie started dating him last year, and outside of me and Donovan's relationship, theirs was the longest-lasting within our group. Even though he was Donovan's best friend, he seemed more like a sycophant than a trustworthy companion. He was also the hugest, most arrogant douche I'd ever met. Of course, he'd go far in life. But it was all I could do to tolerate him. The things we do for love.

"Whatever," I growled.

As Donovan pulled into the driveway, Kip ran out at a trot, meeting us halfway. Dressed in a lime polo shirt with the collar popped, he crawled into the back seat. "Hey! Thanks for the ride, buddy." Kip reached forward, a ludicrous rope bracelet dangling from his wrist, and punched Donovan in the shoulder.

"No problem." I couldn't help but notice Donovan wince from the shoulder jab.

"Kip," I said icily.

"Hi, Elizabeth," he replied without a hint of sarcasm. Kip excelled at disguising his true nature like a predatory, slimy creature. But we knew where we stood with one another. Once, I actually tried to dissuade Addie from dating him. He was a known "playah." And being a "playah hatah", I had to do what was best for my protégé, Addie. "So, you guys hear about Charles Durbin?"

I stole a glance at Donovan to see if the topic might upset him again. He remained solemn but steady. "Yes, so sad."

"Yeah, sucks to be him, right?" Kip giggled.

"Kip! I hardly think this is something to make light of." I narrowed my eyes, threatening him with my best icy glare.

"Hey, whatever. I'm just sayin', that's all." His laughing fit wound down. "I heard he was totally wasted."

"Really?" said Donovan.

"Dude! I heard they found all sorts of drugs in his car and he was way over the limit. I mean, he must've been totally wasted to crash his car into a house."

"Where did you hear about the drugs, Kip?" I asked.

"I don't know, I just heard it, all right?"

"Has it been proven the police found drugs? Did you hear it on the news?"

Donovan looked at me curiously. "Elizabeth, I didn't think you knew Charles. Why are you so interested in this?"

"Look, he was a fellow student. I guess I just care."

"Okay."

"So messed up, dude! Who woulda thought Charles was a major stoner." As Kip grew more excited, it took all of my restraint not to hop in the back and pummel him. "How wasted you gotta be to…"

I counted to ten before speaking, attempting to block out Kip's endless rant. "Kip, was Charles Durbin a friend of yours?"

"No, dude! I didn't know him. I just knew who he was and—"

"Well, then shut up."

****

My girls were lined up at my locker waiting for me. After studying their outfits and exchanging compliments over how nice I looked, our hallway chatter inevitably turned to Charles Durbin. Addie, still looking mortified, got Regina and Bettany up-to-date about what they'd missed. None of them knew Charles, but once again, all of them knew who he was.

As the natural leader of the girls, I offered them appropriate sympathy. I heard no new information regarding the circumstances surrounding Durbin's death—just the same old gossip. I needed to start looking into Durbin's curious death, but had to be careful sifting the facts from the rumors.

The girls stopped chatting and for good reason. "Evil" sashayed down the hallway, flanked by her two clone-like flunkies.

**\*\*\*\***

Last year, Charlotte Drayton was a new student at Clearwell. She had made quite a stir in no time at all. I found her wealthy enough and pretty in a sorta whorish way, I supposed. A Kansas immigrant—her father had transferred jobs from Los Angeles—but you'd never guess it by her porcelain-white skin. After delving into her background and admiring her wardrobe from afar, I made my decision. I approached her about joining us on a trial basis.

I cut into the lunch line and sidled up next to her. Her shirt was too flashy (it cried out "retail!") and her skirt was much too short for one of her purported stature. But I could perform miracles. Look no further than Addie for proof. "Hi, Charlotte, I'm Elizabeth."

"Elizabeth Blackmer. I know who you are." She threw her head back, sweeping her wavy black hair over her shoulders. Too much attention-desperate display. Tsk.

"Why don't you join us today?" I pointed to our table at the front of the cafeteria where the other girls were already adjourned.

She smiled, showing off her ivory white teeth. "Sure, sounds great." She grabbed a tray and pushed it along the metal rollers, studying the day's atrocities. "You wear pearls?" She eyed my necklace enviously.

"Of course." I ran my fingers along the pearls, enjoying the smooth, rich pleasures they embodied. "I'm trending pearls."

"Okay."

Obviously not yet a pearl power believer, but none of the others—excluding Addie—had been at first either. But I could be very persuasive.

When she reached for a cheeseburger, I blocked her arm and tutted. "Not good for the thighs," I whispered.

I grabbed a salad and inclined my head for her to do the same. She complied.

At the table, Charlotte dropped an abrupt snort. The rude equivalent of boys' immature fascination with body gas. "You're all blond! Are you all natural?" Addie looked askance, as if in shame, but the others nodded vigorously. "Well, then, I hope you'll accept a natural brunette."

Actually, we preferred the softer, wholesome image blond hair represented, but we were not bigots. And it was always good to have a token brunette. "Charlotte, I'm more concerned with your wardrobe. Let's chat."

I spent three weeks with Charlotte as my new project like I had the other girls. A good student, she caught on fast, listened carefully, and asked appropriate questions. Like me, she had an unlimited expense account, so purchasing the proper clothing wasn't an issue. At the end of those three weeks, I was proud of her. She looked stunning, preppy—regal, almost.

Too bad her inner beauty didn't match up to the rapturous outer shell I had created.

One day, I sat at our table and noticed we were three shy, including Charlotte. The other girls looked glum and remained quiet. Finally, Addie said, "Elizabeth, Charlotte's being a hater." She kept her voice low but urgency filled it. Regina and Bettany nodded in near unison.

"What are you talking about? Where is everybody?"

"Charlotte started dissing you. Said you're a control freak, a stuck-up beeyotch. She got Andrea and Mona to agree with her."

I dropped my plastic fork into the salad, my appetite having fled. "What? All I've done is try to help that girl. This is the thanks I get?" I raised my hands to the heavens in disbelief.

"Sorry, Elizabeth, I'm just telling you what happened." Addie looked mournful, near tears. "She tried to get me…us…" Regina and Bettany linked hands, appearing too terrified to speak. "…to join her. She said if we went with her, then we could be whoever we want to be, not someone you choose to make us."

"Where are they?"

"But we stayed with you, Elizabeth!" Near panic, Addie latched onto my arm. "We like who we are. It's who we are!" The girls bobbed their heads in agreement. I usually appreciated the fact Regina and Bettany didn't say much. It meant they agreed with me. But, for once, I wanted their input.

"Where is she? Tell me, Addie!" I shot up. Addie, still clutching my arm, tried to hold me back. Finally, she released me and nodded toward the far side of the cafeteria.

Spotting the three traitors, I hurled my way toward them, unrelenting in my quest to see that right won out. "Charlotte," I said, smiling through gritted teeth, "what's this I hear about you hating on me?" I kept my tone even, and civil. A gargantuan struggle.

She stared at me before bursting out in laughter. The two turncoats joined her, wagging their tacky, newly dyed, black hairstyles in the process. "Well, Elizabeth, you heard right." She rolled merrily on her chair, wielding a cheeseburger in one hand. Flaunting it, practically.

"Honestly, I mean, thanks for telling me how to dress, but you're just too, *too* much. Did you seriously think I wanted to spend the rest of my senior year under the thumb of some half-crazed, tyrannical, control freak snob? Someone who tries to tell me who I should be?" She shook her head, her ratty hair flying about. I hoped some would land on her cheeseburger. The other two girls laughed uproariously as if on cue. Blood rushed into my face, my cheeks burning with anger and maybe a little humiliation.

"I tried to help you! You had no friends. I held my hand out…" My voice broke. A hitherto unfathomable notion—*betrayal.*

"Oh, whatever, Elizabeth. You and I both know you do what you do for you and you only. You're not out to help anyone. You just want to build up your little army of mindless robots so you can play with them. Like dolls! You set up your own look-alike entourage of admirers just to build yourself up. To feel better about yourself."

"That's not true." Suddenly I felt like the lonely girl on the first-grade playground again, my balloon of confidence punctured by Charlotte's evil, vocal pinpricks.

"Whatever." Charlotte waved her hand at me, dismissing me brusquely. "Just scoot along now, Elizabeth. Go. Go back to your silly, vapid blond zombies and enjoy the hell out of life." She looked at her giggling tablemates, not even acknowledging my existence. "Go on now, Elizabeth. You heard me. *Shoo.*"

I stood paralyzed, at a loss for words. I stumbled through the cafeteria, my legs weak and wobbly. Attempting to keep my shoulders back and my chin up, a sudden onslaught of tears built up from within. I raced to the bathroom. Locking myself in a stall, I cried, stifling my sobs by stuffing my wrist in my mouth. It wouldn't do to have someone see me crying. They'd think of me as vulnerable.

The birth of my "frenemy". No, that wasn't quite right. The birth of the face of evil. For the first week or so after that awful encounter, I did my best to avoid her. Soon, though, I realized that's not who I was; I cowered from no one. I purposefully brushed by her in the hall, head held high, smiling as if her words had never hurt. I'd say "hello" as bitterly sweet as I could without appearing spiteful. My jaw ached from locking my smile so rigidly into place. How beauty pageant contestants did that on command was beyond me. But by showing her I held no grudge (I did, but outward appearances were everything), I showed the school I was clearly the winner of our battle. And I had right on my side.

Ever since then, we'd been locked in an epic grudge-match. The only reason she threw her hat into the prom queen competition was because I chose to do so first. I couldn't allow her to win. I *had* to win. More rode on the outcome than the most heated presidential election. If I didn't win, the student body would view the heinous lies she had spewed about me as the truth.

Unbelievably, she appeared to be growing in popularity; actively campaigning, handing out cookies, and no doubt offering sexual favors to any guys within breathing distance. She and I were the frontrunners, the others already being also-rans. And she was the one defacing my campaign posters. I mean, who else would do it, right?

\*\*\*\*

Now, here came Charlotte, swinging her hips back and forth and bearing down on me like a whorepedo. Her two companions, TweedleBitch and TweedleJudas, bookended her like matching sluts.

She stopped inches away from my face. "Elizabeth," she said, her icy pronunciation nearly freezing the air between us.

"Hello, Charlotte." Smile locked in place? Check. "I see that *someone's* been ruining my prom queen posters."

"Is that right?" She looked toward her conspirators for corroboration. "That's a shame, isn't it girls? Who could do such a thing?"

"Someone obviously deeply jealous of me." Addie shouldered up next to me. Regina and Bettany, of course, froze, afraid they'd turn to stone if they looked Medusa in the eye.

"I would never do that, Elizabeth." Her fake

71

alligator smile threatened to bite me.

"Nice pearls, Charlotte." I narrowed my eyes at the string of pearls around her neck. My guess was costume jewelry.

"Oh, haven't you heard, Elizabeth? I'm trending them now." She pitched out a hellish yowl, covering her mouth with her fingertips.

My gaze traveled up and down her attire. "I see you're still shopping at thrift stores." The way her mouth pulled down told me I had hit the sweet spot.

"And, Elizabeth, you're looking spectacular in your hand-me-down clothes. I'm thinking circa the fifties?"

*Don't let her get to you!* "I can certainly say I'm going to look glorious in my prom queen crown. Too bad for you."

"We'll see about that, darling, we'll just see. I really must be going now. Ta, ta, for now, darling." She wiggled her slutty fingers at me.

Beaming, I called out, "Skank!"

With a boomerang smirk, she said, "Bitch!"

As she walked down the hallway, we continued calling each other names, both of us smiling as sweetly as could be.

The bell rang and the students scrambled like ants over a tossed candy bar. Which left one person standing in the hall. Tina Bottoms.

\*\*\*\*

When we were kids, I thought Tina and I would grow up together, marry billionaires, have babies, and stroll them together. But it was a childish dream. And she was a childhood friend I outgrew. It wasn't her fault. To better yourself you just needed to let go sometimes.

I met Tina in the first grade. At the time—as hard as it was to believe—I was a shy girl, lacking in confidence and friends. It stung when I saw my classmates playing together, excluding me from their packs. Daddy had transferred to Kansas that year, and I knew no one. So I sat on the playground curb, alone and miserable.

"Hi. What's wrong?" Tina's glasses looked way too big for her small face. She wore short dark hair, very tomboyish. A brace strangled her left leg like a metallic leech. Not fat, but stoutly built, she could've passed for a boy if it weren't for her soft features. For all her faults, though, she supplied the sunshine I needed on my dreary first-grade day.

"Nothing's wrong. *Everything's* wrong."

She sat next to me, toying with a dandelion springing up between us. "You're new, right? I'm Tina."

"I'm Elizabeth." I held out my hand properly.

"So, why are you crying?" She leaned back, her legs kicking idly at the sky.

"I don't have any friends."

"I'll be your friend, 'Lizbeth." From that moment on, Tina always called me 'Lizbeth. The only one I ever allowed to do so. "Really?"

"Sure." She roared with laughter.

"What's so funny?"

She pointed up at the clouds. "Know what that looks like?" I shook my head. "It's Mr. Wilson." She was right. The clouds billowed up in a large round mass, resembling our first-grade teacher's large belly. A bulbous nose jutted out from the puffy oval-shaped head. Capping it all off, a particularly feathery cloud captured Mr. Wilson's crazy, curly perm.

I giggled. "It *is* Mr. Wilson!"

"Told ya."

The rest of that warm afternoon we spent identifying other shapes and people in the drifting clouds. But mostly I remembered the comfort of a friend, someone who liked me for who I was, someone I could count on. I no longer felt alone.

We wasted many days cloud reading. Soon, we were having playdates outside of school, even though Mother didn't approve of Tina's family's financial standing. Her father was a mechanic, her mother a housewife looking after Tina's three younger siblings. It didn't bother me in the least. Her house was loud and alive, the exuberant energy of everyone was a far cry from the quiet etiquette of my home.

The years passed, Tina the one constant in my life. We graduated from cloud watching to boy gazing. We discussed cute boys, cuter boy bands, and shared intimate secrets, certain our confidences were safe with one another.

As eighth grade approached, things changed. I started thinking about my future, my goals. Tina seemed caught in a time warp. She wanted to keep on as the little girls we were. While I grew up, Tina remained perfectly content being the naïve schoolgirl, easily amused by the morphing shapes of clouds. After numerous excuses about having other plans, I finally told her that childish pursuits simply no longer interested me.

So, like putting away a well-loved, but no longer significant teddy bear, I closed the door on our friendship. When Tina called, Mother was only too happy to tell her I wasn't in. I began avoiding her at school. Easy enough to do. As my confidence and bust line grew, so did my circle of friends.

Late that summer, Tina quit calling me. I had already established wealthier, more ambitious friends, preparing myself for my first year in high school. At Clearwell High, I would occasionally see Tina in the hallways, but we passed each other without a glimpse or spoken word; ships that pass in the night.

****

After four years of avoiding Tina, it now fell upon me to ask her about Charles Durbin.

My heart hammered in my chest. I wanted to turn around and run the long way to class. But I kept repeating over and over, "*This is a good thing, a good thing.*" I just dreaded the inevitable fallout. *Elspeth, you owe me big time.*

In the nearly deserted corridor, I braved myself and approached her. "Hi, Tina." I sounded ridiculously chipper, given the circumstances.

She turned with a start. Her expectant smile locked onto her face, then faded. She glared at me for an eternity before she slammed the locker door, sweeping past me in silence.

"Tina! Wait!"

She swiveled on her heels. I noticed the leg brace had vanished as had her unfortunate glasses. Her short hairstyle remained the same, the tips curling in toward her chin. "What do you want, Elizabeth?" The way she bunched her fists at her sides filled me with apprehension.

"I…want to talk to you." I held my books in front

of me like a shield. "How have you been?"

"You have *got* to be kidding me. You blew me off four years ago! Without a single word." She stomped her foot. "You don't get to come up to me now and ask how I'm doing! You don't get to do that!"

My lips trembled through my forced smile. I hated showing weakness, but this was by far one of the hardest things I'd ever had to do. "I'm sorry, Tina...it's just..." I faltered for words. I knew my explanation would sound lame no matter how I pitched it.

"I'm waiting." She crossed her arms and leaned against her locker with a *clump.*

"I apologize for what I did to you." My voice barely registered above a whisper. Eating humble pie sucked. "I guess what I did was wrong—"

"You *guess?* That's your apology? You guess?" When she turned away, I grabbed her arm.

"Wait, Tina. Please?" She swiveled, batting my hand down.

Her nostrils flared, some serious heavy breathing going on. She raised her hands, shaking them beside her head. "*Ooooh!*" We faced off in silence. Finally, she said, "Do you have any idea how much you hurt me, Elizabeth?"

I shook my head, attempting to keep tears of shame at bay. "We were best friends, Elizabeth. Sisters! For eight years. One day you decided we weren't. I wasn't consulted on that decision. I didn't understand what happened." Her voice cracked. "One day we were fine, the next you weren't around anymore."

I reached out to pat her shoulder. She flinched as if my touch contained toxin. "I'm so way sorry, Tina. Maybe if I explain—"

"I'm not finished! You need to know how I felt. I've waited four years to tell you this!"

I looked down at the linoleum; my reflection appeared distorted and ugly, the way I felt at that moment.

"I thought it was me, Elizabeth. I thought I had done something to you. Something horrible! But, I wracked my brain for months. All I could come up with was that you just didn't want to be my friend anymore." She held her arms, swaying like a hanged man in the wind. "I must've cried for three weeks. My parents wanted to call yours, but I stopped them. I didn't want to have my parents fix my friendship problems. After weeks, I finally had the courage to leave my bedroom. The tears stopped. But the pain was still there. The constant pain. I tried to be positive. My parents told me I'd make new friends in high school, but no one could replace what we had."

"We'll always have what we had, Tina." I knew it sounded like a greeting card platitude signifying nothing, but I had to try.

"Oh shut up! I'm talking here! So, when I walked into high school on the first day, the first person I saw was *you.* And your new entourage of stuck-up friends! I tried to ignore you, but every time I turned around, there you were like a bad penny. You're kinda hard to miss."

I smiled at the compliment, but quickly realized she didn't mean it as one.

"So, I tried to make friends. I couldn't. I didn't fit in. I wasn't a jock. I'm not a beauty queen. Not a brain, a preppy..." She puffed out her lower lip in disgust. "I couldn't play an instrument. I tried out for the school play. Do you know where they put me, Elizabeth? Do you?"

"No."

"They put me behind the stage in the set crew! They couldn't even find a small role for me in the damn play. They kept me hidden behind the curtain. I felt like a freak show exhibit. An invisible ghost!"

"You know that's not true, Tina."

She kicked the locker door, which I took as a sign to keep quiet. "It didn't even stop there! You and your evil beeyotch cronies picked on me! You bullied me!"

"Tina, I never—"

"Which part of 'shut up' don't you understand?"

I bit my lip and winced. "You and your Bitch Brigade used to call me Tina Bottom-Dweller! Why? Because I'm not rich, privileged, spoiled? Because I don't dress like a friggin' Barbie doll? Does that ring any bells, Elizabeth? How about it?"

"I honestly never called you that, Tina. I—"

"But you stood by, while your beeyotches did, didn't you? I distinctly remember looking at you for support. And you know what you did? Think hard."

I shook my head, not remembering the incident whatsoever.

"You walked away."

"But I didn't call—"

"You may as well have. When you walked away, it was way worse than calling me names. It was like you didn't know I existed. I wasn't even worth calling names in your high-and-mighty esteem."

I grimaced, ashamed and mortified. I truly didn't remember the incident, and it bothered me. Tina's point was sharp and razor-edged. *Painful. Maybe I am too self-absorbed.*

"But, you know," she continued, "I was used to not existing." She lowered her voice even though we were the only ones in the hall. "And that's when I decided to do something desperate—when my troubles really began."

"What are you talking about, Tina? I don't understand—"

"You really don't know, do you?" Her forced laughter sounded harsh, mirth-free. "Of course you didn't know. How could you in your stupid little world of designer clothing and stuck-up pretentiousness?"

"I'm not pretentious," I squeaked.

Tina karate-chopped the air between us. "What*ever.* You never once even thought about me, did you?"

"Of course I did! But tell me what happened."

"You want to know what happened, Elizabeth?"

I nodded, but wasn't certain if I truly did want to know.

"Fine. I'll tell you." She let out a long exasperated sigh, her shoulders sagging. "Out of sheer loneliness, hopelessness, I decided to befriend the dopers. I thought, surely, they wouldn't dismiss me. I mean, I was probably going to have to impress them by getting high, but I stupidly thought it was something I could do. As dumb as it sounds, I thought I might actually be good at it. So there I was hanging out with them. I started smoking reefer then upped the ante. We started taking designer drugs."

Obviously, I was no stranger to the world of everything "designer," but this was a new one for me.

She must have noticed how baffled I looked

because she said, "Don't you worry your pretty little head about it. So, anyway, we were snorting, huffing. I have very little memory of those days, really. But you know what? At least I had friends."

I felt like I'd been slapped. Numerous times. "I'm really sorry, Tina—"

"Sorry isn't good enough!" She stamped her feet, practically running in place, before calming. "So I thought they were my friends until I ended up in the hospital. If it wasn't an overdose, it was damn close to one."

When I raised my fingertips to my mouth, I felt them trembling over my lips. A ball of nausea built in my stomach, threatening to rise.

"I have no idea what I even took that night. As I said, my memory was just a blur. I had a long time in recovery thinking about my so-called friends. After a while, I realized they *weren't* my friends. I mean, what did we have in common anyway? Doing drugs, not even remembering hanging out?"

"Tina, I had no idea. No one ever told me. Had I known—"

"Just stop it. Stop it! As I said, you were way too busy to bother with me. Your world's so important to you. Besides…" She tossed her hands up, spreading them. "It's not like many people noticed I was gone for two weeks. I'm not exactly the most visible person here at Clearwell."

She stared at me, waiting for me to process her shocking information dump. I had no words, not a clue what to say.

"And here's the funny thing. The stoners didn't come to see me. But others did. Students visited me, wished me well. Students who I had no idea I'd impacted. Turns out, they were like me. Fading away, invisible to the high and mighty at Clearwell. Kids who just wanted to be noticed. For the first time during that horrible year, I didn't feel so miserably alone."

I couldn't help myself and reached out to embrace her again. This time she didn't pull away, but she didn't return the hug either. Her arms remained rigid, glued to her side. "I'm so, so sorry—"

"Get off me!"

I jumped back like I'd touched a hot stove.

"And now, now that I've got a decent enough life going on—not that it could possibly match the wondrously sparkly dream you're living—you try and weasel your way back into my life. For whatever reason. And all you're doing is bringing my pain back."

"That's not what I'm trying to do, Tina."

"We were sisters, Elizabeth. *Cloud-readers!* I told you everything. All my secrets, my dreams, everything." Her voice paled away, a sad shadow of the strength she'd just shown. "You were my everything." Tears streamed down her cheeks, yet her eyes filled with anger. She defiantly, proudly, wiped the tears away with a swift brush of her hand.

"I'm sorry, Tina. Really. So, so sorry."

Tina turned away, slumping down the hallway.

"Tina! Please come back!"

"Just stop it, Elizabeth. Leave me alone."

"Tina! I need to talk to you about Charles Durbin."

She stopped suddenly as if slammed into a glass wall. Her shoulders straightened as she raced back to me. "What could you possibly have to say about Charles?" She growled like a tiger, ready to pounce.

"You didn't even know him!"

At least I had her attention now. No time like the present. With a deep breath, I said, "I want to find out how he died."

Tina groaned. "You have got to be kidding me! First, you try and screw with my head." She extended a finger. "And now you have the gall to sully Charles? What is this? Are you trying to atone for your past sins or something? Are you in some sort of 'Bitches Anonymous'? Am I part of your twelve-step program?"

I backed up, fearful she might take a swing at me.

"Let me tell you something about Charles. He was a true friend, Elizabeth. You know what that means? Maybe you should look up 'friend' in the dictionary. Oh, wait. Your photo is in there for the antonym of friend."

Even though I found her joke less than amusing, she barked out a loud laugh.

"And let me tell you something else about Charles. He was sober! I'm sick and tired of everyone running around saying he died because he was a druggie. Let it go!"

I saw my entryway and took it. "Tina, I want to clear Charles's name. Find out how he died. I think there's something more to it."

"Explain." I had her on the hook, but she remained one very suspicious fish.

"I have reason to believe someone else may be responsible for his death." Seconds ticked by in silence as I swallowed the lump in my throat.

She narrowed her eyes and placed her hands on her hips. "That's what I've been saying. But no one will listen to me." A brief smile lit up her face, reminding me of the inquisitive childhood friend with whom I grew up. "But why are you, of all people, interested in clearing Charles's name?" Her world-weary suspicions immediately dashed the brief "cloud-reader" recall.

"I guess I just don't think it's right that people are talking about his death being drug-related." I offered her a cautious smile. "Especially if he was sober."

"What do you mean you have reason to suspect someone else for his death?"

"Well, from what I've heard, things don't quite add up."

Tina narrowed her eyes, digging her hands into her jeans pockets. "I don't trust you, Elizabeth, farther than I can throw you. Actually, I'll bet I could toss your scrawny ass quite a ways." She grinned, eyes skyward as if contemplating the appealing notion. "Anyway, I don't trust you."

"I get that."

"But, if you're truly interested in clearing Charles's name, and maybe, just maybe, you will be better at it than me because you have connections and people listen to you and all that crap..." She paused as if considering a deal with the devil. "Fine. What do you want to know?"

"Well, not that I don't believe you, I do, but, how do you know Charles wasn't into drugs?"

Tina shook her head slowly. "You really don't know anything about me, do you?"

I supposed I didn't. Not anymore. But now didn't seem like the time to get into it.

"Part of my new life—my new social circle—is the 'Drug-Free Club'." She stared at me, waiting for recognition to set in. I had no idea we had such a club.

"I founded it once I got out of the hospital. Charles was one of the students who visited me. I guess you could say he was the co-founder. It was his idea, really."

"But couldn't Charles have, you know, relapsed?"

"He didn't! Charles was clean long before I was. He'd gone through his problems about a year before me. There's no way he'd ever go back. No way!" She sighed. "Look, the 'Drug-Free Club' might not be a big deal to you, but it's something we're proud of. Nineteen members and growing."

Although the number sounded less than impressive—I thought even the chess club had a larger roster—Tina's pride shined through. "That's great, Tina."

"Yeah, right. You had no idea there even was a Drug-Free Club, did you?"

"Sure I did. I've heard about all the, um, things you guys do and how it's…" When Tina sneered, I gave up the ruse and just dropped it.

"You know, if you or your boyfriend would endorse us, or even join us, our numbers would probably grow. Why don't you use your 'blond power' and put it to good use for a change?"

"I'll talk to Donovan about it." Maybe I would, too. Endorsing a Drug-Free Club might spruce up the résumé quite a bit. "Okay, so Charles was clean. Whom was he hanging out with? Other than the Drug-Free Club, I mean?"

"There's something you need to know about Charles." She leaned in, the menacing glint in her eyes returning. "Unlike me, who was severely ruined for life by someone in the eighth grade, *ahem*…" She glowered at me, her smile bittersweet.

I supposed I deserved that jab.

"Charles…he was different. Sometimes naively so. Charles chose to believe in the best of people. He thought people could change. So it was his endless—I would call it futile—quest to try and, I don't know, coax the druggies back to the clean side."

"Was he ever successful at it?"

"No. But that didn't stop him. He'd take on a new 'project' every so often."

*Ah. Speaking my language—people as projects.* "Who was his last project?"

"Donnie Heidenreich."

"Who?" Who were all these people I didn't know, suddenly coming out of the woodwork? How come they'd never crossed my path before? It was like an alternate world of crazy where new students were, unbeknownst to me, infiltrating the school.

"Yeah, doesn't surprise me you don't know him. He's just a kid. Kinda harmless, I think, but everyone knows he's a stoner. Charles was spending a lotta time with him lately."

"Huh. Could you point him out to me?"

Tina rolled her eyes. "Find him yourself, Elizabeth! I'm not your damn servant."

"Okay, fine," I snapped back. "Can you at least tell me where I can find him?"

A huge grin stretched across her round face. She nodded toward Johnson Drive. "You can find him at the old gas station across the street, at lunch."

"Ewww." The long-abandoned gas station had been transformed into a stoner and cigarette smoker habitat. It was easily within viewing distance of the well-traveled Johnson Drive, but for some reason, teachers and police officers left the dopers alone. They probably thought it was best to keep the never-do-wells doing their never-do-welling off school grounds. Out of sight, out of mind, plus less negative publicity for Clearwell High.

"Yeah, good luck with that," said Tina with a laugh.

"Okay, fine. One last thing. Do you know who's dealing drugs around here?"

Tina's smile snapped back to a fret. With her whiplash expression changes, the girl was practically begging for premature wrinkles. Her gaze darted about the hallway. She opened her mouth and then quickly clamped down. Finally, she said, "No."

"No idea at all?" Given her recent history, I would've sworn she had insider knowledge.

"Look, Elizabeth." She lowered her voice. "I put that life behind me. I do not hang with drug-users anymore. Got it?"

"Okay," I said quietly.

She walked off, strutting more confidently this time.

"Tina?"

"What?"

"Maybe we could do something some time? Maybe we could—"

"Don't push your luck!" She shook her head as she entered the stairwell.

I don't know what possessed me to offer her that olive branch. Maybe simply to assuage my guilt. Or maybe I'd missed her. Just a little bit.

And it looked like Elspeth was right. If it was true the police found drugs in Charles Durbin's car and in his system, it was more than likely someone had planted them, perhaps even dosing him into his death-ride. *Just what were you into, Charles? Or what did you know that was so important it would drive someone to murder you?*

Charles Durbin seemed like one huge, freakin' enigma. And becoming more interesting by the minute. Looked like Charles was my next project. And I had to admit, it felt nice doing something for someone other than myself. As long as I didn't make a habit of it.

Yet I deeply dreaded my impending lunchtime visit to Stonerville. *So help me, God, Elspeth! If I get a reputation as being a druggie, I'll never speak to you again!*

## Chapter Five

*Elspeth*

No way was Elizabeth equipped to visit the doper's domain, so I decided to take this one for the team. Sending Elizabeth into a drug den would be like plopping down a fairy-tale princess onto the frontlines of combat.

At lunchtime, Elizabeth procrastinated in the bathroom. She sat on the toilet, breathing deeply, trying to stoke up some courage. Good luck with that. So, I "pushed" her. Whenever I took over Elizabeth's body, there was always a one-minute "waiting period." It didn't last long in reality, but it was scary. Our personalities—souls, whatever—passed on our way to our destinations. But during those transitional seconds, Elizabeth's body was uninhabited, a hollow shell. I usually saw to it she was asleep safely in bed or at least securely sitting down as she was now.

She felt relieved I was taking over, but wary at the same time. For whatever reason, Elizabeth never wanted me to appear at school. Whatever. Like I was going to cause trouble or something.

So after I shuffled her off to Dream Space, I claimed her body and pushed open the bathroom stall door. I nearly hurled when I glanced at my image in the mirror. Ridiculous clothing, but I didn't have much choice in the matter. I wanted to dress in my full-on, kick-ass attire, but Elizabeth nixed the idea. Said it'd draw too much attention. Well, yeah, kinda the point, but she was the boss. Or so she thought. But right now, I had to suck it up and accept being a pretty, preppy princess. I looked once more in the mirror and sighed. Why couldn't my host have better taste?

I exited the school and traipsed across the large field, trying to adapt to Elizabeth's constricting skirt.

Set on a street corner, the gas station had fallen into poor shape. Straggling weeds pushed through the broken pavement and sidewalk that surrounded the small white-bricked building. The front window and door had been boarded up. Even the graffiti showed signs of age. *Modern Gangstas* had been painted across the rusting, serrated garage door. Some enterprising artist painted a big X through it, with the legend *R.I.P., SUCKAHS!* emblazoned below it, denoting the passing of these relics. An old-fashioned red pump, minus the hose, sat on the crumbling, cement island, a sad memorial for the days when gas was actually pumped for you.

No one hung out in front of the station, but a plume of smoke rose from behind it. Someone coughed, followed by a giggly fit, getting high obviously the cause of hilarity. I stepped through the trash and tires on the side of the building, following the beckoning smoke signal. In the back, a group of five students sat in a circle, some on the sidewalk, others on the grass. More kids lurked farther away, seeking privacy in the shadows of the surrounding trees. Everyone, boys and girls alike, wore T-shirts and ragged jeans. Silence fell over them when they saw me.

"Hey," I said.

Two boys looked at each other, disbelief in their eyes. Finally, after taking a long drag from a cigarette, one spoke. "Um, what? Are you lost or something?" He broke out into high-pitched laughter, his entourage joining him.

"Yeah. Or something." I crossed my arms, impatiently waiting for them to shut the hell up.

"What do you want?" asked a dark-haired girl. "School's back that way." She hitched her thumb across the street.

"Uh-huh. Probably where you should be. Stay in school. Don't do drugs. Drink milk."

The girl hopped to her feet and approached me. She puffed a cloud of smoke into my face. "I know who you are. What? You a narc or something?"

"No narc." I waved the smoke away. "Just looking for someone."

She stepped closer. Underneath her heavy blue eye shadow, her eyes appeared red and glassy. "Who you lookin' for? And why? I mean, shouldn't you be out killing baby seals or something? Like a good conservative cow?" She turned toward the lounging group, looking for approval. Once again, they launched into shrill laughter.

"Shouldn't you be like—oh, I don't know—getting penicillin shots down at the free clinic?" I lifted a corner of my mouth, half-smiling, half-smirking.

"Why don't you just go back and play with your little bitches! We don't want you around here."

I couldn't very well tell her I found Elizabeth's friends as vile as these cretins. The things I had to put up with. "Maybe I just want to see how the other half lives," I said, channeling my best, stuck-up, inner Elizabeth.

A deep, wet sound emanated from within her chest. She heaved her shoulders back and dredged up a loogie. She spat onto Elizabeth's ballet flat.

"Uh-oh," I said. "You really shouldn't have done that." I didn't particularly want to explain to Elizabeth how her beloved shoe had become tarnished. Girl can be unreasonable.

Red-eyes shoved her face into mine. "Maybe you'd better leave, bitch!" Her cheap bracelets jangled when she shot her arms out. I caught one of her wrists and wrenched it behind her, twirling her as I did so.

"Look," I mumbled into her ear, "I came here in peace. I'm just looking to talk to somebody. Don't make me go all ninja on your ass."

Several stoners jumped to their feet, looking uncertain. One boy clapped his hands on his jeans, took a step forward, and then changed his mind. Staring around at his inert crew, he leaned back resignedly against the building with a sigh. Didn't want to ruin a good buzz.

"Let go of me, bitch!" The more she struggled, the higher I jacked her hand up.

"You promise to settle down? You gonna be a good, little girl?"

"Owww! Dammit. Yes! Just let go!" I released the hellion. Even though she didn't have the strength to back up her attitude, I appreciated her fire.

"Super. Now we're all friends." I smiled as sweetly as Elizabeth would've. "Now, if you'll just let me finish. I'm looking for Donnie Heidenreich. Seen him?"

The girl rubbed her wrist, scowling at me. She

jutted her chin toward the back row of trees. "In the tire." The girl rejoined her group, chortles erupting from her cronies.

A large, bald tire rested underneath a tree's shadow. Some kid sprawled on top of it, his sneakers dangling lazily, his arms outstretched to the sides. And totally oblivious to my presence.

Tired of waiting for him to open his eyes, I said, "Hey."

He squinted against the sunrays piercing through the tree branches. "Hey." A dumb smile crept across his face. He dragged his fingers through his long, black hair, tucking several greasy strands behind his ears. "I know you."

"Yeah, well, that makes one of us." I squatted down on the ground next to him.

"You were in a couple of my classes last year. Elizabeth Blackmer." He rubbed his eyes like a toddler waking from a dream.

I ran a quick "Elizabeth Scan"; sort of like a mental computer search. I entered a name, a face, whatever, into Elizabeth's mind, searching her memory banks, seeing if I could pull up a hit. Not sure if it was Elizabeth guiding me to answers, the powers above, or maybe even just an automatic brain function. But it usually worked. Not this time. I came up blank. "Huh. Guess I don't remember you."

"Yeah, well…" He shrugged the laziest shrug I'd ever seen. "I always sit in the back and don't say much. You're always in the front." When he smiled, his eyes scrunched up into tiny slits.

"You're Donnie Heidenreich?"

He nodded. "That's right." He paused, distracted

by the trees like they held the answers to the mystery of life.

I kicked the tire. "Donnie, would you please sit up? I need your full attention. Focus."

"Huh? Oh, yeah." He took his sweet time but managed to squirm up in the tire, sinking his butt into the center of it. "So, what do you want? I mean, it's kinda really weird you're out here and everything."

"Yeah, I'm kinda getting that. But I need to talk to you about Charles Durbin."

His eyes finally opened all the way. "Oh, wow. Man. Wow." He shook his head, fluttering his eyelids rapidly as if struggling to keep bad thoughts away. "God damn it…wow…Charles."

"Donnie, I understand he was spending a lot of time with you before, well…"

"Yeah, dude." He shook his shaggy head again. "Yeah."

Donnie Heidenreich wasn't one of the best conversationalists I'd ever met.

"Stay with me, Donnie. So why was he hanging out with you? I thought he was drug-free. And you, well…" I waved my hand at him, hoping that even his fried synapses would make the connection.

He hung his head, his unruly hair hanging at the sides like long dog ears. "Yeah, that sucks about what happened to Charles. Just, really sucks."

Noticing the wannabe badass girl still glaring at me from the back of the station, I winked at her.

"Yeah, Donnie. It really does suck. But what was he doing with you? This is important."

"Man, well, you know, me and Charles were friends in grade school." He stared at me like this was an alien concept. I indicated I understood. "And we got high together the first time. But Charles, he gave up the high life. Didn't want to do it anymore. Me? Partying's still working out for me." He pumped his fist in the air several times, no doubt to an imaginary metal band jamming in his head.

"Yeah, I can see that." I kicked the tire again, stirring Donnie from his golden memories. "Focus, Donnie, focus."

He nodded dutifully.

"Okay, you guys were grade school friends, and then you both went your own ways." He bobbed his head again. "Why was he hanging out with you again?"

"Charles was…he was a good guy, you know? I don't really know what he was doing, but I guess he thought he was trying to save me." His eyes bulged comically, waiting for me to respond to the unbelievably hysterical notion. I remained unmoved. "He kept telling me that a drug-free life was cool, that it was awesome. He wanted me to join his drug-free group. I mean, dude! Can you imagine?"

"No, not really."

"Anyway, he was working on me a lot lately. I told him, 'Dude! I'm cool with who I am and what I do. I like my lifestyle." He shook his head solemnly. "But Charles wouldn't give up. He kept after me all the time. He got kinda annoying. But, he didn't deserve what happened to him. Sucks, dude. Totally sucks."

"Huh." Seeing I was losing him again, I snapped my fingers several times. "Donnie. Stay with me." He lifted his eyebrows, a placid smile offering nothing. "Was Charles doing drugs? In the end?"

"Dude! No way!" He crossed his hands over one

another, displaying more activity than I thought him capable of. "No friggin' way! Dude was clean. That's why what they're sayin' is so messed up. He wouldn't ever have taken drugs. Never!"

"So, what do you think happened?"

"Somebody gave him drugs." Suddenly he appeared focused, the clarity in his voice soulful.

"Who did it?"

Donnie looked around before waggling his finger at me. I leaned in. He whispered, "I don't know." The answer didn't seem worth the build-up.

"Donnie, is that the truth? I mean, really? Are you sure? You don't need to be afraid to tell me the truth. I want to clear Charles of any involvement with drugs." He said nothing, just shrugging occasionally. "Donnie, were you with Charles the night of his death?"

His jaw dropped. "What? No! I didn't do that to him! Charles was my man. I'd never, never do anything to hurt him. Dude! That's messed up!"

He seemed sincere—at least sincere for him, I supposed—yet I couldn't help but feel he wasn't telling me everything. "So, you have no idea who else he was hangin' with?"

"No! I swear to God!"

"Okay." I took in a deep breath. "Donnie, who's dealing at Clearwell?"

Donnie's hands flopped down into the dirt resignedly. Apparently, he had used up his daily quota of energy. "I don't know."

"You don't know? Well, where do you get your drugs?"

"Dude! I only smoke the weed. I don't do that other crap, even I know it's not cool."

"Okay, so where do you get your smoke?"

"Whoever's packin'. I mean, dude. I don't have a job. And my 'rents don't give me cash. I just go where the smoke is."

I sighed. "So, you just leech onto whoever has it?"

"That's what I'm sayin'." He grabbed me by the arm. I cleared my throat, staring him down until he removed it. "Oh, sorry. Look, there's some wicked shit flying around here lately. Lots of potent 'scrips, painkillers, crap like that. And coke's getting big again. Whenever someone pulls it out, I just sorta haul ass out of there. It's gettin' big. I don't know who's slinging, but they're making a killing at it."

Literally "making a killing at it," I wanted to add, but didn't. I hesitated, wondering how to pose my next question. Just dive right in, I guessed. "Donnie, just between you and me, I can trust you, can't I?" He nodded. "If I were interested in scoring some drugs, where would I go?"

He gave me a double take, laughing uneasily. "Wait, what? You're kidding, right? You?"

"Let's just say I'm curious."

He scratched his head. "Well, don't really know. But Mark Dugan's having a party Saturday night. His parents are out of town. I bet you can score there." He winked. "If you're just curious, all I'm sayin'."

I quickly *Elizabinged* Mark Dugan. Apparently, Elizabeth knew Mark Dugan, having shared several classes with him, although she pretended not to know him. She ignored him in the hallways, virtually wiping him out of her narrowly defined universe. Quiet, large, and surly, everyone had him pegged as a stoner. "Okay, maybe I'll drop by."

"Really?" Donnie's eyes lit up. "Maybe we could like, um, hook up and…"

I cocked my head, and gave him an incredulous Elizabeth look. "Yeah, *not* going to happen, Donnie."

His brief blast of confidence shriveled up. "Oh, yeah. I was just…"

"Okay, Donnie." I offered him a doleful smile and shot to my feet. "If you think of anything else or hear anything else, just let me know."

"How do I contact you? Can I get your phone number?"

"Ahem!" I stood over him, arms akimbo. "Once again, that's not going to happen. I'm not hard to find. Just look for the three-ring circus of blonds."

"Oh, yeah, I knew that," he mumbled.

"Thanks, Donnie."

I scooted off. From behind me, Donnie called back, "Elizabeth?"

"Yeah?"

"Why are you doing this? I mean, really? Why?" He hauled himself out of the tire, yawning.

"Just curious, that's all." As I strolled past the gathered stoners behind the building, the confrontational girl wrinkled her face in disgust.

I pantomimed holding a phone to my ear and mouthed, "Call me," before blowing her a kiss. She growled, prompting her friends into fits of laughter.

I ran across Johnson Drive toward the school. Over the years, I'd acquired a certain extra sense, one of my supercool powers. And that sense absolutely tingled. Someone watching me. I swiveled on my flats. From the corner of the gas station, a kid wearing a T-shirt and jeans stared at me, puffing on a cigarette. When I locked eyes with him, he jolted, then retreated around the edge of the building.

Tim Matthews, new kid at Clearwell this year. Expelled from his previous school. He was also in Elizabeth's environmental science class.

*Gotcha.*

\*\*\*\*

The bell rang just as I entered the school, the end of Elizabeth's lunch period. Time enough to get back to the restroom, hunker down in a stall, and bring Elizabeth back. I did a lot for the lords of limbo, but wouldn't sit through advanced sewing or whatever.

Upon pushing open the bathroom door, a large hand snaked out, clamping onto my wrist.

I whirled around, reflexively balling my fist, and stared up into the mad-dog visage of Arville Hastings, Clearwell vice principal, full-time football aficionado, and resident dictator. Tex had told me some things about Hastings, none of them flattering. Hastings made it his agenda to terrorize the downtrodden and unpopular. Which was apparently why he adored Elizabeth. Elizabeth's memories flashed in my head; a grotesque jumble of put-upon smiles, baby talk, and twittering eyelids meant to pacify Hastings and keep him on Elizabeth's team. *Gag.*

"A minute of your time, if I may, Ms. Blackmer." He clenched his teeth tightly, his protruding eagle-like nose flaring. His box-like head looked so tightly wound, I thought it might pop off and spin down the hallway like a top.

"Oookay, if you'll let go of my arm," I said, failing to manufacture an Elizabethan smile.

He let go, but not before yanking one more time.

"To my office. Now."

As I scuttled behind him, attempting to match his pace, my pulse raced. I couldn't deal with Elizabeth's ploy of batting my lashes and playing the sweet, obliging "Beauty" to Hastings's "Beast." Just not wired that way. And there was no time to bring Elizabeth back.

Hastings barreled into the receiving area, blew by a snooty-looking woman behind the front counter, and pushed his office door open with a bang. Showing his bigger and louder Texas roots. Yee-haw!

"Have a seat, Ms. Blackmer," he ordered.

I plunked down and crossed my ankle over my knee. Quickly correcting my unladylike posture, I straightened my legs, clamping my knees together in the most prudish possible way. Eyeing the Hastings bobblehead lookalike on his desk, I tapped the head. "What can I do for you, Mr. Hastings?"

Extending a meaty finger, Hastings stopped the bouncing bobblehead. He folded his hands, sinking back into his chair, and then whinnied like a wild horse. "Ms. Blackmer. Do you mind telling me just what in the hell you think you're doing?"

"Um, getting an education? Forming my future plans?"

"I think you and I both know what I'm talking about."

I tilted my head and smiled. "Okay, why don't you tell me? I didn't sleep very well last night and—"

"What in God's name were you doing at the gas station just now?"

I wiggled my feet while thinking of an answer. "What do you mean?" Probably not the most appropriate of answers.

"I saw you coming back from there. I'm sure you know what type of rabble goes there. Hardly the people I'd expect you to be hanging out with." He exposed his lower teeth like a territorial dog. "I'm extremely disappointed with you, Ms. Blackmer. I expect better from you."

I shrugged. "What kind of people? They're just students, like everyone else."

He shook his head as if he couldn't believe what he'd just heard. "What kind of people? They're dopers. Drug users, smokers—the dregs of this school!" He narrowed his eyes, studying me as if through a microscope. "Are you high, Ms. Blackmer? That would certainly explain your sudden insubordination!"

"Want me to pee in a cup? I'll pee in a casserole dish and bake it if you'd like." He whipped back his head in shock. Unfortunately, my involuntary chuckle couldn't be stopped. "No, Mr. Hastings, I'm not high. Seriously. If you want me to pee in a cup, I will."

He coughed, looking away briefly before returning his unflinching gaze. "Please, pray tell, why were you over there?" He folded his hands across his bulging-at-the-buttons belly. "Please, do enlighten me. I just can't wait to hear why you would visit such a place." He smiled sardonically and swept his hand at me, inviting me to the dance. "Go on, I'm waiting."

Uh-oh. "Well…" I tried batting my eyes in a horrendous display that must've looked like debris had flown into them. "Well, I wanted to make sure I had the right homework assignment for environmental science. There's a kid in my class I needed to ask. Someone told me he'd be over there."

"Environmental science." He sneered as if that was *much* worse than drug use. "And who is this kid?"

"Um, Tim Matthews." The thick silence hung between us like a suffocating fog. I crossed my legs, remembered myself, and uncrossed them. I flicked my finger at the bobblehead again, grinning up at Hastings.

He slammed his hand onto the bobblehead and yanked it away. "Tim Matthews. He's that new transfer kid, right?" I nodded. "And did you get your assignment?" I nodded again, two bobbleheads in the office. "And would he corroborate your story?"

"Yeah, I guess."

"You guess?"

"Yeah, well, sure, yeah, he'll corroborate it."

Hastings leaned back, scratching his thick eyebrow with the back of a thumbnail. He swayed back and forth in his chair, the chair's hydraulics getting a workout underneath his weight. "Elizabeth, I don't need to tell you drugs are for idiots and losers, do I?"

"No, Mr. Hastings."

"I would hate to see someone like you, someone who has a very bright future ahead, to throw it all away for some wild, stupid, and dangerous joyride." He threw his hands in the air, wiggling his fingers about, making it rain. "How would you like that to end up on your permanent record? On your transcripts? You definitely would not be seeing an Ivy League college then. You can count on that."

"No, sir."

He raised his eyebrows.

"I mean, yes, sir?"

"And what about your chances of becoming prom queen? Did you ever stop to think about how your afternoon tryst could affect the outcome of that?"

I had to roll my eyes at that one. Whatever.

"And what would Donovan think?" He leaned forward, attempting empathy, but not achieving anything remotely similar. "What might that do to him? Or your future together?"

Apparently, I was the only person on the planet who didn't think Donovan Goode walked on water. "I guess that wouldn't be good?"

"No, it would not, Ms. Blackmer!" He pounded his ham hock of a fist onto the desktop. "Do not go over there again, young lady! It's dangerous and you do not want to be hanging out with that rabble over there."

"Mr. Hastings, some of the, ah, 'rabble' don't seem that bad. Not really. I think they're sorta maybe just, I don't know, lost. Maybe kinda misunderstood?"

"What? Where is this coming from, Ms. Blackmer? I cannot believe what I'm hearing!" He pointed a finger at me, his thumb up, ready to pull the trigger. "Look. You and I—up until now—have been on the same page regarding Clearwell and what's best for you. What's best for the school. And now you're talking like a damn—"

"Democrat?" I offered.

His sudden calm creeped me out far more than his righteous indignation. "Ms. Blackmer, do not let this happen again. If I hear of your being in the vicinity of the gas station or hanging out with the druggies, then I will administer a drug test."

"So I'll get to pee in a cup?" I looked around, searching for evidence of a cup. I'd probably have to apologize to Elizabeth later. But I just couldn't help myself sometimes.

"I will administer a test and it will go on your permanent record, ruining your chance at the college of your choice!"

I sighed and counted to ten. "Mr. Hastings, you do not have to worry about me and drugs. Seriously. All I was suggesting was that maybe these other kids— whom you and the school seem to have already given up on—just maybe, they haven't had the breaks I've had. Maybe they're not rich. Maybe they see themselves as failures because you guys do. They're slipping through the cracks. They—"

"Ms. Blackmer!" He raised his eyebrows, sticking his chin toward the door. "We're finished here."

"Okay." I got up to leave, trying to remember Elizabeth's tight-ass posture.

"Ms. Blackmer?"

"Yeah?"

"I mean it. Everything I said. Stay away from the gas station." He prodded two fingers at me, back to his eyes, and repeated the move several times. "I'm watching you."

I slammed the door a little too loudly, awakening Ms. Snooty McSnooty Pants from her huffy chore of shuffling papers. I told her, "He's having a bad hair day. I'd be careful around him if I were you." Her "tsks" and "clucks" accompanied me out the door.

Yeah, Hastings and the rest of the world had already written the stoners off as lost causes. Really pissed me off. I should know. I was once one of them. You make a few bad choices, get some bad breaks, and before you know it, you've gone from zero to one hundred sixty and crash into a house. Like Charles Durbin. Not everyone was born into privilege like

Elizabeth. They were the invisible kids.

And my Elspeth senses were a-tingling. Hastings seemed adamant about my not visiting the gas station. Crazily so. Hiding something? Afraid I'd find something out? Or maybe he was just a dick. The smart money was on all of the above.

\*\*\*\*

As soon as I left the office, I ran smack into Donovan. Literally. *Crap. This day keeps getting worse.*

He flapped his hands while recovering his balance. "Elizabeth? What's going on?"

"Hi, Donovan." I shut my eyes, steeled myself, and kissed him. Kissing a dead fish would be more pleasurable, but as Elizabeth always said, "appearance is everything".

Stunned, Donovan broke our embrace. "Um, Elizabeth? No PDAs."

I probably should have expected every aspect of Elizabeth's life was pure and pristine. "Why? Didn't you like it?"

"Well, yes. It's just we agreed. No public displays of affection."

"I know." It's not that Donovan was a bad guy. From all indications, he was nice, just dreadfully dull, like angel-food cake: sweet, bland, and possessing a sponge-like persona that soaks up everyone within his gravitational pull.

"Well, how are you? I came right away when I heard you were in Hastings's office."

"Oh, that." I dismissed it with a wave. News traveled fast in the halls of Clearwell High. "It was nothing. Hastings was just busting my, um, giving me a hard time about going across the street to the gas station during lunch."

Donovan's eyes widened. "What? Why would you do that?" And here we went again. "That's not an appropriate place for you."

I sighed. Was it any wonder Elizabeth was the way she was? Everyone wanted to put her in their pocket and keep her there. "I had to find out about a homework assignment. Someone told me I could find Tim Matthews there. No big deal."

"Tim Matthews? The transfer student?" Donovan had an uncommon talent for knowing everyone in school. Didn't know where he found the time, but it was probably part of his plan for future world conquest.

"Yep. Anyway, got it all straightened out." I leaned back against the row of lockers, placing one foot flat against them.

"Elizabeth, are you okay?"

"Yeah, why?"

"I don't know. You're just...acting strange." I couldn't hold his concerned gaze. Felt like staring into the eyes of an unwanted puppy in a pet-store window.

"I'm okay, Donovan. Really."

Donovan's "douche-mate," Kip Aldrich ambled up, hands in his designer shorts. "So is it true? Did our little princess get in trouble with big, bad Hastings?"

A well-placed kick to the junk would've obliterated the smarm right out of him, but I held it together. "Shut up, Kip. He just wanted to talk to me, that's all."

"Yeah, right." With his shorts, suspenders, and socks, he looked like some idiotic, overgrown German kid from the forties. "I heard you were busted across the street."

Donovan winced, yet kept his resolve. "That's

enough, Kip. Elizabeth went over there to get a homework assignment."

"Okay, what*ever*. You sure you weren't, you know…" He held his thumb and forefinger to his lips and inhaled loudly.

Donovan whacked Kip on the shoulder, but followed it up with a make-good smile, just a good time between Clearwell's primates. "Come on, Kip. Elizabeth doesn't—"

"I'll handle this, Donovan." I squeezed between the two of them and stared Kip down. "If you have something to say, Kip then say it. Otherwise, you're acting like a catty, gossiping girl."

All semblance of humor vanished. If I didn't know better, I'd think Kip was actually afraid of Elizabeth. "I…I was just playin', that's all. Come on."

"Elizabeth!" Addison Harcourt ran toward us, taking tiny pigeon steps since her legs were tightly harnessed underneath her skirt. "I just heard! Oh my God! Are you all right?"

Seemed I'd become an unwitting passenger on Clearwell's Information Highway.

"I'm fine, Addison." She leaned toward me, her cheek held adjacent to mine. Not knowing what to do, I reluctantly planted a quick kiss on her cheek. She pulled back, staring at me in horror. Still trying to save face, I embraced her, giving her a guy-hug. Her mouth gaped open like a garishly painted fun-house entryway. How in the hell did these silly girls greet one another, anyway?

"All right," belted out Kip. "A little girl-on-girl action!"

"Shut up, Kip," said Addison, before turning back

to me. "I was just so way worried about you."

"Everyone," I shouted, triggering many in the hallway to look our way. "I'm fine. Nothing happened to me. I made the oh-so-huge mistake of asking someone about a homework assignment at the gas station across the street." Addison gasped. "But, as you can see, I'm fine, in one piece, end of story already!"

"Okay, Elizabeth," said Donovan, patronizingly tamping down the air. "I believe you."

Kip cracked an imaginary whip in the air, accompanied by a "whooshing" vocal effect. Addison gave him a shove, failing to hide her smile. Kip slid his arm around her waist, then flashed his arrogant smirk for everyone to enjoy. How I would have loved to rearrange his costly dental work permanently.

"All right, love birds, take care now. We're off to class." He swung Addison in a circle like she was an extension of his body. When he faced us again, he added, "Ciao!" before leaving.

Donovan dropped his hands on my shoulders. "Hey, you're certain everything's fine? I would've gone to get your assignment for you, you know."

"I know. Thanks." I'd say this for the guy. Although he was blander than white bread with the crust cut off, he obviously cared deeply for Elizabeth. "But I'm a big girl." And maybe it was time for Elizabeth to grow up a little bit. She couldn't rely on Daddy Warbucks and Donovan all her life. Even though that appeared to be her plan.

"Just let me know how I can help you, okay?" His immobile brown hairstyle glistened beneath the fluorescent lights. With the amount of product he used, he should have been considered a fire hazard.

"Oh, I keep forgetting to ask you. Charles's funeral is tomorrow. Friday. I won't ask you to take school off for it, but afterward, will you go with me to the visitation at his parents' house?"

"Sure, yes. Of course." It might wield some useful information. "Just pick me up. What time?"

"Sevenish?"

"*Hello,* Elizabeth," screeched a voice behind us. Another harridan from hell, dressed like a schoolgirl in a Japanese anime. She stood, one hand resting on her angled hip. Quickly accessing Elizabeth's memory, Elizabeth's hatred for the girl blew me away. Charlotte Drayton, her enemy. Now *this* was gonna be fun.

"Charlotte."

"Hi, Charlotte," echoed Donovan, his tone unusually cold and reserved.

She tossed her other hip out like a pole dancer while passing boys snuck peeks at her snugly wrapped body. "What's all this I'm hearing about our dear sweet Elizabeth living a double life?" She leered at me, her tongue tip flitting between her teeth.

"What are you talking about, Charlotte?" I asked, knowing the answer. I wondered if even the cafeteria crew knew about my lunchtime visit.

"Doing drugs now?" She tittered into her hand, two idiot look-alike girls behind her following suit. "That's what the scuttlebutt is!"

Even though she had several inches of height on me, I was more than ready to take her down. "First of all, Charlotte, the only 'scuttlebutt' I see around here is your big ass. So why don't you scuttle your butt the hell out of here?" I pointed down the hallway. Donovan appeared torn between shock and awe. Charlotte's mouth clamped down so tight, tiny wrinkles tucked into the corners. "Secondly, I don't do drugs. Never will. But, everyone knows what you do for recreational kicks." I smiled, waiting for her to walk right into it.

She tossed her hair back, looking at her sidekicks for support.

*Come on, take the bait, take the bait!*

Finally, she hefted one dark eyebrow high. "Oh? And what's that, Elizabeth?"

I held out my hand and began ticking off digits. "Well, one, you do the football team. That's the whole team, mind you, excluding the water boy, natch, because even you have to draw the line somewhere. Two…" Second stabbing finger tagged off. "You do the basketball team, including the benched players—and I understand you give an entirely new meaning to 'benching ball players'. Third, oh, I could just go on all day, Charlotte, talking about your slutty, wanton adventures, but I think you get the point."

Charlotte extended her hand, palm up, in front of my face. Slowly, she closed her fingers, her entire arm shaking. She screamed, "Ohhh!" and turned on her heels. "Come on, girls!" Her support team scrambled after her gyrating hips.

"Wow," said Donovan, his mouth agape. "That was…that was either very awesome…or kinda dangerous."

"Oh, I'm not afraid of Charlotte. Big deal."

"Well, sweetheart…" I nearly grimaced at Donovan's pet name for Elizabeth. "We know she plays dirty. I just hope it doesn't come back to bite you."

Not only would Charlotte Drayton bite back, but she would also try and gobble Elizabeth up, regurgitate her, and eat her again out of spite.

****

I pretty much missed my—well, Elizabeth's—class after lunch. But it gave me plenty of time to grab her books for the next class and relinquish her body back to her. I really didn't want any more unnecessary schooling.

After Donovan left me, I spotted two students huddled together in the hallway, engrossed in some serious whispering. One of them I immediately recognized as Tim Matthews, the small T-shirted kid in Elizabeth's science class and gas station voyeur. The other was large, hulking, and wearing an ugly, open flannel shirt—the kind that died with grunge music—over a death metal band T-shirt. With hair cropped close to his head, a scruffy soul-patch balanced out the hair deficit. I didn't need to access Elizabeth's data banks to know he was Marc Dugan. I just felt it. And I would be crashing his party Saturday night.

When they noticed they'd gained my attention, they quickly turned their backs to me, then shot me a few not-so-discreet glances. They strutted off in opposite directions, still watching me.

Cursing much too loudly for the likes of Elizabeth Blackmer, I finally succeeded in opening her damn locker. A folded piece of paper fluttered to the floor. A simple typed statement read, *Let it go. Before someone else gets hurt.*

Huh.

## Chapter Six

*Elizabeth*

"I can't believe what you did today!" Majorly pissed, but bundled up in my cute pink pajamas and bedspread, I probably appeared as a less-than-imposing force of nature.

"Oh, what did I do anyway?" Elspeth rolled her eyes.She kicked her feet off the desk and propelled my desk chair toward the bed like a rocket, the wheels ratcheting across the rug.

When she tried to prop her feet up on my bed, I glowered at her.

"You were going to go over to the gas station, anyway. I did you a favor. You were scared to death and wouldn't have known what to do."

"That doesn't matter." I scrunched my hands into fists and beat the air. "Our deal is you don't mess with my chances of getting into college. Or mess with my image. Now everyone thinks I'm a druggie!"

Elspeth grinned lopsidedly, the grin I'd grown to hate.

"Elizabeth, your pristine and pure image is intact. I gave you a good cover story. Relax."

"Easy for you to say, Elspeth. You don't have to go to school there! With all my friends and my boyfriend and—"

"Yeah. I met some of them today. Just how do you greet your girlfriends, anyway?" She clasped her hands behind her neck. "Do you have some sort of secret handshake or something?"

"What are you talking about? What did you do that you haven't told me about?" I suspected Elspeth didn't make me privy to everything she did when she took over my body. Sometimes I only got glimpses—drips and drabs of memories from our shared mind's faucet. I used to be okay with it when Elspeth dealt with people who didn't matter much to me, the old adage "out of sight, out of mind" proving quite literal in those cases. But now that Elspeth was directly dealing with Donovan, Addie, and the others, I'd most def be in a need-to-know mode.

"Well, I did give your pal, Charlotte, a good smack down."

"Wait, what?"

Elspeth filled me in. I couldn't help but share in her glory over besting Charlotte, but remained uneasy about the inevitable fallout. Charlotte was one who'd never allow me to get the upper hand.

"So, she was actually super pissed? And she didn't say anything?"

"Just goodbye!" Elspeth giggled and kicked her boots into the air. "You shoulda' been there. Well, you know what I mean."

We both laughed giddily. For a moment, it seemed like the world's most paranormal slumber party. "And your vice principal, Hastings…what a tight-ass."

"Oh, God, Elspeth, what happened?" I buried my face in my hands.

"Doesn't matter. Everything's cool." She wrinkled

her nose. "He was, I don't know, really against you going back to the gas station."

"Well, duh. Hello! He doesn't want me hanging out with druggies!"

Elspeth shrugged. "I guess. It's just, I almost get the feeling there's more to it than that."

"What? You think Hastings is dealing drugs? He might be kind of a tight-ass, but he wouldn't do that."

"Okay, whatever. You're missing the bigger issue here." Elspeth reached into her leather jacket, pulled out a wadded-up piece of paper, and tossed it at me. "That note in your locker tells me we're onto something. Someone wants us to stop looking into it."

I unfolded the dirty piece of paper and grimaced. "Elspeth, couldn't you have taken better care of this?"

"Oh, did you want to dust it for fingerprints? Chill out. The real letter's on your desk. This is Dream Space, remember?"

I read the note again. "There's something about this." I studied it carefully before I latched onto a nagging memory. "Wait. The words 'let it go', that's what Tina told me earlier."

Elspeth hopped onto my bed, sitting on her haunches as if preparing to spring into action. "You don't think Tina has something to do with this, do you?"

"I don't know. It just seems funny those were her exact words. That's all I'm saying."

Elspeth sighed and shook her head. "I don't think Tina Bottoms is a drug dealer. I mean, she's pretty strongly against drugs. Especially after, you know."

I cringed at the unspoken accusation. "I guess you're right. It's just a coincidence."

Elspeth clapped her hands. "Okay! Looks like you're going to a drug party Saturday night. Or I guess I am."

"Do you promise not to do anything stupid? Or to call attention to yourself?" I closed my eyes tightly and screamed. No one could hear you scream in Dream Space. It was almost therapeutic. "Why am I involved in this, anyway?"

"Don't worry. I've been around these sorts of parties before. I know how to act. Your reputation will remain pure as snow."

I knew Elspeth meant to placate me, but her underlying tone did anything but.

"If all goes well, we'll bust the drug dealer, find out what happened to Charles Durbin, and you'll be off to Dartmouth, living the princess lifestyle you've always dreamt about."

"Fine." I thrust my finger into her face. "But everything has to be kept on the down-low."

"Down-low, good to go, got it." Elspeth's eyes sparkled. Obviously, she was enjoying this. And it frightened me.

"And no one—I mean it, Elspeth—no one better recognize me in your clothing." My stomach turned at the thought of her wardrobe. If anyone ever caught me in those clothes, it'd be much worse than being outed as a druggie.

"Right," she snapped. "No one will recognize you...us. I'll wear sunglasses or something." She leaned over, dropping her hand on my shoulder. "Just relax, Elizabeth. Nothing's going to go wrong."

And you know what they say about famous last words.

\*\*\*\*

You have got to be kidding me. Twelve-fifteen a.m. and again, a raucous, hideous noise awoke me. Once I realized it wasn't some dream of a far-away tribal land, I tossed on my robe and pulled the window sash. The idiot next door was at it again. But this time, it was something far worse than basketball.

I clambered down the stairwell. Once outside, I cinched my robe closed against the night breeze. As I stomped up the driveway, my slippers slapping against the cement, the ruckus grew. The garage door stood open, light flooding the driveway. Inside, Kevin Bartholomew sat behind a drum kit, pounding away. *Why do boys love to pound on things? Gah.*

He wore headphones, oblivious to anyone and everything around him. With closed eyes, he bobbed his idiotic head. Occasionally, he let slip a ludicrous—almost painful sounding—"yeah" or "uh-huh" in a high-pitched tone, like a drowning cat. I stormed the garage, a pink and fuzzy vessel of fury.

"Hey! *Hey!*" No response. I yanked the headphones off his head, snagging one of his ears in the process. He started, his mouth flapping open like a mouth-breathing buffoon. "Do you mind?" I dangled the headphones in front of him like a carrot in front of a horse.

"Oh, hey." He grinned lazily, his idea of boyish charm, no doubt. "Hi, I—"

"It's late! What is your damage?"

"Oh, sorry." He sighed, relaxing the drumsticks to his side, almost hiding them. Probably hoping I wouldn't break them in half. "I just couldn't sleep again. I didn't know it was so loud, or late—"

"Well, knock it off, Ringo!"

"Ringo? I was thinking more like Meg White or somebody." He hit his symbols once for comedic effect. Not amusing.

I lashed out and snagged the drumsticks from his hands. "I don't know who Meg White is nor do I care. It's late and I have school tomorrow!"

He looked distraught as he stared at the drumsticks. "Um, you're not going to throw those into the bushes again, are you?"

"No! I'm confiscating them!"

"Wait, what?"

"I'm taking them until you learn how to respect your neighbors and their need for sleep! Duh! Just because you can't sleep doesn't give you the right to interfere with mine!"

"When can I get my sticks back?" His voice dropped into timidity, so low I barely heard him.

I growled, raising the sticks above my head, shaking them like Zeus's lightning bolts. I turned on my fluffy heels and stalked out of the garage. When he slapped a hand onto a drum, I swiveled and shot him a death glare.

"Oh, sorry."

I punched the automatic garage door opener. With a grind, the door closed as I ducked underneath it. "Wait," I heard him call out. "The lights are going out! I can't find my way—"

"Go to sleep!" With some satisfaction, I heard him banging around in the dark, crashing into things.

*Moron.*

\*\*\*\*

"Good morning." Usually I found Lance's

optimism infectious. Not today.

"*What*ever," I groused and sunk into my seat.

"Oh, Elizabeth. What's got your saddle pants burred this morning?"

"If you must know, everything's messed up. I have this idiot neighbor who won't let me get any sleep."

Lance cocked a sexually loaded eyebrow.

"No! Not like *that!*" The druggie kid in front of me—always persistent in his choice of T-shirts—turned halfway to watch me from the corner of his eye. "Hello! Do you mind? People trying to have a conversation here!" I spun my fingers for him to face forward. He obliged, scooting low in his chair. "Anyway…" I lowered my voice as I didn't want the entire classroom hearing my problems. "Two nights in a row and I haven't slept—"

"Of course." Lance patted my arm. "We know you need your beauty rest."

Even though his attempt at humor failed miserably, I had to agree with his assessment. "And then there's the whole prom queen thing."

"What about it?"

"That damn Charlotte Drayton. What if she wins? It would be horrible!"

Lance sighed. "Do you really think that might happen, Elizabeth?"

I shook my head, surprised it transformed into a nod.

"Well, how important is it for you to win?"

"*Very.*"

"Okay, here's what we're going to do—"

"'We'?"

"Yes, we. If you want to win, you need me on your

team."

"Why do I need you on my team? I mean, no offense or anything, but we don't exactly run in the same crowds or—"

"Exactly. We need to work on your image."

"What's wrong with my image?"

"Well…" He hesitated, drumming his fingers on our table. "For one thing, you come across as, um, exquisitely bitchy. That's a nice way of putting it."

The doper's shoulders bobbed up and down, giving away his stifled laughter. I rapped my pencil on the back of his seat until he stopped.

"See what I mean?" said Lance with a chuckle.

"Okay, fine. I'll take the 'exquisite' part, but 'bitchy'? You think people really see me as bitchy?"

"Oh, yeah. I mean, what I just told you? You took away the wrong word. You don't even get it."

"Get what?" I waved a hand over myself like a practiced game show hostess. "I can't help it if I'm the product of good breeding and refinement. This is what money and good genes get you."

"Exactly," he said, as if proven right. "Look, Elizabeth, people are not going to vote for you because they can't relate to you. I mean, look at you." His gaze steamrolled over my wardrobe.

"I like my saddle pants."

Lance chortled, swaying in his chair. "You look like you're ready to go horseback riding. You walk around, flaunting your wealth, all high and mighty, like you're above everyone else. No one will vote for you because, well, they resent you."

"You're not helping much here, Lance. I can't help that I'm wealthy."

"Okay, well, you need to get over that kind of attitude. Look at me. I, too, come from a wealthy family." His turn to display his hands over his clothing. Suspenders over a short-sleeved, purple paisley shirt with black slacks. A little too flashy for my tastes, yet undeniably stylish. "I like to wear nice clothes, sure. But I'm nice. I take time out to talk to everyone. You don't do that. You stick to your own 'type' and no one else matters."

"Oh, whatever, Lance! I can't help who I am. And frankly, I don't really feel the need to apologize either."

"'Whatever' back at you. You just proved my point. Listen to yourself."

I folded my arms, throwing my defenses up. "And what would you have me do? How would you go about making me more relatable?" If I wasn't relatable, then I didn't know who was. Yet, I'd taken all of Lance's abuse so far, and part of me was undeniably curious as to what he had to say. Morbidly curious, I supposed.

Lance rubbed his lip, and fiddled with his chin. "It's going to be tough. But I think that if we started with your wardrobe, maybe, just maybe, a personality change might follow. Or at least, a perceived personality change."

"What? You think I'm going to start shopping off the rack or something? No way! Forget it."

"Elizabeth, you don't have to change your entire wardrobe. Just tone it down a little bit. Dress like a teenage girl for once. You look like a snooty, rich collegiate girl."

"Yes."

He sighed loudly. "This is going to be hard."

"Okay. Let's just say for a minute I decide to go

along with your crazy plan. I would have the final say on clothing. You will not put me into anything slutty or less than refined—"

"Elizabeth—"

"I'm not finished. Secondly, I get the final say on my campaign posters."

"Yeah, about that—"

"What?"

"That's another major issue."

"What's wrong with my posters?"

"They show you sitting in front of a fireplace, stroking a cat. Relatable to no one."

I bit my lower lip and felt the pain. But Lance's accusations hurt worse. "Okay, I might—*might*—concede you that point." Which I hated to do, of course. But ever since Charlotte had disfigured my poster, I'd given it a lot of thought. Maybe it wasn't the type of image I needed to win the prom queen crown.

"What would you suggest for a poster?"

"Let me think on that. I'll get back to you."

"Lance? Why do you want to do this? I mean, I appreciate the offer and everything, but why?"

"Let's just say it's sorta an internship. Just like you and Donovan, I'd love to see a career in politics."

"I never knew that."

"I know you didn't. It's part of the problem. You really need to get to know more people outside of your immediate circle. Stop shunning them because of a lack of money or popularity or prestige or whatever! High school life shouldn't be a road paved by people you deem less than worthy. You're missing out on a lot. Tex knew that. Even Donovan understands that."

"Maybe."

"Definitely. Anyway, politics." His voice lowered and then raised his eyebrows. "You and I both know a gay senator in Kansas just ain't gonna fly. So that's why I'm interested in political strategy. Someone behind the scenes. Maybe a campaign manager in the future. I mean, that's where the real power and fun is anyway." He kicked back and crossed his ankles, extending them toward dope boy. "So, I'd like to take your cause on because, well, it'll be good practice, a real challenge. And maybe it'll be good for you in the long run. Time's running out and graduation is just around the corner."

"Huh." I never would have believed I'd be part of a project. Just as I took on my girls, forming them into the young women they deserved to be, here came Lance proposing to change me for the betterment of mankind. Or at least to win the valued title of prom queen. I didn't think I needed to change. Not really. But one thing Lance said—the "perceived change in personality"—stuck with me like pizza to Charlotte's hips. The people had spoken through Lance. Politics was all about the perception of the candidate in the public's eye. And I wanted to be prom queen. Whatever it took. "Okay, Lance, fine. Let's do this."

"Cool. But, Elizabeth, you have to listen to me, okay?"

"Fine."

"For real. If you want to win, you have to listen to me."

"Okay, already! I get it."

"Are you free Saturday afternoon?"

I nodded. Other than Elspeth's stupid doper party later that night, I had no plans.

"Good. Then we'll start—"

The door opened with a bang. Mr. Dawson strutted in, more purpose in his gait than his usual dawdling. Behind him, a tall shaggy haired figure attempted to keep up. When I recognized him, I knew God had decided to mock me this week. My jaw dropped in a very ill-mannered fashion.

"Class, take a chill pill," said Mr. Dawson, tamping down the air. "I'd like you to meet…" He consulted a sheet of paper in his hands. "Kevin Bartholomew."

"Oh my God," whispered Lance. "He's—"

"A total douche," I said quietly.

Lance stared at me like I had gone around the bend. "I was gonna go with dreamy."

The drug-addicted transfer student sat up straight in his chair, something about Kevin awakening him from his typical stupor.

"Kevin's going to be shadowing our science class for the rest of the quarter. He's a student, studying at K.U., wants to become a teacher." Mr. Dawson beamed like a proud father. "With a special emphasis on science. That's wicked cool, Kevin."

Kevin waved awkwardly and then wiped his hand on his pants. "Thank you, Mr. Dawson. Now, I want everyone to just go about their business as usual. Just pretend I'm not here. I'm here to observe and to help when I can." His eyes lit on me as I tried to sink farther into my chair. "Oh, hey, Elizabeth. Had no idea you were in this class." My chin nearly leveled with the lab table. "You think I could get my sticks back?"

Lance stared at me, mouth agape. As did the rest of the class.

\*\*\*\*

Donovan, prompt as always, majestically strolled through the dining room and sidled up next to his king of commerce.

"How are you, Mr. Blackmer?" He grasped his hand, a move I never tired of watching.

Daddy stood up, wincing as if his back pained him. Even Donovan seemed incapable of bringing a smile to his face today. "Donovan, I'd like to speak with you in my study." The severe look exchanged between them worried me.

"Of course, sir. We just need to make the visitation at six—"

"Ah, yes, the Durbin boy, is it?"

"Yes, sir. It's across town and—"

"This will only take a few moments."

He had already fled the dining room before Donovan could reply. Donovan hitched his shoulders up and followed him. I scuttled behind them. Daddy avoided eye contact with me as he slowly closed the door in my face. I tiptoed to the door and pressed my ear against it. All I heard was the hushed, steady murmur of Daddy's voice, occasionally interrupted by Donovan saying "Yes, sir", his enthusiasm gone. When their voices rose, signifying the end of their meeting, I raced back to the dining room.

"Did you have a nice men's chat?" I asked, attempting levity.

More flushed than usual, Donovan focused on the centerpiece fruit bowl on the dining room table. His Adam's apple bobbed up and down, straining as if it pained him to swallow. "We need to go, Elizabeth." He brushed by me. "We'll be late."

Daddy lingered in the dining room doorway's

shadow, a ghost of the larger-than-life man I remember. "Okay. Good night, Daddy."

He mumbled, "Good night," before making a hasty retreat to his study.

Once we reached Donovan's car, I asked, "What was that all about?"

Sliding behind the steering wheel, he shrugged. "Just business."

"Is everything all right? You look, I don't know, upset."

"No. Everything's fine. Just work stuff, that's all."

"Fine." I could tell he wanted to drop the subject, but something didn't quite add up. Maybe he was upset about the visitation. But it was a topic I fully intended to revisit later. And like an elephant (an elegant, thin, and beautiful elephant, natch), I never forgot.

The house sat square in the middle-class section of Shawnee Mission. Even its location screamed mundanity. Cars lined the street in front of the small, yellow house, and several people milling about on the front porch. In the yard was a wreath wired in at an angle, a calling card to let people know this was a domicile of infinite sadness. A single light bulb, dangling from a loose connection, flickered on and off, spreading long shadows across the porch. A swarm of moths flitted in front of it then flew away when the light sporadically died.

In a dark corner of the porch, Tim Matthews leaned against the railing, smoking a cigarette. I almost didn't recognize him without his telltale T-shirt. A natty button-down shirt was tucked into ill-fitting black slacks; an improvement, but not much of one. He stood when we passed him, a single nod exchanged between him and Donovan.

Donovan took a deep breath and rang the doorbell. Bright light poured over us when the door opened. A thin, balding man wearing round spectacles greeted us. If you could call it a greeting. He didn't say a word, but remained stony faced. The lower halves of his glasses' lenses were slightly fogged.

"Uh, hi, sir, I'm Donovan Goode." Donovan smiled more wanly than usual and extended his hand. "This is Elizabeth Blackmer. We're here to pay our respects."

The silent man shook Donovan's hand loosely and stepped aside. Emotionally stuck on autopilot, he trudged off into parts unknown. Obviously shell shocked out of his mind, I presumed him to be Mr. Durbin, Charles's father. I couldn't even imagine losing a loved one. The grief seemed unimaginable.

Quite a few people filled the house; an unexpected number, given how quiet they were. Low-set choral music piped in from a small stereo system in the living room. On the couch sat Tina Bottoms, holding the hand of a crying middle-aged woman. While Donovan pulled me toward them, I hoped Tina wouldn't cause a scene. Definitely the wrong place and time.

"Mrs. Durbin, I'm sorry for your loss," said Donovan, standing with his hands clasped reverentially in front of him.

The woman looked up, her mouth poised to speak, but lapsed back into a crying jag.

"I'm very sorry, Mrs. Durbin," repeated Donovan.

"Hello, Donovan," said Tina. "Elizabeth," she added icily.

"Hi, Tina," said Donovan.

"Tina," I said.

She whispered something to Mrs. Durbin, who fortified herself and asked, "Were you friends of my son?"

"No," Tina answered for us, scowling.

Donovan appeared at an unusual loss for words, so I took the reins. "I'm afraid we weren't very close with Charles, but we realize what a tragic loss this is for you." Mrs. Durbin's eyes closed as she sobbed quietly, brokenhearted.

Tina shot to her feet and grabbed my arm, dragging me after her. Once we were out of earshot of Mrs. Durbin, she said, "Way to go, Elizabeth! You leave a trail of agony wherever you go."

"That's kind of harsh, don't you think?"

"No."

I thought she sadistically enjoyed putting me on the defensive, her idea of payback.

"Come with me." Still grasping my arm, Tina jerked me out onto the front porch. "T-shirt" still hadn't left his post, puffing away, nosy radar on red alert. I inclined my head toward him and whispered, "Tina, let's go to the other side."

"Fine." She followed me to the far end of the porch, as did "T-Shirt's" watchful gaze.

"What have you found out, Elizabeth?" Didn't take long for her to adopt her defensive body language. Arms folded, foot tapping, message received. No patience.

"Nothing yet. Not really. I know Charles was trying to get Donnie Heidenreich to join your drug-free club. I talked to him. He didn't know anything either. But he agreed Charles was clean."

"I already told you that."

"I know. But I'm still looking into it. Really! I want to clear Charles's name as much as you do—find out who did this to him and why."

Tina rolled her eyes like a seasoned pro. Something I hadn't even taught her. Impressive. "Why are you here, Elizabeth? You told me you didn't even know Charles."

"I'm here to support Donovan, I guess. And maybe see what else I can find out." Telling Tina about my mysterious locker note seemed like a bad idea, but it might show her I was serious about my investigation. "There's something else, Tina—"

"I'm waiting."

"Someone put a note in my locker. It said, *Let it go. Before someone else gets hurt.*"

Tina fell back against the railing as if the wind had left her. "Wow. Who was it from?"

"If I knew that, this would be over!"

She massaged her cheeks, deep in thought. "Huh. So, is that enough to take to the cops? I mean, isn't it pretty much evidence Charles was innocent of drug use?"

"Tina, we don't know who the letter's from. And it really doesn't say anything."

"T-shirt" wandered closer to us, his eager ear primed to eavesdrop. "Really? Do you mind? We're trying to have a personal conversation here!"

He hopped, mumbled, "Sorry, sorry, my bad", and sulked back to his corner of depravity. What was his problem, anyway?

"Tina," I said, lowering my voice, "what do you know about him?"

"Who, Tim? Not much. He's a transfer student. Got expelled for something. I think he smokes weed. Other than that, not much. Why?"

"It just seems like he's everywhere, always listening. Something about him rubs me the wrong way."

"You think he's Clearwell's dealer?"

"Not sure. When did the heavy drug usage start at school?"

"I guess, maybe, about three months ago."

"And how long has Tim been here?"

"Huh," was all she said, but I understood her answer completely.

"Yeah." I stole another glance across the porch. The red ember of Tim's cigarette glowed with every inhalation, a one-eyed demon. A chill ran down my back. "Let's go back inside." Walking through the front door, I called back, "Hope you got a good earful!"

"Right. Whatever," he said, his voice wavering slightly.

Donovan, busily grab handing every person within sight, rushed to my side. "Ladies." Tina shook her head and made her way back toward Mrs. Durbin.

"Heeey." The reedy voice startled me. I whirled, staring down into the beady eyes of Donnie Heidenreich. Earlier, Elspeth had "flashed" me about our encounter with him. Slack-jawed and grinning, he turned his attention toward Donovan. "Oh, is this your boyfriend?"

"Hello, Donnie." He stared at Donovan's proffered hand before understanding what the gesture meant.

"Oh, yeah, right." Finally, he shook Donovan's hand. Then he released it and fist-bumped Donovan.

"So, what's going on?" He said it as casually as running into someone at the mall.

"Well, you know," Donovan said, "we're here paying our respects."

"Right, right." I practically saw the slow-burn realization that we were at a visitation catch-up to Donnie's fried brain. Every place treated as a potential party to Donnie, no matter the circumstance. "I hear ya." He swept his long hair behind one ear to reinforce that he was, indeed, "hearing."

I felt Donovan tense up beside me. "Well, we should really make our rounds." Donovan seized my arm, quickly steering me away.

"Let go, Donovan." I was really getting sick and tired of being dragged around.

Donovan released his grip. "Sorry, Elizabeth. It's just, we should be careful about the company we keep." His demeanor immediately brightened, his optimism clearing his head.

"You're right." But it almost seemed like Donnie Heidenreich frightened Donovan. Was Donnie dangerous, as preposterous as that sounded? Seemed like he was only a threat to himself.

"Would you like a drink, Elizabeth? I think I spied a punch bowl in the kitchen."

"That would be nice." While Donovan left, I searched the crowd, looking for a friendly face. I didn't know any of these people, and the few I thought I recognized I'd never spoken to. I placed my back against the wall, trying to blend in with the woodwork, watching the somber proceedings.

From around the corner, a large figure loomed, and then stopped next to me. "Elizabeth Blackmer," he said in a deep voice, carved even deeper from nicotine abuse. "Slumming it?"

I looked up at Marc Dugan, flying a highly inappropriate flannel shirt. At least "T-shirt" had tried to rise to the occasion. I guessed it was a minor miracle he had managed to button his shirt. "Dugan," I replied.

We weren't friends, never would be. He'd been in several classes of mine. All six foot four inches of him. Trying to ignore giant lumberjacks in Clearwell's halls was a daunting task. "Just paying my respects."

"Didn't think you even knew Charles." When he smiled, the odor of smoke wafted off his breath. *Ewww.*

I fanned my hand in front of my face and backed up a step. "I can still pay my respects. It's a free country."

"Whatever."

"Was Charles a friend of yours?"

He shook his head soberly. "Yeah, I knew Charles from way back." He placed his hand on the wall above my head and leaned closer. "Isn't this sorta out of your wheelhouse?"

"Oh, what does that even mean, Dugan? Wheelhouse? I told you, I'm paying my respects. I suggest you go do the same instead of hassling well-meaning mourners." He leaned against the wall, laughing, and I stomped off. *Jackass.*

As I searched for Donovan—who was gone way too long—I passed a small dining room, a mere fraction of our dining space at home. Set back on a buffet, two half-melted candles flickered and shimmered, spotlighting a photograph of Charles Durbin. The candlelight touched at Charles's sweet smile, before retreating and veiling him in shadows. A death shroud.

130

In front of the small shrine lay several other photos and a grade-school yearbook.

I picked up the Rosemore Elementary School yearbook and thumbed through it. I found Charles Durbin in the eighth grade, his hair a bit longer than the more current photo, but the innocent smile remained the same. Next to him stood Marc Dugan, who, even in the eighth grade, looked like a behemoth. His shoulders were squared like a building compared to his scrawny peers. Flipping the page, I saw Donnie Heidenreich. Rosemore School contributed more than their fair share of stoners to the community.

The next face I recognized. All too well. I dropped the book as if the candles' flames leapt out and licked me. With a shaking hand, I picked the book up to make sure my eyes weren't playing tricks on me under the dim light.

Donovan Goode, eighth grade, Rosemore Junior High School. Donovan had told me he didn't know Charles, barely knew who he was. Why would he lie to me? Okay, I reassured myself, their eighth grade was large, so maybe Donovan didn't know him. Possibly.

I turned toward the back of the book, thumbing through the autographs.

*Charles, stay true to yourself, Donovan.*

"There you are," said Donovan. I yelped and dropped the book again.

Donovan, holding two plastic cups of red punch, stared at the book on the floor, speechless. I stretched up and whispered, "You lied to me. You said you didn't know Charles!"

Donovan set the cups on the edge of the buffet. "I can explain, Elizabeth. Just not here. I don't want to cause a scene."

"Then we're leaving—now." Without waiting for him, I strode through the house and out the front door. Behind me, I heard Donovan delivering embarrassed goodbyes. I let myself into the car and thought fleetingly about locking him out since he always asked me to carry his keys in my purse. Once Donovan stepped off the porch, he broke into a sprint toward me. "T-shirt" leaned over the railing, watching the commotion. If it weren't uncouth, I would've flipped him the finger.

Donovan crawled in, frantic and out of breath. "Elizabeth, I didn't lie to you. Not really."

"You said you didn't know Charles Durbin. A lie." I crossed my arms and harrumphed. Maybe I had actually learned a thing or two about defensive body language from Tina.

"Well, it's sorta true. Look, I did know him when we were in junior high school. But once we moved on to Clearwell, I didn't know him. Not at all. We went our separate ways. I think Charles became involved with drugs and I didn't want to follow him down that path. I'm here because of who Charles was in junior high. Not for who he became. He was like a stranger to me. I really, really didn't know him any longer."

Hadn't I, more or less, done the same thing with Tina Bottoms? "I still don't like you not telling me the truth, Donovan. I guess what you're saying makes sense, but just don't ever lie to me again." I caught him with my piercing stare, and held him there. "You hear me? That's not who we are."

Donovan dropped his chin to his chest, properly humbled. "I understand. And I'm sorry." He leaned in

132

for a reconciliatory hug.

I lifted a shoulder, shunning him. "Give it some time." Too cold? Maybe. Probably not. Either way, Donovan needed to know what he did was not cool. And now he had me wondering if he had lied regarding his meeting with Daddy. Or withheld the truth, which was tantamount to a big, fat lie.

As we drove home in silence, I stole a few sideways glimpses at him, wondering if he truly was the man I thought him to be.

## Chapter Seven

*Elizabeth*

"So, how do you know Kevin Bartholomew again?" Lance flipped through a pile of skinny jeans on the sales rack, looking for a pair in my size. Usually a girl never tells a boy her clothing size. But I had nothing to be ashamed of.

"He's my neighbor. And he's a total loser."

"Here. Try these on." He tossed a faded pair of jeans at me.

I held them up, unable to visualize my wearing such an atrocity. I mean, could you just imagine? "I can't believe you're making me wear skinny jeans. They're so tacky."

"Hey, sex sells, Elizabeth." He enjoyed this way too much. "It makes guys desire you and girls relate to you."

"Gah! Skinny jeans. What next? Halter tops?" I rolled the jeans up, hoping to hide them without Lance noticing.

"You read my mind. Kidding." Lance raced toward the back wall, a man on a mission, where an array of plaid miniskirts hung. "So, why is Kevin a loser? And what's the deal with your taking his sticks? Um, is that code for something else?"

I gave the store a quick once-over for a sighting of

anyone I might know. I needn't have bothered. No one I knew would be caught dead in this retail store. "He's just a jerk. He's the guy I told you about who's kept me up two nights in a row by playing basketball and beating on his drums."

"And you took his drumsticks?"

"You're darn right I did! He has no consideration for other people."

Lance furrowed his brow in mock consternation. "Hmmm. Sounds like someone else I know."

"What's that supposed to mean?"

"Oh, whatever. Remember, we're creating a newer, softer Elizabeth." He threw a red and black checked miniskirt at me. "Size small."

"No way. I am not wearing something this short. I thought we were making me softer, not sluttier."

Lance smacked a fist into his palm, already practicing political moves. "We're trying to get you votes. Trust me. Nobody's gonna vote for you in business clothing."

"I don't wear business clothing," I mumbled.

"Anyway, I think Kevin seems like a pretty good guy. He's not gay, is he?" Lance smiled, no doubt pondering the possibilities.

"I don't know. And I don't care. I just know he sucks!" I tried slipping the miniskirt back on a rack. With lightning speed, Lance grabbed it on the rebound and thrust it back toward me. "And now, he's gonna make my life miserable in that stupid environmental science class."

"That's right. He exists only to make your life horrible. Get a clue, Elizabeth." He shook his head while making his way toward a spinner rack of ghastly blouses. I hustled after him, more to hear him out rather than to see what next wardrobe monstrosity lay in waiting. "That's your problem. This is not just your world. You are sharing it with others, you know."

"I know that! I have friends."

"Yeah, you and your tunnel vision brigade of look-alike plastic dolls. You need to step out of your tunnel into the sunlight." He held his chin in his hand while inspecting the gaudy-colored shirts. He pulled out an orange and white striped T-shirt. "Here. You're gonna look awesome in this shirt and your jeans. People will see a whole new you." He grinned proudly at his shopping prowess.

"Lance, this shirt won't even cover my belly button!" I hung the shirt up quickly for fear its tawdriness might rub off on me.

"Oh, I see. You want Charlotte Drayton to become prom queen?" He pulled out his cell phone. "I'll just call her and congratulate her." He shrugged. "She's already got it in the bag."

I yanked the striped eyesore off the rack. "Oh, fine."

Lance slipped his phone back into his pocket. He framed his hands in a square, centering on my face, one eye closed. "Okay, what to do with your hair?"

"You're not touching my hair."

"Elizabeth, your hair is an immovable force of nature. It's straight, rigid, every hair perfectly in place."

"Exactly."

"It makes you look hard. We need to get you some wave."

"Lance."

"Come on, Elizabeth, be the hair." He started

chanting, shaking his fists with every beat. "Be the hair…be the hair…"

"Stop it, Lance. People are staring at us."

"Live a little, Elizabeth. Have some fun. Come on! Be the hair. I know you can do it."

I rolled my eyes, resisting the urge to give in. But I knew when I was on the losing end of a battle. It happened. Rarely. "Whatever." I sighed and plopped my pile of clothing onto a sales display. I mimicked Lance's fist rattling but kept my voice low. "I'm gonna be the hair. Be the hair…be the hair…"

To my great relief, a glum clerk asked us to leave the store. Who would've ever thought my life would be saved by a retail clerk?

Undeterred, Lance said, "Ah, we'll go back later and get your clothes when it's someone else's shift."

I sat on the mall bench, knees tightly together. Lance plunked down next to me and slung an arm over the backrest. "Elizabeth, what were you doing at the gas station the other day?"

"Oh my God! You say there's more out there in the world for me, so I try and expand my horizons, yet that's all people want to talk about! I can't go to the bathroom without someone asking me about it. If you must know, I went over there to talk to someone about an assignment. Happy?"

"Who'd you talk to?"

"Oh, that dumb druggie kid—what's his name— Tim Matthews. I needed to get an environmental science project from him."

"Huh."

"Huh? Why 'huh'?"

Lance kicked his legs out into the aisle, his red

sneakers wiggling to an unheard song. "I don't know. Just funny, I guess. I didn't think you liked that kid. You could've asked me about the assignment. It's just, I don't know, funny, I guess."

I quickly changed the topic. "Okay, what are we going to do about my new posters?"

"Well, I want to take some pictures of you. After you get your new do, of course."

I groaned.

"And I want to put you in some cool clothes and less icy settings."

"Less icy? Like what? I'm not going to go around kissing babies."

"Doubt the unsuspecting parents would like that either. I just want people to see you can have fun. I wish I had my camera in the store back there. That's the kind of Elizabeth I want people to see, to know." He stood up, reaching a hand toward me. "Okay, let's get you to the hair salon, pronto!"

I checked the time on my phone. "Sorry, but I need to get home."

"What? Big date with Donovan?" He batted his eyelashes, making some sorta stupid "woo woo" sound.

"Yeah, something like that."

****

Donovan, of course, wanted to see me that night. His natural disappointment kicked in when I told him I had to study. He volunteered to study with me, but I quickly nixed the idea. I told him I had to go to the library as I needed some quiet time. He gave me a dumbfounded look because who went to a library any more these days? And, truth be told, I was still slightly miffed at him for lying to me. Not majorly miffed, but miffed enough to enjoy making him squirm. It was always good for a boy to be chastened, kept him in line. Besides, no way could I tell him the truth. He either wouldn't believe me, wouldn't let me go, or insist he go with me.

Sure, I was lying to him. Hypocritical? Possibly, but I didn't think so. Elspeth was going to the party, after all, not me.

Mother had vanished somewhere. Daddy, as usual, was locked away in his study. I scowled at the black wig and tight-fitting leather clothes before squeezing into them, almost as if I wanted the clothing to understand I was doing this under duress. It made me feel better, anyway. Sticking my tongue out at my Elspeth mirrored image one final time, I quickly bounded down the stairway, yelling my farewell back toward Daddy's study.

It was just after 9:00 p.m., plenty of time for Marc Dugan's party to be getting its rave on. Night had fallen fast, as it did in the early parts of spring, the air still and moist. The leather pants and jacket clung to me in the humid night. Every time I scratched, the leather whispered back. Maybe Elspeth's clothes were alive.

Marc Dugan lived in Merriam, Kansas, a place I rarely visited. The houses were older, not well kept, and oppressively close together. I pulled into his street and parked the car at the end of the block. It wouldn't do for anyone to spot my car, particularly with the give-away license plate, *Pretty Princess.*

I twirled Elspeth's sunglasses around by the stem. It was incredibly tacky in a post-ironic hipster manner to wear sunglasses at night, but it probably wouldn't be out of place at a druggie party. And my identity had to be preserved at all costs. Elspeth assured me she'd do that.

I grabbed my pepper spray and Taser (something Daddy insisted on my having after all the troubles at Clearwell the past two years), and stuffed them into the jacket pockets along with my keys.

Sitting back in the car seat, I closed my eyes. "Okay, Elspeth. You're on. Don't do anything stupid."

****

*Elspeth*

"When have I ever done anything stupid?"

I yawned, whipped my head back and forth to shake away the sleepies, and exited the car.

The party practically led me there. Loud music cranked out from Dugan's house, windows in neighbors' homes rattling from the thumping bass. A car on blocks sat in the front yard. Several guys holding cups were looking underneath the hood, the mysteries of mechanics observed. Laughter emanated from within the house, punctuated by boisterous screams. One of the front windows took an early hit, an empty beer bottle laying underneath it amongst broken glass shards.

A thin figure in a white T-shirt slipped out of the shadows when I stepped onto the porch. Tim Matthews, constant lurker and underachiever extraordinaire, from Elizabeth's environmental science class. The kid with the uncanny knack of showing up everywhere.

I whipped on my sunglasses and nodded in his direction like a TV show cop.

"Hey," he said, pulling on his cigarette. Tempted to bum one from him, I knew Elizabeth would have a fit. Besides, I quit about thirty years ago. Death will do that to you. I swept by him and entered the house. More like the Apocalypse.

Incredibly raucous music thundered, partygoers yelling to be heard over it. The floor throbbed as if ready to split asunder. A couple was making out on the sofa. Several other people sat next to them, apparently oblivious of the groping acrobatics. The air thickened with cigarette smoke, possibly reefer too. Several guys stopped to stare at me, their girlfriends glowering at them.

People flooded out of a doorway like clowns scattering from a circus trick car. Obviously from the heart of the party. Experience had taught me that a lot of partying was centralized in the kitchen. Closest access to munchies, I supposed. I pushed my way past several wasted guys to gain access.

"You want a beer?" Donnie Heidenreich stood behind the keg, haphazardly pumping it, his hands jerking all over the place.

"No thanks." Mercifully, the kitchen was quieter. "I'm thinking of something a little stronger."

Donnie stared down at the keg, almost as if forgetting his place. "You mean booze?"

I shook my head. "Keep going."

"Right, right." He swiped back his hair and laughed, everything a laugh riot in Donnie-World. "I get ya."

"Well? Anyone carrying around here?" Several people sat perched on the kitchen countertops. Their conversations stopped so they could listen in on ours.

"Probably. Just ask around."

A guy behind me shifted and hopped off the counter. I turned, staring up into his bloodshot eyes. "Can I help you? Or maybe I should ask, can you help me?"

He grinned, said nothing, and left the room.

"Hey, who are you, anyway?" asked Donnie. Still wielding the hand pump, beer dribbled over his hand and onto the floor.

"I'm new. Just lookin' to party."

"You don't go to Clearwell, do you? I think I'd remember someone like you. I'm Donnie, by the way."

"Put your tongue back in your mouth." I patted his arm. "No, I, ah, go to Limbo High."

"Wait, what?"

"Never mind. Donnie, who's selling around here?"

He hitched his shoulders up. "Don't know, dude. But just ask around. If you can't find reefer here, then it ain't to be found." He bellowed out high-pitched laughter again, on a real roll tonight. "Sure I can't hook you up with some brew?"

"Yeah, I'm sure. Got any caffeine?"

Apparently, the question stumped Donnie as his face contorted with confusion. Something finally popped as his eyes lit up. "Oh! Yeah, there're some bottles of pop over there." He jutted his chin toward the kitchen table. Several open, large bottles sat amidst a clutter of potato chips crumpled across a table. I poured diet soda into a plastic cup. Caffeine was the only drug I allowed myself these days, and I hadn't yet experienced it on this trip. Extremely flat, but kick-ass, just like me. Well, my old body, at least. Elizabeth was packing more chest-side. Lucky girl was blessed with everything. Whatever.

"You want some fries with that shake?" The hoary pick up line and oozing smarm belonged to Kip Aldrich, Donovan's cretin of a buddy. What the hell was he doing here? Obviously downplaying his usual preppie attire, he opted for a skin-tight black T-shirt and jeans. He brushed his hand through his sandy hair as if gifting me with a visual treat.

"I can't believe anyone still uses a stupid line like that." I set my cup down on the table behind me, prepared for a verbal battle. I hated guys like Kip. If I didn't have a mission to fulfill, I'd take him down a few notches. *Still might, anyway.* "Why don't you save it for your girlfriend?"

He leaned in closer, uncomfortably so. "What makes you think I have a girlfriend?"

"Because stupid girls always go for stupid guys like you."

His false smile slithered away. He wore a shocked look, like I just kicked him in the junk. Maybe a self-fulfilling prophecy. "You've got a real smart mouth on you, you know that?"

"I do." I smiled, happy with his critique. "And you have a real dumb one."

He jabbed a finger into my face, definitely within biting distance. "Nobody talks to Kip Aldrich like that!"

"Oh, really? Well, I just did. What're you gonna do about it? And really, talking about yourself in the third person? What's up with that?"

His serpentine smile returned as he dropped his finger. "I'm just playin', I'm just playin' with ya, that's all. Look, we got off to a bad start." He draped an arm around my shoulders. "I'm Kip, and you are?"

"I didn't say." I grabbed his wrist and yanked his arm away. One step away from getting Tasered. "And I'm not gonna say."

"Oooh, feisty." He held his hands up like claws. "I like that."

"Yeah, well, don't get too attached to me." Probably a long shot, but I plowed ahead, anyway. "You know where I can score?"

He squinted at me. Did I note recognition behind those arrogant eyes? "No, I don't. Never touch the stuff." He shook his head proudly as if this made him superhuman. It was a long climb up from Mount Douchedom.

"Then what are you doing here? Everyone knows this is the biggest druggie party around."

He waved his plastic cup, beer sloshing up the sides. "I like to party. Booze is my deal. It's more socially acceptable. I go where the party goes."

"Hooray for you. Your parents must be proud."

"Look, don't jack with drugs. Let me buy you a beer." He reached around me and grabbed my cup.

I snatched it back. "Wow, how gallant of you. No way." Kip laughed, trying to downplay how I had just punked him. I stepped around him and past Donnie, still absentmindedly holding the pump. Maybe "no-mindedly"?

The breezeway next to the kitchen opened out into the backyard. Clouds of smoke formed around twenty or so partiers. The plumes drifted up in front of several bug-zapping lamps. Every time another bug crackled to its death, a victorious cheer shot out. I slid open the door and stepped outside. The chatter stopped. Tough crowd. I walked by them, inspecting them like they were in a jail line up.

A girl's voice called out, "Take a picture!" *Awesome.* My new BFF from the gas station. One of her entourage issued a raucous catcall, hoping to provoke an encounter to make their party much more memorable.

"I would, but you might break my camera."

She sputtered, tossed her cup to the ground as her friends roared merrily.

She stepped underneath a lamp's orange glow. "Bitch! When I'm done with you, you won't think you're so hot!" She clenched a fist in front of her face.

"Why? You gonna give me a makeover to look like you?"

More hysterical laughter arose from her companions. She dropped down like a runner at a starting gate before her friends held her back. Strolling away, I waved back at her. "Ta for now."

I walked over to some weathered patio furniture, set my cup on the glass-topped table, and burrowed into a lounge chair. The door slid open and three figures stepped out, hurrying toward me. Marc Dugan, party maestro, led the crew. Behind him, the guy who'd earlier scuttled out of the kitchen. Tim Matthews brought up the rear. They hovered over me, three intimidating shadows.

"Hey," said Marc. He rubbed his elbow as if trying to work out a knot. The other two flanked him in silence.

"Hey."

Dugan's flannelled shoulders heaved up and slumped. "Who are you?"

"I'm Elspeth. New to the area, looking to party. Who are you?"

He shoved his hands into his pockets, rocking back and forth on the balls of his feet. "I'm Marc. This is my house. My party. I don't know you."

"I already said I'm Elspeth." I held my hand out. "Now you know me."

"How'd you hear about my party?"

I inclined my head toward the house. "Oh, I don't know…people talk. It sounded like fun. And maybe the right place for what I'm looking for."

"And what would that be?"

"I said I'm looking to party. I'd like to buy some stuff."

He sat down at the end of a lounge chair. "And as I said, I don't know you. I mean, you come into my party and no one knows who the hell you are." He picked up my cup and examined it. "You drink my stuff…What the hell are you drinking, anyway?" He handed the cup to Tim Matthews, who looked inside, obviously uncertain of what he should do with it.

"Diet soda. It's flat."

"Well, that's just too bad." He snapped his fingers at Tim, who handed the cup to Dugan and he passed it back to me. "Anyway, I think it's weird you just show up here, askin' who's holdin'. Do I look like a drug dealer to you?"

"Kind of. You're rockin' the flannel like a dealer."

"Look, even if I was a dealer—and I'm not— there's no way, no *way* I'd sell you anything. I don't know you!" He stood, again digging his hands into his pockets. "Whatever. Stay. Get wasted if you want to." His two cronies laughed. "But if I were you, I'd be careful about what you say and who you say it to. Some people might not be as friendly as I am." He walked away, stopped, and turned. His sidekicks stumbled into him like something out of a silent comedy. "Are you sure we haven't met?"

"Don't think so."

"There's just something about you that seems familiar. Huh. Weird. Anyway…" One after the other, the three of them chugged back inside, Matthews the caboose of their little train.

While not confessing, nor denying being a drug dealer, Dugan certainly presented his argument in a curious manner. And his two pals followed him around like he was their leader, the supplier of their kicks. Marc Dugan merited further investigation. But since all eyes were on me now, it'd have to wait. But, what the hell, one more sweep through the house wouldn't hurt.

I slammed the rest of my drink, leaving the cup on the table. Another dead soldier, we used to call finished drinks. 'Course, back in my wild-child days, the drinks were a bit stronger. And much less flat.

Couldn't resist waving at my gal pal before reentering the house.

When I saw who was in the kitchen, I quickly dove out of there. *Kevin Bartholomew. Is everyone at this damn party? If Arville Hastings shows up, I'll know I'm in hell. Bypass limbo, go directly to jail!*

Even with his back turned, Kevin appeared uncomfortable. He rubbed his neck, staring at Donnie, who had grown attached to the keg. I had to admit the thought of macking with Kevin again crossed my mind, a little bit of my party girl past growling to be uncaged. But it'd be a huge mistake. At least, now. Probably not cool if he saw me here, especially since he was one of the very few who questioned if Elizabeth and I were one and the same. Time to leave.

I crossed in front of an open door. Voices and

muffled laughter floated up, disembodied sounds in an empty stairwell. Okay, one more room to check out, then I'd leave. Just five more minutes, as I used to tell my mom when she tried to wake me up for school.

My legs grew heavy on the first few steps, leaden weights that didn't want to cooperate.

*What the hell? Not a good time for Elizabeth's feet to go to sleep.*

I leaned against the wall, sliding my shoulder to guide me. Even though my feet still trudged downward, I couldn't feel them any longer. Except for a thousand tiny pinpricks, ticklish, rather than painful. Now my legs appeared miles below me, my feet small in the distance. I grew into a giant, my head in the clouds. A fireball of nausea flared up, threatening to explode in my stomach.

Fireflies from nowhere danced in front of me, small lights blinking in and out. Sweat built underneath my wig and crawled down my face. My scalp itched, burned, caterpillars wriggling on my head.

*Focus, Elspeth, focus!*

Somehow, I made it to the bottom of the steps. A clock on the basement wall spun in a circle, multiplying into three replicas. I toed at the carpet, inch by inch, seeking solid footing. But the floor heaved like a boat's deck, threatening to toss me into the ocean. My ankles buckled. I thrust a hand toward the wall to break my fall. From a distance (possibly miles away, although that didn't seem possible), several human blurs moved, leaving pink and red trails in their wake. The room swirled into a miasma of lights, colors, and shadows, bending in on one another. Faces melted away, just bags of featureless skin. Voices slowed to subterranean groans. Distorted laughter buzzed by me—through me—from all directions. I tried to dredge up a plea for help, not sure if I made a sound. My vocal cords went on strike.

Liquid figures swam by me, washing up the tidal wave of stairs. One person? Two? Twenty, maybe. The basement revolved, a tilt-o-whirl of duplicate rooms. A strobe light flashed on and off inside my head. I tripped, and fell, a long journey down. I tried to break my fall but my hands caved under me, useless, as I rolled onto my shoulder. Flopping my dead fish of a hand around, it landed on something. Closing one eye, I made out the framework of a sofa. With a last surge, I hauled myself onto the sofa. Thought I could lean forward, put my head in my lap, and stop the world from spinning. My head demanded a different scenario. I fell back into the soft, inviting cushions.

Loud music. Thumping. Brain frying. I strained to filter it out, but my mind had too many leaks.

Even then, I heard the smallest of voices. A buzzing gnat. Quiet, but persistent.

*"Elspeth, get up! Get up now!"*

*Elizabeth.*

Wait. She couldn't be here.

*Can she? I'm here. I thought I heard myself laugh but it didn't sound like me. Not one bit.*

*"Elspeth, for God's sake, get up! Now! We're in danger!"*

Elizabeth again. Okay. Rocking around in my head. *My* head. Head's exploding.

Needles of sharp agony gave way to feathers of fuzziness. *Nice.* But...*unsafe.*

A vague impression of a person floated over me,

drifting closer. A smear of a hand reached toward my face.

Then I joined Elizabeth in oblivion. Black as death.

And I knew the colors of death.

****

*"Elspeth! Wake the hell up!"*

A sharp sting. Pain traveled from my cheek to spike my brain. *Clear pain.* Vivid, glorious pain!

I sat up, still nauseous, but my sight restored to a singular vision. "What?"

*"Wake up!"* Elizabeth stood over me, hand outstretched to deliver another slap.

Elizabeth's bedroom—Dream Space. I latched onto Elizabeth's wrist before her blow landed. "I'm awake!"

*"No, you're not! You're—we're—still back at the party! We're in trouble!"*

A few seconds and I blinked myself into awareness. "Damn it! One of those little bastards dosed me!"

*"Oh my God! I'm not a druggie!"* Near tears, Elizabeth pulled out full panic mode. *"You've got to wake up for real!"*

"Okay, let me think." I rubbed my temples, attempting to block out Elizabeth's hysteria. She was right. We were in danger. Right now, her body was unoccupied. Both of us were vulnerable. "I've got to go back." I didn't relish the idea. It meant I'd be back in a drug-induced stupor. Behavior I had sworn off a long time ago. And I had no idea how long I'd been passed out or where I might end up. But I needed to get Elizabeth—us—to safety.

*"Go!"*

I lay back on the bed and closed my eyes. The past

several hours rushed through my mind like a runaway train, images and faces speeding by as I clawed my way up from the void.

****

"Shit! What the hell?" Lights pricked my eyes, like a cop shoving a flashlight in my face. A low, mechanical rumbling noise reverberated. To my right, trees flew by, branches bending in the wind.

"Are you okay?" Kevin Bartholomew sat perched on the edge of a car seat, clinging onto the steering wheel, stealing panicked glances at me.

"What…where are we?" My head throbbed, my mouth tasted of cotton, and my throat sandpaper dry. Yet nausea and triple-vision had passed. My quick trip to Dream Space must've wiped the drugs out of my system somehow. But things still didn't add up. I reached across and yanked the wheel. "Pull over! Now!"

"Jesus!" The car bumped over a curb, Kevin wigging out behind the wheel. He slammed the gear into park and stared at me, panting like a dog. "I'm trying to save your life here!"

"Tell me what happened." I blinked, wiping away the smog from my brain's skyline.

"First of all, are you all right?"

"Yeah, I think so."

"I'm taking you to the emergency room. You were passed out. I couldn't wake you! I was scared crapless!"

I had to smile. I couldn't remember how long it'd been since someone worried about me. "I'm okay. No need for the hospital. But, I need to know what happened."

A hand dashed through his hair, his gaze glued to

the windshield. He seemed afraid to look at me, fearful I'd crumble back into the comatose world. "I'm not sure. People were running upstairs, laughing. I don't know, it was hard to hear in there. I asked someone what was going on. They said someone had passed out in the basement. There were a lot of drugs and crap going on at that damn party." He looked at me, waiting for an answer of some sort.

I waggled my hand to brush the moss off him.

"Well, I went down there…found you on the sofa. I couldn't wake you. I yelled for someone to call an ambulance. Then, the host of the party—whatever the hell his name is—and some other guy told me to cool it. Said they didn't want trouble. It probably wasn't the smartest thing to do, but I was outnumbered and I knew you needed help…I carried you out to my car." His words tumbled out into one endless, hurried sentence. "Are you sure you're okay?"

"Right as rain. Question is, are you okay?" He answered me with a silent, open-mouthed gawp. With a smile, I gently pressed his drooping chin up. Poor guy, he'd been through a lot. "First of all, thanks. Second, who was down there with me?"

"What? Why is that important? Maybe we should still get you checked out—"

"I told you I'm fine. Who was down there with me?"

"I don't know. Nobody, I think."

"Hmmm. You sure?"

"Yes…no! I don't know! It's not like I was taking notes about who was partying in the basement! Look, what did you take? You know you really shouldn't do drugs."

"Yeah, yeah, I know. I don't do drugs. One of those little bitches dosed me with something."

"What? Wow…really?" He let himself off the hook, relaxed, and shook his head. "For real?"

"Yeah. The only thing I had was friggin' diet soda. Flat soda! Whatever it was they gave me dissolved fast in liquid." My shoulders hitched up with a leather snap. "Guess I'm lucky things didn't get worse, it seems to be wearing off already."

"Well, if you won't let me take you to the ER, do you at least want to—"

"I'm okay. Just let it go."

I loved the calm silence before he asked, "Why were you at the party? If you don't do drugs? Looked to me like that was pretty much the reason for the party."

"Okay, Kevin, why were you there?"

He sputtered like a dolphin attempting to speak. "I had no idea the party was going to be like that. I just, well, some of the students were talking about it and said I should go. I thought it might be a way to connect with them. Okay, a few beers maybe. A lot has changed since I went to high school."

"Really, Kevin? Really? Where'd you go to high school? Beverly Hills 90210?"

"Cute." He flailed his hands about, trying to steer the conversation back toward me. "Okay, I told you why I was there. Now, you tell me your reason."

What could I tell him? Sure, he apparently saved me, but did I really trust him? Believe him? All I knew about him was that he couldn't sleep, was a science geek, and was a fairly good kisser. Well, fairly adequate kisser. Kinda weird he attended the party, though, even taking into consideration his excuse. And who would know better about manufacturing designer drugs than a science geek?

Before I could answer him with a typical Elspethian "non-answer," he reached into the back seat. "Oh. Um, there's something else I think you should know." He tossed something into my lap. My faux-hawk wig looked like a dead black cat. Crap!

"Look, Elizabeth or Elspeth, whatever! I don't know what you're doing. I can't figure out if you're playing games or really messed up, but—"

"Where'd you get this?" My heart skipped and jump roped up into my throat. And where were my damn sunglasses?

"It was sitting next to you on the sofa. Anyway, if you went there in your Elspeth disguise, I think everyone knows about your, um, double identity now."

*Double-down on crap!* "Crap, crap…crappity-crap—"

"People were all over the basement, looking at you before I got to you. I'm just taking a guess here, but without your wig—and, um, it looks like someone wiped off some of your dark makeup—you're obviously Elizabeth. Or, Elspeth, if that's who you truly are."

In sixty seconds flat, the worst night ever raced into being the End of the World. This news was not going to make Elizabeth happy. "Crap."

"Crap? All you can say is *crap?*"

"Shit?"

"Really? Your secret, whatever has just been exposed, and that's all you have to say? How about some explanations, Elizabeth, Elspeth, whoever?"

"While I do appreciate your helping me, I really

don't owe you any explanations, Kevin. I'm not exactly a helpless little flower. But since you're an above-mediocre kisser—"

"Above-mediocre?" His indignation deflated like a flat tire. Fragile male ego.

"Stay on track, Kevin." I patted his hand in my most condescending manner. "I, um, I'm trying to find out who's dealing drugs at Clearwell."

"What? Why?"

"Because it's the right thing to do. You heard about that Charles Durbin kid? The one who crashed his car into a house and died?"

"Yeah."

"Well, I think someone dosed him, too. Maybe even the same drug. I'd like to clear his name. So, I came up with a disguise. Elspeth."

"Why?"

"Is that all you can say, 'why'?" I sighed. For a science whiz, Kevin was a little slow on the uptake. "Because to infiltrate the stoners, no one's going to take 'Elizabeth' seriously. I mean, have you seen her?" *Whoops.* "I mean, I have a stellar reputation at Clearwell."

"Well, I don't know anything about your reputation, but this seems kinda not thought-out very well, Elizabeth. It sounds dangerous. Why don't you leave it to the cops?"

I threw my hands up in exasperation. "Because they haven't done jack! They can't find out who's behind this by eating donuts. I need to be in there. Hands on. Duh!" I tossed that last "duh" in there because it sounded very Elizabethian. Best to start running damage control ASAP.

"I'm trying to understand this. I really am. But why did you pull your disguise on me several nights ago?"

"Just trying it out. See if I could fool the neighbor boy." I flashed him a smile, hoping to dazzle him into forgetting about the holes in my story.

"I don't know. I think—"

"Yeah, yeah, yeah, Kevin. You need to keep this quiet, okay? Just let me do what I need to do, all right?"

"I guess." He sounded less than sincere regarding his "guess." "I just don't think your, um, secret identity is going to be so secret after tonight."

"Let me worry about that." I jammed a finger toward the windshield. "Now, could you please take me home?"

Several times, he reached for the car keys hanging from the ignition, and then failed to contact. I guess his strategy was to keep us parked on the street forever to keep me out of harm's way. Yet another male wanting to take care of precious, naïve, helpless little Elizabeth.

"Start the damn car already!"

When we pulled up in front of Elizabeth's house, Kevin said, "Why would someone dose you?"

"I don't know. Maybe I'm getting close to finding out who the Clearwell dealer is and they want to send me a message. Or worse."

"Or worse?"

"Yeah. You heard what they did to Charles Durbin. They could've killed me. Maybe they wanted to—"

"You should not be doing this, Elizabeth!"

"I'm a big girl." Smiling, I opened the car door. He didn't look very reassured.

"Wait! If you need my help, you know where to find me. Okay?"

"Sure." I leaned in and gave him a quick peck on the cheek. "My hero."

Hard to tell in the dark, but he may've been blushing. "I mean it, Elizabeth. I'm here."

"Thanks, Kevin." I waited for him to pull into his driveway before I climbed the trellis up to Elizabeth's bedroom.

While his offer was appreciated, no way would I take him up on it. My battle. And I was super pissed. One of those little punks dosed me, sent me on a hellish drug trip. I swore off drugs a long time ago. The reason for my death pretty much. Someone made me break my oath. I intended on finding Clearwell's drug dealing murderer, force-feed him his stash, and personally burn his empire to the ground.

Things were deeply personal. *It's on, bitches.*

## Chapter Eight

*Elspeth*

"I'm really, *really* sorry about tonight, but it wasn't my fault."

"How in the hell can you say that, Elspeth?"

Dream Space again. Home, sweet home. Yeah, right.

"All of this is your fault! If you had never come into my life, none of this—none of this—would have happened! Everything's your fault!"

"Sit down, Elizabeth." I snagged her pink robe belt and pulled her to the bed beside me. "I know things look terrible right now."

"Terrible. *Terrible?*" She jerked away from me and bolted to her feet. "My life, as I know it, is over!"

"Your life's not over, Elizabeth." The pink force of nature whipping about the room did make my pleas for calm and acceptance seem kinda puny. "Yeah, you might face a few speed bumps—"

"Speed bumps?"

"Mmmm-hmmm. It's like that chick you like sings, *Whatever doesn't kill us makes us stronger.* But, you will get through this. I'll do everything I can to—"

"You've done more than enough, Elspeth!"

"Look, what's the worst thing that's gonna happen? So, someone might gossip or something about your having passed out at a party. Big deal. It happens."

"It doesn't happen to me!"

"So, deny it. Or tell the truth that you were dosed or whatever. You won't die from this. You'll get through it. Pinky promise."

"Gah!" She jiggled her fists at me, her pink sleeves slipping down arms. "I almost did die, Elspeth. Maybe next time, we won't be so lucky!"

"Well, I guess there is that," I mumbled. "But chill. Everything will work out."

"And what about the clothes I was wearing?" She pointed a long, polished fingernail at me, her nose wrinkling in disgust. "The wig and the makeup. How am I going to explain those?"

"Um, you have good taste?" Not the most appropriate time for humor, I admitted, but Hurricane Elizabeth needed taming. After hopping off the bed, I anchored my hands firmly on her shoulders. "I am sorry, Elizabeth. But, I've got good insight from my people that everything will be all right."

Her mouth downturned, and her lips pulled inward. But I detected a brief glimmer of hope in her eyes. Just a smidgeon. "Really?"

"Really." Not really, but work with what you have. "Settle down and let's talk this through." I guided her back toward her bed. We sat next to one another, shoulder to shoulder. Suffragette sisters. "Remember, deniability is a powerful tool. It's worked for politicians for centuries." Language Elizabeth could relate to. "When people ask what you were doing at a doper party, dressed in a smokin' hot outfit and hairstyle…" My grin took on a life all its own. "Just say it wasn't you. Get your PR guy, Lance, on the job. It'll work, trust me."

"Every time you ask me to trust you, things just get worse."

I did feel sorry for Elizabeth. She looked like a small young girl, hurt by name-calling bullies. The kind of fragile girl all the men in her life wanted to mold her into. Say what you will about her, but in her own weird way, Elizabeth was a fierce warrior. Or at least could be. Those around her constantly underestimated her.

"You really think it'll work, Elspeth?"

"Really, truly, cross my heart and hope to die…if I wasn't already dead."

To my amazement, she let slip a small chuckle. "Okay."

"Now, business. You know some jackass dosed us tonight."

"Oh my God!" She buried her face in shame. "I'm a druggie!"

"You're not a druggie." I stretched out next to her, ignoring her disgust at my boots on the bed. It's not like you can leave dirt in Dream Space. "Do you have any idea who could have done this to us?"

"No. Duh! I wasn't there. I mean, I saw bits and pieces of what happened at the party. It could've been anybody!"

I shut my eyes, concentrated, and relived what I could remember about the party. "I don't think so, Elizabeth. I had control of my drink for most of the night, but a couple of times, I didn't. I had sat it down on the table behind me when that douche, Kip, showed up—"

"Yeah, what's up with that?"

I much preferred her fury aimed elsewhere. Baby

160

steps, I guessed.

"What was he doing there? Oh my God, he didn't see me, did he? How will I explain that to Donovan?"

"Relax. I thought it was weird he was there, too. I mean, him all lacrosse and dickish and everything. But, I'm pretty sure he didn't know I was you. So, he grabbed the cup, maybe he dosed us. But he only held it for a second. Not sure if that was enough time for him to act."

"Okay, Kip sucks and everything, but even I have a hard time believing he's capable of something like that."

"I'm just tossin' out names here." I sat up and extended a finger. "Donnie Heidenreich was in the kitchen when my glass was on the table. He could've done it while I was fending off Kip—"

"Wait! 'Fending off'? He's going out with Addie!"

"Bigger issues, Elizabeth. Then there's the entire Marc Dugan Mafia encounter—"

"Dugan held it, right? And that little sleazeball, 'T-Shirt,' man-handled your cup, too."

"Yeah, Tim Matthews."

"I knew there was something about that creepy kid I didn't like. He shows up everywhere, always watching, always eavesdropping."

"Elizabeth, you don't like anybody. Although, you're right. Tim Matthews does have a habit of turning up like a bad acid trip, if you'll excuse my metaphor." Elizabeth didn't get my joke. Tough crowd. "Maybe I'll start with him—"

"Start what?"

"Revenge on the ass-hats who dosed us, killed Charles Durbin, and then it's time to take back the night." I sprung to my feet, primed for action. "Wait! That's too long a description. Maybe an acronym or something."

Elizabeth groaned to the ceiling. "Why me, God?"

"I keep asking Him that myself." Elizabeth lifted her eyebrows, anxious to hear the secrets of the afterlife. "Just kidding." Told you, I couldn't help myself sometimes.

**\*\*\*\***

*Elizabeth*

Donovan raced into the kitchen, ignoring Daddy for the first time ever. His face drained, whiter than our finest teacups, his eyes abnormally large. His hand, cold to the touch, fell on mine, and gripped my fingers. Daddy briefly glimpsed over the top of his newspaper and muttered an indifferent greeting, more like a clearing of his throat.

"Morning, sir," Donovan said, uncharacteristically mush-mouthed. "We need to go, Elizabeth."

"I need to finish my cappuccino."

Leaning over, he whispered, "I need to talk to you *now*." Forcefulness was something I didn't expect from Donovan. With everyone else, sure, but certainly not on me. I had to say, it was sort of sexy.

"Fine."

Donovan strode ahead of me, rushing toward the front door. As a seeming afterthought, he held the door open for me and then dashed in front. After slamming my car door way too hard, he jumped in, glaring at me.

"What?" While pretending to fidget with my pearls, I ran subterfuge, hiding a large, dry gulp. Dread filled me.

He flipped his phone open, punched in a few

commands, and presented the incriminating evidence to me. A photo of me passed out on a disgusting sofa. Hair matted against my face, filthy looking. Black eyeliner bled down my face like the tears of a gothic mime. Elspeth's black miniskirt rode high on my thighs. Unbelievably, but mercifully so, my legs remained pressed tightly together.

My stomach performed several somersaults.

"Explain!" demanded Donovan. "Tell me this isn't you, Elizabeth!" The look in his eyes said it all and it hurt me. His girlfriend, high school overachiever by day, hooker by night.

"Where did you get this?" Caught between fear and anger, my voice rose to an abnormally high pitch. My common response to both emotions, unfortunately. "Did Kip send it to you?"

Donovan appeared flustered, one suddenly premature wrinkle denting his forehead. "Kip? What? What does Kip have to do with this?"

I stared down into my lap, ashamed of myself. "Never mind," I said quietly.

"You do not get to say, 'never mind,' Elizabeth! I'm owed an explanation. What's going on?"

"Where did you get the picture?" Attempting to soldier on, my will had left the battlefield.

"What does that matter? Who cares, and I don't know! Someone sent it to me during the night. Anonymously! Look, Elizabeth, we're supposed to trust one another. Tell me what's going on!"

With the back of my hand, I wiped away tears. "Okay. I'm trying to find out what happened to…Charles Durbin."

"What?" Donovan calmed. My tears always

performed miracles on him. This time, though, the tears were genuine, no game in play. He scooted across the seat and draped an arm around my shoulders. "We know what happened to Charles. It's a tragedy. Really, it is, but we know he died using drugs. What you're saying doesn't make any sense." He placed his fingertips underneath my chin, tipping my head up. "Elizabeth, are you doing drugs?"

"What? No!" I couldn't believe he, of all people, would ask me that. A scythe may as well have ripped through the harvest of my soul. "You know better than that!"

"This picture, Elizabeth...it looks like you're passed out. Were you drinking?"

"No, Donovan, honestly."

"I'm trying to be patient here. Please explain everything. Slowly."

"Okay. I think somebody dosed Charles Durbin. They sent him off in his car, knowing he was so high, he'd crash. I'm trying to find out who did it and why."

"Oh, for God's sake! What makes you think someone did that to him?"

"Because, I've been looking into it, Donovan. Charles was apparently a good kid. His death doesn't make any sense. He was an ex-druggie, but he was clean before he died. He was a member of the Drug-Free Club and—"

"How do you know this? I didn't even know it!"

"Tina Bottoms told me."

"Tina? I didn't think you even spoke to her anymore." I'd never known anyone who had a clearer picture of the world than Donovan. So when he looked lost, confused, my heart went out to him. My fault.

"I don't. Well, I didn't. That doesn't matter right now. I just, I don't know, I guess I want to do something good for someone. For a change." The sentiment hung in the air, so thick and real, I imagined reaching out and cradling it to my chest like a kitten. I hadn't realized until now how true it'd become. I did want to do something good. "Even if he is dead," I added in a quiet voice.

He pointed at the damn photo again, like I wasn't sick of looking at it already. "But what does dressing up like that and acting like that have to do with Charles?" It didn't escape my attention that he seemed unable to mention the specifics of the damning photo. I didn't blame him.

"If I'm going to find out who killed Charles, then I have to disguise myself." I grabbed the phone, snapped it shut, and tossed it to the floor like a burger wrapper.

"That's ludicrous." As soon as he started laughing, he abruptly grounded himself. Barely. "Everyone's going to know it's you, Elizabeth."

"I thought it might work."

"Where were you?"

"Okay, don't get mad, Donovan...I was at Marc Dugan's party."

Donovan's eyelids fluttered like butterfly wings. "That doper?"

"I heard it was going to be a big drug party. I thought it might be a good place to nose around."

Donovan groaned, his head lolling about. "Marc Dugan is the biggest druggie at Clearwell. He even started in grade school. I should know. I went to junior high school with him. He's bad news! You need to stay away from him!"

"Do not tell me what I can or can't do, Donovan!" I shoved a feisty finger into his face, my battle armor slowly welding itself back together again. "I know what I'm doing!"

"Oh, my God." His voice trailed off as he realized the tides of war were turning. Rightfully so. "So, tell me, why do you look wasted in the picture, Elizabeth?"

"I think someone might've slipped me a drug or—"

"That's what I'm trying to tell you! This is beyond you! Why don't we call the police and let them know your suspicions? You need to—"

"Are you finished?"

"I guess so."

"This is important to me, Donovan." I kept my voice low, yet balanced and in total control. "I need to do this. I would hope you'd support me."

He waved his hands around ineffectually, just missing a white flag. "I can't support your death!" he snapped, one last salvo.

"I know, Donovan. I'm going to be careful from now on. Really." This time I consoled him. I scooted closer, one hand on his chest, the other behind his neck.

"Earlier you mentioned Kip. How does he fit into this?"

"He was at the party."

"What? Kip doesn't do drugs. Why was he there?"

"I guess he just likes parties. I don't know. He's your stupid friend."

"Did he try to help you, at least?" Poor Donovan. He looked like his entire world was crumbling, as he stood by helpless, unable to do anything about it. I knew the feeling well.

"I don't really know. I was sorta out of it. I don't

think he had anything to do with it, if that's what you're asking."

He appeared relieved, accepting small comfort where he could. Even though one of the world's worst examples of mankind had restored his faith. "And I didn't see your car in the drive this morning. Thank God you didn't drive. But how did you get home?"

"Um, my neighbor gave me a ride." Even though I had nothing to feel guilty about, for some reason, I hated telling Donovan about Kevin. "He was at the party."

"He? He, who?" Okay, Donovan wore jealousy well, another trait I hadn't seen before.

"Just my stupid neighbor who's home from college. He's also watching my environmental science class or something. He's a total idiot, but I'm glad he was there to give me a ride."

"Huh." His simple declaration spoke volumes, but he let it go as he did many things. Yet another one of his talents. "I hate this." With a world-weary sigh, he drew his shoulders back, straight and proud. "Okay, I'll go along with this harebrained scheme as long as you don't go to any more parties."

"I can live with that."

"And you keep me in the loop. I'll help you." He stared at me, eyebrows raised to heaven. "Understood?" I nodded. "I don't want you doing this by yourself."

"Fine." An easy enough stipulation to agree to. But I didn't plan on holding up my end of the bargain. Of course, I'd ask Donovan for help if I truly needed it. But I had to do this on my own (with Elspeth's help, I supposed). Compelled to do so. Why, I couldn't really say. Maybe it was one of those inner voice dealios you heard about from time to time. Perhaps it was a simple matter of pride.

More than likely, I simply had something to prove. Maybe even to myself. "Okay. Done deal. Now, would you be a sweetheart," I said, batting my eyes, "and take me to my car? Pretty please?"

"Where is it?"

"Um, on Marc Dugan's street." I had to raise my voice to give Donovan the address over his protests. Drama king.

Thank God my car hadn't been vandalized. "Thanks, Donovan." I leaned over and gave him a reassuring, full-on kiss. Didn't care if anyone in the neighborhood saw, either.

"Elizabeth, since you were drugged, don't you think we should call the police?"

So dogged, so determined. So damned annoying. "No. I want to finish this. Then I'll bring the police in. Besides, I'm fully recovered. No side effects or anything."

\*\*\*\*

I was used to people staring at me. Came with the territory. But when I walked by the students today, giggling and pointing ensued, something suited to many students other than me. Voices hushed as I strolled closer.

Addie and the girls stood in front of my locker. Judging by their horrified faces, you'd think they'd just heard our favorite boy band went down in a plane crash.

"Addie, what's going on?"

"Oh my God, Elizabeth!" She clutched her books to her chest. "Um…" With a mouth-widening grimace, she inclined her head toward the opposite wall.

A horrific poster hung above the lockers. The photo of me passed out the heinous centerpiece. Below the photo, it read, *Do You Want THIS As Your Prom Queen?*

It only took seconds to rip the poster down. "No...*no!*" I wadded it up, tossed it to the ground, and stomped on it for good measure, trying to erase it forever. "How many are there, Addie?" My stomach churned, threatening to expel my morning's egg-white omelet. "How many?"

Addie shook her head. "They're everywhere. Is that you? What were you doing?"

"I...it's not how it looks. It's a joke!" My world was quickly going up in smoke; everything I'd worked so hard for was being added to my funeral pyre. Several juniors walked by me, smirking. "It's a joke!" I screamed.

Like a skanky moth drawn to a flame, Charlotte, the heat-seeking bitch missile from hell, found me, her target. "Well, Elizabeth, looks like you had a fun night."

"Oh, shut up!" My hands trembled, and my face flushed with rage. "Are you behind these posters?"

She grinned, flashing her bleached teeth. "Maybe, maybe not. But you certainly can't blame me for what you did to yourself."

"It's a joke! I wasn't really passed out."

"Hmmm, funny joke. And what's with your outfit? Sluts 'R Us have a big sale?" Charlotte twisted a lock of her hair around a finger. I wanted to twist her head off.

"Oh, that's really cute, Charlotte. Especially

coming from someone who shops at Hooker Warehouse. Take…*these…posters…down…now!*"

"Or what?"

"Or you'll be sorry!"

Charlotte furrowed her Cro-Magnon unibrow as if in deep concentration. "Hmmm. No. No, I don't think so. Besides, from where I'm standing, you're the sorry one." She strutted off, her gargantuan hips swaying left and right, threatening to knock down passing students. "I'm going to be all a-twitter about this," she called back. "See you from the stage on prom night!"

Squashing the urge to take her to the ground, I turned to Addie. "We've got to take these posters down!"

"Are you sure it's a joke, Elizabeth?" She appeared uncertain. Not a new look for her, by any means, but one that was not helping now. "I mean, it really looks like you're, you know, out of it."

"Trust me. You know I don't do drugs or drink, Addie!" I felt eyes scorching me, heard derisive snickers barely stifled. My heart raced faster than my pony in an open field. Caught in an inescapable whirlpool, I felt my entire life and future sucked into Charlotte's "whore-nado" wake.

"You! In my office. Now." Mr. Hastings held what I presumed to be one of the vile posters rolled up in his ham-fisted hand, swatting it against his leg. Grimmer than usual, his lantern jaw extended to the point of impossibility. He hurled down the hallway, bumping into students like a rage-filled bowling ball.

"Oh. My. God." Addie stared at me, her mouth straining in an unbecoming rectangle.

As I walked toward Mr. Hastings's office, I kept

my head high. But as the surrounding laughter and whispers rose, my head sank lower until all I saw were my feet plodding along. My posture had never taken such a ruthless beating.

I knocked on the office door and was met by a shout. "Enter!"

Sitting down quietly, I folded my hands in my lap. Hastings unrolled the poster and held it up for examination.

"Explain!"

I looked at the poster as if I hadn't seen it before. "Oh, that. Well, Mr. Hastings, it was just a joke."

"A joke? In what world is this funny, Ms. Blackmer?"

"I guess I wanted to show my fellow students I have a sense of humor." As far as lies go, it seemed like a pretty good one, even though it hadn't worked out very well so far. And the day had just begun.

"Do you see me laughing? Do I look like I'm laughing to you, Ms. Blackmer?" He pointed his thumbs back at his stony face, his thick eyebrows slanted down. "I don't think passing out is something to laugh at, do you?"

"No, sir."

"It looks real to me, Ms. Blackmer. If I didn't know better, I'd say you were passed out."

"No! You know me better than that, Mr. Hastings." I attempted to bat my eyelashes and smile, but my face wouldn't cooperate. My lips quivered and my lashes fluttered like Ms. Swanson's nervous, annoying tic. "I do not drink or do drugs."

When he exhaled harshly through his nose, several sheets of paper lifted off his desk like kites. "I'm concerned about you, Ms. Blackmer. I really had high hopes for you and your future. But lately, it seems you're intent on squandering your bright potential. Hanging out with dopers and now this!" He whacked the poster down onto his desk. "You're going to throw it all away! And these clothes you're wearing in the picture." He clucked and shook his head. "This isn't you, Ms. Blackmer. This is not funny!"

The surreal nature of it all nearly caused me to break out into hysterical laughter. The temptation struck me to ask him what he did find funny. But from deep down somewhere, a small voice of reason managed to ground me. "I apologize for the picture, Mr. Hastings. It was truly meant as a joke. I didn't think—"

"That's the problem, Ms. Blackmer. You didn't think!"

"Yes, sir."

"I certainly hope this doesn't hurt your chances of being elected prom queen."

"Yes, sir."

"Now, I'm going to give you a final warning. Stay away from the dopers." His finger punctuated the air with stabbing force. "No more 'jokes'! And stay away from the gas station across the street!"

"Yes, sir."

"Do I make myself understood?"

I didn't trust myself to speak. A true rarity, I couldn't find my voice. And I felt embarrassing tears breaking through my barriers.

Mr. Hastings waved his hand while staring out the window. He wouldn't even acknowledge me with a grim farewell glance. "You may go."

Donovan stood outside Hastings's door, struggling

with a heavy armful of the hateful posters. "Elizabeth, are you okay?" The question of the day and the answer remained the same. No. He embraced me and pulled me toward him. "I'm sorry about the posters. I took down as many as I could find."

My tears dampened his oxford shirt. "They're so mean." The floodgates opened as I sobbed into his chest, burying my face so onlookers wouldn't see me crying. "So unfair."

"Shhh, it's okay, Elizabeth."

"No, it's not! My life is ruined."

"That's not true and you know it. This is just a little thing. People will forget about it by tomorrow."

"But what am I going to do the rest of today?"

"Maybe you should go to the nurse's office? Or go home sick."

"Maybe." I tapped my forehead against Donovan's chest, hoping his inner strength would magically wear off on me. "But that's what the haters would like to see. I won't give into terrorism."

"That's my girl. You're Elizabeth Blackmer. Don't you *ever* forget it."

"Damn that Charlotte." I pushed away from Donovan, trying to jump-start my resolve. It helped when there was an actual face to the enemy.

"Is she the one who made the posters?"

"Pretty sure. She was certainly tickled by them. But how did she get the picture?"

"I'm guessing from the same person who sent it to me. Are you sure you're going to be okay? I'm already late for class."

"I'll be fine. Go to class." I kissed him quickly on the lips. "Thanks, Donovan."

He gave me a heart-melting smile and trotted down the hall.

I absolutely abhorred the idea of going to my first class, especially since T-Shirt was in there. No, I needed some time to get the red out of my eyes and gather my thoughts. Maybe hide out in the bathroom for a while.

Someone was really out to sabotage me. First, they physically endangered me with drugs and then they worked on destroying my reputation. Was I perceived as a threat to the drug dealer? Closing in on the truth? No matter. Because now, both Elspeth and I were mad. *Mean* mad.

\*\*\*\*

As I suspected, the day went on forever and felt like torture. I heard people sniggering at me, but at least they had the courtesy to do so behind my back, something I was better equipped to handle. When students gawped at me like I had some sorta STD, I met their gaze and smiled sweetly. Donovan knew what he was talking about. I was Elizabeth Blackmer, damn it, and made of stern stuff. And today's news seemed to be already fading.

Addie pushed her fork around her salad, pretending to eat. "Elizabeth, are you—"

"I swear to God, Addie, if another person asks if I'm doing okay, I'm going to pull a total bitch-fit. I'm fine." Regina and Bettany were apparently still too traumatized to speak. "I think all the posters are down, thanks to Donovan."

"I can't believe Charlotte would do something like that."

"Well, I can. She's a mean, fat skank!" The girls

174

nodded in agreement.

"Girl, we need to talk." Out of breath, Lance dropped down at the table. Uninvited, even. "Hey, girls." Regina and Bettany stared at the curious Gaysian in their midst. "Where were you in class this morning?"

"Whatever. I'm sure you've seen the poster."

"Kinda hard to miss."

When he pulled out one of the folded posters from his jacket pocket, I promptly shredded it into perfect strips of trash.

"You got some 'splainin' to do."

"It was a joke, nothing more. I didn't think it'd be all over school."

"I don't know, Elizabeth. It looks kinda real to me."

"It's a joke! I don't do drugs or drink. Why do I have to explain this to everyone?"

From the way his lips twitched, I knew Lance was heavily debating his answer. A smart boy, he moved on. "Okay, whatever. Either way, it's not good news for our campaign."

"Yeah, kinda gathered that."

"Okay, we need spin control." His finger played over his lips, mental cogs at work. "But how in the world am I gonna spin this? You're like my Watergate."

I grimaced at the gross comparison.

Addie asked, "Is she a junior?"

Lance stopped giggling when he saw Addie's puzzled look. Ignoring her—actually more often than not, the best way to handle Addie—Lance turned back to me. "You say it's a joke? Fine, whatever. We'll come out with a series of posters, each one of you in a different outfit, doing something silly."

"I don't do silly!"

"You wanna win or what? The only possible way to spin this is to play up the joke factor. Our campaign will play on your sense of humor. We'll be able to hide this poster in plain sight." He nodded at the torn remnants on the table. "By making it look like it was planned along with our other 'funny' posters. You'll be the prom queen of comedy!"

My stomach roiled. *I am decidedly not funny.*

"I don't get it," said Addie.

"Don't you worry your pretty little head over it," said Lance.

"Lance, this idea sucks as much as this stupid, wrong poster. I don't want to be the laughingstock at Clearwell!"

"I think it might be a little too late for that," he said.

"Excuse me?"

"Never mind."

My back against the wall, hope appeared futile. But at least it was a positive idea, moving forward, not dwelling on the past. As super-unappealing as it sounded. "Do you really think it'll work?"

"Can't do any more harm than what's already been done. But, yeah, I think it might just work. Okay, gotta bounce, I got work to do. We're gonna have to get together later."

Political aspirations nipping at his tail, Lance raced out of the cafeteria and out into the commons. He knocked into some kid, rebounded. No, not just any kid. T-Shirt. Lance whirled, waved apologetic hands. T-Shirt kept his gaze glued on me the entire time. When I caught his eye, he stepped back and vanished behind the cafeteria door.

I thought it was high time—no pun intended, although it was rather good—Elspeth had her little chat with T-Shirt. I knew she was looking forward to it so much.

\*\*\*\*

*Elspeth*

Waking up in a toilet stall sucks, but hey, that's limbo for you.

Elizabeth seemed pretty pissed about the photo leaking out. Again, she demanded I not call attention to myself. Meaning, I had to wear her clothes. Okay, ugh and fine. Swinging into action looking like a prepster sorta sucked the fun out of it, but I was game either way.

I pocketed Elizabeth's Taser and pepper spray. As the Boy Scouts said—or maybe it was the Bible?—always be prepared.

Three-thirty and it didn't take long for the hallways to clear. But like the most dedicated dopers, Tim Matthews spent a lot of his after-school hours across the street. I just needed to take the long route so Hastings didn't spot me.

Through the main hall window, I saw that the gas station had its party mode rocking. Smoke rose from behind it like a miniature mushroom cloud. Yet Matthews was walking away from the party. He appeared antsy, nervously looking over his shoulder.

*And just where are you going, T-Shirt?*

He crossed the front commons grounds, heading toward the east side of the school. I raced back down the hallway, slowed in front of the offices, picked up speed again. When I pushed open the east door, Matthews had just passed in front of me. I shut the door, counted to ten, then burst outside. *Gone.*

Just past the gym, I caught sight of him entering the empty football field. Keeping a safe distance, I followed him. Then he vanished underneath a set of bleachers. Trying to keep Elizabeth's damn ballet flats from slapping on the metal bleachers was a chore, but I quietly climbed the bleachers, positioning myself above Matthews. Below me, he spoke in a hushed tone, either bughouse crazy talking to himself or making a phone call. Why the need for such privacy?

His words were impossible to make out, and his tone smacked of pure panic.

Taser in hand, I slipped through the bleachers and jumped. My knees landed squarely on Matthews's back, bringing him down into the dirt as he richly deserved.

"What the hell?"

I think that's what he said. Hard to tell since his face bit the ground.

With a sudden surge of energy, Mathews tossed me off and scrambled to his feet. He came at me, flailing his arms around like a windmill. A lucky punch swiped the side of my head, knocking me back. As I regained my footing, he rushed me, head down and arms out. I pulled the Taser's trigger and twin hooks snagged him in the chest. His legs turned into jelly. He dropped to the ground, spasming and flopping like a fish out of water. I turned off the device and straddled his back, practically riding a bucking bronco. Took a few minutes for him to stop.

"Okay, Tim, isn't it?" He groaned, whether out of

relief or pain, I couldn't be certain. "Now, I've turned off the Taser, but I'm ready to give you another jolt if you don't behave. Got it?" No reply, not even a moan this time. I displayed the Taser in front of his face with relish. "*Got it?*"

"Elizabeth? What…what the hell…are you doing?" His voice sounded faint and thin, high-pitched like that of a cartoon mouse.

"Quiet. I'll ask the questions. Now, what are you doing under the bleachers?"

"Nothing. Making a phone call. It's a free country."

"Well, that's debatable. But I'll ask again, what were you doing?" I dangled the Taser in front of him again. I could really get used to this kick-ass toy.

"Making a call!"

"Who were you calling, Tim? Maybe making a drug deal? You holding?"

"What? No!"

"Tim, I'm getting tired of your uncooperative ways. Gettin' kinda boring. Maybe another jolt will show you the light." I would have been lying if I wasn't looking forward to his challenging me.

"No! Wait! I wasn't making a drug deal! I swear!"

"Tim, if it's not you, then who is it? Who's the drug dealer? Who killed Charles Durbin?"

His shoulders twisted as he tried to throw me off. So tiresome and predictable. Rapping the Taser against his head put an immediate stop to his fidgeting. "I don't know," he finally said.

"Who drugged me? At the party the other night? Was it you?"

"No! I wouldn't do that!"

"Then who did it?"

"I don't know. Look, why are you doing this?"

"Because I stand for truth, justice, and the American way. But Super-Chick's losing her patience. Let's see just what Tim Matthews has on him. And if I find drugs, then I'll know you're lying to me, and do you know what I do to liars? Time to get reacquainted with my friend, Mr. Taser." I patted down his sides, and slid my hands down his scrawny back.

When I yanked out his wallet, he swung his arm back defensively. "Ah, ah, *ah!*" I nudged him with my foot until he rolled over. Brandishing the Taser over him, I searched his front pockets. My hand brushed up against something hard underneath his T-shirt. Presuming it was not a six-pack, I yanked his shirt up.

"No! Don't!"

A small black electric device adhered to his chest, a wire stretched taut and running into his jeans. "Wait, you're a cop?" Matthews pursed his lips and pouted like a kid, saying nothing. "You're an undercover cop?" I fell onto his stomach, sitting on him. "Crap. But…but you have acne!"

"Just keep it down, Elizabeth. And real nice acne comment. And let me the hell up!"

"Oh, sorry." I hopped up. Matthews stood, pulled his shirt down, and brushed the dirt off his jeans. "Why didn't you tell me?"

"It's called undercover for a reason!"

"Does Hastings know?"

"He called us. Yes, he knows! He's the only one who knew except for you now!" His look of shame suggested his manhood was in question. Boyhood, maybe? Just how old was this guy?

"So, Hastings called you in. To investigate the drug dealer? What are you? Like, fifteen?"

"I look young. Clean living. Look, Elizabeth, you can't tell anyone about me. I'm getting close to nailing the dealer. And I don't want to be compromised on my first mission!"

"Well, that depends—"

"What? What do you mean 'that depends'? I'm the cop here!" He shot his gaze around the bleacher's shadows, then lowered his voice, going even deeper undercover, I supposed. "You can't make deals with cops. I should have you arrested."

"Let's not be hasty, Tim. I'll keep your secret if you let me know what you've found out."

He laughed bitterly. "I'm not going to do that."

"Okay then, wait till all your little drug buddies find out about you." I turned to leave, flourishing my fingers in the air. "See ya."

"Wait! Dammit, wait!"

"I knew you'd see it my way."

"I can't do this. If word gets out, my career is over before it's begun!"

"Seems like you don't have much of a choice, Tim."

"Fine! God dammit!" He folded his arms, tapped the ground with a foot—the best hissy fit I'd seen in some time. I stared at him expectantly, didn't say a word. Two could play in the same playground.

"Okay, I don't have much. The drugs really started flowing through Clearwell about three months ago. Whoever's doing it has been very discreet and careful. He's well-organized—"

"He? You know it's a he? Or are you just, you

know, being sexist?"

Since he ignored the question, I assumed he was sexist. "Apparently, I'm either hanging out with the wrong people or they're too scared to talk. No one's told me who their dealer is. The closest I've got is one kid who said he scored over the Internet. The deal was made anonymously and there was a secret drop place. He paid the dealer using an electronic third party—we haven't had any luck tracing it back to him."

"Where was the drop place?"

Matthews inclined his head toward the school. "The gas station—at night."

"Huh."

"As I said, whoever our dealer is, he's smart and careful. Never seen anything like it before. He—"

"Yeah, I really admire him."

"And he knows his way around a science lab."

"Why do you say that?"

"The synthetic drugs he's come up with. They're new, homemade. He's gotta have some sort of scientific knowledge."

"Okay, so really, you don't know anything?"

"I've told you what I know. He's cagey. But I will get him. Now, you. What's this all to you? I didn't take you for a doper, but after the party the other night—"

"Someone dosed me. I don't do drugs. And I'm pissed."

"Huh. Okay, I get that, but why are you in the middle of this?"

"I guess I just want to see justice done. There's a murderer out there."

"We don't know that, Elizabeth."

"Oh, yeah, we do know it. I know Charles Durbin

was murdered. He didn't do drugs. Someone intentionally dosed him, stuck him in a car. They may as well have held a gun to his head and pulled the trigger."

"You have proof of this?"

"Let's just call it feminine instinct." I zapped him a smile. "Well, Timbo, I really must be going."

"Wait! You won't tell anyone, right?"

"Sure, Tim. Our little secret." I feigned locking my lips. He flinched when I tossed him the invisible key. "But you will keep me in the loop, right?"

"Elizabeth, why don't you leave the police work to me? To us? If there is a murderer, you shouldn't be involved."

"What? And let you have all the fun? I don't think so." I raced out onto the football field before Matthews could get all law enforcement on me.

"Don't you get in the way of my investigation, Elizabeth!" he called out.

"Don't you get in the way of mine, five-o!"

## Chapter Nine

*Elizabeth/Elspeth*

Full of nervous energy and nowhere to let it explode, I needed to do something—anything—regarding Charles Durbin, but had no clue what to do. My life felt center-stuck on Fate's median. So when Mother informed me she had invited the newest minister of our church to dinner, I decided just to roll with it. Maybe a little bit of normal was what I needed. Normal seemed in short supply these days.

"So, Elizabeth, I understand you're going to Dartmouth next year." Minister Mackintosh's eyebrows glowed bushy and white as snow, his face a sunburned red. His mouth perpetually hung open, his tongue lolling about. Santa Claus gift-wrapped and tied with a clerical collar.

"That's right, Mr. Mackintosh." At least I hoped Dartmouth would still want me after all of Elspeth's shenanigans.

Daddy narrowed his eyes as if experiencing a sudden migraine. He remained quiet, leaving the bulk of the conversation to the rest of us. I wouldn't categorize Daddy or Mother as super religious, but I thought they viewed their minister dinners as buying them goodwill, sort of laying down the pavement on the road to heaven.

"What are you going to study?" asked the minister.

And that's when "normal" packed its bags. Bright lights poked the perimeter of my vision, growing into frightening lightning strikes. Sweat beaded across my forehead, my hands clammy and numb. My head spun like a merry-go-round, my stomach roiling, trying to keep up. I slipped into a dream-state, a waking nightmare, only remotely connected to my body.

Then I remembered nothing.

"Elizabeth?"

*What the hell?*

Someone called Elizabeth's name. Nowhere to be found. I'd lost contact with her. Blankets of brightness pulled back from my eyes to expose the tableau in front of me. Seated at Elizabeth's dining room table, I faced her parents and a fat, red-faced man.

"Elizabeth, Mr. Mackintosh asked you a question."

*Why am I here?* Elizabeth didn't call for me. And now I was stuck in some hellish Norman Rockwellian portrait of Americana. *I'd rather be chasing after murderous drug dealers.* "Um, what?"

Elizabeth's father scowled at me. Her mother said, "Mr. Mackintosh asked you what you're going to study at Dartmouth." When she pressed her lips together, the color drained from her face.

"Oh, well…" *Damn. What did Elizabeth say she wanted to study? Guess I'd better pay more attention to her in the future.* "Uh, beerology?" The first thing that popped into my head, and I thought the eyeballs looking at me were going to pop out of their heads.

The ruddy-looking man sputtered, his face growing impossibly redder.

"*Elizabeth!*" The mom turned to the stranger and

apologized. "Elizabeth is joking. Such a wry sense of humor."

The man dabbed his lips with a napkin, and gave a wussy smile.

Elizabeth's dad, of course, frowned, apparently his everlasting look. "She's going to study politics."

"Oh, is that right?" A speedy recovery on the big man's part, no Heimlich maneuver necessary. "Well, I would hope one day when you're a wealthy senator, you won't forget to donate to the church." He grinned, his large teeth the better to eat me with.

"Yeah, okay." I shrugged. Silence all around. Dinner parties were terrifying.

"Is there any particular area of politics you're interested in?" The old guy just wouldn't give up.

*Elizabeth, help me out here!* "Um, I don't know. A liberal interest?"

Elizabeth's dad coughed. There was more coughing going on than at a doctor's office. In the future, I hoped they stuck to soup—leave any hard food in the kitchen. "I believe she's joking again with you, Paul."

"Paul" gave me a puzzled look, obviously seeing no joke. "I see. Well, I certainly appreciate your inviting me to dinner. It smells wonderful." He drew in a deep, unnecessary breath, actor extraordinaire.

"It's our pleasure, Paul," said Elizabeth's mother. "We've got to feed our minister so you can continue to nourish our souls." I joined in everyone's merry laughter as best I could. *Any time now, Elizabeth!*

"Well." Paul folded his hands underneath his waddle that would have given turkeys a serious case of envy. "Why don't we give thanks to God before we indulge in your delightful meal." He stretched his hands out.

Reluctantly, I grabbed his hand following Elizabeth's mother's example.

"I say grace so often I usually take great pleasure in hearing others do so. Particularly younger people. They can be so refreshing." I did not like where this was going. "Elizabeth? Would you care to do the honors?"

I swallowed, the audible click loud in my ears. *Elizabeth, where the hell are you?* "Um, why don't you do it, Mom?"

Her head snapped back like a demon had suddenly possessed her. "Elizabeth!" Even though she regained her ice queen composure, her look nearly gave me frostbite. "Please do as Mr. Mackintosh asked."

Elizabeth's father nodded grimly. "Elizabeth…"

"Okay, fine, whatever." I cleared my throat, hoping to buy time. Kill time. I hadn't prayed since, well, never. "Okay, uh…dear God…who is great and who is good, let us thank you for our food. Um…Amen." I released Paul's hand, opened my eyes, and smiled. Smiles were in short supply around the table from hell.

"Well," said Paul after a long silence. "That was…" He hung his head, staring down into his empty plate, no doubt contemplating the heathen he was about to break bread with.

"Elizabeth Blackmer! Say a proper prayer. *Now.*"

"Do as your mother says, Elizabeth," instructed her dad.

The center of attention, no way out. This was way worse than getting dosed the other night. "Okay, let's give it another go." I clenched my eyes shut, this time actually praying Elizabeth would wake up. "Uh, I'd like to give the Big Guy in the Sky a shout-out and a fist-bump. Thank you for the food we're about to eat…and share…and stuff. Um, please help the poor and the sick more than the rich…"

Elizabeth's dad coughed, probably a new coughing world record.

"Get us through hard times…" *Like this damn dinner party.* "And help the cops catch the drug dealer at Clearwell High. Keep doing what you're doing, Big Guy, and roll with the punches. Amen!" I clapped my hands together, sonic thunder from heaven. Once again, blank stares met me.

"That was, nice, Elizabeth," said Paul. While I knew he didn't really think it was nice, I was thrilled he had apparently washed his hands on my God-skills. "Ah, you mentioned in your prayer a drug dealer? At your school?"

"Yeah. No one knows who he is. I hope they bust him soon. One person's dead from it so far."

At the far end of the table, Elizabeth's father's eyes raised, the first time he'd shown an interest in this farce. "Are the police any closer to finding out who this dealer is, Elizabeth?"

"No, not really. At least, I guess not. I hope they catch the bast…um…jerk soon, though. Before someone else kicks it."

"Honestly, Elizabeth," said her mother. "What has gotten into you tonight?"

"I don't know, the devil, I guess?" I grinned, once again the only person doing so.

****

*Elspeth*

"Your father wants to see you, young lady." Elizabeth's mom whirled on her high heels, mechanically stalking off like an angry automaton. Definitely close to blowing a gasket. I hopped off Elizabeth's bed and trudged downstairs.

Nearly two and a half hours had passed without a peep from Elizabeth. Usually, I could sense her lurking somewhere, sometimes even able to exchange a few words. But now it was like she wasn't there at all. She simply ceased to exist. She had me seriously worried. And I really, *really* didn't want to spend the rest of my life in Elizabeth's plaid skirts.

I knocked on the study door.

"Come in."

"Um, hi, Dad. You wanted to see me?"

He looked up from his laptop and snapped it shut. "Sit down, Elizabeth." Scooping up some papers, he quickly slid them into a manila envelope and put them in a drawer. With his gaze firmly glued on me, he locked the drawer. The click sounded ear-shattering in the quiet study. Folding his hands, he took his sweet time getting comfortable. Just like being in Hastings's office all over again. "What was wrong with you tonight, Elizabeth?"

"What do you mean?" I sat, remembering to clamp my legs tight together. Mustn't be vulgar!

"You know what I mean. Your behavior tonight at dinner, well, it was very unlike you."

"Um, sorry. I didn't think it was that bad." I attempted a smile. But smiles didn't work very well in this household.

"Why did you behave that way? We'll be lucky if Mr. Mackintosh doesn't tell the entire congregation about this."

"I don't know. I guess I was just sorta sowing my wild teenage oats." His grimace told me he didn't buy it, so I changed course. "Really, Dad, I'm sorry. I was just having a little fun, I guess."

"'A little fun, you guess'. Elizabeth, are you on drugs?"

"No." I really wished people would quit asking me that. "Seriously, Dad, I'm not on drugs."

"You're certainly not acting like yourself." *You got that right.* "If you are on drugs, you'd tell me, wouldn't you? So we could get you some help?"

"Yes, I'd tell you. I'm not on drugs."

"It's just unusual, your behavior." He took off his glasses and rubbed his eyes. "You've never called me 'Dad' before tonight." *Uh-oh.* "I think that's also unusual."

Crap. That's right. Elizabeth annoyingly called him Daddy. "Maybe I'm just trying to grow up a little bit, Daddy."

"Well, don't grow up too quickly, princess." *He does have a heart, after all!* "With your new obsession over the drug dealer at school, I have to wonder what you're really going through." He frowned. The Tin Man had just lost his newfound heart.

"I wouldn't call it an obsession, Daddy. It's just sorta troubling. I think the drug dealer killed that Durbin kid."

He batted his eyelids, trying to blink the crazy from his brain, no doubt. "This sounds like a matter for the police, Elizabeth. Don't poke around in affairs that are none of your concern."

"Daddy, it was a boy at my school. That sorta

makes it my concern."

He leaned across his desk with intent, as if ready to drop a bombshell. "As I instructed you, Elizabeth, do not poke around in this. You might uncover something you do not want to find out or worse. Everyone has secrets."

Huh. This conversation had just taken a turn for the weird. What was he trying to tell me? "Um, okay."

"Now, have you finished your homework?"

I nodded. *No* shouted my brain. No way I was doing Elizabeth's homework.

"Fine. Get to bed now."

"Good night, Daddy."

I had my hand on the door, ready to make my escape, when he called out, "Elizabeth?"

"Yes?"

"No matter what happens, I want you to know I love you. You understand that, don't you?"

"Yes, Daddy. I, um, love you, too." I closed the door, listening through it. I heard the rattle of the key in his desk drawer as he took out the folder he had been so rushed to hide from me.

"Everyone has secrets," he'd said. I wondered what his were.

**\*\*\*\***

"Get up!" I awoke to a pink pony pummeling my face.

"Elizabeth! Thank God you're back!" So relieved to see her, I actually tossed my arms around her. She responded with another smack from her damn stuffed pony.

"Is there anything in my life you're not planning on destroying?" Elizabeth delivered more abuse to

Snowcone as she slapped it against her leg. "Great. Now we're going to be ostracized from the church because of you."

"Don't sweat it." I stretched out on her bed, fingers entwined behind my neck. "It all worked out, but don't ever make me go through another dinner party again. Where were you? I was worried."

She flopped down next to me with a sigh. "I don't know. It was weird. First, I was at the dinner table, then I wasn't."

"Were you conscious? In Dream Space?"

She shook her head, her blond helmet of hair refusing to move with her. Obviously, Lance hadn't yet been successful in getting the starch out. "I don't think so. It was like I was nowhere. I don't remember anything. But…"

"What?"

"The way how you felt when you got dosed at the party? It was like that. It was like we were dosed again."

"Crap. That might explain it."

"Explain what?"

"I think because of our 'special condition' we had a drug flashback."

"Oh, wonderful!" She slapped her palms over her eyes and crashed onto the bed. "I am a druggie."

"Whatever. You're not a druggie. But we're going to have to be careful in case it happens again. And it pisses me off. I'm going to get this bastard. He's really screwing with us."

"Tell me about it! You think these flashbacks will wear off?"

"They should. Over time, probably." Elizabeth

moaned. "As I said, we'll need to be careful. Just don't go AWOL when there's another dinner party."

"Like I can help it."

"You know something? After having spent some time in your shoes, I guess your life's not as easy as I thought it was."

She glared at me, poised between rage and relief. "Just because I'm rich and pretty, doesn't mean life is a bed of roses, Elspeth. Welcome to my world."

"You can have it!" We shared a much-needed laugh. "So, I guess you're aware Tim Matthews is an undercover cop, right?"

"Yeah, I saw the whole deal. Did you really have to Taser a cop?"

"I know, right?" I grinned, reliving the golden moment. "Anyway, he knows nothing. We're further into our investigation than he is."

"Oh, yeah, right. In denial much?"

"No, really. I mean, the fact that you got that note and we were dosed tells me we are on the right track. We just need to stay on it, not get derailed."

"Fine. I can't wait for this to be over. So, what next?"

"Not sure. It's a work in progress." I hesitated, and debated telling Elizabeth about her father's suspicious behavior. "Elizabeth?"

"Hmmm?"

"There's something up with your dad. He's hiding something." As I told her about my encounter with her dad, Elizabeth's eyes grew wide, large enough to rival Snowcone's grotesquely manga-styled eyes.

"You seriously don't think Daddy's involved in this drug business, do you?"

"No, well, at least I don't think so. But I know he's hiding something. You want me to look into it?"

"Oh, my God! Is he in trouble? What's going on with my world?" Spinning in a circle, she stuck her arms out like airplane wings. "Just make it stop." She growled at the ceiling, and then brought herself down. "Let me think about it, okay, Elspeth? One thing at a time."

I knew what she was doing. Defense systems up. If you pretended the problem didn't exist, it simply didn't. Maybe that was how her world worked, but not mine. Even if Elizabeth didn't want me investigating her dad, I was still going to. For her benefit.

At least that was my good intention. Until it went so incredibly, horrifically bad.

****

When Elizabeth finally gave up her battle with consciousness, I took over. I couldn't wait to get into my clothing again; hell, they practically beckoned me. *"Wear me, Elspeth."*

Sorry, my friends. Another time. My leather battle gear would be hard to explain if Elizabeth's dad caught me.

I opened the bedroom door, adjusted my eyes to the darkened hallway, and listened. A few tics and plops, the sounds of a house settling after a weary day of hosting living occupants. Other than that, dead silence.

I tiptoed out into the carpeted hallway, grasped blindly for the banister rail, and let it guide me toward the stairwell. Moonlight dribbled in through the large window above the stairwell, illuminating my descent. I abandoned stealth-mode once on the lower level—since

Elizabeth's parents' bedroom was also on the second floor—and shuffled into the hallway leading to the study. The moonlight abandoned me in the windowless corridor as I dragged my fingertips across the walls. Earlier, I'd thought about looking for a flashlight, but had no idea where the Blackmers kept them. Probably in a closet dedicated to nothing but flashlights.

After a few false starts, my hand found the brass knob. Crap. Locked. But I expected it. I grabbed the nail file and a bobby pin from Elizabeth's robe pocket, knelt, and went to work. Lock picking was a talent I acquired before entering the world of limbo. In my youth, it came in handy, allowing my friends and me to sneak into the back door of over-age concerts. Even had a lock-picking kit once. Wished I had it now.

I inserted the top of the bobby pin into the hole underneath the knob, the nail file below that. Carefully wriggling them around, I heard a reassuring click. The door swung open. Fumbling for the light switch, I flipped it on and was momentarily blinded by the miniature chandelier sparkling from the ceiling. I turned on the desktop lamp, raced back, and snapped the overhead light off. A yellow oval of light spotlighted a portion of the desktop. How could anyone, other than a bat, work in such dimness?

Elizabeth's dad's laptop had vanished. Probably tucked safely underneath his pillow, keeping his secrets close. Although I would have loved to take a peek at his computer, no way was I going into his bedroom. And really, I had no idea what I was even looking for. But I'd bet my best boots he was hiding something. Captain Obviously Mysterious.

As I suspected, his drawer remained locked. I

performed a quick search for the key, but came up empty-handed. It was an older lock, though, a cinch to pick. Unfortunately, I couldn't relock the drawer, but Elizabeth's dad was old—he'd probably just think he forgot to lock it. Seconds later, the drawer opened with a frog's croak, the sole contents the manila folder Mr. Blackmer had hidden away earlier.

Quickly, I flipped through the contents. Page after page of notes on individuals and companies with handwritten asides scrawled in the margins. One scribbled note read, *Ready to pull his investment. Send reassurance note.* Attached to this page was a printed letter, full of boring business-speak, blah, blah, blah. The letter concluded, *Please be assured our offshore investments are extremely solvent and the promised interest will continue now on a twice a year schedule instead of bi-monthly due to the complex nature of our interests.*

Boring much? I had no idea what it all meant, and maybe that was the point. I was no expert in the high falutin' high-finance world, but even to these novice eyes, it read purposefully vague. Really sketchy.

On a whim, I pulled Elizabeth's phone from her robe pocket. I snapped photos of various pages and carefully put them back in order. Yet I had no idea what to do with the photos. Maybe I was just looking for bad guys in all the wrong places.

I replaced the folder in the drawer, closing it tightly. A shrill, loud buzz went off in my hand, sending me into a heart-racing adrenaline rush. Elizabeth just received a late night text.

—*I TOLD YOU TO LEAVE IT ALONE!*—

Rude, making a threat in all caps. And apparently,

the mystery texter was an insomniac. I immediately fired back, *—OR WHAT?—* The text bounced back as undeliverable.

Stumbling back down the hallway, I glanced through the tall, multi-paned windows flanking the front doors. A shadowy figure slowly walked down the street, uncertainty forming his every step. I punched in the security code by the door—"Elizabeth scans" were awesome. Too bad I didn't have this power when I was in high school.

I stepped outside.

The tall figure stopped in front of the Bartholomew driveway.

Running after him, I nearly tripped in Elizabeth's ridiculously floppy slippers. "Kevin, wait up!"

Obviously startled, he jumped. I seemed to have that effect on him. "Oh, hey, Elizabeth." His voice raised a little higher than usual. Too old to be suffering from adolescent voice changing, it had to be something else. Like I had caught him red-handed at something devious.

"So, what are you doing out this late?" I cinched the robe tight, adhering to Elizabeth's stone-age ideas of propriety.

He dropped his arms to his sides with an exasperated slap. "Couldn't sleep, as usual."

"Huh. Insomniac, are you?" The dots connected with ease. But the resulting picture unsettled me. Surely, Kevin was not the mystery texter. Right? "So, what? You're just out walking?"

His gaze flitted left and right before finally settling on me. "Well, you know about my other night-time activities. Thought I'd try something a little quieter. So

Stuart R. West

I wouldn't wake you."

"Considerate. So why can't you sleep? Something buggin' you?"

"Just the usual stuff. Fears about the future, that sort of thing." He sat down on the curb. I dropped beside him. "I'm beginning to wonder if teaching is what I want to do."

"Well, what would you do instead? I don't think you're going to get very far with basketball or drumming."

"Yeah, thanks." He leaned back, looking up at the stars sprinkling the sky. "I don't know. Just having doubts."

He seemed sincere enough. Maybe he was just taking an innocent stroll. At 2:00 a.m. on a school night. Not lurking in front of Elizabeth's house right before I got the text. "Awww, what's the matter, Kevin?" I pouted my lips. "Have the big, bad high school students been picking on you?"

He chuckled. "No, nothing like that. I actually like most of them. I'm only, what, one or two years older than they are. No, I just don't know if I want to spend the rest of my life in a classroom. I mean, I just escaped high school not so long ago."

"Yeah, I think I get that."

"Maybe I want to do something more meaningful with my life." He picked a pebble up from the street, rolled it between his fingers, studying it like a modern marvel.

"Really, Kevin, really?" Riding on his self-pity train grew tiresome. Next stop, Inspiration Station. All aboard! "What could possibly be more meaningful than teaching kids?" Well, it didn't really hold true for me, but there was no sense in purposefully derailing my argument.

"Yeah, but science? Do any of them really care? Am I wasting my time?"

I sighed, long and loud enough for him to understand my annoyance. "Okay, so look, maybe you don't want to teach science. Maybe you do. Doesn't matter. What matters is these kids need some guidance, someone to teach them what's morally correct, teach them about what to expect in the real world. Otherwise…" I shrugged. "They're just gonna keep learning from reality TV and all that crap. If you wanna quit science, fine. Be a quitter. But even if you do teach science, doesn't mean you can't squeeze in social lessons every day." I thumped his shoulder, maybe a little too roughly. But he deserved it. "I thought you're supposed to be some sorta smart guy."

He turned to me, brown eyes wide under the moonlight. "And you surprise me, Elizabeth. You seem wise beyond your years. You talk about your classmates like, well, like you're not one of them."

I stretched my legs into the street, crossing them at the ankles. "Guess you might say I'm an old soul."

"I guess." He tossed his philosophical pebble across the street. "Thanks for the advice. You've actually given me some things to think about."

"Don't mention it."

"Elizabeth?"

"Yeah?"

"How are you doing? I mean, after the party the other night. You weren't in class today, and I saw one of those posters of you."

And here we go. Too late to hop back on the self-pity train instead? "Yeah, well, no worries. I'm awesome, as always." I shot him my best flirtatious grin.

"Yeah, I guess you are. Just seems like you're going through a lot in a short time."

"I can handle myself."

"I don't doubt that." He smiled briefly, a gorgeous smile, before donning his dour sourpuss mask again. "So, how goes your, um, investigation?"

"It's going."

"So, I guess you're not going to talk to me about it?"

"You're a great guesser but just an average kisser."

"There you go again. You're gonna give this guy a complex, you know."

"More guys could do with complexes."

He scrunched his eyebrows in confusion.

"Fewer douches." He formed an "O" with his mouth and nodded. Maybe I was taking a wild leap in faith, or placing my belief into misguided intuition, or maybe hints from above —sideways, wherever—were being fed to me, but I suddenly felt I could trust Kevin. Or maybe I was just a sucker for brown eyes and good looks. "Kevin?"

"Hmmm?"

"Do you know anything about the world of finance?"

"Hello. Science guy." He poked himself with his thumb. "One of the reasons I went into teaching and science is because I can't stand corporate greediness. Why?"

"I don't know, it's not important now, not really." But that was a lie. It was important, I just knew it. Elspeth senses tingling. "Okay, how are you with computers and decrypting and all that crap?"

"I can get around. I'm no expert, by any means. But you know something? My roommate at K.U., he's pretty much a genius in both of those areas. He's gonna rule the world some day. Scares the hell out of me. You know what they say about quiet guys." He looked at me, awaiting my acknowledgment. I responded with a vacant, intolerant stare. With things getting interesting, I needed him to stay on track. "Well, anyway, we get along okay."

"You think he might be interested in doing a little work for me? I mean, I could pay him and everything." Elizabeth didn't share her dad's aptitude for financial talents. She would never notice a few missing bucks from her much-bragged-about unlimited expense account. "I'm not even sure if I can get to the computer in question yet, but just in case, would you ask him?"

"Well, yeah, I guess. But what kinda work are we talking about here?"

I sensed he was about to turn all adult on me. So tiresome being right all the time.

"We're not talking anything illegal, are we?"

"No, no, at least not on my part. I just want to know if I get my hands on a copy of a hard-drive, can your boy figure out the files? Even if they're encrypted?"

"Does this have anything to do with the drug dealer?" He pressed on, turning more and more serious, more and more boring.

"Completely unrelated." I hoped. "But I think the files are gonna be full of financial gibberish. Can your guy help or not?"

"If anybody can, he can. He's a friggin' genius."

"Cool. If you could plant the seed in his ear that it might be coming his way, I'd appreciate it. But, Kevin..." I glared, Elizabeth's icy eyes searing him. "You need to be completely quiet about this. You can't even bring it up to me when you see me. When I want to talk about it, I'll contact you. Understand? Get it?"

"Yeah, okay, I get it already." But his dumbfounded look told a different story.

"Okay, I need you to do me one last favor." I pulled out Elizabeth's phone and began tapping the keypad.

"What?"

"Give me your phone number."

His smirk irritated the living hell out of me. Where was that pin to stick into his ego-filled balloon? "Just give me the number, Kevin. And this does not mean you get to text or call me without my explicit approval." Wow. I was getting good at being Elizabeth.

"Okay, okay." After he rattled off his digits, I sent him the photos I took earlier, and immediately deleted them from Elizabeth's phone.

"Just keep these for me for a while, okay?"

He stared at one of them, his eyes confused slits. "What are they? I can't even read these."

"Never mind. Just keep them until I say differently."

"Okay." He snapped his phone shut and saluted me. "I guess that means I'm your dutiful slave."

"Careful what you wish for."

"Oh, I've been wishing for lots of things." The leer came back. Time to resurrect his confidence lacking, yet endearing, inner child again.

"Kevin?" I halfway sang.

"Yeah?"

"Were you walking up and down the street in front of my house hoping to get my attention?" I smiled at him, head cocked, knowing I had just gained the upper hand.

"What?" He chuckled, began stuttering. "That's crazy! Why would I do something like that?" His voice ground down, spitting like a faulty lawn mower. "No. Okay, maybe. I don't know. All right! Yes."

So easy to break. Barely a challenge.

"Kevin?" I continued my annoying singsong delivery. "Do you like me?" I spun a lock of Elizabeth's hair around my finger, taunting him. "Does somebody have a crush?"

Even in the moonlight, Kevin's face turned three shades of red. "I was just worried about you, that's all! You weren't in class and you seem to be just as much awake at night as I am!"

"That's because you wake me up."

"Okay, okay, fine. Just worried about you."

"I think it's sweet." I grabbed his face and pulled him toward me. Our lips met, lingered, played over one another's. His hands, soft and gentle as you'd expect a science teacher's to be, fell on mine. We kissed until it sounded like he might stroke out. I pushed him back and jumped to my feet. He held his arms up toward me like a toddler wanting Mama to pick him up. After a lengthy performance of deep concentration, I shook my head solemnly and frowned. "Yep. Just as I remembered. Just an okay kisser."

"What? Come on! You're driving me crazy! I shouldn't even be kissing you! You're one of my students and—"

"Oh, sack up, Kevin. You're not a teacher yet. You're a student. And I've almost graduated from high school. Deal with it. Or don't. Okay. Gotta bounce." I turned, fairly running toward Elizabeth's home. I didn't want Kevin to see my grin. I had lied again. He was a good kisser.

"Elizabeth!" he called out, as loud as a whisper could travel. "I don't get you!"

I swiveled, still jogging backward. "Exactly."

A real pity, too, that he'd never be able to get me, either.

Chapter Ten

*Elizabeth*

"Elizabeth?" For once, Daddy appeared to be more interested in me than his boring old newspaper. "Did you get up during the night?"

"No, of course not. Daddy? Last night, why did you say, 'no matter what happens, know that I'll always love you?' You're not sick or anything, right?"

He folded the paper in eight perfect sections the way he tended to his handkerchiefs, but it seemed a ploy to buy time. "Never mind, princess. I was just feeling melancholy, I suppose." His smile looked forced, painful. "I remembered when you were younger, so small, so perfect, the entire world at your feet." This time, his smile seemed genuine, heartfelt, and worry-free.

The doorbell rang. Mother made a big to-do over Donovan from the hallway.

"Good morning! Hello, Mr. Blackmer." Donovan only merited a nod from Daddy, handshakes a forgotten art. "And how are you this morning, Elizabeth?"

"Very well, thank you for asking." I gave him a quick, cheek-to-cheek hug, and felt a touch of uncustomary stubble on his face.

Mother strolled in, working a killer dress, ready for another hard day at the country club. "Elizabeth is feeling much better this morning." She flickered her long, fake eyelashes at me, and then Donovan.

"Oh, were you sick last night, Elizabeth?"

"No, no. Don't be silly." I waved my hands at Donovan, dispelling the notion of pesky germs. "I was just feeling silly."

"That's certainly one way of putting it," said Mother, lips pressed together tighter than her knees.

"Anyway…" I lingered a little bit longer than usual with my customary Daddy neck hug. "Gotta get to school."

"Bye, honey. Have a nice day."

"I will."

Outside, I saw concern on Donovan's face. The way everyone looked at me these days. "Silly? You're never silly."

"Don't fret, Donovan. I was just trying to shake up dinner last night with Reverend Mackintosh. Those dinners can be so boring."

"This I've got to hear."

After giving him a censored version of the dinner party last night, Donovan chuckled, a good sign. "Honestly, Elizabeth, it's a little late for you to start rebelling, isn't it?"

"Oh, whatever. Donovan?"

"Yes?"

"What's going on with Daddy?"

He focused on the road in front of him, considering my question. "What do you mean?"

"Well, Daddy's been acting really weird lately. Like something's going on with him. Donovan, I've got a right to know. If something's going on—and you know about it—then you've got to tell me. He's my daddy!"

Donovan remained quiet. He slowed the car, pulled into a grocery store parking lot, chunked it into park. The sorrow in his brown puppy-dog eyes nearly melted me. Before panic kicked in. "I don't know if it's my place to tell you, Elizabeth—"

"Just tell me, Donovan!"

"Okay, you're right. It's your father, your family. I, uh, I don't think your father's doing very well." The bombshell exploded, shrapnel tearing into my brain.

"Oh, my God! Is he sick?"

"No, no, nothing like that." When he caressed my shoulder, I leaned into him. "As far as I know his health is fine. But, I don't think he's doing very well financially."

As long as I could remember, Daddy had been a financial god, rock solid in his brilliance and business acumen. No way. "That's crazy."

"I hate telling you this. But, I really don't think it is crazy."

Surely, he was wrong. He had to be. But like a good journalist, Donovan never stated anything unless his facts were verified. And the expanding cement block in my stomach agreed.

"Listen to me, Elizabeth." His hand continued stroking my shoulder, like his life depended on it. "Some time back, your dad sorta withdrew at work. When I first started working for him, he was excited— thrilled—to teach me everything he could. And I was more than happy to be his errand boy and coffee guy. But, then his mood...it became darker. Whenever he took a phone call, he closed his doors, something he never used to do. The small talk dried up. He'd say cryptic things to me, on occasion—"

"Cryptic? Like what?"

"He told me 'nothing's ever certain in the financial world'."

"That's just Daddy, Donovan! He's trying to teach you a lesson about investing!"

When he shook his head, morning sunlight glinted off his hair gel. "I don't think so. He kept saying strange things, became much more secretive. And then he took me aside one evening and told me he couldn't continue to pay me. At first, I thought it was something I'd done, maybe my job performance wasn't up to his high standards. He reassured me that wasn't the case. He said there was no one he'd rather have working for him, even told me he thought of me like a son. But he said business is down due to the state of the economy. I told him things would pick up and I'd work for free just so I could learn from him." Donovan grinned, reveling in his undeniably awesome art of brown-nosing before he came crashing back to reality. "He finally agreed—said he'd make my pay retroactive once the economy turns around. But it hasn't yet and he finally told me this week he wouldn't be able to pay me at all."

"Oh, my God." I felt tears building, fought to keep them at bay. No way was I going to school bleary-eyed, mascara running down my cheeks like a cheap floozy.

"But, Elizabeth, please don't let your father know I told you this. He made me swear I wouldn't tell you. He worries about you." He shifted, looked down as if he had something to be ashamed of. "I told him I wouldn't. But you mean the world to me, Elizabeth. So, I felt you should know. I don't like keeping secrets from you."

I bit down on a knuckle, forcing physical pain to engulf my emotional turmoil. "What does it mean? How bad do you think his company's doing?"

"I don't know. Really. But if I had to guess, I'd say it's pretty dire."

Was the world I knew—maybe even took for granted sometimes—about to change drastically? Would I be living next to Marc Dugan, eating dog food, and wearing clothing from second-hand stores? My very future, one I'd envisioned since an early age, suddenly seemed uncertain.

The cement block my stomach cultivated burgeoned into a boulder. It threatened to roll right through me. I needed to hear—to feel—something comfortable and safe. The way I felt when Daddy held me in his arms.

Then something odd happened. The stomach boulder shattered into smithereens, replaced by a steely inner armor forged from the fires of adversity. Here I was, prematurely bemoaning my fate as a food stamp shopper, when I hadn't even thought about Daddy. About what *he* was going through. He'd been harboring this dark secret, the pain obviously eating away at him to the point he'd visibly aged before my eyes. And I'd been totally, selfishly oblivious to it all. I needed to get to the truth. Maybe even see if I could help him.

I'd take Elspeth up on her offer to investigate matters. No matter the outcome.

****

Even though I was a firm believer of both hands on the wheel at all times, Donovan sweetly held my hand for the rest of the trip. We rode in silence, but our unspoken love and support didn't need vocalizing, symbolized by our entwined hands. Not even a fiery car crash could tear us asunder. I guessed it was true what they said: tragedy brought people closer.

We only broke our physical bond when Donovan rushed out to open my car door. Then we resumed our handholding through the parking lot and into school, Hastings's wrath be hanged!

I didn't care.

I felt newly empowered, prepared to face any challenge thrown in my path. Donovan grounded me, standing ready to ignite my fuse and propel me into the path of misfortune and frenemies alike. A rush of excitement filled me when I saw my first challenge awaiting me at my locker.

Kip had an arm slung around Addie's shoulders, his hand uncomfortably close to cupping her breast. Regina and Bettany were nowhere to be seen. I imagined they took a hike when they saw Kip, either loathing to be a third (and fourth) wheel, or flat-out loathing him. I, on the other hand, wasn't going to back down. I had unfinished business with Kip.

"Addie, you look wonderful," I trilled, letting the hallway know that Elizabeth Blackmer was back. Okay, so I overstated it. Addie looked fine—perhaps not wonderful—in her light blue button-down shirt, matching Alice band, and long Bermuda shorts. Bending forward at the hips, we kissed the air between us.

"And you look fantastic as always, Elizabeth." As she admired my wardrobe (white polo shirt, orange cardigan, tan khakis all tastefully tied together with a ribbon belt), I noticed Donovan and Kip exchanging a serious glare.

"Kip." It took all the control I could muster not to launch into immediate name-calling.

"Hey, what's up, guys?" He reached out to Donovan for a guy's one-armed hug, and found himself frozen out. He braved on, nonetheless, with a fist-bump. Hesitantly, Donovan returned it.

"Hey, Kip." Poor Donovan. He just didn't have anger in his arsenal. But I did.

"So, Kip, did you enjoy the party the other night?" I hadn't seen him since the party. Too busy dodging practically everyone yesterday. And I had to tread carefully. I didn't want everyone knowing I'd been drugged. My royalty was riding on the awful poster being perceived as a joke.

Kip, appearing flustered for the first time, maybe ever, floundered around for a coherent reply. "I guess. Just one of those things," he said with a shrug.

Brave, yet foolish, Addie rose to his defense. "It's okay, Elizabeth. Kip told me all about the party. He knew that was you in disguise, um, playing your practical joke and everything." Her lips were spread wide in an agonizing smile, the closest she'd ever come to a battle-stance. I hoped Addie didn't get caught in the path of my friendly fire.

"Oh, really? So, you knew it was me when you hit on me, Kip?"

"Um, yeah, I was just playin' witcha', just playin'. Really." He shot looks all around, a rather pathetic and desperate plea for understanding. "It was a killer disguise. But I knew it was Elizabeth all along."

"Are you sure about that?" Donovan crossed his arms. Being a man of nonviolence, I knew he was restraining himself from tearing Kip a new one.

"Hellz yeah." He pulled Addie toward him, arms snaking all over her body like she was a hostage. "Everybody knows I'm faithful to my girl Addie, here."

"Don't worry, you guys. Kip and I don't have any secrets." Addie looked up into Kip's eyes. Her adulation told me I'd have no luck changing her mind, and I knew better than to try. When it came to affairs of the heart, it was best to stay out. Usually. "Isn't that right, Kippie?"

"Yeppie!"

I hated when they spoke that way.

"Addie, so you think it's okay for your boyfriend…" I sneered for maximum impact. "To go to these parties? Especially without you?"

"Well, yeah. He told me he was going."

Kip nodded. "Everyone knows the Kipster lives for partyin'. What's the big deal?" He shrugged, his shoulders tight in his golf shirt. "Besides, Elizabeth, you were there without Donovan."

"Elizabeth was there campaigning, Kip," said Donovan. "That's a better reason than going to get your drink on! I knew Elizabeth was going."

Donovan's chivalrous lie stoked the fires of my love for him even higher. And hotter. "That's right, Kip," I said. "And just out of curiosity, where were you when I was, ah, getting my picture taken?" I couldn't even fake a smile, didn't even try. Just impossible to do while facing the jerk who may've dosed me.

"Hey, I, um, left shortly after I talked to you. Wasn't much of a party, anyway." He rolled his shoulders as if cranking his douche-moves up again. "It was long past time for me to bounce."

"He came to visit me," said Addie. She couldn't

understand our animosity and truth be told, it did feel like I was picking on her. But she was guilty by association.

"What time was that?" I asked.

"What?"

"What time did he come see you, Addie?"

"Oh, I guess probably about ten thirty."

If this was true, Kip couldn't have taken the photo. Elspeth placed her passing out around eleven or later. But Kip still could've been behind Elspeth's dosing.

"Hey, what's the big deal, guys?" said Kip, sniggering through every word. "We're all buds here, right?"

"I suppose so." Donovan rubbed the back of his neck, almost as if to force his aggression away.

"Cool, cool," said Kip.

"I'll tell you what's not cool!" said the hell-spawn behind me. Charlotte and her ever-present harpies, always turning up at the most inopportune moments. I wished the war on terrorism extended to high school.

When I said, "You, I'm guessing," Kip hooted. Addie dragged him off, even though it looked like he wanted to stay for the fireworks.

"You ratted me out to Hastings!" Charlotte dug her knuckles into her ship-sized hips. "You told him I made those slut posters of you and put them up everywhere."

"First of all, Charlotte, I did not tell Hastings you did it. He probably guessed it was you and got it right. It seems like something totally evil that you'd do—"

"I told Hastings," said Donovan.

"What?" Charlotte turned her ire toward Donovan.

"I told Hastings. It was a mean and cruel thing you did." Not intimidated in the least, Donovan stood his ground.

Charlotte puckered her whorishly red lips into a small nubbin. "Let me just say this, Donovan! I may have made the posters—emphasis on may have, I'm not saying I did. But even if I did, it's your girlfriend who was dressed like a slut at a druggie party. Not me. She's the one who deserves detention!"

"It was a joke, Charlotte," said Donovan. "She was campaigning for—"

"For what? The druggie vote?" Charlotte raised her double chins to the ceiling, screeching like a gibbon. "Everyone knows they don't even vote!" Her sidekick chimpanzees joined in, no doubt preparing to fling their waste at us. "And you, dear Elizabeth. What? Can't you even fight your own battles anymore? Even if you won this battle, the war's just begun. The true victor will be decided next weekend. I wouldn't want to be in your shoes now. Everyone knows you were really passed out at that party. If they don't, I'm on it, and I'll let everyone know. Ta for now."

As she and her big-boned bookends waddled off, I swore I heard the gateway to hell clanging shut behind her, leaving the stench of sulfur and cheap perfume behind.

I turned to Donovan, reached for his hand, and mouthed, "Thank you."

He smiled.

It was at this precise moment I knew I wanted to finally consummate our relationship.

\*\*\*\*

"Okay, so at lunchtime, I want to take some pictures of you." Lance yanked out a bag from underneath his desk and held it aloft. "I've got props."

He displayed a mischievous grin, the kind that taunted *you're in trouble now.*

"What kind of props?"

"You'll see."

Tim Matthews turned around, staring at me expectantly.

"Can I help you?" Cop or no cop, our relationship hadn't changed. I didn't appreciate his constant eavesdropping. "The front of the classroom is that way." I pointed toward the chalkboard. Slinking down in his chair, he faced forward.

Mr. Dawson entered the class, Kevin nipping in behind him. When Kevin tossed me a wave, I responded with an eye roll.

"He likes you," whispered Lance, barely keeping his amusement in register.

"Oh, shut up."

"Okay, class, let's all chill and get down to some bidness. I have your latest assignment graded," said Mr. Dawson. Marching triumphantly down the aisle, he slapped papers down in front of the students, a hint of sadism in his eyes. "Some of you did very well. Gotta give it up to you homies! Others? Well…" He hovered over our table, swaying, glaring down. Lance beamed at his "A" grade. "Ms. Blackmer…" The heart-wrenching "C-" sat in front of me like a blood-filled crescent moon.

Stunned, I turned to Lance, who wisely dropped his smile. "Oh, um, sorry, Elizabeth."

"This is so totally not fair! You're my lab partner! We turned in practically the same findings. How could I possibly get a C-?" Lance didn't say a word, knowing anything he'd say would just make matters worse.

"This totally sucks. Why doesn't he like me? I do all the homework! I hand in—"

"I don't know, Elizabeth, maybe he just…" When I glowered at him, Lance snapped his mouth shut like a mousetrap.

All throughout class, I studied my paper, looking for clues. The lousy grade seemed to take on a life of its own, growing in stature, torturing me. A huge scarlet letter. To make matters worse, Kevin kept stealing glances and grinning at me. What's up with that? Did he find my horrible grade amusing? Or was it something else?

I stormed Mr. Dawson's desk before the bell rang. Couldn't wait any longer. I swept by Kevin, ignoring him completely, and thrust the damning paper in front of Mr. Dawson.

"Mr. Dawson. Why did I get a C-?"

He lifted his eyebrows in a practiced professorial manner. "It's average work, Ms. Blackmer. Nothing better." Kevin squirmed next to him, pretending not to listen in. Yeah, right.

"But this is totally unfair. Lance turned in the same findings and he got an A-! What do you have against me, anyway?" The anger rose in my voice. I needed to find my happy yoga place before I said something I'd regret.

Mr. Dawson sighed and leaned back in his chair. "Ms. Blackmer, sometimes life isn't fair."

That was his explanation? Some kind of hippy nonsense hokum? He was not getting off that easy. "This is—"

"Maybe I gave you an average grade, Ms. Blackmer, because I know you're capable of much better work." He smiled, not a very pleasant sight. His tiny teeth were in such shambles, I wished he'd go back to frowning at me. "Fo' rizzle." He just had to add that. It yanked me out of my serene place and set me on fire.

"Yeah, nobody says that anymore, Mr. Dawson! And I did the stupid assignment the way you—"

His hand shot up like a buyer at Mother's auctions. "Quite finished? Yes, you did the assignment, but as I said, I believe you're capable of much more. I expect much more."

A scream built in my chest, ready to be unleashed. How in the world was it possible to do more than what was asked of me? "I don't understand."

"Ms. Blackmer, I know your type all too well. The important things in your life are all superficial. Money's not really that important, not in the grand scheme of things. Yet money appears to be your motivating factor. I just want you to open your mind, expand your horizons."

More hippy agenda. "But this is environmental science!"

"Yes, it is." Mr. Dawson stared at me blankly before reaching into his desk. "I'll tell you what." He scrawled something down on a piece of paper. A buck said it was recycled paper. "Go see this person."

*Derrick Gyrich* with an address next to it. "What is this?"

"He's a friend of mine. Go visit him, talk to him. Do it and I'll give you some extra credit." A corner of his mouth lifted. "Get your grade raised to a B+."

"But what does he have to do with environmental science?"

"Just go see him. He's cool, he's cool."

"I'll go with you," peeped Kevin.

Great, just what I needed. "My boyfriend will take me, Kevin!"

"You have a boyfriend?" I didn't have time to deal with this nitwit.

I stalked out of the room, making sure I gave the door a good, therapeutic slam. So I was going to have to go hug a tree-hugger, sing *Kumbaya,* whatever.

When the hallway emptied, I let out a loud, angry yowl.

\*\*\*\*

"I don't know, Elizabeth, maybe Dawson wants you to recycle cans with his buddy."

"Lance, I'm so glad I can supply amusement to your otherwise boring life. How long is this going to take, anyway?" With his back against the sun, he fiddled endlessly with the camera. Seemed like I'd been sitting on the picnic table for hours, making me very uncomfortable. Worse than uncomfortable. Mortified. I looked ridiculous in the football helmet and jersey.

"As long as it takes for you to win prom queen." I couldn't fault his logic there. "Now smile."

My jaw muscles ached. I'd been smiling a lot lately. Especially when it didn't seem appropriate. "This is stupid, Lance."

He lowered his camera. "Look, we're trying to show the school you have a sense of humor. Remember? We're going for the jock vote here." He shrugged. "I guess you've already got the druggie vote."

"Not funny, Lance."

"It's sorta funny." Lance snapped a few photos and then whipped out his bag of tricks. Sore jaw or not, it dropped when I saw the contents: dark-framed glasses with a piece of tape wrapped around the center, a slide rule, and a horrid-looking plaid jacket. "Now put these on."

"You have got to be kidding me."

"Hey, nerds vote, too."

"Oh, good God." I ripped off the helmet and jersey and donned the atrocious attire over my regular wardrobe. *Just keep reminding yourself, prom queen, prom queen…*

"You look great," said Lance with a laugh. "Now, say cheese."

"Just get this over with." I glanced around the commons, hoping none of my friends were out. For a beautiful day, the commons seemed unusually abandoned. A few couples strolled across the grass, hands linked. Several stoners slumbered underneath a tree, no doubt dreaming of their next high. From behind the closest oak tree, a figure stepped out. Large, imposing, his signature flannel shirt flapping in the breeze. He sauntered toward us slowly, his dirty tennis shoes kicking out to the sides.

"So, what happened to you at my party, Blackmer?" Dugan grinned. Stubble speckled his face, surrounding his ridiculous soul-patch. "Did you find the drugs you were looking for?"

"Dugan. What brings you out from underneath your rock?" I yanked off the nerd glasses and glowered at him. Lance, atypically quiet and perched at the far end of the picnic table, focused his attention on his camera as if we didn't exist. "And I don't do drugs!" I turned to Lance, who had all but disappeared into his little A/V geek world. "Am I going to have to get a T-shirt that says that?"

"Hey, you're the one who came to my party asking for drugs, dressed like…" Dugan licked his lips. Gross. "Some party slut."

"It was just a joke, Dugan."

"Huh. Some joke. That picture of you passed out wasn't very funny."

I stood and stared up into his cold, gray eyes. "You wouldn't happen to know anything about that, would you?"

"What are you talking about? You said it was your joke. I mean, all I know is it really looked like you passed out. Bad trip or something."

"Yeah, or something," I spat.

"Hey, it doesn't matter to me if you're into drugs. Whatever. Just don't get all high and mighty on me for something you did." His earlier amiable tone slipped away into menace. "I'm the one who should be pissed. You came into my home looking for drugs. I don't have those kinds of parties."

"Not what it looked like to me."

"You know something, Blackmer?" He took a step closer. "If you really want drugs—"

"Why? Are you offering?"

A long pause. "Why don't you just do what every other little rebellious rich girl does and go buy some bath salts? Seems much more your style."

"And what was Charles Durbin's style?"

His smile melted away like drippings from a candle. Lowering his voice, he said, "Once again, I don't know what you're talking about."

I matched his barely audible tone. "I think maybe you do."

Another step closer. So close, his nicotine-tinged breath nearly made me gag. "And I think you should just stick to your wonderful world of prom queens, gay boy-bands, and fashion designer clothes. You don't know what you're talking about. You don't know anything." He stared at Lance, who was still wearing his invisibility cloak, then back at me. His fists curled up. Terrified he might take a swing at me, I still didn't back down. Elspeth would be proud of me.

Finally, without saying a word, he walked away, his bearing tense at first, before relaxing into a typical stoner gait.

"Interesting friends you have," said Lance, finally rejoining my world.

"Yeah, thanks for the back-up."

"What? You kidding me? I'm a nice guy, but I'm not stupid. That animal could eat me up and crap me out before breakfast."

"Lovely."

"Why are you talking to that guy, anyway? What is your damage with everything drugs all of a sudden?"

"I wish I knew." And yes, I really wished I did know. I wanted my old life back. I missed my old life. This scary, new world of drugs and violence was not for me.

"What?"

"Never mind. Let's just say I'm doing research."

"Whatever." Lance shrugged, the threat of Dugan easily rolling off his shoulders. Wished it were that easy for me. "Let's get back to work, unless you want to go across the street to the gas station and get your high on."

"Shut up!" I kicked at his leg, but fast as a

jackrabbit, he hopped to safety.

Nothing was going right today.

**\*\*\*\***

The girls clustered around my locker in their proper places. The shock of yesterday's poster now all but forgotten, things appeared to be stabilizing. Outfits were compared, gossip shared, all of my problems temporarily on hold.

"So that's how you're going to clear Charles's name?" I whirled around. Tina stood before me, her face flushed. Of course. Practically the only person who hadn't weighed in on the poster ordeal yet. "You think this is funny, Elizabeth?" With her shoulders pulled back, she jutted out her chin boldly.

"Tina, it's not what you think."

"I should have known better than to think you'd try and do something good."

"Tina—"

"What's got Tina Bottom-Dweller's panties all up in a bunch?" Regina and Bettany giggled in unison as Addie said it. "Don't you have some lesbian cause to go to or something?"

"I am not a lesbian, bitch!"

The girls "ooohhed."

"What are you going to do, Tina Bottom-Dweller? Have your girlfriend beat me up?" said Addie.

"Why do you have to be such a hater?"

Addie knocked Tina's extended forefinger away with a laugh. "Oh, get over yourself, Tina Bottom-Dweller. You're the hater, not me!"

"That doesn't even make sense. I've never said anything about you stupid girls!"

"Stop it," I screamed. Addie stared at me with a

furrowed brow, uncomprehending. My God. She had no clue what she was doing. She was a monster. And I had created her in my own image. *Frankenbitch's monster.* "Just stop it, Addie. Leave her alone."

"What're you talking about?" Addie hitched a nonchalant thumb toward Tina as if she weren't there. "It's just Tina Bottom-Dweller."

"Stop calling her that."

Addie glowered at me, the sense of betrayal in her eyes overwhelming. "Come on, girls," she huffed. Initially taken aback, Regina and Bettany followed behind her as she paraded down the hall. She turned back and said, "What has gotten into you lately, Elizabeth?" As if my answer didn't matter, she snapped her blond head forward and stalked away.

"Tina, I'm sorry about that."

"Guess I'm used to it." Her casual acceptance seemed far worse than a major hysterical meltdown. I'd never had to face such name-calling, bullying, even. Comparatively speaking, my worries and troubles seemed so ordinary.

"Again, I'm sorry. Really. It won't happen again."

"Whatever. Now, what was that poster all about? I thought you were trying to find out what happened to Charles. Not get wasted!"

"Tina, it's not what it looks like. Believe me, I am trying to find out the truth. I went to that stupid party looking for answers. But someone dosed me."

Tina blinked at me before realization set in. "Oh my God! Are you all right?"

"More or less."

"Who did it?"

"Good question. But I'm willing to bet it's the same

person who drugged Charles. I'm getting closer—"

"Maybe it's time to call the cops."

"That's probably the smart thing to do. But, I don't have any proof or anything, really. And now, since they drugged me, it's personal."

"Who do you think it is? What about that new kid? Tim Matthews?"

I shook my head. "I know it's not him."

"How do you know?"

"I just know. I think I've got it narrowed down to three or four people. I just need him to slip up or strike again."

"Just be careful. Really. I mean, we're not besties or anything, but I don't want anything bad to happen to you." The tentative smile she let slip warmed my heart. "I guess."

"I'll be careful, Tina."

"Thanks for that, by the way. I mean, you standing up for me."

"You're welcome. Let me know if it happens again." She nodded. "Tina?"

"Mmmm?"

"Do you still read clouds?"

Maybe it was the poor fluorescent lighting, maybe not. But Tina suddenly looked older than her years. The twinkle in her eyes was gone, her vibrancy vanished. "No. I put that behind me some time ago."

I watched as she walked away, determinedly holding her head high. No longer a little girl, but a woman who graduated from the school of hard knocks.

Chapter Eleven

*Elizabeth*

"Oh my God, Donovan. This is so way stupid." I took my aggression out on my hair, brushing it with unfettered fury.

Donovan grinned. "Well, you may think it's stupid, but it's extra credit. It can't be all bad. Besides, you need to keep your grades up."

"Whatever." I looked out the car window at the beautiful spring day I should have been enjoying. Instead, I was on my way to see some dumb guy for some dumb reason that made no dumb sense. When I'd called the guy earlier, he sounded curt, as if I was disturbing him. It wasn't like I was thrilled to talk to him or anything. I just wanted to get it over with.

"At least this is something safe you're doing." Donovan's "worry eyes" always worked their magic on me. I drew my hand softly down his cheek.

"My prince." I hadn't yet told him of my decision regarding our relationship. I wanted to keep it a surprise. And I'd chosen the right time. Prom night—after we were crowned king and queen. Nothing seemed more romantic, so perfect.

Barking dogs announced our arrival on Grenada Street. One-level boxes of houses crammed in next to one another, barely enough room for a person to pass between them. Sun and neglect had burned the lawns. The neighborhood looked trapped in a time warp, no car newer than late 90s models.

Gyrich's house sported a dingy gray color, possibly white at one time. Paint chips peeled off the sides like a snake sloughing its skin. A long, weathered porch fronted the house, the railing splintered and ragged. A single, barren tree sat close to the porch, its missing leaves replaced by beer bottles hanging on the branches.

"Gag. Welcome to hell."

Donovan laughed at my misery. "It won't be all that bad," he said, although it sounded like he thought the opposite. "I think."

"It's a beer bottle tree! He probably listens to country music!"

"Elizabeth, do you want me to go in with you?"

"No. This is something I have to do on my own, I guess. I do appreciate giving me a ride, though."

"Anytime."

Small dandelions poked through the cracks in the sidewalk, straining for life. When I stepped up onto the porch, the wooden platform groaned, threatening to drop me into the pits of redneck hell.

A sun-damaged curtain pulled back from the door when I knocked. "Yes?" he said.

"Um, hi, Mr. Gyrich. I'm Elizabeth Blackmer. Mr. Dawson sent me."

Derrick Gyrich studied me. Very pronounced cheekbones and a hawk-like nose gave the impression of the longest face I'd ever seen. Gray speckles dotted his full head of red, wavy hair, matching his unkempt lumberjack's beard.

"So, you're one of Petey's students?"

"Um, yeah." I assumed "Petey" was Mr. Dawson.

"Well, come in, I suppose." The door opened with a creak and he ushered me in. His loud, chaotic Hawaiian shirt stung my eyes. "Sorry, the place is a mess."

Understatement of the year. An overhead fan rattled sheets of paper strewn throughout the room. Three unfinished TV dinner packages sat on the coffee table. A mountain of clothes, predominantly Hawaiian shirts, sat in a corner of the room. Flies buzzed at the windows, seeking escape from a den too gross even for them. A flat-screen TV blared in the corner, a reporter yammering on about Afghanistan.

"It's fine." And I was a liar!

"Let me get a good look at you. Elizabeth, right?" I nodded. His gaze roving up and down my body creeped me out. *Nice extra credit, Petey!* Suddenly his head rocked back and his eyes grew into huge ovals. "Oh, huh."

"Ah, is something wrong, Mr. Gyrich?"

He shook his head, almost as if trying to dismiss a nightmare. "No, no. Nothing's wrong. And it's Derrick, by the way. I'm not that old."

*Well, yes, you are. Like fifty or so.* "Okay."

"Have a seat." He waved across the war-torn room at nothing in particular.

"Where?"

With a sigh, he snatched up an armful of papers off the sofa. I sat on the edge of the sofa, hoping the scary, inexplicable stains wouldn't rub off on me. He crashed down next to me.

"Now, why are you here?" He flung an arm over

the back of the sofa, intensely scrutinizing me with psychiatrist eyes.

"I have no idea."

"Fine. Tell me about yourself."

"Well, I'm Elizabeth Blackmer, Clearwell High senior, hopeful prom queen." He seemed less than impressed. "I have a great boyfriend, Donovan Goode. He's, ah, out in the car." I pointed toward the street, hoping to put the kibosh on any serial killer intentions Gyrich might harbor. "I get good grades—except for Mr. Dawson's class. I'm going to Dartmouth—"

"What are you going to study?"

"Business, finance, possibly politics—"

He smiled, his jaw stretching to the point of snapping like a rubber band. "Now I know why you're here. Petey's done it again. Every time he gets on his high horse, he sends me his self-centered, overachievers to straighten out."

"I'm not self-centered," I said in a near-whisper.

"Well, Petey must think you are. Otherwise, you wouldn't be here." He sighed, staring out the dust-covered window. "He really owes me. Anyway, tell me something, Elizabeth. What are your true goals in life?"

"My goals?"

"Yeah. You know, what are you striving for? What do you want your life to mean?"

"I guess I'd like to be wealthy, have a great career, and maybe even become famous. Live in an awesome mansion with my adoring husband and three children—"

"Three children?"

I nodded firmly. "That's what I want in life."

"I see." He ran his fingers through his mess of a beard, spelunking for hidden treasures, I supposed. "Let me tell you something about myself. Many years ago, I was quite like you. I had big dreams, high hopes of being rich. To live the life of a king!" He threw his arms up in the air dramatically, madly thrashing them about. I was one step away from running for the door. "And I achieved my goals. I went to Harvard, graduated at the top of my class. I went to law school. I became a celebrated—and very wealthy—corporate lawyer for one of the biggest companies in the world. I was stinking, filthy rich. And I thought I had it all."

"Doesn't sound too bad." I stared around his hovel in disbelief. Either he was a liar or he really sucked at investing his money.

"Well, that's what I thought." He pulled his legs up underneath him and leaned in toward me. "But then, I got some news that ripped my world apart. I was diagnosed as being HIV positive."

"Oh…*oh!* I'm sorry."

He chuckled, blowing off my empathy with a wave of his hand. "It's okay, Elizabeth. But at the time, I didn't think it was okay. I began to reevaluate my life, thinking about what's truly important and what wasn't. It was time to do some housecleaning."

Yeah, too bad he didn't start here in his house.

"For all my wealth, my money, my real estate, my business successes and prowess in the courtroom, none of it seemed that important anymore. Just what had I accomplished? I made myself rich, sure, but sometimes at the expense of others. And I made a greedy, soulless corporation richer in its quest to squash the little guy." He brought his fist down hard into his palm. "I asked myself, is that all there is to life? I became painfully aware of those who I'd previously taken for granted, those who weren't as fortunate as me, living in poverty and despair. It was time to help others. I quit my job, donated my fortune to charities. I ended up here—Kansas City, Kansas—working at a shelter for battered women." He presented his hands in front of me as if showing off how empty they were. "Living the dream," he added with an ironic snort.

"You really gave it all up?"

"I did. And I haven't regretted it. Ever."

"Huh."

"And that's why you're here." He closed one eye and pinpointed me with his finger. "Petey sent you here because he sees you as bright, intelligent, highly motivated, but you've set your sights on all the wrong goals in life. It's time for you to open your eyes. There's much more to life than some greedy pipedream, built on ludicrous notions of what constitutes success. It's time to consider…the world." He paused, waiting for me to comment.

"What's wrong with pursuing wealth? I mean, it's what I've been taught all my life."

"Well, sure, it doesn't mean it's wrong. For some people, it's what's best for them, I imagine. But I think Petey sees something special in you, Elizabeth. Maybe he thinks that with your skills, your intelligence, your drive, it'd be a shame to waste your talents in the corporate world. I'm just asking you to think about what I've said."

"I will." Frankly, it surprised me I was already considering what he said. My life had been in such topsy-turvy turmoil of late, my head felt ready to explode. And now this man had given me something new to think about, something that was contrary to everything I'd learned, everything I'd dreamed about. Yet he made sense. In a sorta weird way.

"There's something else I want to ask you about, Elizabeth. I was born with a special power. Before you think I'm nuts, let me explain. It's a silly power. Something that has never been very useful, really. But, I can see auras."

"What?"

"I can see a person's aura shimmering about them. It doesn't happen all the time. And I can't control when I do it, but I can see them. And auras tell me a great deal about people. My question is..." He sat back and winked. "Why do you have two auras?"

"Ah, huh." Well, if he could tell me about his special powers, I supposed I could trust him with mine. "Okay, now you're really going to think this is crazy, but..." As I told him about my strange relationship with Elspeth, to my surprise he responded with genuine interest and curiosity. "Okay, now which one of us is nuts?"

"You're not crazy, Elizabeth. I believe you. Remember, I can see both of your auras. And I must say, they're both incredibly strong, burning bright and passionate. I think Petey made the right decision about you. You can go far. Just do it."

I smiled. "Thanks, Derrick. I appreciate it."

"No problem. But do me a favor and be careful about this drug business."

"Of course. But will you do me a favor in return?"

"Sure, name it."

"Please keep what I told you a secret. Don't let Petey, um, Mr. Dawson, know about it, okay?"

He laughed. "No problem there! Petey still doesn't

believe I can see auras. Scientists." He blew out a raspberry as he rose to his feet. "Okay, I think I've said everything I have to say."

Practically on autopilot, I tossed my arms around him and hugged. Obviously shocked—almost as much as me—he took a moment to respond. "Derrick, how long do you have?" I asked quietly. "I mean, well, you know."

Laughing, he broke our embrace. "Elizabeth, I'll probably live a full and long life. Being HIV positive is not the death sentence everyone once thought it was. Maybe you should pay more attention in science class."

"Are you kidding me? I go to a Kansas school. They don't cover HIV!"

He let out a loud guffaw. "Yeah, tell me about it. Makes me wonder what I'm even doing in Kansas. I guess I thought it'd be a challenge."

"Is it?"

"Oh, yeah." He walked me toward the door. "Hey, Elizabeth?"

"Hmmm?"

"You're welcome to visit any time you'd like. You know, just to catch up. And I'd really like to know where you end up and how you're doing."

I offered him another hug. "I'll be back."

****

The next morning was a strange one, one that would end in a totally unexpected and heart-wrenching manner. Just not for me, for once.

Teachers herded us down the hallway to our yearly anti-drug rally. Maybe if it'd been held several months ago, Charles Durbin would still be alive. Maybe not. The anti-drug rallies seemed only to preach to the converted, the druggies taking great pleasure in deriding the message.

Donovan reached for my hand, and squeezed it tight. He always knew what I needed. Ever since I defended Tina, Addie and the girls had been giving me the cold shoulder. I felt bothered my friends had abandoned me, but the more I thought about it, the more I wondered just what kind of friends they were. Watching their cruel behavior the day before made me see them in a new light. I supposed they'd always been like that, and I just chose to turn a blind eye, having been caught up in my own life.

Lately, though, it seemed like God or the Fates—or whatever—was conspiring to force me to reevaluate things. The awful poster, the possibility of Daddy not doing well financially, the reappearance of Tina, my meeting with Derrick, and my efforts to clear Charles Durbin's name…everything seemed to happen at once and it could not be just coincidence. I'd been sent one giant, flashing, neon message meant for my eyes only. *Don't be so selfish.*

I noticed Lance had already been hard at work. My "nerd poster" hung over a row of lockers, the words *"Elizabeth Blackmer—Prom Queen with a Sense of Humor"* underneath it. Most of the students giggled at it in passing. I just hoped they were laughing with me and not at me.

Farther down the hall, Charlotte and her thugs gawked at the football player variation of my poster, clucking like hens. Upon seeing me, Charlotte snapped her fingers and said, "Nice try, darling. But it's not going to work. Everyone knows what you're all about these days."

Before I could launch into retaliatory action, Donovan tugged me back. "Don't let them get to you," he whispered—right, as usual. They were not worth my energy. I strolled by, ignoring them. But I couldn't help myself. I swiveled around and mouthed "Bitch!" Okay, maybe they did get to me. A little.

When we entered the gym, Mr. Hastings and several coaches prodded us up the bleachers like cattle. Merry laughter and raucous conversation filled the air. Hardly what one would expect from an anti-drug rally. While we stalled on the steps, Kevin Bartholomew rose from his seat.

"Hi, Elizabeth."

Trapped and nowhere to go with the line of students not moving. "Kevin," I said. "This is my boyfriend, Donovan. Donovan, this is Kevin, my neighbor. You know, the one I told you about."

Immediately shifting into politician mode, Donovan smiled, a smile guaranteed to win the hearts of everyone across the country. Donovan finished their handshake with a triumphant hand on top. "So you're the neighbor. Nice to meet you, Kevin." The words were there, but Donovan delivered them with an uncustomary frostiness. Kevin winced as Donovan bore down, their hands still locked in a death-grip. *Boys.*

"And you're, ah, Elizabeth's boyfriend." Kevin looked shell-shocked, confused. Just what was Elspeth not telling me?

"That's right," said Donovan, his response a forceful declaration of his status.

"Hmmm, okay." Kevin squirmed, attempting to reclaim his hand. "Well, it was nice, um, meeting you." Donovan finally released his victorious hold. Kevin flopped down onto the bleacher, shaking his shaggy head.

I slipped my hand around Donovan's arm, urging him up the stairs. To the left, Donnie Heidenreich sat with several other underachievers, laughing at something no doubt inane, yet somehow profound, in their drug-addled brains. Several rows behind them sat Tim Matthews, surveying the crowd in a very obvious manner. How his cover hadn't been blown yet seemed like some kind of miracle. Towering over the other students, Marc Dugan, fashioning his seemingly endless wardrobe of flannel, scowled at me. *Hail, hail, the gang's all here.*

We sat close to the top of the bleachers. On the gym floor, the school band churned out a wildly inappropriate rah-rah march, unaware they were supposed to be playing as a unit. Cheerleaders worked the crowd, totally clueless grins spread across their spray-tanned faces. The one male cheerleader, embarrassing in his red and black form-fitting outfit, desperately tried to enthuse a largely disinterested audience.

Looking out over the sea of heads, I saw Kip, Addie, Bettany, and Regina making their way up the opposite bleacher. Their shrill squeals of delight at seeing whom they eventually sat with nearly sent me ballistic. Charlotte and her two slutlets scooted over, making room for their new friends. Charlotte stood and wiggled her hot-dog fingers at me. Tempted as I was to wiggle one particular finger back at her, I wouldn't stoop to her crass level. I could not believe my traitorous, so-called friends. I bit my lower lip, forcing myself not to shed tears. Donovan wrapped an arm around me, holding me tight.

"Everything will be okay," he said.

"Promise?"

"I promise."

"Testing! Testing!" bellowed Mr. Hastings. The microphone squelched back, prompting many hoots from the students. Hastings scowled at the room and continued. "Quiet down, students. Now, as you know, it's time for our annual anti-drug rally." Cheers erupted as if entertainment was to be expected. "This year—thanks to Clearwell's Drug-Free Club—led by..." Hastings consulted a note card. "Tina Bottoms—"

Addie yelled out, "Tina Bottom-Dweller!" The crowd broke out into catcalls, several members taking up the rallying cry of "Tina Bottom-Dweller!" Had I been sitting in the other bleachers, I would've slapped Addie, not caring what others thought.

"Quiet!" Hastings's evil glare promised a boatload of detentions. "Tina Bottoms has arranged for a very special anti-drug rally this year." He pointed at several people seated in folding chairs behind him, obviously unaware which one was Tina. Tina stood, pulled a hand out of her pocket, and waved. I clapped as loud as I could, never minding the manners. She practically dove back for the shelter of her chair, relieved her moment of fame had ended.

"This year, Ms. Bottoms has arranged for several parents from across the country to join us and tell us of their experiences of having lost loved ones to drugs." He once again passed his hand over the collection of people behind him. "Now, I want every one of you to give them your full attention and be polite. They're here doing you a favor, and rudeness will not be tolerated!"

Too bad Mr. Hastings didn't adhere to his own anti-rudeness rule.

Like a good game show host, he switched gears and said, "And now, here they are. Give them a round of applause." The crowd did as ordered. Feeling the need to get one last word in, Hastings returned to the microphone and said, "And don't do drugs!"

I had a hard time paying attention to the sad testimonials while Charlotte, Addie, and company flaunted their newly forged alliance in front of me. After forty-five minutes or so, the stories all started blending together: tragic tales of the loss of sons, daughters, and friends, to drug use.

Then a woman, possibly in her early sixties, took the stage. Obviously gorgeous at one point, she still looked handsome in an aristocratic way. Long jet-black hair flowed down to her waist with one silver streak on the side, a badge of honor for the suffering she'd lived through.

"Hello, my name's Cheryl," she said, her voice strong, belying her small body. "I lost my daughter to drugs in the 80s."

I felt a sharp pang in my head, jolting me upright on the bleacher. Donovan placed his hand on my back, gently massaging it. Another bang, a frying pan slamming into my brain. I gritted my teeth, trying to ignore the pain, fervently hoping to not experience another drug flashback.

"She was only seventeen when she died. She was always somewhat wild, prone to adventurous behavior, which more often than not, got her into trouble." A few laughs from the like-minded troublemakers in the audience. And my head kept pounding as if a miner had pick-axed his way out of my brain.

The pain gave way to sounds. An inner voice. Someone desperately trying to gain my attention by rapping on my mind's window. *Elspeth.*

"But one night, my daughter took it too far. After a big night of partying, she was found the next morning, dead in an alley behind a New York nightclub. Alone."

*"Oh my God, Elizabeth! Let me out! Please, please let me out! Let me out now, Elizabeth! Please! Please! Please!"* Elspeth's voice gained in volume until it sounded like she was screaming right into my ear. I'd never experienced such incredible passion from her before.

The black-haired woman, who had been so strong and commanding up until now, released an anguished sob. "That was the short, sad life of my daughter Elspeth." My *God.* Elspeth's mother.

*"Please, Elizabeth! Let me out! I have to see her! Please...please..."* Elspeth's voice slowed to a crawl, her voice harsh. I could feel her tears sprinkling onto my brain, a warm, sad shower of sorrow.

I lowered my head and closed my eyes. *Okay, Elspeth...*

\*\*\*\*

*Elspeth*

The auditorium blurred. I snapped to attention, my eyes moistened with tears.

*Mom.*

Fighting the urge to shrug Donovan's damn hand off, I let it stay. The support kinda felt good.

*Mother.*

I could not believe it. She looked older, more tired, but undeniably the woman who had raised me, fought with me, loved me…whom I had let down. Tears rolled down my cheeks, Elizabeth's makeup now a mess. Donovan held my hand. I leaned into him, hiding my face on his shoulder. Pure agony watching Mom cry. Every time I dared to peek between my fingers, my tears started up again. I covered my mouth to stifle my sobs.

I only picked up sporadic words from her story— *our* story. My mind raced in numerous directions like children scattering on a playground. Unable to focus, I played out every possible scenario under the sun. More than anything, I wanted to speak with her one final time, maybe even touch her. Give her words of comfort. Anything. Something. Let the caretakers of happy limbo land be damned. I was doing it.

Mom finished her speech to a quiet crowd. Her shoulders shuddered as she took a deep breath and thanked the audience for having her. I jumped to my feet, cheering like a loon. The audience followed suit, the applause thunderous. Hastings commandeered the microphone, shouting something about getting to class. I pushed my way through the students and launched down the steps ahead of the crowd. I heard Donovan calling out, but he'd have to wait. Mom sat down in a folding chair, wiping away the last of her tears.

The first one off the bleachers, I practically vaulted onto the gym floor. I blew by Hastings, no time for jackasses, and made my way toward Mom.

Standing in front of her, I said, "Excuse me? Mrs. Chambers?"

She looked up, startled. Her red-rimmed eyes relaxed into the kind, loving look I used to take for granted. The look I thought I'd never see again. "Yes?"

She stood.

"I just…wanted to tell you…how much your story touched me." How I longed to hop into her arms and be held. And cry. And hear her soothing words, telling me things would be all right. *Things always get better,* she used to say.

"Well, thank you. But may I ask how you knew my last name? I didn't give it in my presentation."

"Um, Tina Bottoms told me your name before the rally. She said your story was really strong."

She smiled sweetly. "How nice. What's your name?"

"Elizabeth. Elizabeth Blackmer." I held my hand out to her. She accepted it. I didn't want to let go.

"Have you lost someone to drug use, Elizabeth?"

"No. Not really." She stared at me quizzically. "But your story touched me. I want to do something about the drug problem here at school." I shifted nervously, staring at my feet while swallowing the lump in my throat.

"That's very admirable."

"Thank you." I didn't know any subtle way to ask about Dad, so I just forged in. "How is your husband doing, Mrs. Chambers? I mean, with the death of your daughter?"

She averted her eyes, never a good sign. "Mr. Chambers is no longer with us, I'm afraid."

"Oh."

She smiled sorrowfully, momentarily retreating to the past. "It was just a few years after losing Elspeth. The doctors said he died of a heart attack. I think it was a broken heart. I know that's not a very scientific explanation, but he never really recovered from…"

"Oh, I'm so, so sorry. I'm sorry." *Dad.* My tears poured out. My hands flew to my face, shaking like an alcoholic with tremors. "I'm really sorry."

Mom stared at me, no doubt wondering what was up with this psycho. But she reached her arms out toward me. I fell into them and burrowed in. She stroked my hair, whispering "Shhh" and "It'll be all right." The two of us stood entwined, both crying rivers. The hug lasted forever and still not long enough. For one beautiful moment, frozen in time, nothing had changed.

"There, there, Elizabeth. It'll be all right. My goodness, you certainly are taking this personally. Shhh, shhh. It's not your fault."

But it was. It truly was. And I wanted to tell her so. But I couldn't. "Mrs. Chambers?"

"Hmmm?"

"You know your daughter loved you, right?"

She stepped back, blinking, her mascara running down her cheeks. "I know that, dear, I know that."

"I mean, even if she was wild, she was just confused, young, but she never stopped loving you or her dad."

Mom tilted her head like a dog hearing a curious sound. "I know. It's very nice, if not a little strange for you to say so."

I managed a small chuckle. "I guess. It's just that your story really moved me." And there I was again, repeating myself.

"You know something? It's funny."

"What's funny?"

"Oh, well, you remind me of her in a way. Elspeth, that is."

I tried to raise my eyebrows, but my eyes felt too swollen to comply. "Really?"

"Something about your spirit, or maybe the way you carry yourself." She opened her purse and reached for a tissue. I picked up the faintest, but most familiar of scents. A mixture of cosmetics and tissues, the comforting way Mom's purse always smelled. "Oh, I'm just being silly. I get pretty worked up over these things, too." She blotted her eyes with the tissue.

"It's okay, Mrs. Chambers. Really."

"I honestly don't know why I'm boring you with all this. There isn't a moment I wished it would never have happened. I'd give anything to have my little girl back, but…" She paused, taking her time to form her thoughts. "It hasn't all been for naught. Some good has come from it. The fact I'm reaching students like you, it almost makes it…"

Seeing her struggling with her words, I saved her with another hug. I could have done this all day. I had a lot of time to make up for. "I know, Mrs. Chambers, I know." We stood for some time, locked in our slow dance—she, holding a girl who reminded her of her dead daughter and me, desperately clinging to my mother. "You know, she's proud of you."

"What?"

"I mean, I'm sure your daughter is proud of you for what you're doing. Talking to students and everything."

"That's a very nice thing to say, dear. Believe me, it means the world to me."

"No problem."

"Okay, Elizabeth. It's been a real pleasure meeting you. But I must be going." She smiled. "We're off to another school."

"Goodbye, Mrs. Chambers. It was great meeting you, too."

One final hug—one for the road. It'd have to tide me over for some time.

Before she left the auditorium, she turned toward me, waving.

I waved back and whispered, "Goodbye, Mom."

Chapter Twelve

*Elspeth*

"Are you sure you're okay, Elspeth?"

"I'm fine. Thanks for asking." I turned toward Elizabeth, both of us lying on her bed. This softer side of Elizabeth was unusual; it rarely surfaced.

"Well, I know it was tough. I just wish you didn't have to go through that today."

I sat up, resting on my elbow. "Are you kidding me? I've wanted to see my mom for thirty years now! I wanted that more than anything. Yeah, it was tough, but..." I shrugged. "I got a little closure. Maybe Mom did, too. In a weird way."

"Yeah." Elizabeth reached across and timidly patted my shoulder. "Sorry about your dad."

"Me, too."

After my draining encounter with Mom, I'd sought solace in the dark confines of the nether regions, letting Elizabeth have her body back. I'd had more than enough mental trauma for one day.

But now there was work to do. Looking forward to it, too. Nothing cleared the mind better than some down-and-dirty action. "Speaking of dads...you sure you want to find out what's going on with your dad?"

Elizabeth winced. "Am I ready? Probably not. But I have to know. And I don't see him telling me what's going on any time soon. He's always been secretive about his work."

"Or maybe he just didn't think you were ever interested enough." Yeah, I took a cheap shot. But the best way to keep my emotions at bay was by donning armor forged of sarcasm and defensiveness. "Sorry," I quickly added.

"As much as I hate to say it, I think you're right. Kinda. I always did think his work was boring. But we have to do this. I need to know."

"Okay. I just hope you don't find out something you don't want to, Elizabeth."

"Yeah, me, too. Are you sure *you're* up for this?"

"Oh, yeah!" I jacked my leather-clad arm into the air. "Nothing like a good bit of skullduggery to blow out the cobwebs. Believe me, I need this."

"Okay. What's the plan?"

"All right. There's no way I can access your dad's laptop at your house. He pretty much keeps it under lock and key—"

"How do you know this?"

"Um, I did a little preliminary investigation myself a couple of nights ago." I grinned, hoping to disarm her.

"You did what?"

"It's not important right now. Okay, so, I'm going to have to try and get into his computer at his office. That's probably where he has all his important crap, anyway." Elizabeth nodded. "Now, how are we going to get in?"

"Well, Daddy's building has a security guard on the bottom floor who's kinda psycho about letting people in or out without signing in. But he knows me. It's five o'clock. If we go now, I can probably just tell him I'm visiting Daddy."

"Okay, cool."

"But there's another night watchman who checks out the floors around the clock. You'll have to watch out for him. And Daddy keeps his office locked. How are you going to get in?"

"Leave that to me. I've got my ways."

"Whatever, Elspeth. Just be careful and don't get caught."

"Never."

"Never? Never to what? Being careful or getting caught?"

"Ah, semantics. Never had much use for them. Did you get me the flash-drive? One with a lot of capacity?"

"Yeah." Elizabeth flicked it open like a switchblade knife. "So you're planning on downloading his hard-drive?"

"Uh-huh. Or at least all the files that look mysterious."

"And what will we do with the files once you get them? I mean, neither one of us really knows about the business or anything."

"Got it covered, Elizabeth."

"How?"

"Um, Kevin says he knows a guy who should be able to make sense of the files. Decrypt 'em if necessary."

Elizabeth's eyes opened wide before narrowing into small, furious slits. "What? And when did you talk to Kevin about this?" She spat out his name, like he fell below her contempt.

"Ah, I, um, saw him a couple of nights ago."

"And when were you going to tell me this, Elspeth?"

Elizabeth jumped to her feet, glaring down at me in her best parental fashion.

"Today. Now."

"What else are you not telling me?"

"I might've accidentally kissed Kevin."

"Nooo! My God, this just gets worse and worse!" She placed her fingertips on her temples, rubbing them madly. "You can't do that, Elspeth. It's my body! What if Donovan finds out?"

"Relax. Donovan's not going to find out. Unless you tell him." Okay, I did feel like a heel for kissing Kevin. But it seemed well worth it. "Sorry, Elizabeth. I'll be more…considerate."

"You'd better be!"

"Let's get to work. Make sure you pack my clothes." My dark attire was better suited for stealthy night work as opposed to Elizabeth's all-the-colors-of-the-rainbow wardrobe. This time I picked my high-top tennis shoes instead of my usually favored Doc Martens or leather boots. Not as stylin' kicks, but much better for covert operations.

Elizabeth sighed deeply and laid down next to me, both of us closing our eyes, waiting for Dream Space to kick us out.

****

*Elizabeth*

Before leaving, I asked Mother if Daddy had come home from work. I needn't have bothered. He never returned home before eight o'clock anymore. I kissed Mother goodbye, told her I was going to Donovan's, and set out for downtown.

I pulled into the parking garage beneath Daddy's building. The parking attendant had already fled for the evening—the gate sat up, admittance free to night owls. Standing on the sidewalk, I looked up at all twenty-four stories of the red-bricked structure, one of the tallest buildings downtown. Old as the hills, built maybe way back in the forties, I'd always wondered why Daddy still worked in such a decrepit building. Obviously, he could've afforded to upgrade. He once told me he wanted to stay put because he was old school, and it was traditional for investment analysts to work downtown or something like that.

Actually, the ancient age of the building might work to our advantage. There weren't any security cameras and gizmos; just a couple of crotchety guards, dogged in their determination to watch television, who scowled at anyone who dared enter. Unlike the newer skyscrapers that entombed workers in tightly sealed, white-collar coffins of glass and concrete, this building featured windows that opened up. Rusted fire escape platforms and ladders clung to the north and south sides of the building—relics of an ancient past—where people could actually, you know, escape to safety. Didn't know why "progress" did away with them.

I entered the rotating door. Immediately, the walrus behind the reception desk accosted me. Startled, he kicked his feet off his desk and stood, his potbelly threatening to overturn the various knick-knacks covering the desk. "Is that you, Elizabeth?"

"Hi, Tommy. Just here to visit Daddy." I hoisted up the sack containing Elspeth's clothing as a visual aid. "Is he still here?"

Tommy scrambled to check his computer screen, and double-checked his handwritten logs. "These damn computers," he said, his mustache huffing underneath his breath. "Oh, sorry."

"It's okay," I said. "I've heard worse."

"Looks to me like he's still up there. Yup."

"Thanks." I headed for the elevators.

"Hey! You want me to ring him and tell him you're coming up?"

"No thanks. I'm gonna surprise him." I punched the up button.

"Well, okay then." Tommy plopped back down in his chair, the air wheezing out of the tortured cushion. "Let him know I asked."

"I will." I hit the button again. These ancient elevators always took forever. Finally, announcing its lengthy arrival with a "ding", the doors slid open. I entered, staring at myself in the mirror surrounded by baroque, nearly gothic carvings. *Elevator of the damned.*

The numbers slowly lit up and hopscotched back and forth, crawling up the panel until landing on lucky number twenty-one. When the doors pulled back, I stuck my head out, looking in both directions. Finding the hallway empty, I made my way to the women's restroom at the end of the hall.

I kept the lights turned off and flicked on my small penlight. Sitting down in the last stall, I closed my eyes…

\*\*\*\*

*Elspeth*

I dreamed. I never dreamed. It seemed one of limbo's unspoken rules was that you were in either limbo or the real world; your brain was never allowed to travel on its own. Whenever I crossed the ocean of limbo, I was either asleep or aware of Elizabeth's actions, an unwilling observer to her rich-girl antics.

But this felt different. A full on, honest to God dream.

I strolled through a New York park where my dad used to take me when I was a child, dressed in my full black leather duds. Birds appeared comfortable in my presence, surrounding me, chirping their greetings. Friggin' Snow White. A group of balloons sat bunched to the limb of a tree, oddly unmoving in the breeze-free air. I walked along the sidewalk, and several people with blurs for faces stood still as statues as I passed them. I spotted the bench Dad and I used to spend hours on, watching people. Sitting down, I stretched out my legs. Jaunty, repetitious music repeated endlessly as if from a broken merry-go-round. I closed my eyes, letting the sun wash over my face.

"Hi, Elspeth," said a familiar voice.

The sun scorched white light into my eyes when I opened them. A shadowy figure hovered over me. "Hi."

"Beautiful day," said Dad as he casually sat next to me. He looked elegant in a tailored dark suit, something I was sure he never owned. Used to be more of a jeans and T-shirt kinda dad. Even though he didn't look a day older than when I last saw him, he still pretended to have more hair than nature granted. Thin strands of hair stretched across the top of his baldpate, fooling no one.

"Dad." I reached across and hugged him.

"How have you been, Elspeth?" His warm smile blazed brighter than the burning sun.

"Okay. Weird, but I'm fine."

He nodded and chuckled, the dad-like chuckle that was a cross between condescension and true, openhearted love. "I've been keeping up with you, you know."

"Really?"

"Really. You're something else, you know that?"

"I guess." I felt like a young girl again, giving myself over to my dad's infinite wealth of knowledge and rock-solid protection. "Dad, I'm sorry for the, you know, pain I caused you and Mom."

"I know." When he held his hand out, a blue bird alit on his fingers. He stroked its head before releasing it into the still air. "But I couldn't be more proud of you than I am now."

"Thanks." We sat in silence for a moment. Dad began humming a lullaby he used to sing to me. Soon, we were both singing gloriously at the top of our lungs. As the song came to an end, I scooted closer to him, resting my head on his shoulder. "I miss you, Dad."

"I miss you, too, honey." He stroked my hair. "Your mom misses you as well. I understand you saw her today."

"Yeah. Dad?"

"Hmmm?"

"Are you happy? Where you are now, I mean?"

He jutted out his jaw, his lips tucked inward. Then he grinned. "I think so. I miss you and Mom. But I'll see you both again."

"Really?"

"Really, *really.*" Fatherly concern darkened his face. Now that look I didn't miss so much. "Elspeth, please be careful with what you're doing. Things are not as they seem. And they're about to get very perilous."

"I know. I've been hearing a lot of that lately. But I'm always careful. I learned my lesson the hard way, as you know."

He laughed. "Okay. You always were a tough nut. Nothing's going to stop you from doing what you feel you need to do. But, please take my warning seriously. Others have deemed it dangerous enough to send me to warn you. And you're much too valuable to the future to lose right now."

"Huh." I knew better than to ask him who the "others" were or what the future held for me. I'd played the game with the limbo masters, getting nowhere. "Dad, is this real?"

He cupped my face in his hands. "What is real, Elspeth? You're involved with two different realities. Can anyone really say what's real?"

"Yeah, thanks for the answer. Spoken like a true politician."

"Do you think this is real, Elspeth?"

"I'd like to believe it is."

"Then it is."

"I love you, Dad."

"Love you, too, pumpkin." He kissed my cheek, releasing me from the dream.

****

*Elspeth*

I woke up on a hard toilet seat in the dark, my cheeks wet with tears. I'd thought that well had long run dry this morning, but it hadn't. Apparently, I was a miracle of moisture, akin to the weeping statue of Mary. Still slightly groggy, I smiled at the fond memory of my dad's visit, already sadly fading away as dreams do.

Reality came crashing back as I remembered what I had to do. I shook away my sleep, stood up, and stretched. A paper sack fell off my lap, plopping onto the floor.

*Right.* I turned the penlight on, set it on top of the toilet paper box, and changed. Then I stuffed Elizabeth's clothes into the sack. Elizabeth's cell phone read nine-thirty on the dot. Probably due to the dream, I'd been out longer than planned. That was all right, though, as everyone—excluding the two security guards—should have cleared out by now. I stashed the sack behind the toilet and left the bathroom.

Darkness blanketed the main corridor except for a red Exit sign at the far end. I scooted down the hallway, checking out the office numbers as I zipped by. As per Elizabeth's directions, the office numbered 2112 sat in the farthest north corner. Blackmer Investment Consulting, Inc., stated the gold plate next to the door.

Penlight in mouth, I pulled out a nail file and a very small screwdriver and set to work on the lock. Straining to hear the small clicks, I twisted the knob. The door swung open, the creak at the end of its journey sounding loud in the empty office. Several black chairs and a matching leather sofa flanked a huge, exotic-looking potted plant. Straight ahead, the receptionist's desk anchored the room, immaculate and ordered. Above the desk, a large photograph of Elizabeth's dad, looking grim and mean as ever, hung on the wall. *Who would invest with this guy?* Various plaques and awards surrounded his narcissistic photo, like arrows pointing toward his glaring success. Several smaller offices occupied the left side, while on the right I spotted a single closed door. My penlight lit upon another plaque, golden glints shining like tiny stars in the dark night skies. *Harold Blackmer, President.* And another lock. *Sigh.*

Since the lock appeared to be as old as the building, I had no trouble getting the door open. Shutting the door behind me, I saw the computer resting atop his desk. Realizing this sort of dexterous work might require more luminosity, I boldly snapped on the over-head light, the fluorescents taking their time to flicker into existence.

I sat down at the desk and turned on the computer. When it asked me for a password, I momentarily panicked. *Why in hell didn't Elizabeth tell me about this?*

Drumming my fingers on the desktop, a thought occurred. What did Elizabeth's dad always call her, even giving her a personalized license plate with the pet name upon it? Easy enough. *Princess.* And gross. The screen blanked out before welcoming me back. Got it in one! I nearly let out an elated whoop before I reined in my premature victory dance.

I stuck the flash-drive into the USB portal, waiting for it to appear onscreen. The deadly dull computer courses I had taken in limbo finally paid off. I studied the hard-drive, wondering where to begin. Endless folders for "Investors", "Potential Investors", "Questionable Investors" nearly knocked me comatose. The list went on and on. Recalling the documents I had discovered the other night, I clicked on a folder entitled "Offshore Investing." Opening a sample file, the results slowly crawled up on the screen—nothing more than oblique symbols, numbers. Total gibberish. Encrypted. Well, that generally meant secrets.

*Oh, the hell with it.* I started downloading the entire hard-drive, encrypted or not.

Twenty more minutes. Twenty excruciating, intense minutes was how long the damn computer said it would take. I stood up, pacing nervously. I rifled through the desk drawers, looking for other incriminating evidence, but, really, just trying to stay busy. In the bottom drawer (easily picked, of course), I found several letters from the United States Securities and Exchange Commission. Even though most of it flew over my head, the general gist appeared to be that Elizabeth's dad would soon be under investigation for fraud. At least that was what I thought they were jabbering about. I wanted to take the letters, thought better of it, and snapped a few photos with Elizabeth's phone.

Something clattered and then jangled in the hallway. I stiffened with terror. My heart tore at my chest. I held my breath, listening for follow-up sounds. A door opening and shutting?

Eight minutes left to download the hard-drive.

I ran to the light switch, clawed at it, and shut the office into darkness. The after-flash of the fluorescents left a slight, flickering blueprint of the room in my brain. I opened Elizabeth's dad's door and, on tiptoes, ran to the outer door leading to the hallway. When I peered through the float glass, I saw a flashlight's beam bouncing up and down the hallway, vanishing and suddenly reappearing. Slow, labored footsteps shuffled across the hallway floor. Doorknobs rattled, growing louder. *The security guard.* Elizabeth gave me no indication he'd be so thorough as to check for unlocked doors. *Crap!* The only way to relock it was with a key from the outside. Hadn't they ever heard of modern innovations?

I raced blindly through the office, bumping my shin on the receptionist's desk. Stifling a howl, I opened Mr. Blackmer's door, then shut it with a nearly imperceptible click. Six minutes left, and the guard was closing in. I took a risk, turning on the flashlight. Yanking back the curtains, I saw that the windows unclasped and pushed up, providing enough room for me to climb out. The window opened with surprising ease. Below the double-stacked windows sat a brick ledge, extending no more than eight inches in length. It would have to do.

The doorknob shaking grew louder, a ghost dragging his chains down a haunted house stairway. Then the guard started whistling. The Carpenters, I think. *Ugh.* But it helped me pinpoint his location. By my reckoning, just one office away. With one foot out the window, I noticed the computer screen glowing. I tumbled back in, rolling with a gymnast's skill, and flicked the screen off.

I levered one leg over the windowsill. Carefully digging my toes onto the ledge, I secured solid footing. I tossed my arms above me, wedging my hands against the overhanging sill. Then I brought my other leg across and out, just as the outer doorknob rattled. The whistling stopped. The door opened, creaking.

My arms shook. If muscles could scream, mine surely would. They strained, pressing against the upper sill. Forced into a half-squat, my shaking knees extended out into the open sky, twenty-one floors off the ground.

Then I realized I had left the window open. Carefully releasing my right hand, I brought the window down slowly to not upset my balance. My back protested with pain as I forced my arm behind me. The window shut just as the inner office door opened. Fluorescent lights sprayed out next to me. I huddled into the corner like a crab. All four limbs trembled from fear and exertion.

The curtains were pulled back. No way to close them behind me. A beam of light splashed across the window, its arc falling dead across the skyline. I shut my eyes and held on tight. From inside the office, the lights turned off, the sound of the door closing following it.

Tiny green and yellow specks of light crawled from the corner of my vision line like a deadly fungus. A vortex of dizziness made my head spin. Sweat oozed from nowhere, soaking me from head to foot. My fingers slipped from the moisture, and I clawed blindly at the cornice.

The light show completely overtook my vision.

*Dear God, not now! Not another drug flashback! Not now!*

Then blackness swam around me…

\*\*\*\*

*Elizabeth*

My eyes blinked open. I felt tired, dizzy. My arms ached, and my legs shook. Intense pressure. *Weird.* I looked straight ahead of me and saw nothing but the night sky, the sound of traffic eerie and far away. *Dreaming.* I relaxed. Until I looked down.

*Oh my God, oh my God, oh my God!*

Far below me, cars looked like mere toys. Elspeth's wig slipped off my head, flapping through the sky like a bat. I snapped my head back, cracking it hard against the concrete. I let the pain wake me up. Daring a glimpse upward, I saw I was jammed into a window frame, the sill the only thing keeping me from plummeting to my death. I forced my arms and legs even stiffer, hoping to bond my position. My muscles felt unwilling, ready to give out.

A sudden grinding sound erupted to my right.

*Chank. Guzzzz…*

I would've screamed if my voice had not dried up.

The mechanical sound grew louder until it settled into a steady, whizzing sound. Daddy's old-fashioned window air-conditioned unit. I felt my fingers slipping above me. I dug in deeper until they hurt.

*Don't look down, don't look down!*

I did look down and nearly fainted. A cool breeze brushed my face, giving me momentary relief. I snapped my eyes shut.

*Please, God, I won't ever be selfish again! Just help me out of this!*

\*\*\*\*

*Elspeth*

Total darkness, nothing around. I pulled myself off the floor (assuming that was what it was), and turned, looking for a hint of light. Nothing but inky, unforgiving blackness. I slapped myself, trying to wake up.

That's when I remembered. Elizabeth was out on the window ledge. I freaked. Scurrying back and forth, I looked for something, anything, a wall to guide me toward light and cognizance. Still an infinite maze of night.

I sat down. Shut my eyes. Concentrated.

"Don't panic, Elizabeth. Just stay put. I'm coming back." I kept repeating the mantra over and over, hoping it'd pull me back and save both our asses.

\*\*\*\*

*Elizabeth*

Tears gushed through my shut eyes, the saltiness dribbling into my mouth. I could not hold on much longer.

My legs wobbled. My right hand slowly slithered off the concrete, fingers sliding away. I watched helplessly as my hand flapped out into the air with a sickening *whoosh.* For a brief second, I teetered on the window ledge, both arms flapping for balance. And then, in one heart-freezing moment, I knew momentum and gravity wanted me. Before I went over, I twisted and lunged for the air conditioner.

*Got it! Barely.*

My chin scraped on the metal casing when I caught the unit. Half-contorted, my feet unbelievably still planted on the sill, my arms wrapped around the box. But my fingers were slithering away, slowly, inexorably. My back felt wrenched from my position, painful, yet numb. Making moves no larger than millimeters, I turned one foot around and then the other.

*"I'm coming, Elizabeth! Hold on!"* Elspeth shouting from somewhere deep within my mind. *"Hold on!"*

Wooziness overtook me, my vision uncertain. I scrabbled at the back of the unit, fighting for a better grip. My hold didn't take. Gravity my enemy, sweat the agent provocateur.

The rods supporting the air conditioner to the wall snapped off, jolting me into one last Herculean burst of effort to grab behind the box. One hand jammed behind it. My fingers exploded with pain as I grabbed something hot. But it felt solid. I swung my other arm up and over.

*I did it!*

An awful groaning sound, metallic in nature, ripped from the back of the air conditioner. The braces were giving away, slowly, surely, most definitely.

My last thoughts were what it would be like watching the earth rise toward me as I fell to my death. And whether everyone would think I'd committed suicide. All I needed.

****

*Elspeth*

I opened my eyes and saw that Elizabeth had grabbed onto the air conditioner. But it was loosening with a slow crawl of a rasp.

*Not much time till we go over.*

Releasing my right hand, I slapped it up against the window and pushed. One inch open. Two inches. It gave way, sliding more easily toward the top. A bracket tore away with a jarring jerk. I fell back, one hand wrapped around the dangling box, the other grabbing the open window frame, my arms stretched to the limit.

*It's now or never.*

I released my left hand and aimed for the window.

*Yes!*

The box, sounding like the last call of the dinosaurs, pulled away from the wall and twirled away into the night. A solid crash echoed from far below.

My nearly numb legs were still planted on the sill. When I swung one leg up to the window, the other followed involuntarily. I missed the target. Both legs dropped, dangling against the side of the building. Only my arms kept me alive. I took in a deep breath, let out a scream, and pulled. I got my head almost inside the window and then slumped back. I yanked again, weakened, then rested. If you could call it that. I had to get a leg up there to propel me over the top. Taking three deep breaths, I hauled myself back up, head level to the window. I risked releasing my right arm for a brief second and crammed it through the window.

*It's there! Just a little bit more...*

My right leg flipped up. The shoe slipped into the open window and held.

*Victory!*

With one last surge of energy, I tugged myself up, throwing my upper torso weight through the window. I fell to the wonderful floor, letting my other leg follow of its own accord.

I must've lain on the floor for fully ten minutes until my heart decided the danger had passed.

"That was fun," I said, pretty much just to hear my voice, reassuring myself I wasn't dead all over again. I jumped to my feet, still shaky, and grabbed the flash-drive.

First things first. I had to retrieve Elizabeth's clothes. I figured I was already in enough trouble with her as it was. Wouldn't want to leave her clothes behind.

The stairs were my first choice, but my legs weren't having it. When the elevator arrived, I nearly collapsed inside, then rode it down to the second floor. I got out, scanned the hallway, and ran for the stairwell. On a whim, I stumbled down to the basement where a door sign said *Emergency Exit Only. Alarm Will Sound.* Realizing no matter what happened, there was no way it could be any worse than what I—we—had just gone through.

Bracing myself, I burst through the door. The alarm clanged around me as I found myself in the parking garage. Seeing Elizabeth's car, I fumbled for her keys. I jumped in and said, "Okay, Elizabeth, take us the hell out of here."

Chapter Thirteen

*Elspeth*

"What did you think you were doing, Elspeth?" I'd seen Elizabeth pissed before. Never this much, though. She had climbed new heights on her mountain of indignation. Totally in my face, she thrashed her hands in the air. "I can't believe you crawled out onto Daddy's ledge!"

"Elizabeth, you wanted me to break into your dad's office." Even the simplest of shrugs shot lightning bolts into my shoulders.

"I didn't say you could put my body in jeopardy. I just can't believe it! *Ooh!*"

"Yeah, it was kinda scary. Not a good time for us to have one of our flashbacks. Or whatever you want to call them." I took a flying leap onto her pink-covered bed. Obviously downplaying it, I attempted to calm her. But truth time? It had scared the hell outta me. Heights weren't really my thing.

Elizabeth sighed and settled down next to me. "When are these stupid flashbacks going to stop?"

"Soon, I think." Under my breath, I added, "Maybe."

"Maybe isn't good enough. We almost died!"

"But we didn't. Everything's cool. We got what we wanted." I tossed the flash-drive up, caught it, and then threw it high again. Elizabeth snagged it mid-air. "You want me to run it over to Kevin tonight?"

"Oh, no! You've paid enough visits to him. I still can't believe you kissed him!"

Too bad. The thought of tripping over there tonight filled me with anticipation. "Fine, whatever. But you know what to ask him, right?"

"I think I can figure it out, Elspeth." She held up the flash-drive, eyeing it warily, wondering what unspoken mysteries it held. "What do you think's on it?"

"I'm not sure. But you need to be prepared for the worst. I didn't really understand what I saw in your dad's office, but it seemed kinda sketchy."

"Oh, God." Her head banged against the headboard, and then she threw an arm over her eyes. "Daddy—"

"Hey, hey." I draped my arm over her shoulders. "You can handle whatever life throws your way. You've proven that time and again. Just give that gizmo to Kevin. Have his guy look at it. Then we'll take it from there. You'd rather know than not know, right?"

"I suppose." Not very definitive.

"Everything'll be cool. No matter what. Besides, prom is the day after tomorrow. You've been looking forward to it for a long time. Don't let anything ruin it for you." My smile wavered, possibly betraying how I truly felt about the stupid prom. But Elizabeth had earned the right to be happy, even if it was through such artificial, dumb, and unimportant things like proms.

"I guess you're right." A slow smile burned across her face. "Elizabeth?"

"Hmmm?"

"When is this going to end? I mean, this whole drug thing?"

I considered the question. I didn't know, but I had a burning gut instinct it would all come to a head soon. *Count on the gut.* "Soon, I hope."

But in a strange way, I didn't want it to end. Not just yet. It meant being banished again to the land of the ever-smiling and humdrum limbo-ites.

"I hope so, too."

"Hey, Elizabeth?"

"Yes?"

"I'm gonna need a new wig."

She snapped off the lights without saying a word.

****

*Elizabeth*

Friday morning, the day before prom. Even though my adrenaline still pumped from the previous night's cliff-hanging date with death, the thought about being crowned Clearwell's prom queen stoked my fires. At long last, all of my hard work was about to come to fruition. The drug dealers, the death of Charles Durbin, even whatever it was Daddy was up to, all paled in comparison to the exhilaration I had experienced. I wanted my golden moment, unfettered by trauma and danger. The drug dealer had been around for months; he could wait a few more days.

Daddy stewed in a particularly foul mood that morning when the phone rang. He answered it with a growl, moving slowly as if his bones pained him. He turned his back toward us while he chatted, his shoulders drooping lower with each grunt.

"What is it, Harold?" asked Mother as soon as he hung up. When he fell into his chair, Mother likewise collapsed across from him, her face ivory white. I wondered how much she truly knew about Daddy's problems.

"There was a break-in at my office last night."

"Oh my God!" Mother's knuckles went for her mouth. "What did they take?"

Daddy lifted one side of his mouth, the closest he'd come to a smile in a while. "That's what's odd. It appears nothing was stolen."

"How do they know someone broke in?" asked Mother. I hid behind my croissant, covering a dry clack in my throat with a sip from my teacup.

Lines webbed across Daddy's forehead. "Doors and drawers were picked, and the air conditioner unit was wrenched off and tossed into the street."

"Oh my. Vandals, I suppose."

"I suppose." With a disgruntled toss of his napkin, Daddy stood and stumbled his way into his den. I heard the click of the lock as he barricaded himself from the outside world.

"Mother?"

"Yes, dear?" Although visually stunning, Mother's smiles always lacked warmth.

"Is Daddy all right?"

"He's going through some difficult times at work, dear. Nothing he can't handle."

"Is…is he in trouble?"

Mother's eyes drifted, flitting away from me to the corners of the dining room. She squinted as if spotting a dust bunny. "He's going to be fine."

"Are we in financial trouble?"

Her lower lip quivered, dropped a few times. She had opened her mouth, ready to speak when the doorbell rang. Her lips snapped back into a smile, her cheekbones preternaturally high. "That'll be Donovan." The lyrical quality returned to her voice. She bolted up, practically running for the door, escaping her daughter, the Grand Inquisitor.

****

Hand in hand with Donovan, we strolled down the sidewalk. I felt like royalty already. Yes, maybe I was being slightly anticipatory about the outcome, but the sea of students parted for us, letting us saunter between them with an unspoken reverence. Against all odds, Lance's ridiculous campaign seemed to be working. Clearwell's fickle student body had already put Dugan's party behind them.

The sun bore down, particularly warm, shining its golden spotlight on us. My king stood at my side, my handsome Donovan, greeting his constituents, doling out complements and fair-minded judgments. For the first time in weeks, I felt great.

Not even the evil pretender to the throne, Charlotte, or her newly acquired two-faced acolytes, could ruin my day. *My special day's eve.* They gathered around Charlotte's locker, the way they used to flock toward mine. I walked by them, ignoring their jealous titters and whispers. I carried my chin and shoulders straight, my head up in the clouds. Donovan gave me a reassuring smile once we passed the gauntlet of witches. I stared deeply into his soulful brown eyes. Little did he realize what wonders he had to look forward to post-prom.

As soon as I walked into environmental science class, Tim Matthews's typically clueless, open-mouthed gawp met me. But I put his needy pleas for attention on hold along with all my other problems. Just a couple of days to live like an ordinary prom queen were all I desired at the moment.

"Morning, sunshine," said Lance.

"Morning. Unbelievably, I think your posters are working."

"Glad you noticed. I've heard lots of people talking about them…even in the right way."

"Wait, there's a wrong way?"

"Don't worry about it." Lance's typical life-guiding principle. "Even bad publicity is good. You're in the public eye now."

I dropped my voice when a fleeting moment of uncertainty darkened my thoughts. "Do you really think I'll win?"

"Yeah, I kinda do, now. I mean your biggest competition is Suzy." He shrugged his shoulders, dismissing the cheerleader as inconsequential. "I don't think she's a problem. And then there's Charlotte—"

"Yeah." Tempted to call her a heinous name, I refrained. I was above that. *Royalty.*

"It's funny, though. From what I gather, people are now talking about her like they were about you."

"How's that?"

"Well, you know, kinda bitchy, stuck up, rich…bitchy."

"Um, you said 'bitchy' twice."

"Did I? My bad."

"But people are changing their minds about me?"

"Yeah, I think they are. You have a really good chance at winning. I truly believe so."

"Thank you. You know, you've been a good friend." I didn't know what came over me. I tossed him a quick hug. "Thank you."

Obviously shocked, Lance flinched in my embrace before relaxing. "No problem. I actually kinda had fun doing it."

Mr. Dawson walked into the room, self-importance in his stride. Kevin raced after him like some copy-making office lackey. Mr. Dawson pointed at us, still embracing, and said, "All right, you two. Break it up. That's what hotel rooms are for. Ya feel me?"

We stared at one another before bursting into laughter. Hard to believe, but apparently Mr. Dawson remained unaware of Lance's sexual orientation. Most of the classroom joined in our laughter. Mr. Dawson, flustered, stared at Kevin for enlightenment. He responded with a shrug.

Throughout class, Lance and I had a terrible time concentrating, falling prey to sudden giggling fits. The harder we fought it, the more our barely stifled chuckles bubbled to the surface. I thought we had reached the point of no return when Lance put his head down on his desk. The back of his neck glowed bright red. His head bounced up and down as if bobbing for apples.

Unable to erase the silly grin on my face, I approached Mr. Dawson once the bell rang.

"Yes?"

"Mr. Dawson?" His furry eyebrows raised behind his glasses as if they were independent organisms. "I visited Mr. Gyrich, like you suggested."

He leaned back, smugly folding his arms across his chest. "That's cool, that's cool. What did you learn, Ms. Blackmer?"

Actually, I had had a nice experience, but maybe not for the reasons Mr. Dawson intended. But I knew what he wanted to hear. Always give the people what they want. "I learned there's more to life than pursuing capitalism for the sake of money."

"That's totally rad, Ms. Blackmer...rad!" *Gag!* I sorta thought "rad" went out of vogue way back in the, like, the nineties or something. I stopped myself from telling him so. Why not accept his gift graciously? Oddly enough, I took pride in myself. I was making progress. Not only with Mr. Dawson but in the way I handled the situation.

He opened a book in front of him and hastily scribbled something down. "And as I told you, Ms. Blackmer, you'll receive extra credit for this. Now, please don't forget what you've learned and apply it toward your future. Keep it real."

He stood up and held a hand out to me. "I believe you'll go far in life. But, don't squander your potential on fame and fortune. Any fool can achieve that if they have the financial means to begin with." He couldn't hide his barely contained sneer, his contempt visible. Okay, Mr. Dawson was not "rad" with privileged people. "But it takes someone special, with leadership qualities and intelligence, to use their talents to make the world a better place. I see that in you. You just needed a wake-up call. Remember to chillax."

"Thank you, Mr. Dawson." I flashed a look to Kevin, inclined my head toward the hallway several times. He looked baffled—his every day appearance—before he finally followed me out of the classroom.

I immediately nuked his stupid, school-boy grin. "This is not a booty call, Kevin!"

"I, uh, didn't think it was." I reached into my purse. "Here's the flash-drive that we, um, talked about."

"Oh, right." Eager to please, he almost dropped it when he grabbed for it. "Turns out I'm seeing my guy tonight. Gotta go back to campus for something. I'll see if he can give it a look."

"How much will it cost?"

"Don't worry about it, Elizabeth. I'll take care of it."

No way would I accept his unwanted act of chivalry. The last thing I needed was to be in his debt. "Oh, no you're not. How much?" I whipped out my checkbook. While he waffled around, I scrawled out a blank check. "Here!" I thrust it into his hands. "Just let me know what the final tally is."

"What is it you're hoping to find?"

"The truth. No matter what it is. I need to know what Daddy's mixed up in."

"Okay, but it might be, you know—"

"I'm a big girl."

"Elizabeth…" As soon as he reached for my elbow, I yanked it away. "Sorry, sorry. I just, I didn't know you had a boyfriend."

"Well, now you know."

"Um, why did you kiss me then?"

Elspeth's lesson in practical deniability was the first thing I thought of. "I, um, didn't." I looked him in the eyes, knowing my unflinching gaze would win the day. Sure enough, he faltered, staring down at the floor.

"But, you did. Twice!"

"No I didn't."

He chortled, halfway to hysteria. "Yes, you did!" He rolled his eyes for effect, not very becoming. Leave it to the pros.

I didn't despise Kevin. Not really. Annoying? You better believe it. But I took pity and let him slightly off the hook. Besides, no one enjoyed questioning his own sanity. "Oh, you thought that was a kiss? It's just how I was raised to greet neighbors."

"Well, the neighbors must be keeping the lip balm industry in business," he said quietly. Then he tried to retract his huge mistake. Too late. "Sorry. It's just…it didn't seem like a neighborly welcome. That's all I'm sayin'."

"Sometimes things are not what they seem." I flitted away, thinking about those words. Where had I heard them recently?

****

All day long, people continued to stare at me. Obvious looks of admiration. But as the day grew longer, I couldn't shake the feeling I was being watched. Paranoia gobbled up my earlier exhilaration appetizer. I saw—thought I saw—fleeting shadows, unnatural, almost, scurrying off into dark corners of hallways and classrooms. Students snapped their heads away quickly when I caught them looking at me. And like a bad penny, Donnie Heidenreich kept popping up everywhere. He appeared less carefree than usual, nervously twitching as if something filled his mind. Hard as that was to believe.

Since my traitorous friends had abandoned me at lunch for Charlotte's table of sluttery, I needed some backup friends. Stat. Out of desperation, I joined Lance and a few of his drama department pals. They appeared as uncomfortable in my presence as I felt in theirs. Lance over-compensated, trying to make me feel welcome, but the others remained quiet, burying their heads in their lunches like ostriches in the sand.

"Tomorrow's your day, Elizabeth," said Lance, trying to drum up enthusiasm. The others stared at their food without comment. *And these are drama guys?* "Time to get crowned!"

"I guess that makes you some sort of knight or something, since you helped me gain the crown on your royal quest."

"Sir Lance-a-Lot," he roared, finally drawing a few chuckles out of his comatose tablemates.

"And I shall henceforth be known as Queen Elizabeth!" My newly knighted round table once again fell silent. A shadow fell over my lunch tray. Someone behind me.

Lance stopped chattering, staring over my head. "Um, Elizabeth…"

Donnie Heidenreich rocked back and forth on his feet, his head swiveling in constant motion like a security camera. His ever-present slacker's smile had vanished, making him appear like a bound up ball of anxiety. I could almost feel it radiating off him in heat waves. "Hey, uh, Elizabeth?"

I stood. "What's wrong?"

"Can I, um, talk to you? Just for a minute?"

I nodded, and then realized by his silence that he wanted privacy. He turned and hurried out of the cafeteria, almost as if afraid to be seen with me. *I know, right?*

We stopped in the commons. "What's going on, Donnie?"

He looked pale, definitely out of breath. His eyes swelled with panic, hardly the party-boy persona he usually perpetuated. Perspiration broke out underneath his mop of long hair, sliding down his face. "Remember what you asked me about?"

"Um, yes." I had no clue which specific detail he referred to, but decided it best not to interrupt him.

"Well, I think I found out what happened to Charles. I know who killed him. Who the dealer is." Someone brushed by us, their loud eruption of laughter making Donnie jump. Reflexively, he clamped a hand over his mouth.

My heart raced, thumping. So close to the truth. I swallowed, my throat rising, then settling. "Who is it?"

He shut his eyes as if trying to keep a brutal nightmare at bay. "Not here. I don't want him to find out. I don't even want him to see me talking to you." When he opened his eyes, I noticed his pupils weren't dilated. *Unusual.* "Just, not now. I gotta go."

Frustration beat me like a drum, to say the least. But from what I knew about Donnie, things had to happen in his own way, his own sweet time. "Okay, Donnie, where?"

"You know where the skate park is?"

I sighed. Skate parks were so not my usual domain. "Which one?"

He looked at me, flabbergasted, as if there was only one stupid skate park. "The Clearwell Skate Park."

"Okay, I think I know where it is."

"Can you meet me there at seven? Tonight?"

"Fine."

He twisted away, making a half circle like a dog before it lies down. Then he quietly said, "Don't tell anyone, okay?"

"Of course I won't."

He nodded before taking off, checking all

directions like a good pedestrian. He stumbled, but for once, his mishap had nothing to do with being high. When he regained his footing, he kept his gaze firmly locked on the ground. Absolutely terrified.

And so was I.

Elspeth had been right. It looked like Game Over was near.

**\*\*\*\***

We planned for me to drive to the skate park, and then let Elspeth take over (wearing my clothing, of course). But lately, our plans had not worked out so well.

Apprehension clawed at my stomach like an escape-minded gerbil in a terrarium. I wanted nothing more than to put an end to this—just in time for prom— yet I also felt incredibly tense. If Donnie's information checked out, we still had the problem of what to do with it. Did I turn it over to Tim Matthews and let him take care of it? Elspeth fought me tooth and nail on that gloriously safe option. She wanted to be in on the takedown. She'd made a vow to herself never to take drugs again. Someone broke that vow for her. I understood. If someone ruined my life, I'd want payback myself. Yet all we'd have was Donnie's word. No proof, no evidence. How would we flush out the dealer? Too much stress!

Also, Donnie's obvious terror bothered me. Nothing—not grades, his future, anything—had ever fazed him in the past. Was my life in danger? I wished I could enlist Donovan as back up. But he wouldn't approve. He'd try to talk me out of playing girl detective. No sense worrying him unnecessarily at any rate.

I had rolled up the top on my yellow convertible (because I hated the wind mussing my hair), and still had about a mile to go to the skate park. No more than fifteen minutes to get there on time. That's when the colors of fear started to encroach upon my vision again. Dots of apprehensive orange and ringlets of yellow anxiety swam in front of my eyes before exploding into a world of black...

\*\*\*\*

*Elspeth*

My own audible gasp dredged me up into the waking realm. I clenched something hard with my hands. Houses and trees passed by me at a rapid pace. I woke behind the wheel of Elizabeth's car.

"I can't drive, Elizabeth," I screamed. I punched the two pedals underneath my feet, figuring it couldn't hurt. The car jerked, stuttered, sped up again. My hands instinctively twisted the steering wheel, forcing the car to bounce up into a yard. A giant tree trunk raced toward me. I yanked the wheel left. The front bumper responded with a crunch when it barreled over the curb. Ahead, a car exited an intersection, crawling like a turtle across my path. I laid on the horn. That much I could figure out.

The driver sped up, barely clearing my path. With a few taps, I figured out which was the gas and the brake pedals. I hammered the brake down. Tires squealed as I fishtailed into the street. I completed a circle, inching closer toward a parked car. Closer. I locked my arms straight, willing the damn demon car to stop. My eyes shut, my teeth clenched as I waited for the inevitable collision. Elizabeth's car shuddered to an abrupt halt, thrusting me forward. My head cracked against the steering wheel.

I finally allowed myself to breathe once I knew the car wouldn't move again. With the engine still idling, I had my foot jammed hard upon the brake. The parked car sat less than two inches from me.

*Okay, think, Elspeth.*

With a mile to go, I knew I could not drive it. But I had to get there. I'd have to run the mile. Could not leave Elizabeth's car in the street, though. I carefully edged my foot off the brake, and the car crept forward. I slammed on the brake again, forcing the car to understand I had taken charge. I continued like this, moving the car ahead, millimeter by millimeter, stopping and starting until I cleared the parked car. I twisted the steering wheel to the right as far as it would go. The front tire lifted into a yard, providing a nice, solid anchor. Satisfied I had cleared the street, I turned off the ignition with a cheer and locked the doors. I began running toward the skate park, Elizabeth's stupid flats slapping down the street.

****

I arrived about ten after seven. The early spring night's dusk had fallen. A full moon lit upon the creepy bronze statues heralding the skate park's entryway. I bent over, one hand on a statue, the other on my knee, trying to catch my breath. One statue appeared to be a chopped-off head, another amputated legs atop a skateboard. A bad artist's work, vandalism, or ominous portents?

The park looked and sounded empty. No voices, shouts, laughter, or echoes of skateboard wheels ringing through the man-made hollows. A car's headlights swept through the park before flitting off like a firefly.

No overhead lights, only the moon as my lonely guide.

I descended a ramp into the bowl-like structure. "Donnie?" I whispered. A nocturnal creature of some indefinable nature responded with a *chirrup.* "Donnie?" I repeated louder. *Something's wrong.*

Lightning struck the back of my skull. The accompanying sound was soft, yet sickening. The cement rushed up to meet me. I rolled slightly to take the brunt of the impact with my shoulder.

*Hello, darkness, welcome back.*

\*\*\*\*

I woke completely shrouded in black. Again.

*Where am I?* Limbo? The place where I was consigned when the "drug flashbacks" happened?

No, didn't seem to fit. Everything seemed quieter. That wasn't quite accurate, either.

Sounds drifted toward me from far away. Muffled noises. Deeply muted thumps, groans, creatures bemoaning their destiny. My breath came out shallow, hot, rebounding into my face. I stretched my hands slowly out.

*Tump.*

The touch of cool metal. Blindly feeling my way around my surroundings, I realized a small compartment of some sort encased me. Enclosed on all sides.

*A coffin.*

My ears plugged up, the distant sounds diminishing. My stomach lurched as the container shifted, tilting me. It wavered before tipping. I fell slowly, almost weightlessly, floating down into the depths of nothingness.

"*Wake up, Elspeth!*" Elizabeth's words blasted

through my brain, mental firecrackers exploding with urgency.

I placed a hand against the platform I lay on.

*Wet.*

A few inches of liquid, cold and uninviting. I heard water trickling in from somewhere, determinedly and inevitably coming like Christmas, only not so joyous. Running my fingers about, I found the source. A small leak but expanding with alarming speed. The water dribbled in along a horizontal line, a miniature waterfall. Soon, it gushed in. I stuck my face underneath the water, bringing myself into full consciousness.

Another loud scraping sound came from outside my tomb. A startling plummet of several feet followed, tossing me against a metal wall.

My heart pole-vaulted into my throat.

*I'm in a car trunk. Under water.*

I pounded on the trunk lid, my knuckles bloodied by my useless efforts. I reached around, groping for something. Anything. My hand fell into a small indentation, then grazed over a plastic bag. Inside the bag, I felt a tool; sleek, long, bent…a lug nut wrench. I pounded it against the trunk, the noise shrill and sharp. I jammed the wrench into the small sliver where the water poured in. I got up on my knees and leaned on the wrench's handle. Nothing. You can't lift infinite pounds of water. I dropped the worthless wrench, now half-submersed. And slipping deeper with each downward pitch.

I always thought it a cliché that your life passed before your eyes while you're dying. You think I'd know, right? But I heard Dad's voice, clear as day.

"Elspeth, in a lot of older cars, the back seat's

removable." Always a car fanatic, always trying to interest me in his hobby.

When I asked why, he'd answered, "So people don't find themselves locked in the trunk."

At the time, I had filed it away with an eye roll, shoved it into my mental trash file. I remember thinking how stupid it was for someone to get locked in a car trunk.

*And here we are. Thanks, Dad.*

Lying on my back, I pulled my knees up and kicked. And kicked again. Elspeth, the battering ram. Each kick folded the back seat farther into the car. One more kick and the seat collapsed with a reassuring *floomph*. Music to my plugged-up ears. Feet first, I scrabbled into the back seat.

Slight illumination filtered out from the windshield. By the dashboard's still-lit lights, I made out a body in the front seat. Donnie, head slumped onto his chest. His breathing sounded light, his pulse barely registering. But he was still alive. And so was I. At least for now.

Water rushed in through the tattered stripping surrounding the windows. The floorboards were completely submerged. Looking out the window, I saw only darkness.

*How deep are we? How long have we been sinking?*

I bit my tongue hard, drawing warrior's blood. *I'm no damn quitter.* Even if it seemed I had limited options.

Liquid death cascaded through the vents and other openings. I had to move fast. Reaching across Donnie, I explored the door panel. My hand gripped a handle and

I nearly let out a whoop. Donnie drove a junker. Old-fashioned, roll-down windows. I checked Donnie for a seat belt, not surprised there wasn't one.

I wrapped one arm around Donnie, bounced him around a bit to gauge what I'd be dealing with. Slight of frame, but it'd still be a struggle to swim us both to the surface.

*Move, Elspeth. Quit thinking and just do it!*

A one-handed swim. The only way. My other hand would be clamped around Donnie's nose and mouth, ensuring he didn't drown.

I grasped the window handle and pushed down. Unmoving. "God damn it!" I forced my weight upon it. Still rigid and not going anywhere. The car heaved forward again, its parts whimpering under the water pressure. I pulled Donnie next to me on the passenger side. My teeth chattered. Soaking wet and freezing. Last chance, unless I wanted to die a lonely and cold death.

*Again.*

I shoved the handle, and let out a strength-mustering cry. *Movement!* Just a little, but it budged.

"Okay, Donnie, let's do this." I knew he couldn't hear me, but it helped me feel I wasn't alone. And maybe I was just buying time. I'd never been more terrified. Deep breath and roll! Exerting all my strength, I cranked the son-of-a-bitch down. Water flooded in, blasting me, forcing my cheeks back and my eyes closed. I developed a rhythm, rotating the handle and holding on for dear, sweet life. I put every muscle to use. The water battered me, a severely pissed-off force of nature. Holding Donnie's face up toward the car's roof, the cabin had nearly filled—what I was waiting for. Couldn't very well fight the onslaught of water. I took in one last breath before I plunged underwater.

With Donnie's nose plugged between my thumb and forefinger, my other three fingers clamped over his mouth. I managed Donnie's head into the crook of my arm. With my stoner booty, I lashed my feet out. Using one arm to clear the car, I pulled Donnie alongside me.

Dark, too dark, impossible to tell which way was up. Using the car's position as my guide—and going on strong faith it hadn't completely capsized—I assumed we were still upright. It was all I had to go by.

*Here we go.* I kicked off the car's hood and lifted, my arm digging into the water in front of me. I felt a whooshing sensation from behind me. The car flipped over. The resulting undertow pushed against me, propelling me faster toward the top.

If that's where we were headed.

Struggling, I strained to see through the darkness. Looking for any sign of light, anything at all. If I made a mistake and reached the bottom, game over.

Donnie, the dead-weight anchor, slowed me down considerably. But paddling and pulling like crazy, I felt progress. Couldn't really tell, couldn't see. But I had to be making progress. Had to be!

Still no light, not even a glimmer of hope. My lungs burned, totally expanded, and demanded a sweet intake of life-sustaining oxygen. I grew completely disoriented, a stranger in a strange world. I swallowed, heard the sound internally, a reassuring sign life still coursed through me. I pulled against the water one over-handed swing at a time. The more I paddled, the more energy it took. I needed a breath.

*Can't hold on.*

I'm not sure if I prayed or not (crazier things have happened). But a dim light pierced the darkness. A tiny flashlight beam of moonlight, life's beacon.

*I'm near the surface!*

I kicked the water away, increasing my speed. The blurry, yellow circle grew. *Ripples!* Ripples above me! I reached, stretched. Lungs on fire, ready to explode. My right hand broke water. I shot up, and took in a deep gasping plea for air.

Leaning back slightly, I cradled Donnie against my chest, treading the water with my legs and free arm. When the air sufficiently filled my lungs, I looked around, trying to get my bearings.

Trees and woods surrounded us. I appeared to be in the middle of a relatively small pond or lake. But not so small you couldn't bury a car with two people in it.

I swam to the edge of the lake and nearly kissed the mud. I pulled Donnie ashore like a sailor hauling in that day's fishing net. Laying him flat on the ground, I saw his chest, unmoving. I tossed his head back and gave him mouth-to-mouth resuscitation, followed by chest palpitations.

"Come on, Donnie, dammit! Come back!" I repeated the procedure. He finally choked, coughed, spat up water. I fell back into the dirt, relieved. But he immediately fell asleep again. I straddled him, felt his pulse. Still alive, just not responding. I slapped him, lightly at first then harder. "Donnie! Come on! Talk to me!" Deeply, blissfully asleep—not very encouraging. I needed to get help.

I grabbed Elizabeth's phone out of my pocket but knew it was a lost cause. Dead. I jumped up and down, trying to look beyond the trees, scanning the area.

Lights sparkled in the distance. But I had to leave Donnie behind. I couldn't carry him. I set off on my second jog of the night.

An old, near-death dog greeted me in a yard with a lackadaisical, phlegmy bark. The front lights of the seen-better-days farming home flipped on. This quieted the dog, his work for the night completed. An ancient face peered out the screen door. "Who's out there?"

"Um, hi, sir, there's someone in trouble down by the pond!" I jacked a thumb behind me.

"What happened?" Instant distrust in his voice, sadly the way of the world.

"Some kid's car went into the pond. I saw the accident and pulled him out. But he needs help! Can you please call an ambulance?"

"Ayuh. I'll do that, missy. Are you okay?"

"Yeah."

"No drugs or booze?"

"No, sir. I don't do that."

"Ayuh. Good girl. Wait here a spell. I'll call for help and then we'll go tend to your friend."

As he disappeared into the house, I disappeared into the night.

**** 

I stumbled my way through the woods, following the sounds of traffic, using the distant highway lights as my map. Finally, I reached a sparsely traveled highway. About a mile down the road, a well-lit building sat just off the highway. A road marker claimed it as Alternate 69. Never heard of it. Just hoped I was headed in the right direction.

I took the exit ramp and climbed the incline with heavy legs. I reached the parking lot of Deuel's Truck-

Stop & Good Eats. My eyes tightened against the harsh, buzzing lights, a shocking contrast to the unremitting darkness out of which I'd crawled.

A few trucks were parked haphazardly in the lot. I looked through the diner's window. Just a couple of sleepy truck drivers staring into their coffee cups, pondering the meaning of life. A plump, yet friendly-looking waitress came outside. Her smile vanished once she saw my condition.

"Honey, are you okay?"

"Yeah, I'm good. There was an accident. I, uh, need to call the police. Could I maybe borrow change for a call?"

"Sure, honey." She reached into her apron pocket, pulled out some coins, and handed them to me. "You sure you're okay? You look like fifty miles of hard-traveled road."

"I'm fine. Thanks. Where are we, anyway?"

"Claremorton, Kansas. Can I get you a cup? Food?"

"I'm good, thanks. How far is it to Clearwell?"

She sputtered out a laugh. "Girly, you're a good thirty-five miles south of there! Now, really, what's going on?"

I smiled. "Just a small accident. I'll work it out with the police." I turned before she could finish her interrogation.

A sole phone booth sat in the parking lot, a sure sign I was far from civilization. I didn't know who else to call, so after getting his number from the phone company, I bit the bullet and dialed.

On the fourth ring, he answered. "Kevin? It's Elizabeth."

A pause. "Oh, hey. I just got back from K.U. Listen, my roommate says he'll look at the flash-drive tonight and—"

"Never mind that now. I need your help."

"What kind of help?"

"How about giving a girl a ride?"

I sat down on the curb and waited. An ambulance, followed by two police cars, sped down the highway in the direction of the lake. After thirty minutes of my avoiding the increasingly suspicious diner waitress, Kevin finally pulled up. Not a minute too soon, either. The waitress had been staring out the window at me, phone in hand.

I clambered into the car before he came to a complete stop.

He stared at me, stunned. "What happened to you?"

"Long story. But right now, get me the hell out of here!" I pointed down the highway.

Once we were far away from the scene of the crime, I told Kevin what happened.

"Wow…wow. So, someone knocked you out and put you and Donnie Heidenreich into a car? And dumped you into a pond? To kill you?" He nearly swerved off the highway while gawping at me. I grabbed the wheel and tugged us back on course. I had had enough fun with cars for one night.

"Yeah, that's about the size of it." I rubbed my hands up and down Elizabeth's khaki shorts, hoping to dry them. My skin began to chafe.

"Oh, sorry," he said, noticing my discomfort. "You want some heat?" I nodded. "Did you, um, see who did this to you?"

"No. It was dark. He snuck up behind me and whacked me. Hard." I rubbed the back of my head, and felt a round bump of pain.

"Damn."

"But you can't tell anyone about this, Kevin. I mean it!"

"Elizabeth, this is out of your ballpark now. Someone tried to kill you. You need to call the police and let them handle it."

I shook my head, Elizabeth's wet locks slapping against my face. "Not yet, Kevin. I need to finish this. So far, this son-of-a-bitch has dosed me and now dumped me into a lake. I have to get him. Besides, calling in the police now is just gonna make him go into hiding. Then I'll never get him."

"This is crazy!"

Yes, it was. Frustrating, too. I had come so close to finding out who the killer was, then had the answer yanked out from underneath me. But if Donnie hung on, I could still talk to him. "Yeah, it's crazy. But it's the way it has to be."

Kevin exhaled loudly. "I don't know."

"Kevin!" I shot him one of Elizabeth's patented cold glares. "You can't say anything."

We drove in silence until we reached Elizabeth's car. "Okay, I don't understand why you're launching a one-woman strike team on the war against drugs. I mean, I guess I do. But, really, it goes against every bit of common sense I have. You're in danger. I don't like this."

"You don't have a say in the matter."

He looked into his lap and mumbled, "What if I do? What if I decide to call the cops for your own good?"

"Because if you do, well, you don't want to cross me." His concern touched me. Just as much as his half-veiled threats to call the cops pissed me off. "Give me a couple more days, all right? If I don't find out what I'm looking for by then, you can call in the National Guard for all I care. But just be quiet for now. Please. Do it for me."

He hesitantly nodded. "Well, I hope your friend's going to be all right."

"Technically speaking, he's not a friend, more of an acquaintance. But yeah, I hope he'll be okay, too."

Kevin scrambled for his phone. "I've got an idea."

"What?"

He did a quick Internet search and showed me the resulting phone number. "I'll bet they took him to Shawnee Mission Medical Center. It's the closest large hospital to Claremorton. You wanna see how he's doing?"

After a few minutes of hacking through some red tape, he reached a floor nurse in the know. "Hi, I'm calling about Donnie Heidenreich—maybe brought in there about thirty minutes or so ago. I think his car went into a pond in Claremorton?" He looked at me and held his thumb up. "How's he doing?" A pause. "Oh, yeah, I'm his brother." He creased his brow, looked worried. "I see. What? No, I don't know what kind of drugs he was doing." Losing his nerve, he wound the conversation up fast. "Thanks…no, that's okay…bye." He slapped the phone shut.

"Well, the good news is they think he's stabilized. The bad news is he's in a coma. They're not sure when—if—he'll come out of it. They're pretty sure he's got a ton of drugs in his system, but they're not sure what they are."

I sighed and dragged a finger across the window. "Damn it."

"The nurse did say someone apparently saved him from drowning on top of everything else. That would be you." He stared at me expectantly. I said nothing.

"Okay, Kevin, about the flash-drive—"

"Oh, yeah, um, okay. Just give me a minute. It's not every day I hear someone I care about was almost murdered." His eyes snapped wide open once he realized what he'd said. "I mean, um—"

I chuckled. "Whatever, Kevin. About the flash-drive?"

"Okay, my roomie says he should have something to tell me tomorrow."

"Cool. Just let me know, okay?"

"Yeah, of course."

I crawled out of the car, desiring to reward him with an appreciative kiss. Decided to meet the urge halfway. I leaned back in, planted one on his cheek. "Thanks, Kevin. You seem to be making a habit out of giving an endangered girl a ride."

A tiny, wry smile crossed his lips for the first time that night. "Okay," he said, almost painfully bashful.

Being a noble knight, he waited for me to drive off. Wasn't gonna happen. I waved him on as he reluctantly drove away.

I could easily give into this white knight of mine, but sadly, Elizabeth's beholden to her one and only king.

\*\*\*\*

Once Elizabeth reclaimed her body, she fumed all

the way home. Big surprise. Even in my half-cognizant state, I knew I was in for a major throw-down. Once in Dream Space, she let it rip.

"First," she began calmly, "you get us dosed. Second, you piss off my reverend. Third, you put us out on a ledge twenty-one stories up!" By the time she listed the inevitable "four," she had reached shrieking levels. "Fourth, you get us knocked out, locked in a trunk, and then dumped into a lake! This is going to stop now!" She marched loudly in front of her bed like a gung-ho soldier. She swiveled, and poked a finger into my face. "I demand to talk to your superiors, Elspeth. You've almost gotten me killed at least twice now! Our partnership is over!" She tapped her foot against her rug. "You hear me! Come on, give me their number!"

I couldn't help but smile. "It's not like you can reach them on speed-dial or anything." I narrowed my eyes toward the ceiling as if in deep thought and tapped my chin. "Maybe you can 'friend' them or something on the Internet—"

"This is not funny. Seriously! You almost got us killed. Twice!"

"I know it's not funny, Elizabeth. Believe me. I'm just as pissed as you are. But, you're taking it out on the wrong person. I'm not responsible for any of this." I reconsidered. "Well, maybe, the reverend dinner thing," I added quietly.

"You just don't know when to quit." She tossed herself onto her bed, digging her face deep into her pillow, the way she usually ended her hissy fits. "Aghh!" She kicked her feet in a child-like tantrum.

I waited patiently for her to work it out. I had all

the time in the world. Two worlds, actually. When she ran out of gas, I said, "You're right. It does need to stop. And now that he's gone after us twice, I'd think you'd want to get this bastard as much as I do."

She rolled over, eyes red. "I just want to live out my final days of high school in peace. I just want to be prom queen. Why can't I be normal? School days are supposed to be the best days of my life!"

"Who told you that? They lied. But, whatever. We're going to get this guy. Trust me on that. And I can't wait to personally take him down. For Charles, for Donnie, for you and me, for anyone else whom he's hurt that we don't even know about." I sat up and tossed her a solemn look. "I can't believe you want to back away from this fight. Not when we're so close to the truth." I tapped her playfully on the shoulder. "You'll get your chance to shine. You will be prom queen. I just know it."

"Really? I mean, are you just saying that? Or do you really, *really* know it?"

"Take it as you will. I just have a good feeling."

"Okay," she said, seeing the silver lining in my words even though they were mostly lies. "Fine. Whatever. But Donnie's in a coma. You can't just go to the hospital, walk in, and yell him out of it until he tells you who the damn dealer is."

"Elizabeth, just because Donnie's in a coma doesn't mean I can't talk to him."

Chapter Fourteen

*Elspeth*

The desk nurse scowled at me. Not a fan of my leather attire, apparently. I tossed her a wave before riding the elevator to the fourth floor. An older man and woman lingered outside of Donnie's room. No words passed between them, their faces drawn with grief. The man placed a hand on the woman's shoulder and gave her a weak smile. Donnie's parents.

I sat down next to a young boy in the waiting room, a miniature replica of Donnie. "Are you Donnie's brother?"

"He's in a coma," he said matter-of-factly.

"Well, you know something? I think Donnie's gonna come out of it."

His eyes lit up with hope. "You really think so?"

"Yep. He's a scrapper. Kinda like his little brother." I ruffled his hair.

"Are you Donnie's girlfriend?"

"No. Just a friend. You hang in there, all right? Have faith. You'll have your brother back."

"Okay." But I didn't think he believed me for a minute.

I left the room quickly, grief not being my thing. Donnie's parents still stood in their unwavering hallway vigil. "Excuse me, Mr. Heidenreich? Mrs. Heidenreich?

Would it be okay if I see Donnie?"

Mrs. Heidenreich took one look at me and burst into tears. Not the results I had hoped for. "Are you Donnie's friend?"

I stuck my hand out. "Yeah. I'm Elspeth. I'm sorry about Donnie. But could I have a few words alone with him?"

Mr. Heidenreich wrapped his arm around his wife's shoulders and pulled her aside. He turned back and nodded his head up and down glumly. A heart-wrenching sight, they shared the same, hollow-eyed set my mother wore.

I said, "I think he'll be all right. You have to believe that." My words were meant to be strong, to lend support, but they weren't accepted as such. Mr. Heidenreich shot me a glare, full of fury. I imagined they'd been given their fair share of well-meaning sentiment, probably sick of it.

But, maybe—just maybe—I could pull Donnie out.

Donnie lay peacefully slumbering in the room, no doubt visions of bongs dancing in his head. Oxygen pumped into his nose, various machines dinging around him. His chest rose and fell, keeping beat with the mechanical orchestration. Alive, yet dead. Something I could identify with.

"Okay, Donnie," I said, kicking off my boots. "Scoot over, I'm coming in." I crawled into the narrow bed, having to turn sideways to fit. I closed my eyes and waited for darkness to whisk me away.

****

A thundering clatter of noise, deep in bass, bombastic in its intensity. I fumbled my way through the darkness, following the sounds. The hallway I entered narrowed with each step, barely allowing me a passageway. The noise grew louder, artillery blasting, bombs exploding. A thin sliver of light lit upon my feet. A door. When I pushed the door open, bright light dazzled me. Donnie sat on a sofa in the cluttered, small room, working his fingers over a video console. On the large screen television, computer-animated soldiers merrily slaughtered zombies.

Dropping down next to him, I snatched the remote and turned the television off.

Donnie stared at me, unable to wrap his head around my appearance. "Hey, it's you." His grin looked kinda dumb and typical, the only grin in his limited arsenal. And still dressed in the same clothes he wore when we were tossed into the pond—a black metal T-shirt, grungy jeans, grass-stained tennis shoes.

"It's me," I said. "Donnie, you really, really need to come back. You can't waste your life in here."

He studied his hovel, assessing the fast food wrappers strewn everywhere. "But I like it here. This is like heaven, dude!" Donnie's idea of heaven was endless junk food and video games.

"Believe it or not, there're a lot of people out there who care about you."

He looked regretful, almost ashamed. Didn't think he had it in him.

"I know. But can't I stay a little longer? I mean, dude! This is awesome. I'm happy in here. I can do what I want and just be me."

Reason had no place in Donnie's nirvana, so I gave in resignedly. "Okay, Donnie, fine. But just a little bit longer. All right?" He nodded, happy to be given a reprieve. "If you don't come out soon, I'm going to come back and drag your scrawny little ass out of here. Got it?"

"Got it. So like, whoa, are you real?"

I remembered Dad's words from my dream. "Do you think I'm real?"

"I think you're kinda hot—"

"Let's stay focused."

"Hey! Did you kiss me? Out by the pond?" He ran his thumbs absentmindedly over the console as if the television was still on.

"That wasn't a kiss. I gave you mouth-to-mouth. I saved you from drowning."

"Oh. Felt like a kiss."

"Focus, Donnie, focus. Now, we've met before. I'm Elspeth."

"Wait. I thought you were Elizabeth in disguise."

I rolled my eyes and wished I had a hammer. Might knock some common sense into his head. "Doesn't matter. Let's stay on topic. You told Elizabeth you had information. Something about Charles Durbin and the drug dealer who dosed him up."

"Oh, yeah...yeah." He appeared puzzled, searching his scant brain cells for recall. "Yeah, I think I know what happened. I'll tell you." He flashed his yellow teeth into a leer. "But you have to do something for me."

"Oh, for...what?"

"You gotta make out with me."

"You've got to be kidding."

"No, dude. For real! I mean, like you're hot. Smokin' hot! And I'm in paradise. It's the one thing to make it perfect."

For God's sake. The things I had to do. But I knew

it was the only way he'd talk. Punk. "Fine. But absolutely no tongue. Got me?" He nodded in eager anticipation. Leaning in, he closed his eyes and extended his lips like an angelfish.

The briefest of pecks and I pulled out. With his eyes still shut, he clawed at the air, smacking his lips, ready for round two.

"Playtime's over, Donnie. I fulfilled my part of the bargain, now it's time for you to do the same."

He opened his eyes and sighed contentedly. "Okay, well, turns out Charles Durbin found out who Clearwell's drug dealer is. An old friend of his from junior high school. Charles was a good guy, but really kinda uncool. He went up to his buddy, told him he knew he was dealin', and asked the dude to stop, to go straight. Charles offered him a deal. If he stopped dealing, Charles wouldn't go to the cops. Dude refused. No big surprise. Then he took Charles out, pumped him full of drugs, and put him behind the wheel of his car."

"How do you know this?"

"Dude! I've got a network of spies! My reach goes across the school!" When I cocked an eyebrow, he saw I didn't buy it. "Okay, fine. I overheard him talking about it on his phone. I was at the gas station, taking a leak in the woods. I guess he didn't know I was there. When he started yelling, I hunkered down behind a tree and listened. It all sorta came out about Charles. He also said he was worried about Elizabeth, um, you, whatever, finding out about Charles. Said something has to be done."

"So you told Elizabeth. What happened last night when you were supposed to meet her?"

He reached beside him, pulled out what looked like

a half-eaten donut that had seen healthier days. "Hungry?"

I glared at him until he continued.

"Well, when I got to the skate park, the dude jumped me. He had some older guy with him, too. They took me out to my car, and shoved me into the back seat. The older guy pulled out a gun and held it on me. He—he forced me to down all sorts of pills, things I never do. I'm all about the smoke, dude!"

"Yeah, so you've said."

"Anyway, what was I gonna do? It was either go out on a high or get shot. Didn't take no brain surgeon to figure out which way's better. Next thing I know, I'm flying. Dizzy. Then I wake up here." He spread his hands about his glorious den of depravity.

"How'd they find out about Elizabeth meeting you in the skate park?"

"Don't know, really. Maybe he overheard me talking to Elizabeth—"

"I don't think so. There wasn't anyone around when you talked to her. I think they used you as bait. The dealer probably knew you were in the woods." The laughable notion of Donnie being stealthy added credence to my theory. "I think he was worried about Elizabeth poking around, saw you two talking earlier and set a trap. He was probably watching you, probably followed you to the park."

"Whoa." Definitely a slow burn, but realization finally smacked Donnie upside the head. "Dick!"

"Yeah. Now, who is this dick, Donnie?"

First my hands, then my shoulders started shaking. Donnie's visage wobbled, became bleary, then vanished. I heard a voice from far away, quiet, yet urgent.

"Tell me, Donnie," I shouted. Suddenly, I yanked back down the hallway like someone had lassoed me and pulled. My feet lifted, and then I flew backward. The walls zipped by.

But before I left, I heard Donnie's answer, nothing more than a whisper.

My eyes popped open. Mr. Heidenreich hovered over me. "Just what in God's name do you think you're doing, young lady?" Livid, his face nearly purple. With his hands gripping my shoulders, he shook me like a maraca.

"Um…" I sat up, groggy with a hangover. "I was praying for Donnie."

While Mr. Heidenreich bellowed his outrage, I hopped off the bed and raced out into the hallway.

Time to go get the bad guy.

\*\*\*\*

*Elizabeth*

More than elated, butterflies of excitement fluttered in my belly. Not only because of the prom tonight, but we finally knew who the drug dealer and murderer of Charles Durbin was. Normalcy would return soon. Elspeth would return to wherever and leave me to pursue my future dreams.

Of course, there was the tricky issue of how to bring down the dealer. Elspeth wanted to flat out assault the douche and beat a confession out of him. I harbored doubts about how that scenario might play out, but whatever. Everything was almost over!

I had a great feeling—supported by Elspeth's supernatural insight—that I would take home the crown. The perfect capper to my senior year, a shining star on my permanent record. Dartmouth would be thrilled to have me attending the year following. Optimism returned to my life after taking a brief vacation.

I pulled into our driveway, and checked the time. Three hours and a bit until Donovan swept me away. Plenty of time to do my hair, apply makeup, double-check the dress Mother picked out for me for unsightly wrinkles. Giddy!

"Um, Elizabeth?"

Kevin lurked behind the bushes, waving frantically. And suddenly my giddiness flipped into anxiety.

"Hey, uh, I need to talk to you." He ridiculously placed his hand alongside his face like it'd muffle his voice or something. And he wanted to teach science? "It's about your dad."

Absolutely not. No way was I letting Kevin ruin my prom. I applied a mental patch to my happiness balloon before it started leaking again. "Can't it wait, Kevin? I've got to get ready for the prom."

"It's kinda important." He jammed his hands into his pockets and kicked at the grass, literally beating around the bush. "There's something you should know."

"Whatever." I stalked toward him, dreading any news deemed more important than the prom.

I followed him into his open garage and he closed the door behind us. "My roommate called this morning." He displayed the flash-drive between thumb and index finger. "He found out some interesting things."

I snatched the flash-drive away from him as if it'd snatch away bad news as well. "Kevin, if it's about his financial woes, I already know he's not doing very well. Please spare me your drama and just get on with it. Well?"

He grimaced, barely glancing at me. "I, uh, really don't know how to tell you this. And keep in mind that a lot of this is conjecture on my roomie's behalf. It took him a while to decrypt the files, but he saw enough to figure out what's going on. Now, he didn't understand everything, but he really does know what he's talking about and—"

"Kevin! The clock is ticking!" I glanced at my wrist for impact, even though I never wear watches.

"Okay, you wanna sit down?" He pointed at the stool behind his drum set.

"Oh, my God! Just friggin' tell me already."

He headed for the stool and collapsed onto it, twisting left and right. "I, well, my roommate thinks your dad's involved in a Ponzi scheme." He practically folded into himself, his shoulders bunched up for protection.

"Ponzi? What? Like that old guy on the show, 'Happy Days'?"

I glowered at him until he swallowed back his annoying chuckle. "Um, a Ponzi scheme is, well, it's a scam. An investor tells his clients he's got a great opportunity for them. They give him their money. Incredible returns are promised. Impossible returns, really. Your dad told his investors they'd be getting ten percent monthly interest on their investments."

"Yeah, big deal. So what? Daddy's a great businessman. Like that's a crime."

"You don't understand. He doesn't really have anything for them to invest in. It's all made up. From what my roommate could tell, your dad's enticing these investors with some fictional off-shore investments. There's no proof any such thing exists."

When I fell back a step, Kevin jumped off the stool and raced toward me. "It's a lie, Elizabeth. And it won't last forever."

My high-flying balloon of giddiness had just sprung a huge leak, whizzing around my head, trickling away the promises of a happy future. "You don't know this is true!" I hated him for telling me this. I lashed out, slapping his chest. "It's not true. It can't be true!"

Kevin came closer, his hands raised in a pacifying manner. "I'm sorry. But, I think it is true. I'm really, really sorry—"

"No!" When he grabbed my shoulders, I swung my arms up, batting him away. "You're a liar!" I kicked at the closed garage door. The door's rattling mirrored how I felt; hollow and vulnerable. "Let me out of here."

"Elizabeth—"

"Let me out now!"

He walked toward the garage door button, shaking his head. I wanted to rip the empathy off his face and feed it to him. "I'm sorry. I truly am. I understand—"

"You don't understand anything!" The door began to rise, and I raised my voice to be heard over it. "It's not true! None of it! Daddy wouldn't do that. And you're ruining my prom! And I'm crying. I can't be a prom queen with puffy, red eyes!"

"Uh, Elizabeth?" Kevin stared over my shoulder, his eyes wide. "Elizabeth?"

The door cranked to a halt behind me. Daddy stood on Kevin's driveway, his shadow long and thin from the late afternoon sun.

"Elizabeth," he said quietly, "I need to talk with you." His face was ashen, his mouth drawn tighter than shoelaces. He shot Kevin a brief glance, and dismissed him immediately. "Come with me."

I quickly wiped the tears from my cheeks and brushed past Daddy. High tailing it through the yard, I hoped all signs of crying would disappear before he caught up to me.

"Elizabeth?" he called out. "Wait a minute, princess." Nearly out of breath, he bent over with his hands on his knees. "What were you and the neighbor boy talking about?"

"Nothing. Nothing at all."

He looked into my eyes, and knew I lied. Then he did something he hadn't done in a very long time. He held his arms out and pulled me in tight. I buried my face into his chest, didn't want to let go. His arms bestowed the emotional and physical comfort I'd missed so much over the past several years. Hand in hand, we walked to the house, our silence more unbearable than any possible words.

****

Daddy's "secret chambers" were usually reserved for men and business chats.

It was going to be bad. And judging by the way Daddy refused to look me in the eyes, I had a sinking feeling everything Kevin told me was true.

"Elizabeth." He strained for an all too scant smile. "I want to tell you the truth before you hear it anywhere else." I sat on the edge of my seat, waiting for the bomb to drop. "As you know, times have been hard, particularly hard, on the upper class lately. The economy is at an all-time low and it's been affecting my business over the last several years. I've been struggling to keep us afloat, fighting a losing battle because people have become tighter with their money, less willing to take chances in today's unstable money market. I was drowning, running out of options—"

"I know that feeling," I said.

"Please, let me finish telling you this. It's hard enough as it is." His voice faltered. He gripped the corners of his oak desk and locked his arms, a small life raft in his storm-tossed sea of woes. "I made a decision…in retrospect, a very bad decision. I set up a…"

Daddy was never at a loss for words. He started a few times, uttered a couple of nonsensical syllables, and then stopped. Always a man of incredible pride, it must have been torture for him. I helped him along. "A Ponzi scheme?" I asked.

He blinked at me, a hint of surprise in his eyes. "Well, I'd rather not think of it as that, but for lack of a better term, I suppose so." He let out a long sigh, his breath wheezing from his nose. "I told my investors I had a special opportunity for them, something that would gain them great rewards. But in reality…" When he spread his hands, they trembled. He dropped them to his desk to steady them. "I had no such opportunity. To keep them aboard, I gave them back a little bit of their own already invested money. But you need to understand something, Elizabeth. I had every intention of paying them back in full with interest." He smacked a fist into his palm. "Every intention. I thought things would turn around. I did a little investing with their money, hoping it'd yield the proper returns." He slumped back in his chair, defeated. "But it didn't. I just got in over my head, losing more and more money—"

"Oh, Daddy." My heart shriveled up into a raisin. "Daddy…"

"Shhh, Elizabeth. Shhh." Unbelievably, he smiled. Not a pained, forced, uninterested smile, either. "I want you to know my feelings for you and your mother haven't changed and they never will. I love you, princess, always and forever." The sunlight, trickling in through the curtained windows, had now begun to set. Shadows fell over his features, his eyes shrouded in darkness, perfectly complementing the somber mood. "No matter what happens."

"What…what's going to happen, Daddy?" Suddenly, I transported back a decade. I blubbered like a little girl incapable of understanding the harsh realities of the outside world. I just wanted my daddy, the rock that was always unyielding, always there, always dependable. Why couldn't things go back to the way they were? But my make-believe time machine jettisoned me back to the present. The inevitable now.

"On Monday morning, I'm going to turn myself in to the US Securities and Exchange Commission. I'm going to present my case to them…plead for mercy. If I come forward, they might go easier on me." But his words sounded weak. My lifelong rock nothing more than a small pebble in a huge rock quarry. "A couple nights ago, someone broke into my office. Someone's already investigating me. They opened my desk and went through my files. It's just a matter of time, Elizabeth."

My inner turmoil flared radioactive, my coils ready to melt down. Had we not broken into Daddy's office, we might not even be having this conversation. "Daddy, I'm so, so sorry."

"Shhh, Elizabeth." Again with the heart-breaking ghost of a smile. He walked around his desk and knelt before me. Wrapping his arms around my back, he squeezed me tight. "It's not your fault. This is all my fault, princess. I made a very bad decision." His voice rose, then wavered. As soon as he began to cry, I doubled-down on my tears. Never in my life had I seen him cry. Honestly, I didn't believe him capable of tears. "I love you, princess, now, more than ever. And I'm so dreadfully sorry I haven't been here for you lately. I'm so very sorry."

We stayed that way for a long time. Words weren't spoken, only mournful sobs of regret. Regret for what might happen and what should have happened. When the ship of tears finally sailed, we remained close. He cradled me in his strong, warm arms, making up for lost time.

"Elizabeth, all I ever wanted out of life was to provide for you and your mother. To give you the life you deserve…that you're accustomed to. I'm afraid I failed you."

"Daddy, no! You're not a failure!"

"That's nice of you to say. But it feels like failure to me."

"What's going to happen? I mean, what will the Commission do to you?"

When he stood up, his knees cracked like twin finger-snaps. He sat down next to me. "I may have to go away for a little while, princess." Before I started moaning again, he shushed me. "And I'm afraid they're going to freeze all of my assets."

"Freeze your assets." As if the statement somehow extended its icy reach into the room, my voice sounded cold and far away.

He nodded and made a clicking sound with his tongue against his lips. "I'm sorry to tell you this, but Dartmouth is probably out of the question. At least for now."

"What?" My stomach hopped up into my throat.

"We won't be able to afford it." He leaned in, meeting my blurry gaze.

"No Dartmouth?" I couldn't match up the meek, mouse-like voice in the room with my own.

"I'm afraid so. But your mother has made money over the years, working at bake sales, charities and…" He shrugged his shoulders as if uncertain what it was Mother did with her days. "I've spoken with her about this, Elizabeth. Worst-case scenario, we do have enough money that the SEC has no right to touch…to send you to junior college."

My world imploded. "No…no…" I saw double. I felt dizzy. I wanted to throw up. But unlike the drug flashbacks, still completely in the here and now, even though I wanted to wake from this horrible nightmare. *Please, God, let it be a nightmare!*

"Not junior college. *Nooo!*" I bayed at the ceiling like a dog, my fists upraised at the uncaring gods who were punking me and enjoying every sadistic second of it. *Junior college.* My entire life had been focused on one thing and one thing only: getting into the Ivy League school of my choice. So close, too. Yet, one small slip of fate, and I was banished to junior college. My dreams gone. *Poof.* Up in smoke. All the good things I'd done lately—clearing Charles Durbin's name—should've bought me extra credit with God, the fates, whatever.

"Daddy, no. No, no, no…" I continued to repeat it, hoping to counteract my dire fate.

"Elizabeth, it'll be all right." Daddy hugged me again, tears all around. "I promise you—no matter what happens—things will work out."

"Do you truly believe that?"

This time he displayed a strong resolve in his voice, firmness chiseled onto his face. "I truly do. This is just a minor setback for you. Junior college is a waiting station. There's still time to get into Dartmouth, just not right now. I promise you, we'll get you there, one way or another. I have faith. You must have faith as well. We Blackmers are not quitters. You have your entire life ahead of you, Elizabeth." He tipped my chin up with his fingertip. "And what a great life you're going to have."

For the first time, I couldn't see a future. It used to be clear as day. Now it seemed darker than Charlotte Drayton's soul. I wanted desperately to believe Daddy's words, but…but…I couldn't.

But. This was *Daddy;* Daddy who was always right, always my support, always the one I depended upon. And he was finally back after taking an extended, emotional holiday. "Oh, Daddy, I'm so selfish, thinking about—"

"Shhh, it's okay. I understand."

"What…what can I do for you?"

His eyes sparkled as he cupped his hands alongside my cheeks. "I want you to go to prom tonight and have the best damn prom of your life."

"Daddy, no. It hardly seems important…not now."

"You listen to me, Elizabeth Blackmer. I'm still your father! And I'm telling you that you're going with

Donovan tonight. You're going to have the time of your life, and you're going to be crowned prom queen. The best, most beautiful prom queen in Clearwell's history. It's what you've strived for and it's what you deserve."

"I don't know—"

"Well, I know. I mean it, Elizabeth. Don't let my stupid mistakes impede your happiness. Do you hear me? If you want to help me, that's what you can do."

"How's that supposed to help you?"

He smiled again, appearing like a man half his age. "Because, princess, the one thing I care most about in this world is you. It may not have seemed like it the past couple of years, but it's true. If you're happy, I'm happy. I love you…always will…more than anything." He kissed my forehead.

"I love you, too, Daddy."

One of the things I'd fervently wished for over the past two years had finally come true tonight. Daddy found his way back to me. It was too bad it took a tragedy for it to happen. Ironically, he was ready to leave again. This time more than emotionally.

****

I closed my eyes, and waited for the comfort of dark oblivion to whisk me away.

A few minutes later, Elspeth slid onto the bed beside me. "I'm sorry about your dad, Elizabeth. I know it sucks."

I snorted. "Sucks is putting it mildly."

"You know there are worse things in life than—"

"What could possibly be worse?" How dare she minimize my anguish? "Daddy might be going away to prison. We're going to lose our money. We'll probably have to live in some sort of hovel or apartment." I wrinkled my nose in disgust at the notion of such squalor. "And I'm going to have to go to *junior* college!"

"Hey, at least you're alive. At least you get the opportunity to go to junior college, Elizabeth."

Elspeth was always hard to read. I couldn't tell if she was mocking me or something else. A blank slate, she merely stared at me.

"You don't understand." Although part of me had to admit she was right, I felt I had earned my despair. I wanted to wear it like a Brownie merit badge jabbed into my chest by a clumsy troop leader. The more my wound bled, the more I would embrace the pain, the only absolute I had in my life.

"Oh, right, Elizabeth. You think you have a monopoly on crap in your life?" Elspeth half-sneered, half-smiled. "Hello! Dead person, here." She turned her thumbs on herself. "Even though I hated school, there were times I wondered what it would've been like to go to junior college. If I'd have been so lucky."

"It's just..." I stopped before I unleashed another avalanche of tears. Even though the tears weren't real in Dream Space, I had grown sick of them.

"I know, Liz." Elspeth linked her arm around mine and rested her head on my shoulder. Surprised by her compassion, I didn't even correct her calling me "Liz."

"I hear junior college isn't so bad. And like your dad said, it's not forever. You need to buck up and look toward the future. That's what you've always done in the past."

I released a shuddering sigh, a valve finally shutting off my tears. "It might not be bad, but it's not what I wanted."

Elspeth cocked her head, and gave me a confident grin. "You'll get there."

"Yeah, I will."

Elspeth hopped off the bed, twirled, and faced me. "That's the Elizabeth I've come to know and inhabit." She clapped her hands together with a loud smack, finalizing the last moment of my pity party. "Okay! Time to put on your winning prom dress. Donovan will be here in an hour or so."

"Elspeth, the stupid prom just doesn't seem important now."

"Yeah, well, that's what I've been sayin' all along. But quit your bitchin'. Time to go!" She grabbed an imaginary shovel and pantomimed digging underneath me. "Come on. I mean it. This is important to you. Don't make me go all bad-ass on you. Get up! Princes to kiss and crowns to wear and all that junk."

I bit my lower lip, finally gave in and laughed. It felt good. "Fine. You win."

\*\*\*\*

Looking in the mirror, I cringed. The flesh around my eyes appeared swollen from crying, my eyes bloodshot. I had to admit, though, I still looked killer. My designer dress glowed resplendently blue, perfectly setting off my blond hair and blue eyes. The keyhole front—slightly naughty enough to tastefully show a hint of cleavage, but not too much—carried jewels on the straps. I fretted about the short length, several inches higher above my knees than usual, but I had sexiness on my mind. I wore matching earrings, dangling down against my cheekbones. Jewels also lined my silver-strapped heels. Once I won prom queen, the crown would be the perfect accessory.

I whirled in front of the mirror, taking myself in from every possible angle. The complete package. Then I thought about how much it all cost. My sunny disposition clouded over with sadness. I'd gladly take the dress back and give the money to Daddy to help him pay off his investors.

The doorbell rang. Mother called up, "Elizabeth! Donovan's here!" The sprightly cheery tone in her voice rang contrary to the drama going on in our house.

****

Earlier, Mother had caught me when I came out of Daddy's study. She'd been crying as well, a nearly empty martini glass in her well-manicured hand. "Elizabeth, I'm sorry, love."

I glared at her. "How long did you know this was going on, Mother?"

She stared into her glass as she swirled it about. "I just found out." Her left eye twitched once, a dead giveaway she lied. "That's not quite true. I've known for a while."

"How long's a while?" For some reason, I felt less forgiving to Mother than Daddy. Daddy screwed up. But Mother conspired to keep it from me.

"It doesn't matter, dear. What's important is both your father and I love you very much." Her voice broke. She slumped against the wall, her free hand flying to cover her eyes. "We'll get through this…somehow we will."

How thoughtless of me. Of course, she faced life changes as well. And she had had many more years than I did to grow accustomed to an idle rich lifestyle. I had to put my petty concerns aside. We needed to stick together, now more than ever. The Blackmer women, forging a new life together, alone against the world. I reached for her.

We embraced for a long time. "I love you, too, Mother." I had experienced more physical displays of affection from my parents in the last half hour than I had in the last two years combined. Maybe something good would come of this, after all.

\*\*\*\*

"Elizabeth, don't keep Donovan waiting." Her stark command snapped me out of my reverie.

I braced myself, took a deep breath, and admired my image one last time in the mirror. Not bad for someone whose world had just slipped out of the universe. I gave myself one last, inner pep talk and could almost hear Elspeth cheering me on.

I walked onto the landing, slowly, dramatically. I had dreamt of this moment, wanting to make a ginormous impact. By the looks on everyone's faces, I had totally succeeded.

At the bottom of the stairwell, Daddy lowered the camera to gaze upon me. His eyes lit up with satisfaction, his smile proud. Mother audibly gasped and clasped her hands together underneath her chin. Donovan stared with wide, unblinking eyes, boyishly endearing.

Daddy's bulb flashed, stinging my tired eyes. I made my way down the stairs, enjoying the moment. "You look stunning, dear. Doesn't she, Harold?" All Daddy could do was nod in agreement. Good. If he choked up again, I was sure to follow his lead.

"You look…fantastic, Elizabeth," Donovan said.

Donovan looked very handsome, himself, nicely tucked into his jet-black tuxedo. His purple velvet vest pinned a long black tie firmly in place. Even though I had helped him pick out his attire, I kept my dress under wraps. The teasing hints I had dropped had the desired effect. Fumbling with a box, he pulled out a corsage. Not once did his gaze leave me as if afraid I'd fade from memory like a wondrous dream. Deep in his soulful brown eyes, I detected awe and lust, a tantalizing combination. It put a smile on my lips.

I reached the bottom of the stairs as he finally wrestled the corsage from its container. "This is for you." He slipped it onto my wrist with a soft touch, taking care not to break his porcelain doll. I held it up by my ear, pushed back a lock of hair, and posed for another picture.

Donovan's expression suddenly switched over to concern. He leaned in and whispered, "Are you okay?"

I whispered back, "I'll explain later. Let's just get through this."

Donovan shook Mother's hand lightly and turned to deliver a manly squeeze to Daddy's hand. "We really must be going, sir."

"Fine. Fine. Let me get one more photo of the two of you." Donovan and I lined up as instructed, our arms naturally falling around each other's backs.

He snapped the photo, forever commemorating a dream come true. The handsome man I loved and would spend the rest of my life with was taking me to my crowning prom; my beaming parents looking on with well-deserved honor for having raised me so well. *My fairy tale.*

Yet, I couldn't completely ignore the absolute charade of it all. It might be the last time we'd be together as a family for a while. My father's imminent departure sadly tainted what I thought would be one of my life-defining moments.

I grimaced just as Daddy took another photograph.

Looking back, I wish I would've cherished the moment longer, warts and all.

Chapter Fifteen

*Elizabeth*

"Okay. What's wrong, Elizabeth?" Before starting his engine, Donovan turned squarely in his seat to confront me. "I can tell you've been crying."

"Oh, my God. Is it that obvious?" I flipped down the visor to examine myself. I had hoped my bloated face would've smoothed out by now, but my body had different ideas.

"No, you're fine. You look, well, stunning. Now, tell me, what's wrong? Maybe I can help."

I shook my head. "Nobody can help." I told him everything, naturally leaving out how we broke into Daddy's office and downloaded his hard-drive.

"Wow." He grabbed my hand, his fingers intertwining with mine. "I'm really sorry. What can I do to help?"

"Nothing," I spat out, too harshly. I felt horrible when I saw the hurt in his eyes. He wasn't the enemy. "Sorry, sorry. It's just, there's nothing anyone can do at this point. It's something I'm going to have to deal with by myself."

"You don't have to cope with it by yourself. I'm here for you." He held my hand high and kissed the palm. "Always have been, always will."

"Promise?" I batted my eyes at him, my flirtatious

side brought out by his gallantry.

"Promise. You know I will be."

"I know." Our hands dropped to the seat, still connected. "It's just…junior college. *Gah.*"

"Elizabeth, there are scholarships. Your grades and achievements are outstanding. You'd be an ideal candidate for—"

"It's too late for this year. I was counting on our money, but now, that ship has sunk."

"Never give up hope. Never! You'll get to Dartmouth. I'm sure of it."

His words helped boost my dire mood. I pulled him toward me. The kiss felt special. Different. Not a mere kiss of affection reserved for high school hallways. This time I kissed him with fiery passion, our tongues exploring, our heavy breath unified. Hormones fueled my desire. I wanted Donovan. And I would have him. After the prom. I wanted to experience lovemaking with him and seek comfort in his strong arms. The kiss was just an appetizer for what was to come.

We came up for air. My eyes darted back and forth, taking in both of his. "I love you, Donovan."

"I love you, too. Always."

\*\*\*\*

When we entered the gymnasium, blaring Hawaiian music assaulted my ears, rattling my teeth. This year's theme was inexplicably "Hawaiian Luau." The themes were always sorta nonsensical, but this year the prom crew really went all out. The backdrop of the stage displayed a fully painted vista of a sun setting over deep blue ocean waves. Sand covered the stage floor. Several not very convincing paper-mache coconut trees extended from barely concealed buckets.

A bamboo hut with an arched straw roof sat at the center of the stage, presumably where the royalty would be announced. The decorations totally detracted from what the night was really all about.

Mr. Hastings stood just inside the door, accosting students with a Breathalyzer. His red Hawaiian shirt bulged at the seams. "Ms. Blackmer," he said while hoisting an eyebrow along with the device, "please blow."

I did as instructed, no sense arguing. Hastings already thought I was a stoner. He stared at the results, disbelieving as ever. "How are you, Donovan?"

"Very well. Thanks for asking, Mr. Hastings." Donovan grasped Hastings's hand and actually shook a smile out of him.

"Here." Hastings handed Donovan a purple lei. He held one out for me and I respectfully declined. A cheesy lei definitely wouldn't work with my carefully calibrated outfit.

Lance raced toward us, an unstoppable ball of energy. "Elizabeth, you look great!" Even though he directed his compliment toward me, I couldn't help but notice him checking out Donovan. As were many girls. "Hi, Donovan." He lingered a little too long on Donovan's handshake.

"You look pretty dapper yourself, Lance." Utilizing ninety percent style and ten percent over the top, Lance wore a red blazer and checkered vest. Red highlights streaked through his dark hair. "Did you bring a date?"

He widened his eyes exaggeratedly. "What? Here? You're kidding me."

It was strictly against Clearwell's rules for same-sex couples to go to a dance together. Yet, I grew curious if he had a significant other. To my shame, I realized I'd never asked him. "Do you have a boyfriend?"

"I'm not one to kiss and tell," he said with a wink. "But enough about me. This is your night, Elizabeth. You ready?"

I suppose so."

"Hey, cheer up, girl. Our posters did the job. You're going to win!"

"If you say so."

Lance squinted, and shook his head doubtfully. "What's the matter? You should be flying high as a kite."

"She just had a little bad news," offered Donovan.

"Well, get over it, Queen Elizabeth." Lance bowed toward me.

"Thank you, Sir Lance-A-Lot." I curtsied in my most regal manner.

Some would-be musician tortured a ukulele over the loudspeakers, a high-pitched voice moaning along. The chaperoning teachers looked none too happy in their Hawaiian shirts and grass skirts as they stomped through the gathered students, searching for signs of foul play. "Hawaii" never seemed so oppressive.

"Donovan? Would you get me a glass of punch?" He obediently trotted off.

"Elizabeth?" Tina looked plain, yet pretty, in a simple blue dress. But my jaw dropped upon seeing her daringly exposed shoulders. She looked like a completely different woman. "Can I talk to you? Alone?"

Taking the clue, Lance bounded off, the only

person happy to be here.

"Elizabeth, I heard what happened to Donnie Heidenreich. It sounds like exactly what happened to Charles." She flicked at her hair, obviously uncomfortable with the newly implanted waves.

"Tina, it is what happened to Charles. They got to Donnie, too. They drugged him and sent his car into a lake."

"Oh, my God. How do you know this?"

"Trust me. I just do." I leaned down and lowered my voice. Yet I still practically had to scream to be heard above the music. "I can't go into details now, but I think I know who the dealer is. And who did this to Donnie and Charles."

Tina rolled her hands the way she used to do when she grew flummoxed. *The wheels on the bus go round and round.* Yet whereas I once found it annoying, I now felt an odd tinge of nostalgia for her nervous tic. "Well, who is it? And are you going to be able to clear Charles's name?"

"I think so. But, right now, it's best if you stay out of it. For your own safety."

"Why don't you call the cops, already?"

Good question, really. But Elspeth's stubborn streak kept me from doing so. "Because, I don't really have any evidence yet."

"Well, then, how can you be so sure?"

"I know I'm asking a lot from you, especially after our past. But trust me."

Tina stared at me for a long, quiet moment, pondering if I'd earned her trust. "Okay, Elizabeth. Fine. I just hope you get results."

"I will."

"Thanks. I mean, thanks for what you're doing for Charles."

"You're welcome. I'm happy to, well, to be able to help, I guess." And I was, too. As a matter of fact, it seemed more important to me now than winning the stupid prom queen crown. "Oh, and Tina?" She lifted her eyebrows. "You look nice tonight."

Tina grinned, a natural and toothy smile, a look well suited to her. Redness colored her cheeks, her eyes sparkling. She wandered off, a confident kick in her step.

Call it a sixth sense or whatever, but recently I'd developed a more acute awareness of my surroundings. I felt eyes peering into my back. I turned, facing the bleachers. Tim Matthews stood behind the folded bleachers, barely visible in the shadows. For the first time, he looked like a cop in his ill-fitting—no doubt off the racks—natty suit. Except for the braces.

"T-shir…um, Tim. You know there're programs for guys like you. It's called Lurkers Anonymous. Is that what they teach you cops?"

He chopped the air with several knife-like motions. "Keep it down." I joined him in the darkness. "I'm trying to remain undercover, you know."

"Yeah, well, dressed in your detective suit?"

He took inventory of his clothing, looking at his arms, then his legs. "What's wrong with my suit?"

"Nothing, forget it. What have you found out?"

"That's my question for you. The Heidenreich kid's still in a coma. What do you know about that?"

"Nothing."

"Yeah? That's funny. A farmer called it in. Said there was a blond teenage girl who told him about the accident. The description he gave resembles you." He attempted a television cop's steely gaze. Looked more like a childish pout. The braces just weren't very intimidating.

"Huh. Imagine that. But like I said, I don't know anything about it. I was home studying like a good girl. But from what I've heard, it sounds like the same thing that happened to Charles Durbin."

He stepped forward, shadows slipping away from his face. The blue overhead floodlights cast his face in an eerie, deathly pallor. "What do you mean?"

"I think Donnie was dosed just like Charles Durbin."

"Are you withholding information from me? You know that's against the law, right?"

"Calm down, junior G-man. All I'm saying is it sounds like a similar situation. Surely you've figured that out by now."

"I knew that," he said, sounding extremely uncertain.

"Of course you did." I spotted Donovan, two drinks in hand, looking over the heads of the crowd for me. "Ta ta for now. Time to go take my crown."

Just in time, I stepped out from the bleachers and grabbed a cup from Donovan's hand. "Thank you."

"You're quite welcome." I curled my hand around his arm. Resting my head on his shoulder, I wondered what it would be like to do the same in a horizontal position. *Naked.*

And that's when all hell broke loose.

"Well, well, if it isn't Elizabeth Blackhead, prom queen 'also ran and never won'." Charlotte had stuffed herself into a slutty black number, the skirt not much more than a bandanna. She looked like a rotten banana. "I'm surprised you even bothered to show up. Are you here to cheer on my victory?"

I rolled my eyes. "I thought I smelled something bad." Donovan immediately grappled for my hand. "Hello, Char-slut." Her entourage, including Addie, Kip, and the girls, let out a collective gasp. "You're looking absolutely whorish this evening."

"And don't you look slut-tacular? Just wait, my dear. We'll see who has the smart mouth once I bring home the gold." She threw out a hip and tossed her long, dark hair off her shoulders.

"You don't stand a chance, Elizabeth," spat Addie. "Charlotte's going to win!" Kip kept his mouth shut, but grinned widely, probably hoping for a girl fight.

"No, Charlotte's not going to be crowned prom queen...drag queen, maybe."

Charlotte's lips spread into a ghastly sneer. "Care to make a bet on it?"

"I would, but I only bet on horses, not with them."

Charlotte rattled a fist at me, an invisible tambourine in her hand. "Come on, girls. Let's not spend any more time than we have to on losers." She swiveled on her hooker shoes, ankles snapping angrily back at me. Her toady army fell in line. Kip, the last in the frog parade, shrugged at Donovan before catching up with the other creatures.

"Maybe Charlotte is going to win."

"No, don't say that. You're Elizabeth Blackmer, dammit. You don't quit."

My hero. Always the right thing to say. "I'm going to the restroom." I handed Donovan my drink. As I made my way out of the gym, the nightmarish hula music continued to worm its way into my brain.

And there he stood. Marc Dugan in front of the bathrooms.

I had no idea he'd even be at the prom. It was definitely not his thing. Shockingly, his favored flannel shirt had taken a flyer. Instead, he wore a white dress shirt tucked into khaki pants. His long hair had been slicked back and bound in a small knot. On his arm hung the slutty girl whom Elspeth had an encounter with at the gas station, poured into a small red slip of a dress. It barely covered her crotch. Obviously bored, she smacked her gum, trying to gain Dugan's notice. But Dugan's serious discussion with several surrounding goons demanded his full attention.

Dugan looked up and caught my eye. A reptilian smile slithered across his face. He held up his hand, extended his index finger at me, thumb up. He closed one eye, took aim, and dropped his thumb, mouthing "bang." Then he and his cronies entered the bathroom.

Just enough to bring out a seriously pissed off Elspeth.

****

*Elspeth*

I wobbled in Elizabeth's shoes for a few seconds. I took a risk, making the transference standing up and in front of people. But no way in hell I was missing out on this.

As I pushed past the red-dressed harpy, she shrieked at me, saying I couldn't go into the bathroom. I brushed by her and threw back the door. Dugan bent over, showing me "plumber crack," two fingers slipped inside his shoe. He stared at me from underneath his arm before straightening. His cronies exchanged glances, decided to leave. Good decision. They slunk by me, not daring to look at the crazy chick in the dudes' bathroom. Fine. Whatever. All I cared about was Dugan.

The bastard who had tried to kill me.

"What do you want?" The growl reverberated like an alley-dog's before it attacked.

"I want you to pay for what you did to me. For what you did to Donnie. And to Charles Durbin."

"You're crazy. But even if I did something, who's going to make me pay? You?" He burst out laughing.

*Yeah, just keep on laughing.*

"You bet your ass." I grabbed the pepper spray out of Elizabeth's purse. Holding it up, I rushed him. His hands raised to his face. Not quick enough. Perfect shot to the eyes. Cursing, he fell back against the sink, his arms windmilling about. One of his fists clocked my ear good. I bounced off a toilet stall door like a pinball. Using my momentum, I leapt onto his back, ear boxing him with no mercy.

"What did you do to me, bitch?" With his eyes nearly shut and arms flapping in front of him, he looked like Frankenstein's monster fending off villagers.

Riding him like an untamed bronco, I couldn't help myself and hooted, "Yee-haw."

He turned in a circle, closing in against the wall. *Uh-oh.* "Get off me, you crazy bitch!"

Repeatedly, he battered me against the stone wall. With each slam, my breath left me. But I clung tight. "God *damn* it!"

Fire started low in my back and burned its way up my spine. My legs weakened, dropped from around his waist. I slid to the floor.

*I have to get up!*

A steel-tipped shoe kicked at my chest. Before he pulled back his foot again, I snatched his ankle and yanked hard. He plummeted backward, his head impacting the floor with a satisfying crack. Maybe not so satisfying for him. Now on all fours, I leapt for the pepper spray by his arm. He swatted it away, the vial spinning across the floor like a top.

Dugan squinted, practically half-blind. Closing his eyes, he launched himself at me. I rolled, sprang up, and brought my elbow down into his back. Felt good. While I crawled after the pepper spray and Elizabeth's purse, Dugan climbed to his feet.

"You crazy bitch," were his last sentiments before he retreated into the hallway.

As soon as I pulled the door open, a fist skyrocketed into my face. Little yellow dots welcomed me as I rolled along the lockers. But my vision cleared just in time to see Dugan's she-devil date pulling her fist back again. "Leave him alone, bitch!" Same vocabulary teacher as Dugan's, apparently.

I seized her fist, squeezing hard. I wrenched her arm and tugged it behind her back, and she pirouetted like a dance partner. "Playtime's over. Don't you have an STD or something to go get?" I tossed her aside like so much trash. She sidled down along the lockers to the floor, crying.

From down the darkened end of the hallway, I heard a commotion. "She's crazy," Dugan called out. "Someone stop her!" Other students backed up against the lockers, watching the fracas. I spotted Dugan at the end of the hallway, running like his life depended on it. Pretty much did, too.

Breaking into a mid-strut, I kicked off one of Elizabeth's shoes and popped it into my hand. I hurled it down the hallway. It rebounded into a locker with a clang. I knew I couldn't hit him at this distance. But I wanted him to know I was coming. For good measure, I heaved the other shoe as far as I could. Damn shoes were in the way, anyway.

I grabbed the Taser from Elizabeth's purse and flung the purse to the floor. Holding the Taser at arm's length, I stalked down the hallway with purpose in my eyes and vengeance in my soul.

"What in the name of the gods?" Elizabeth's environmental science teacher stood in the open door of the teacher's lounge, wearing a grass skirt over his suit.

"Nothing to see here," I said, waving him back into the lounge.

The door slammed shut at the far end of the hall. I picked my pace up, running past gasping students, disregarding their shrieks. I opened the door, and peered down the stairwell. Two flights down, Dugan was racing for the basement. Taking three stairs at a time, I jumped to the bottom landing. He swung the door shut.

*Almost got you.*

I burst through the door, caught the tail end of Dugan entering the boy's locker room.

The locker room sat in darkness, the only illumination coming from the red Exit sign. A water faucet leaked slow drops inside the shower room. My panty-hosed feet felt cold on the cement floor.

I stopped and listened carefully. Breathing. Closer now. I crept toward the sound. In the last row of lockers. Taser ready, I squatted down. He'd be swinging high. Then I pounced around the corner. A powerhouse swing released a whoosh of air above me. Estimating his crotch's whereabouts, I landed a solid blow there. He shrieked, doubled over. A fist swam up, sliced me underneath the chin. I wobbled back. My head clanged into a locker. I hit my tailbone on the floor while my legs popped up onto the bench. He darted out the closest door.

*I can't believe this guy. Doesn't he know when he's beaten?*

I stood, wagged my head, and ran into the narrow corridor. To Swimming Pool, the sign stated. In front of me, the door clicked shut. Crouching, I prepared to yank open the door. Then I heard a splash.

Inside the pool room, Chiaroscuro water reflections played over the walls and ceiling. Ludicrously, I spotted Dugan dog paddling in the center of the pool.

"Stay away from me, you crazy bitch!" Dugan spat out water every third word or so. He dipped in and out, trying to cleanse his eyes. "You're crazy!"

I flipped on the overhead light, grabbed a folding chair leaning against the wall. Straddling the chair backward, I rested my arms on the back. I lined up Dugan in the Taser's sites. "What, Dugan? You gonna swim to safety?"

"I didn't do nothin'!" He kept paddling his arms, a kid going nowhere, figuratively and literally.

"Well, define 'nothing'. Let's start with drug dealing. How about attempted murder and, you know, murder?"

"You can't prove anything!"

"Bet I can. I'd like to take a look in your shoes. Not looking forward to the smell, though."

A long pause, just the sloshing of water. "You can't look in my shoes! I'll have you arrested!"

"Oh, that's rich, Dugan." I sighed, and flourished the Taser in front of him. "Look, we can play games all night, but I'm getting bored. And I've got to go get crowned in a little while. Now…" I frowned as if deep in thought. "I'm no science geek. I suspect you're the one who makes designer drugs. But if I were to shoot you with this Taser, while you're in the pool…" I grimaced, inhaling loudly through my teeth for show. "*Yikes!* If it doesn't electrocute you, I'm sure it'll be very uncomfortable."

Dugan attempted to open his eyes, failed, then returned them to red slits. "You can't…Help! Someone help me!"

"Oh, shut up. Don't say I didn't warn you." I stood up, went to the edge of the pool, and made a big production out of aiming the Taser at him.

"No! Wait! Please!"

"Well? You have something to say to me? May as well confess. Donnie came out of his coma and said you tried to kill him, anyway." A worthy lie. Might hurry this farce along. "Just a matter of time before the cops come."

"All right! All right! Just put the Taser away!"

"I don't think so. Not yet. Talk."

"I did it."

Like pulling teeth. "Did what, Dugan?"

"I drugged Donnie. Pushed his car into the lake…with you in the trunk."

"Okay. It's a start. What else did you do?"

"I deal drugs. And I drugged Charles Durbin."

Oh, the hell with what I had promised him. I took

aim. *"Wait! Don't!"*

"Did you drug me? At your party?"

"Yes....*yes!*" When he covered his face with his hands, he bobbed, sputtered. His arms throttled back at the water. Apparently not much of a swimmer.

"Why?"

"You were all up into stuff that wasn't your damn business. I had a good deal going. You were going to screw it up. Just like Charles."

"Okay. Also…"

"Also what?"

"Also say 'I'm the biggest douchiest douche that ever douched'." He looked at me incredulously then smirked. His smirk nearly triggered the Taser. "Say it!"

"I'm the biggest douche—"

"No. The biggest *douchiest* douche…"

"I'm the biggest douchiest douche that ever douched! Happy now?"

"More than you could dream."

Dugan's unexpected laughter came out hoarse and desperate. "You don't even know what you're uncovering here, do you?"

I sat down by the edge of the pool. "What are you talking about?"

"I'm not in this alone, you know." He spat water out again with vitriol. "I have a partner. He supplied me with the start-up funding for our operation."

Unexpected, but I supposed it really shouldn't have been. Behind every jackass, there's a bigger jackass with cash. "Who is it?"

As soon as he told me, the door clattered open. Tim Matthews barreled in, his face white and glistening with sweat. "What in the hell is going on here? Kids were saying you were chasing Dugan through the school with a damn Taser!"

I pointed toward Dugan. "There's your drug dealer, Matthews."

"Say again."

"He just confessed everything. And check his shoes. That's where today's specials are."

"Tim? What the hell?" Dugan looked extra stupid, switching his gaze between us.

"You're sure?" Greed overwhelmed Tim's smile. I supposed this bust would be a nice feather in his cop cap.

"I'm sure."

I got up to leave, dreading the last horrible thing that needed to be done. And Elizabeth was going to have to take the bullet. It strangely devastated me. So much sadness. And so much more to come.

"One more thing." I turned to Dugan and fired the Taser. His body twitched and jerked in the water, a convulsive aqua ballet. I dropped the Taser. I didn't really think it'd electrocute him. Didn't really care. I needed the cathartic moment.

"Oh my God," Tim said as he dove into the water. Mustn't let the murderer drown.

I sent Elizabeth back to the prom with a heavy heart.

****

*Elizabeth*

I walked into the gym in a daze. My shoes gone, my dress torn, my pantyhose destroyed, my hair disheveled, makeup all running and smeared; I looked a bloody mess. But it was nothing but a stain on my inner devastation.

Within the Hawaiian hut, Donovan beamed, newly crowned, and smiling at his constituents. I slowly made my way to the front of the stage, the students whispering and clearing a path for me as if I had the plague.

Hastings stood next to Donovan, note cards holding the winners' names in hand. Donovan furrowed his brow and mouthed, "What happened?" I snubbed him.

Hastings shot me a look. "We're going to have words later!" Then he continued with the wondrous proceedings. "And now, what you've all been waiting for. It's time to announce our annual prom queen!" He stared at the audience expectantly. Sporadic applause dribbled out, mostly nervous laughter. "Can we have a drum roll?" Hastings looked at the disc jockey, who just shrugged. "Okay, fine." He listed the candidates slowly, agonizingly enunciating each syllable. "And your prom queen is...Elizabeth Blackmer!" He pointed at me and frowned again. "Uh, let's hear it for your prom queen!" He stood back and applauded.

I walked up the steps, and positioned myself next to Donovan. Didn't look at him. Those who hadn't already noticed me tittered over my devastated appearance.

The disc jockey blasted out pompous regal music. He just as abruptly squelched it off when I grabbed the microphone. Hastings leaned over and whispered, "We need to have a talk, young lady." With a phony smile, he stood tall and placed the silly tiara on my head.

Donovan appeared anxious. He reached over, cupped a hand over the microphone, and said, "What happened? Are you okay?" He gingerly placed his arm on my back. I knocked it away with my elbow.

I looked out into the audience, couldn't see anyone. Kinda like how I'd never seen most of the student body before. The glare of the spotlight burned my eyes, representative of so many students' bright lights that I should've taken the time to look at, to appreciate, to know.

I cleared my throat and let it rip. "My whole life…is a lie. Everything I thought I knew, everything I've devoted my entire life to isn't true. My Daddy…Dad…he's going to jail for illegal activities." Several gasps rose from the faceless audience. "He taught me to strive for excellence—that hard work and success matters. Well, it doesn't. He didn't even adhere to his own teachings. He lied. And cheated people. Now we're going to lose our money, probably our house… my horse." I choked, but shook it off. "I'm won't be going to Dartmouth. I'm going to…" I couldn't bring myself to say it. "And my friends. My so-called friends!" I waved a hand vaguely out toward the audience. "They're a bunch of monsters! They're nothing but mean, spoiled bitches!" A few laughs and cheers rang out from the crowd. "And the first chance they got, they betrayed me. But that wasn't the cruelest betrayal." I turned to Donovan. "Here stands your prom king, who many of you found worthy of your votes. Well, let me tell you something. He's not worthy."

Students' murmurs and whispers rippled and grew like a tidal wave.

"Elizabeth," said Donovan, still trying to wrest an arm around me. I backed away from him.

Hastings stormed across the stage. "That's enough, Ms. Blackmer!"

I ran to the opposite side of the stage, microphone still in hand, barely escaping Hastings's lunge. "Your prom king is a drug dealer." Silence dropped like a blanket over the audience. I looked at Donovan, now hanging his head. He slowly removed his crown, dropping it to the floor with a hollow *thump*. The crown wobbled on the floor before coming to a stop. It seemed so tarnished now, so inconsequential, so unwanted.

Like me.

I dared a glance at Donovan. His deep brown eyes, once so beautiful and puppy-dog-like, now looked pathetic. "He funded Marc Dugan's drug dealing venture. He lied to me. He lied to all of you."

"Elizabeth…" Donovan's voice broke with pain and I hoped more than a little guilt.

"So…" I took off my tiara, and made a face at it. "I'm not worthy of being your prom queen either. I appreciate your voting for me, but it just doesn't matter anymore. It's not important. Why don't you give it to somebody who is worthy of it? Someone like Tina Bottoms, maybe. She's more worthy than me. She's a nice person."

"No," shouted Tina's unmistakable voice.

I actually managed a small smile. Years of practice. "Okay, so Tina doesn't want it. Give it to Charlotte Drayton. I just don't care…"

From the back of the gym, Charlotte let out a huge squeal. Her footsteps skittered across the gym floor, and then she stormed the stage. Racing toward me like a horse, she snatched the crown out of my hands, nearly tumbling out of her dress. She held it up victoriously and dropped it on her mane. Waiting for applause, quiet indifference met her.

"It just doesn't matter…" The microphone screamed when I dropped it. Trying to keep my head up, I began the seemingly endless trek off the stage.

"Elizabeth! Please stop!" Donovan clutched my wrist. "Let me explain! Please!" I looked into the eyes of the man I had planned to give everything up for. Tears streamed down his cheeks. Crocodile tears? "Please!"

I firmly removed his hand and dropped it like the microphone. "You're a drug dealer, Donovan. What else is there to say?"

"No! I mean, all I did was give Dugan some money! Then it grew out of control. When I suspected what he'd done to Charles, I got out. I told him I didn't want anything to do with it anymore! I didn't even talk to him again."

I pummeled his chest with my fists. "Why did you do it, Donovan? Tell me! Tell me."

"Elizabeth, I'm so sorry. I did it, well, because I didn't have any money. I had some savings. That's what I gave Dugan over the last several months. But it wasn't enough. I'm not rich like you. I needed money to keep up with the clothes you thought I should wear, to give you the lifestyle you deserve. The boyfriend you deserve."

"You are not going to blame this on me! And I don't deserve a drug dealer."

Donovan winced. "I'm not blaming you, Elizabeth. I made a stupid mistake. Your dad quit paying me. But he once told me when opportunity knocks, you jump at the door before someone else does. Drugs are a product people want. Supply and demand. It was my shot at making a lot of money fast. I talked to Dugan…I knew he was into drugs. He thought we could make good money. My plan was to finance several initial operations, then get out."

"It's not supply and demand. It's drug dealing! Why did you do this to us?" I buried my face into his chest. Not for comfort. But to hide my shame, my pain. "Why? I would've done anything for you. Why?"

He caressed my hair with long, loving strokes. "I'm sorry. I tried to warn you to stay away from the whole drug thing. I sent you the notes." His sobbing broke my heart, but I wouldn't give in. "If you would've left everything alone, we could've gone on. I'm sorry."

The disc jockey, obviously uncomfortable with the all-misery floorshow, started playing a slow song. Donovan swayed back and forth, pulling me close to him. My hands slipped into his, once the most natural reaction in the world. We circled slowly, turning round and round, ultimately going nowhere. One last dance.

"I love you, Elizabeth. Now and always," he whispered.

I nodded, my head bobbing on his shoulder. "I know and that's why this hurts so much. Because I love you, too, or at least the man I thought you were."

A clatter arose at the back of the gym followed by stomping footfalls. The overhead lights flipped on. Squinting against the harsh light, I saw several police officers approaching the stage. A student pointed toward us.

I kissed Donovan one final time. "Goodbye, Donovan."

\*\*\*\*

*Elspeth*

"I'm sorry, Elizabeth. Really. I know you're miserable." I cradled her in my arms, the way my mom held me when I was sick or scared of the lightning.

"Thanks." Her eyes looked nearly swollen shut, her nose red and irritated. Tissues littered the floor like random clumps of snow.

"But you really, really need to get out of bed and do something. You've been lying here for two days now. Go spend some time with your dad, get out and do something."

"Why? What's the point?"

"Elizabeth," I said with more than a little exasperation, "yes, you've been through a lotta crap, but you've done a lot of good. You nailed, well, two drug dealers." My bad triggered a fresh crying jag. "Sorry. But, really, you put away the bad guy. You cleared Charles Durbin's name. You gave everyone a really memorable prom."

Elizabeth snorted out a laugh between sobs. "Not funny, Elspeth."

"Maybe it is a little bit." I held my thumb and finger apart, the way we'd done before this mess started. "You were quite a sight."

"Oh, God! Don't remind me." Her hands flew to her face. "But it doesn't matter anymore. I won't have Donovan or Daddy."

"I bet they go easy on Donovan. First offense and all. And I understand he's cooperating fully. He'll probably get a slap on the wrist or a really small sentence." Even though I offered words of encouragement, an involuntary sneer slipped through. "Then you can get back together with him, if you want to."

Elizabeth sat up, considering the thought. "I don't know. I don't think I can go back to him, not after what he did."

"That's my girl. Don't give him a second chance. I happen to know—from higher sources—that your next guy is just around the corner." I didn't really, but I knew it was true. Girls like Elizabeth never lacked for male attention.

"Really?"

"Really. And you know something? Yes, what you went through sucks, but you're a better person for it." She looked at me and scoffed. "No, I mean it. The old Elizabeth wouldn't have done what you did for Charles Durbin. And what you said at the prom? Totally kickass!" I messed her hair up. Usually, she would've screamed at me to stop. But she was past caring about appearances. Maybe for the first time in her life. "I like the new Elizabeth. That is, if you'll ever get out of bed. Things will get better, trust me."

"You know, a lot of people have said that to me lately. And some of them, I shouldn't have trusted."

"That's part of life. Deal with it. Hard lesson, I know, but you are better for it."

"If you say so."

A small victory. But little by little, I chinked away at her armadillo shell. A glimmer of hope sparkled in her eyes.

"Now, are you going to get out of bed?"

"I guess so."

"Good." I stood up and clapped my hands. "Well, get going!"

"Okay." She shuddered, and slowly crawled out of bed. Drained, she plopped right back. "Just five more minutes."

"Fine. Just don't be a slacker like Donnie." I sighed, preparing for more sadness. "Elizabeth, I guess it's time for me to get going, too."

"What?" She bolted up, her lower lip quivering. Maybe I could continue to shock her out of bed. "You're going to leave me, too?"

I smiled sadly at her, for both of us, really. "I don't have any say in it. It's just the way it rolls."

"Why is everyone leaving me?" she shouted.

I hugged her, a more frequent deal between us lately. "Hey, you know me. Just when you least expect it, I'll be back. I'm good about that, you know."

"I never thought I'd say this, but, I'm going to miss you."

"Elizabeth, you took the words right out of my mouth." To my astonishment, I started crying, too. "Dammit. Look what you made me do. Pass the stupid tissues." We sat next to one another, a nose-honking symphony between us.

"But first—and before you get out of bed, if you ever do—I'd like to take one last nighttime stroll."

"Wait, what?"

"I promise I'll be good. 'Night, Elizabeth."

Probably a rotten trick, but I put her out before she could object. She needed the rest, anyway.

\*\*\*\*

I savored the cool breeze against my skin. One final time.

In limbo, the wind never blew, clouds didn't fill the sky, never anything. Just year-round nice weather and, "hey, have a nice day" greetings from the vapid inhabitants. Sometimes I wondered if I ended up in limbo by mistake. I didn't exactly have what you'd call a sunny disposition.

I dreaded going back. Even if this particular mortal visit had been my most dangerous assignment yet. But I wouldn't have traded it for anything in this—or any other—world. I kissed a boy several times (Donnie's peck didn't count, neither did Donovan's—ugh) and I saw my mother one last time.

Disappointment kicked me in the gut when I stopped in front of Kevin's house. All lights were off. Then I saw a figure sitting in the darkness on the front stoop. I probably should have felt some guilt that I was thrilled with his insomnia.

He hadn't spotted me yet, and I planned on keeping it that way. I promised Elizabeth I'd be good and honestly, the poor girl has suffered enough without having to deal with more awkward advances from the neighbor kid. Just one last glimpse…

Ah, the hell with it.

I ran straight toward him. He sat up, startled. "Whoa. Elizabeth?"

"Yes." When he stood, I grabbed his ears like handlebars and kissed him passionately. I released him and he fell back, winded. Obviously, I knew how to rock his world. "You know something, Kevin?"

He panted, unable to find his words. "What's…that?"

"I lied. You are a good kisser." I turned, shouting out, "Gotta go."

"Elizabeth! Wait! I heard what happened! I've been concerned but didn't want to bother you. Are you all right?"

"Yeah. I'm fine." Sudden inspiration smacked me

upside the head. Time to do Elizabeth a solid. "But I want you to come see me…maybe even ask me out."

Always leaving them wanting more, I ran, grinning all the way back to bed. Then I hopped the short train to limbo.

**** 

*Elizabeth*

I finally did get out of bed. At least physically. I moved with a foggy brain and a heavy heart, almost as if in a coma. I tried to stay busy, practically sleepwalking through the most menial of chores. Like an IV restoring precious life fluids, though, I soon felt my life slowly being restored drip by drip. But every time I dared to hope for a silver lining, my mind drew back the black curtains, exposing the stage farce my life had been.

I helped Daddy get his files in order for his visit to the SEC. We didn't speak about his upcoming departure. I think we were both holding onto the slim chance he might not go away. Few words were exchanged between us, but it felt fine. On occasion, Daddy would stop and smile at me. Those smiles said more than words possibly could.

Both Mother and Daddy acted surprisingly understanding about what Donovan had done. Daddy, of course, embraced his shock at first. He thought of Donovan as the son he never had. Well, as the saying goes, like father, like son. Maybe they could share a prison cell. These days, gallows humor was my only source of amusement.

Late that Sunday afternoon, the doorbell rang. Tina Bottoms stood on my doorstep. Immediately, I sensed her demeanor seemed softer than what I'd experienced recently. For a moment, I felt swept back to our childhood when she'd stand on my doorstep, bashfully asking to play. "Hi, Elizabeth."

"Hi."

"I was…worried about you. Thought I'd stop by and see you." She studied my appearance in an obvious manner. I didn't need her wide-eyed shock to let me know I looked awful. "I guess you've had better days."

I shrugged. "I'm doing the best I can."

"I'm sorry about Donovan. That came as quite a shock."

"Tell me about it." Just being able to talk about it seemed an improvement over my endless crying jags. Maybe I'd entered the acceptance mode of the grieving stages.

"I also wanted to thank you. You did what you said you would. You cleared Charles's name. Hey, by the way, Donnie Heidenreich's out of his coma. He told the cops Dugan drugged him."

"Good. I'm happy for Donnie's family." A detached sort of happy. I didn't feel happy. A hollow place burrowed inside me like my soul had been scooped out. And suddenly, the floodgates opened again. "Oh, Tina, what am I going to do?" I practically collapsed on top of her, my voice garbled.

"Everything will work out for the best." She wrapped her arms around me, patting my back like a consoling parent. "Hey, I have an idea." She broke our embrace and held her hand out to me. "Come with me."

"But I look like a mess. I can't go anywhere like this." I rubbed my raw nose and sniffed. Completely unladylike, but I didn't care.

"It'll be okay. Nobody will see us." Reluctantly, I

took her hand. She led me to the middle of my large front yard. "Down you go."

"What?"

"Oh, just lie down already." Grinning mischievously, Tina fairly pushed me into the grass. With a *flump,* she fell down next to me. "Okay, look." She pointed to the sky. Slow, white clouds—marshmallows drifting nowhere in a hurry—crossed the expansive, blue sky. "What do you see?"

"Nothing."

"Boring! Look, there's Hastings." She pointed toward a particularly boxy-shaped cloud, an angular section jutting out like Hastings's nose.

I chuckled. "I see it." I picked out a peculiar hourglass-formed cloud. "And there's Charlotte Drayton. Slutty as ever."

We laughed, calling out clouds for a good hour. Even though we stretched matters at times, I felt a closeness to someone. And it felt good. I welcomed back the young girl I thought I'd left behind years ago.

"Tina?"

"Hmmm?" A long blade of grass dangled from the corner of her mouth while she contemplated her sky canvas.

"Will you be my friend...again?" I reached for her hand.

"Yes," she said without hesitation.

We held hands the rest of that warm spring day, looking into the sky and reading clouds.

\*\*\*\*

Later that night, my eyes had nearly fully recovered thanks to Tina's unexpected intervention. Then the damn doorbell rang again. *Grand Central*

*Station.*

"Elizabeth, hi." Hands in his pockets, Kevin absolutely oozed insecurity. "How are you?"

"I'm fine. Well, that's not totally true. But whatever."

"I'm really sorry about everything that's been going on. I just wanted to check on you, you know, like you said to do?"

"Wait, what?"

"Ah, never mind. Hey, I was wondering...would you like to go get a cup of coffee?"

"I don't drink coffee."

"Oh. Espresso? You drink espresso?"

"I do drink espresso."

He smiled, the dimples in his cheeks working overtime. "Well?"

"Oh. You mean like a date?" I knew what he meant, but I enjoyed watching him squirm. Maybe, I was back.

"Um, yeah. Exactly like a date." He reverted to childhood, kicking at the stoop nervously.

"Well, I can't go tonight. Daddy...he—"

"Oh, yeah, of course. Well, um, how about tomorrow night?"

I smiled. "I think I'd like that."

\*\*\*\*

*Elspeth*

Susan rolled over on her bed, eyes bright with excitement. "So, you kissed a boy? Three times?"

I nodded. "Yep. Got a little tongue action in there, too."

"Elspeth!" Susan tried to act proper, but her inner fires blazed. "You've got to tell me everything!"

"Not much to tell, really. But, okay—"

The pink phone interrupted storytime. Susan answered it, looked at me, and hung up. "Ms. Pillows wants to see you." Susan appeared disappointed again. Poor girl, I did hope she got outta here soon on a mission.

When I knocked on Ms. Pillows's door, she sang out, "Come in." As soon as I entered, her assistant fled.

I popped my feet up onto her desk, and got comfy. She cleared her throat, finger pointed at my kicks. I pulled them off and crossed an ankle over my knee.

"Well, now, Elspeth..." I always suspected the papers she shuffled were nothing more than a prop. From the few glimpses I'd had of them, they appeared blank. Maybe they were written in special, secret, invisible angel ink. "I understand you had quite a time on your last visit." She stacked the papers loudly.

"I guess so. We put away a couple of drug dealers."

"Yes." She peered at me warily over the top of her glasses. "I also understand you put your host in danger on several occasions."

"Hey, that wasn't my fault."

"Be that as it may, we can't be inflicting danger upon our hosts. A good host is hard to find, after all."

"After all," I agreed.

"And you took drugs?"

"No! I mean, the drug dealer dosed me. Believe me, it wasn't my decision."

She harrumphed loudly. "And you talked to your mother. Is this true?"

I blinked, finally agreed. "Yes. I talked to her. But she didn't know it was me."

"I see. And what's this about your kissing a boy? Three times?"

They did know everything! I wrinkled my brow and acted puzzled. "Now that I don't know anything about."

Ms. Pillows pressed her lips together and tilted her towering hairstyle. "Yes, well…" She packed the papers together again, taking her sweet time. I bet she and Hastings studied together at Intimidation University.

"I have to say that although you use extremely different and sometimes reckless methods, you do get results."

"Thanks."

"As it turns out, there's another problem in Clearwell. You're going out again."

"What? Shut up!"

"I will most certainly not shut up, young lady."

I tossed her a conciliatory grin. Too much trouble explaining to her that it was just slang. "Of course not."

"Now. Before we get down to the nitty-gritty of your next mission, is there anything else you'd like to say?"

"Yeah."

"Well?"

"Kick-ass!" I enjoyed her many shades of red very much.

## A word about the author...

Stuart R. West is a lifelong resident of Kansas, which he considers both a curse and a blessing. It's a curse because...well, it's Kansas. But it's great because...well, it's Kansas. Lots of cool, strange and creepy things happen in the Midwest, and Stuart takes advantage of them in his books. Call it "Kansas Noir." Stuart writes thrillers, horror and mysteries usually tinged with humor, both for adult and young adult audiences.

Stuart spent 25 years in the corporate sector and had to bail, splitting his time between writing and real estate. He's married to a professor of pharmacy (who greatly appreciates the fact he cooks dinner for her every night) and has a 29 year old daughter who's dabbling in the nefarious world of banking.

If you're still reading this, you may as well head on over to Stuart's blog at: http://stuartrwest.blogspot.com/ It's what all the cool kids are doing.

Thank you for purchasing
this publication of The Wild Rose Press, Inc.

For questions or more information
contact us at
info@thewildrosepress.com.

The Wild Rose Press, Inc.
www.thewildrosepress.com